TEMPLE OF THE

Foreword

Writing thrillers is a strange, very rewarding, and sometimes hazardous business. Over the last twenty years my search for background material has taken me into some dangerous places because dangerous places are interesting places.

For *Savant* I got caught up in the 1991 Kurdish uprising in Northern Iraq in the aftermath of the Gulf War. A minibus I was travelling in with the company of some heavily armed pershmarga guerrillas (they climbed aboard at a bus stop) was shot up by an Iraqi helicopter gunship and I ended up in a Kirkut hospital. Today the approaching heavy *wap-wap-wap* beat of Southern Electric's big Sikorsky helicopter doing its regular low-flying power line inspection patrols in my very rural part of Surrey/West Sussex has me crawling under my desk.

For *Mirage* I managed to stray into a buffer zone between Israel and the Lebanon, and suffered the ignominy of being rescued by a United Nations UNIFIL patrol when some Syrians started shooting across a valley at me. Look at the map and you find a point where Syria, the Lebanon, and Israel meet. That's exactly where I was – a singularly stupid place to be at any time, but particularly so during a UN-monitored peace.

In South Africa in the late 1970s, my eagerness to find out about gold movements during the Second World War for *Churchill's Gold* did not endear me to the authorities. Their hostility puzzled me, because it was all so long ago; until Gerard de Koch, the then Deputy Director of the South Africa Reserve Bank, explained to me that little had changed over the years regarding the movement of bullion.

In an overcrowded Hong Kong refugee camp, I listened with horror to first-hand accounts of the terrible atrocities perpetrated by pirates against Vietnamese boat people escaping across the South China Sea – material that I used in *Torus*.

All this chasing after human-conflict fire engines blinded me to the thriller potential of the area in which I live. I craved major battlegrounds as backgrounds to my stories and felt that my sleepy part of Surrey/West Sussex simply did not measure up in the action stakes. It took several significant events to open my eyes.

The first was when my local parish council bought the field that adjoins my house. Field? It was more of a hillock. There was a furore when the council announced their plan to use bulldozers to level the field to provide a large enough area for a football pitch.

"You can't do that!" complained some villagers. "It's a plague field! You'll be digging up hundreds of corpses."

Old records indicated that the field had been used as a mass burial ground for victims of the seventeenth-century plague outbreak. The bodies had been shipped from London to Godalming by barge and thence by wagon to my village. Some of the seemingly bottomless swallow holes in the area had also been used for the disposal of bodies.

The uproar delayed the football pitch. Test bores were made and the samples sent for analysis. No macabre evidence was found. The heavy Weald clay around here is so acid that buried organic matter disappears completely within 100 years or so.

What was interesting about the whole affair was not so much the chemical properties of the soil, but the revival of strange and ancient superstitions. Some older villagers firmly believe that the bodies of hanged witches are buried in the plague field because their bodies could not be destroyed by quicklime. There is a belief that disturbing their bones would bring about some form of hellish retribution.

The next incident was much more prosaic. It happened when I was driving south on the A285 from Petworth. Three miles south of the town, the almost dead-straight A285 ends in a sharp ninety-degree left-hand turn. I had foolishly let my attention wander so that instead of taking the bend I continued in a straight line, and braked to a standstill on the approach road to Seaford College, not believing that I could have made such a monumentally stupid mistake. Luckily for me, it's such a regular occurrence that the college authorities have removed their huge wrought-iron gates, but had a vehicle been coming in the opposite direction the chances are that I wouldn't be writing about it today. I survived, but a character in this trilogy doesn't.

The third event started on a truly terrifying night in October 1987 when hurricane-force winds raged with demented fury across southern England. We stood outside, anxiously watching a large ash tree thrashing to destruction, expecting it to fall on the house.

A bright, sunny morning revealed the extent of the appalling devastation: trees uprooted, houses without roofs, the roads lethal with tangles of fizzing, sparking power lines. An overhead power distribution system built up over half a century destroyed in less than three hours. Like many other villages in the area, we were without electricity for nearly two weeks.

During that brief but memorable period our lives underwent a most profound change. We had to rise at dawn, get all our chores done during the hours of daylight, and go to bed when it got dark. We had no heating and no means of cooking. To keep warm meant sawing fallen trees into logs. There were no newspapers or telephones and, without electricity, no television. Our link with the outside world was the local radio station. Southern Electric adopted the slogan *We're coming and we care* and set up a communal canteen in the local school – our only source of hot meals other than smoky, greenwood barbecues in the garden. To this day I can never work up any enthusiasm for barbecues.

There were two remarkable aspects of that period: the community spirit that prevailed with everyone helping everyone, and the unsuspected ingenuity that people drew on when it came to solving problems. A near neighbour fitted an aircraft propeller to an electric motor and mounted it on a pole to provide wind-generated electricity. I was writing *Mirage* at the time. My typewriter, unused since 1981, had seized up, so I rigged a small generator to run a Radio Shack Model 100 laptop. When the electricity was eventually restored, getting power back was almost as much of a shock as losing it.

I believe it was about this time that the germ of an idea for this trilogy – the notion of a modern community pitched back into the eighteenth century and how they rose to meet the challenge – began to form. The trouble was that the idea lacked focus. It was nothing more than an interesting concept that was relegated to my overcrowded back burner.

The catalyst came with the realisation that Petworth, a few miles south of me, was a town with some very unusual features. Just how unusual, you can find out by reading on. I might as well come clean and admit here and now that my Pentworth in this story is based on Petworth and that every place I've mentioned does exist, although I've taken a few liberties. I've enlarged the Market Square, and dignified the town with a Town Council rather than a parish council. It goes without saying that any resemblance between the inhabitants of my Pentworth and the real Petworth is purely coincidental, and I hope that the morris men sides around here will overlook the liberties I've taken with their Sussex tradition dances.

The biggest change concerns the actual Temple of the Winds. Yes – it does exist. Just as well, because the strange myths surrounding it, which I've described in this book, are far more bizarre than anything I could invent. I'm actually writing this foreword on its high, legend-shrouded scarp, and I can almost hear the demon-like gargoyle, carved in sandstone by the gales of a million years, sniffing the winds that invade his temple. The spooky atmosphere here is getting to me; the irritation of Alfred, Lord Tennyson's ghost at my moving of his favourite spot a few miles south to a more dramatically convenient location just has to be a product of my imagination.

A correction: Ellen's cave, with its Palaeolithic wall paintings of hunting scenes of 40,000 years ago, doesn't exist. But – as I look out from the Temple of the Winds across the folds and humps of the sun-dappled downs of West Sussex where vast herds of bison once roamed, preyed on by cave lions, sabre-tooth tigers, and our clever ancestors – it's easy to believe that the cave is out there somewhere beneath the ancient landscape – waiting to be discovered.

James Follett, The Temple of the Winds, West Sussex, 1999

One

Vikki Taylor saw the long shadow cast across the rutted lane by the late afternoon sun and froze in terror.

Her knuckles, gripping the handlebars of her new twelve-speed bicycle that she was pushing along the rutted track, went bone-white. But only on her right hand, for her left hand was artificial. Such was her fear that an involuntary trickle of urine escaped and soaked into her panties. Her pounding heart felt as though it were trying to smash through her ribcage.

She kept perfectly still and so did the shadow.

What may have been a small creature close behind her made a metallic scrabbling noise with its claws on the loose stones. Vikki heard the sound but was too hypnotised by the terror that lay ahead to turn around.

Run! Run! This is where Debbie French was raped a year ago! For God's sake, run!

But she was unable to move. Her legs were jelly, and if she let go of the bicycle she would surely collapse. The cosy, familiar surroundings of the West Sussex countryside that she had known all her life underwent a profound and frightening change. The sunlight dappling through the trees and reflected from the puddles left by the storm of three nights ago became a harsh, unnatural glare, and the chatter of birds in the hedgerows celebrating the arrival of spring died away to an eerie silence.

The cause of the shadow was a man, hidden by the girth of an old oak some twenty metres ahead. He remained motionless, like a sentinel. Despite her stomach-churning fear, this puzzled Vikki. If he were waiting in ambush, surely he could see his own shadow and realise that it gave him away?

The sensation of dread heightened. Supposing there really had been a UFO that had landed during Tuesday night's storm? After all, several people claimed to have seen something dropping from the sky, even though the ufologists that had descended on Pentworth the next day had found nothing. Maybe it had left an alien behind?

1

Maybe the UFO would return when the alien had kidnapped some-one?

She told herself not to be so silly. Whatever it was, it wasn't trying to hide. From the bold silhouette thrown on the ground she could see that he wasn't even crouching close to the tree, but was standing erect, legs apart, holding what could be a shotgun. Perhaps he was one of Asquith Prescott's cottagers? His gamekeeper awaiting a fox? But surely he would be holding the shotgun at the ready? And what sort of hat was he wearing? It was more like a headdress – tall fronds that caught the breeze, and were the only thing about the shadow that moved. Yet there was something oddly familiar about the headdress – she knew that she had seen it before.

Gradually Vikki brought her terror sufficiently under control to will her legs to move, and a sharp downward push on the palm of her artificial left hand caused its cleverly articulated fingers to tighten their grip on the handlebars. Slowly, one trembling step at a time, she backed away without taking her eyes off the strange shadow for an instant . . .

Ten paces . . . Twenty paces . . .

She reached the spot where the lane's asphalt ended, where she was forced to dismount each day on her way home from school. It would be easy now to jump on to her bicycle and pedal furiously away. The track was slightly downhill towards the safety of St Catherine's – whatever it was behind the tree would never catch her. But there was a strange compulsion about the shadow. She continued staring at the old oak and the figure that lay beyond. Her thumping heart merged with a new, distant sound that caused the ground to shake in unison with the primeval, savage beat. It was a sound she had never heard before in her fifteen years and yet she knew what it was: a full impi – 500 warriors beating their assegais on their ox-hide shields and stamping – the slow, insidious beat of the main cohort – the buffalo's head – designed to focus the attention of the enemy while the horns spread out through the long grass to complete their deadly encircling manoeuvre. The heavy beat quickened – there would be one beat for every spirit being avenged by the war party, followed by a burst of hollering cries, a sudden unnerving silence, and then the pounding of spears on the inside of shields and the stamping would resume.

How do I know this?

But she did. Just as she knew that the impi was an 'izimpohlo' – a brigade of unmarried warriors. They were a mile away and about to wipe out a Butelezi kraal – the hated enemy.

The rich, storm-soaked colours of the English countryside swam around her – a crazy kaleidoscope of colours and patterns. The lines of chestnut fencing posts and hedgerows that divided the fields on the storm-sodden plain that bounded the northern slopes of the South Downs dissolved into a vista of yellowing elephant grass and red soil. What had been broad oaks were now a group of scrawny thorn trees, cowering under a blistering sun.

He's still there!

She began walking towards the trees, not noticing the sharp stones beneath her bare feet or that she no longer had her bicycle. She didn't even notice that the customary dead weight of her artificial left hand had also gone; her entire consciousness was fixed on the motionless shadow. The pounding and stamping stopped suddenly. The buffalo's head would start closing in now, shields held forward at an angle and the warriors packed tightly together to make them appear fewer in number than they were. The enemy would be fooled – they always were – and would send an inadequate defence force to meet the approaching menace. Suddenly the buffalo's head would spread out, stabbing spears flashing out from shields abruptly turned square on, the attacking army would seem to double in size in an instant. The effect would be devastating. The enemy, having hurled their spears and now weaponless, overwhelmed in a few bloody moments of savage carnage.

How do I know this?

But she ignored the corner of her reason that was trying to retain a firm grip on reality and concentrated on placing one foot before the other – not looking down – eyes fixed straight ahead to where the owner of the shadow would soon come into view. Her steps faltered at the sight of the powerful fist clutching the assegai, and then the warrior was before her. She stopped, raised her eyes to his face, and the beauty of his fine, aristocratic, chiselled features caused her to breath to spasm in her throat. It was a face that she knew: the man made flesh.

"Dario!" she whispered in recognition.

It was the name she had given him when she had first seen him several weeks before; it had seemed in keeping with his height and majestic bearing.

"Dario!" she breathed again, and went closer.

Not a muscle moved in that perfect body; the large, liquid eyes watching her were neither threatening or welcoming. Apart from the crane-feather headdress he was naked, because that was the mighty king's ruling. No strings of crocodile teeth or ornaments that an enemy might hear; no armlets that might catch the sun; no body decorations to identify individual warriors because the king's rigorous training suppressed individuality. Unit markings on shields, coloured headdresses for the benefit of the commander directing the battle from a nearby hillside with signals, and that was all.

Vikki's terror gave way to wonder, such was the hypnotic power of those bewitching eyes. But she could not keep her gaze from the splendours of his magnificent body. She was now close enough to touch him had she the courage. His skin was the colour of Inspector Harvey Evans' sunflower honey, gleaming like polished ebony under its sheen of ox-tallow. The long, pointed shield that he held in front of him was covered in the finest leopard skin, the broad blade of his assegai sandstone-polished to glinting perfection, the stabbing spear's short haft a matt sheen from its treatment with hot beeswax to improve grip.

The eyes gazing down at Vikki softened, strengthening her returning courage. Compelled by the aristocratic perfection of his features, she reached up on tiptoe and touched his chin, automatically using her real hand as she always did. He made no move. Emboldened, she traced the line of his forehead with her fingertip and drew it down the bridge of his finely sculptured nose. The contact sent thrills of an intensity such as she had never experienced before coursing through her.

A mile distant the cries of battle were over. It was finished hardly before it had begun. And now the real killing started: the slaughter of the old men, women and children. The mass murder was not mindless but to ensure that the secrets of the mighty king's military tactics did not spread. Babies would be spared – they would not remember – and in twelve years the males would make warriors of the 'Fasimba' children's regiments – the 'Haze', because their slight forms enabled them to move unseen when the grass was short and enemy kraals would not be expecting an attack.

Dario was a picket: one of perhaps twenty or thirty warriors surrounding the village at a distance to ensure that no one escaped.

This time Vikki did not worry about her strange acquisition of knowledge; all her attention was focused on her right forefinger, which was stroking Dario's lips, daring him to accept the invitation by opening his mouth. He wouldn't, of course – the unmarried girls in her village often made this ancient, teasing offer of *ukahlobongo* to returning hunters whom they had singled out as future husbands. It was an invitation to practise imitation sexual intercourse using the girl's arms, thighs and even feet. The king's law forbade sexual

4

intercourse during a campaign for even his married warriors, but *ukahlobongo* sex play was regarded as acceptable and even encouraged, although many warriors refused, believing that the inevitable outcome of such delightful encounters drained their strength.

But Dario *did* accept!

His beautiful lips parted and Vikki's mischievous, teasing fingers were gripped between dazzling, bark-scrubbed white teeth, sucking gently, releasing a liquid warmth that suffused the centre of her being. She gave a little gasp at her boldness and its inevitable consequence. To withdraw the offer to a king's warrior could bring shame and a hideous punishment if he felt slighted. The village duenna whispered the fate of such girls who were sent north to the royal kraal at Bulawayo. It was said that a terrible operation was performed on them: girls that had denied pleasure would never know pleasure – therefore a mixture of custom, ritual, fear and a good deal of curiosity overruled Vikki's inhibitions and guided her hand to his chest.

Dario lowered the shield a little so that she could span her fingers across several ribs. She marvelled at the sleek hardness of his muscles beneath the smooth, oiled skin. His half smile was reassuring. She moved closer, her breasts now pressing against his shield, and crouched slightly so that she could slide both hands around him and caress his iron-hard buttocks and realised with a distant shock that she had feeling through the prosthetic fingertips of her left hand.

He suddenly seemed indifferent to her presence, his eyes scanning the veldt, but this was part of the game of *ukahlobongo*. He might appear indifferent but the wondrous tensing and relaxing of his gluteus muscles beneath her sensually exploring fingertips told a different story, especially when she teased the little hollow at the base of his spine. Her heartbeat quickened when she felt him lowering the shield. For the first time she looked down and saw that her striped school blouse and tie and sensible Marks and Spencer bra were gone. She was surprised but not alarmed to see that her skin was the same colour as his, her breasts much fuller than normal, her nipples dark and prominent.

But what held her fascinated attention was *IT* . . . So dark and slender, vein-laced, and rising up, forcing its way into the valley between her breasts with a bewildering, insistent strength. She instinctively knew what she had to do even though the village girls who had practised *ukahlobongo* had not gone into details. She squeezed her breasts together against him and began moving them up and down, gently at first and then more quickly to keep pace with his breathing. That her left hand was now real and not a brilliant creation in titanium and silicon seemed perfectly normal.

The distant cries and screams of the butchery went unheard. She concentrated on lifting herself up and pushing down, using her whole body now, sometimes quickly, sometimes slowly, and all the time revelling in the power she was exercising over this magnificent warrior as she rolled the oiled sleeve of skin back and forth. A glance showed that his eyes were still open, searching the long grass for shadows fleeing from the doomed village, but his lips were parted in a silent grimace and his teeth tightly clenched.

It ended with a sudden warmth spreading across her breasts and between her thighs. She straightened and stepped back, smiling at him while working the milky fluid into her skin to be sure of absorbing the strength he had given her. And then the sun went in and the blinding glare on the yellow bush was no more.

Panic seized her when she saw that he was fading. She gave a little cry of anguish, thinking she had taken too much of his power, and reached forward to embrace him, to beg his forgiveness. But it was too late – a shimmering outline that blended with the distant hills and he was gone. Tears blurred her vision. The elephant grass took on the brilliant greens of spring and she found herself staring south towards the rolling hills of the downs. A breeze played coldly on her pale exposed breasts, her left hand again its customary leaden weight, clinging by suction to her wrist, behind her an approaching diesel engine slowing to a tick-over.

An old-fashioned bulb horn sounded.

She quickly hitched her bra into place, buttoned her blouse, straightened her tie – all performed with her one-handed skill – and stepped guiltily from behind the tree. A mud-splattered tractor had stopped before her bicycle that she had left lying across the track some twenty metres away. With her emotions a jumble of charged eroticism, guilt, confusion, and fear, she ran towards the machine and wheeled it clear.

David Weir leaned out the cab of his antique John Deere tractor and grinned down at her. He was a lean, debonair forty-year-old, sandy haired, grey eyes. A broken nose enhancing his aristocratic features. He possessed an unconscious, easy-going charm, and his bachelor status was one that several Pentworth ladies were in favour of changing.

Five years previously he had decided that he wanted more open air than three weeks a year salmon fishing in Scotland, and exercise that didn't require gymnasium fees. He sold his share in a successful Westminster art gallery to his partner and bought the rundown Temple Farm. Another gentleman farmer, said the locals, and waited with interest to see how long it took for him to fall flat on his face. They reckoned without David's flair for showmanship, which had made his gallery a success, and his capacity for innovation and hard work.

Armed with a bank loan and a grant from Brussels, he had harnessed his boundless fascination with the past, and had turned Temple Farm into a living rural museum with its smaller fields cultivated by implements that dated back to the early seventeenth century. Theme farms were becoming big business. Temple Farm as a museum and its stream of paying visitors was a source of friction between himself and some fellow councillors on Pentworth Town Council, particularly now that he had improved his winter turnover by turning a Dutch barn into an Ice Age annexe. But as long as he kept the farm going as a farm, there was little authority could do: there were no laws that required farmers to use modern equipment. He was fond of pointing out that Pentworth was an antique shop town that now had an antique farm. He had obtained planning consent from the District Council for a car park and farm shop, and the farm shop sold tickets to visit the farm.

"Hallo, Vikki," he said cheerily, his voice pleasingly cultivated without sounding affected. "Thought it was your bike. Careless of you, m'dear."

Vikki matched his smile and gripped the handlebars tightly with her good hand to control her trembling. She liked David Weir. Last summer she had spent a hot afternoon with him riding on an ancient, juddering combine harvester. She had been wearing shorts and all the time he had kept a hand on her thigh to hold her steady on her insecure perch. She had never forgotten the touch of his palm, the knotted veins on his forearm – which she had found incredibly sexy – or the animal smell of his sweat. Vikki's best friend, Sarah Gale, had boasted that he had done 'it' to her last summer, but Sarah was a noted liar and had failed to provide details despite Vikki's eager questioning.

"Hallo, Dave," she replied, pleased that her voice sounded so steady. "I was watching some badgers; you frightened them off." And also pleased that she had sufficient control to think up a plausible lie so quickly.

He nodded. "There's an old sett in that field. Probably flooded out of their usual sett by the storm. Thunder and lightning put paid to Prescott's milk yields. Never known that to happen before. Four trees down, too. Pentworth Lake's still the colour of mustard after four days. Always a bad sign." He broke off and leaned forward to study Vikki's left hand with genuine interest. "Is that the new one your dad was telling me about?"

Vikki smiled. She preferred David Weir's friendly, open approach to that of those who pointedly avoided the subject. She proudly held up what looked like a normal left hand for inspection. It was the silicon skin's imperfections – some blemishes and even a few matching freckles on the wrist – that made the hand look near-perfect. "New? I've had it a month. And Dad had a spare made."

"Amazing," said David admiringly. "You'd never know. It's a work of art. And to think that I thought that British Aerospace made only aircraft and things that go bang. Is that huge watch strap all that holds it in place?"

"Suction. It's a perfect moulded fit. There's a little vacuum pump just under the skin on the wrist. Four presses and it's on. I can even go swimming with it if I'm careful. The watch is just to hide the join. And I can open and close the fingers and thumb by pressing on the palm."

"Certainly a huge improvement on the old one," said David. He jerked his thumb at the high-sided trailer behind the tractor that was laden with storm-ravaged leeks. "Try it out by helping yourself. Last of the season. What the storm didn't flatten, the UFO spotters finished off. They were convinced my leeks had been flattened by a mothership. I threatened to flatten a few of them with a tractor. Persistent devils. Worse than twitchers."

"We had some climbing into the school grounds – looking for a Silent Vulcan, they said."

"That's what the press called it. Thank God they've got bored and gone home. Anyway – you help yourself. I'm not going to get much for them. Washed through with dirt, they are."

"I hate leeks, Dave."

"They're for your lovely mother, m'dear."

Vikki's quick gesture that caused her artificial fingers and thumb to close on the vegetables was so natural that David missed what happened. She repeated the motion more slowly, demonstrating her skill by even using her left hand to cram the bedraggled leeks into her saddlebag.

"Well, I'll be . . .." David breathed in wonder. "That's amazing, Vikki. Anyway – don't forget to tell your mother where the leeks came from."

"I think she'd prefer flowers, Dave."

David laughed good-naturedly and thought how lovely Vikki looked. She had inherited her mother's ash-blonde hair and green eyes, and she had shot up recently so that mother and daughter looked like sisters. But what was truly remarkable about Vikki was her bright vivaciousness – her infectious, sparkling exuberance that refused concessions to her disability. "Now that's something I might just be tempted to try on her daughter in a couple of years."

"You'd be wasting your money," Vikki retorted but inwardly delighted with this confidence-building flirtation.

"Oh – they'd only be cheap flowers." With that parting shot and a cheery wave, he revved up and let in the clutch. The tractor rumbled off, splashing through storm puddles.

Vikki wheeled her machine a little way and paused at the spot where Dario had been standing. She stood, lost in thought for some moments, wondering why this particular daydream about Dario had been so powerful and so detailed. Mrs Simmons had taught her class about the Zulus and the Zulu Wars but, as one would expect of a teacher in a Catholic girls' school, she had never gone into details about their sexual practices. She started walking.

Perhaps I read it somewhere?

Unlikely. She knew that she would have remembered such startling details. Something made a noise behind her as she started wheeling her bicycle. She turned around and caught a fleeting glimpse of a multi-legged shadow darting under a hedge.

A giant crab? Oh, God – I am seeing things today.

She stared hard at the spot where the strange creature had disappeared but was unable to discern anything. She decided that it was probably a hungry squirrel emerging from hibernation to test the lengthening spring days. Odd, though – it had a mechanical look about it.

Ten minutes later, still in deep thought about her strange daydream and unaware that she was being followed by the strange device, she arrived home, or rather the building site that had been home for the past two years since the Taylors had moved from a modern estate on the edge of Pentworth.

One day Stewards House, so named because it once been a farm steward's house, and the adjoining labourer's cottage that her father was knocking into one, would be a single dwelling, but that day seemed even further off than when they had first moved in.

"It'll be finished the day the bloody mortgage is paid off," Anne

Taylor was fond of saying although she was not so fond of having to say it.

Jack Taylor's problem was that he always got bored with a task before finishing it. As a consequence of having two cottages to work on, and a job with British Aerospace that took him out of the country for long periods, there was always an abundance of new jobs to hold his interest until they had advanced to the halfway stage and crossed the sod-it-let's-do-something-else threshold.

Himmler, the Taylors' fastidious Siamese cat, had already quit, with Anne often threatening to follow suite. In Himmler's case, he felt quite strongly that he was entitled to decent, civilised standards, where a respectable cat could get its proper ration of twenty-three hours' sleep per day and not have to spend its precious hunting, eating and shagging hour washing cement and plaster dust from its fur. Whereas cats usually suffered from hairballs, Himmler got lumps of cement. After coughing up his third pellet of Portland quickset he decided that enough was enough and moved in with Mrs Johnson in a nearby cottage – a senile old lady who could not recollect having bought or being given a Siamese cat, but fed him anyway because he seemed to expect it and turned nasty when she forgot.

Vikki padlocked her bicycle to a discarded cast-iron radiator in the doorless garage and went to the back of the house clutching the leeks.

The crablike device that had followed her took cover under a hedge and completed its transmission of the data it had collected on the girl. While she had been distracted by the powerful daydream, the strange machine had crept up behind her and removed a tiny blood and tissue sample from her leg.

The samples had been analysed and it was decided that more information was needed. Meanwhile there was much for the device to do. It would return that night.

As Vikki went to the back of the house she noticed that a stonemason, industriously watched by three shovel-leaning helpers, was laying paving slabs around the new but empty swimming pool. That was the nice thing about living on a building site – every time she arrived home from school a new surprise would be awaiting her. The workmen eyed her appreciatively as she entered the kitchen door.

"Sister?" enquired the stonemason. "Daughter."

"Bloody hell."

Anne Taylor's large kitchen consisted of two rooms knocked into one. It was an oasis of order in a desert of chaos. It was finished. Not on account of any great effort by Jack Taylor, but because, in desperation, Anne had withdrawn several thousand euros left to her by her mother from her building society account and paid a Chichester firm to build her a kitchen. They were in and out in a fortnight, leaving gloriously finished acres of limed oak cupboards, tiled worktops, a breakfast bar, and a gleaming Portuguese ceramic floor. They had even installed a television, lit the place with low-voltage lights, and hung strings of Spanish onions. All this was achieved while Jack was installing a radiator that leaked. And the few euros plus a seductive smile that Anne slipped the foreman fitter resulted in a proper door with a lock on the downstairs lavatory. Being able to have a pee without having to keep a foot planted on the door had become a forgotten luxury.

"Mind my floor," Anne warned as her daughter trailed in, dumped the leeks in the sink, and turned on the cold tap to wash out the worst of the dirt. Seeing Vikki's skills with her new hand did much to assuage the cancerous guilt that had haunted Anne ever since that terrible day of the accident when Vikki was four. The old hand had been little more than a clumsy plastic moulding; with the new hand Vikki could even turn a tap on and off. That Vikki's bright personality allowed no room for reproach over the accident served only to heighten Anne's guilt.

"Where did you get those?"

"Dave Weir. A token of his undying love. Storm-damaged. The UFO hunters thought they'd been flattened by the Silent Vulcan."

"Right now I'm cooking your dad a token of my undying hatred," said Anne, flicking a strand of spaghetti at the wall. She missed and had to unpick it from a crucifix. "Or rather, I was."

Vikki joined her mother at the Aga. She was a few centimetres shorter than Anne, who had longer legs, but her growth hormones were still at work on the problem.

"Poor Dad. What's he done now?"

"Guess what those clowns in the paddock will be doing tomorrow."

"Wiring up the pool filter?"

"They've done that. And the underwater lights. They'll be filling it."

The news delighted Vikki. "Oh – magic! It'll be finished at last."

"Watching a pump filling a swimming pool – a gruelling Saturday job for them. Let's hope they don't run the borehole dry."

"Not after all that rain, Mum."

11

"And *then* they'll do the new septic tank." Anne was about to make a scathing comment about her husband's idea of priorities but stilled her tongue. The pool had been installed because Vikki loved swimming – there was nothing that Jack Taylor would not do for his beloved daughter. It was virtually the only thing that was holding Jack and Anne's marriage together. "Still," Anne concluded, "at least it'll be something that's finished."

"And a spot of sexual bribery could get the garage door hung," Vikki suggested, tasting the sauce.

"From you or me?"

"You, of course, Mum – you're so experienced in such matters. They don't teach eyelash fluttering at St Catherine's the way you learned it."

"Well, I'll certainly have the chance," said Anne, catching her daughter's impudent look and trying not to laugh. "Phone call from your father just now. He's flown back to Riyadh this afternoon and won't be home for another week. A Saudi prince has crashed his Tornado. All the King's men are putting the prince back together again, and British Aerospace men are putting the Tornado back together again."

Vikki was disappointed but said nothing. She adored her father.

"And a phone call from Ellen Duncan," Anne continued. "She wondered if you could start work an hour earlier in the shop tomorrow morning. She's had a lot of mail orders in this week. I told her you could."

Vikki loved her Saturday job in Ellen Duncan's herbal shop, and the extra hour's work brought the boots she was saving for a little nearer. "I could go to Saturday mass right after work," she decided. "Save going on Sunday."

"Well, mind you do."

"I always do, Mother dear – you're the one that skives off with migraines."

"You need a shower, young lady."

For a terrible moment Vikki thought that there must be evidence about her of her recent encounter, and was immensely relieved when she realised that mother was referring to her mud-splattered legs.

Ten minutes later, after a shower, wearing a towelling dressing gown and clutching her clothes, Vikki climbed the nearly perpendicular flight of stairs to her tiny garret bedroom tucked into a south-facing roof hip on the second floor. The alarming creak and groan of the narrow stairs assured her of privacy, and the steep climb minimised parental disapproval of the permanent wall-to-wall carpet of underwear. Best of all, the room was finished, because Dad never got bored with any job that benefited his daughter. It had a generous built-in wardrobe with linked sliding doors that could be opened and closed with one hand, drawers that glided at a touch, Mary Quant wallpaper, and a washbasin with a hospital lever-operated mixer tap. A dormer window with motorised curtains set into a slate roof looked across the farmland of Prescott Estates Plc.

James Dean had joined her poster collection since she had seen a re-run of *Rebel Without a Cause* on television, but the prime wall space at the foot of her bed went to Dario. The huge, life-size poster of the Zulu warrior had been a special Christmas offer in a girls' magazine. Anne had clapped her hands in delight when Vikki had unfolded the giant envelope's contents.

"He's beautiful!" she exclaimed. "I expect he needs such a big shield. Amazing, those guys. I went out with the leader of a steel band before I met your dad. The only man I've ever known who could make my eyes water."

Vikki had burst out laughing and her dad had gone off in a huff to grout some tiles.

Dario's liquid brown eyes greeted Vikki when she entered the sanctuary of her bedroom.

"Hallo, Dario."

The eyes watched her as she rinsed her panties and draped them over the radiator. She sat on her bed and cupped her chin on her hand, returning the warrior's gaze and thinking over the moments of the strange daydream encounter, more worried now that she had time to think as she replayed those disturbingly vivid events beneath the oak tree.

"Why was it all so real, Dario?" she asked the poster. "I could feel your skin, the veins on your arms, and your –" an inward squirm of embarrassment and guilt – "well – everything."

Dario remained silent.

Perhaps I'm going mad? Talking to a poster . . . Don't be silly, Vikki – you talk to Benji.

She propped herself against the headboard and put her arms around the huge bear – the sole surviving cuddly toy of her childhood. But not even the reassuring feel of Benji's threadbare fur could take her thoughts off her recent encounter or banish the worries crowding in. The dressing gown fell away from her legs as she drew her knees to her chin. She was lost in thought for a few moments then realised that Dario could see her nakedness. Suddenly embarrassed, she covered herself with her right hand before realising

13

the absurdity of the gesture. Luckily Vikki was of a happy disposition and she could laugh at herself; nevertheless, her hand stayed in place and her knees parted. Very soon her breathing quickened.

She and the Zulu warrior had some unfinished business.

Two

A rnie Trinder and Nevil Rigsby were having a bad day.

The two men were Department of Trade and Industry investigators from the Radio Communication Agency in Southampton. They were wet, cold, tired, hungry, thirsty, aching in every joint, and generally about as pissed off as two men who had spent five hours falling about a storm-drenched landscape wearing inadequate clothing could possibly be. Being mistaken for particularly tenacious ufologists and threatened by a farmer with a shotgun if they didn't get off his land hadn't helped, although the general belief among the locals that they were UFO-hunting was useful cover for what they were really up to.

Rigsby was of the shorter of the two. What he lacked in stature and breath, he made up for with fat and sweat. Clipped to his rucksack was an assortment of instruments that included a wide-band scanning radio receiver with a direction-finding loop antenna, a hand-bearing compass, a map case, and binoculars. Other burdens included large balls of mud clinging to his feet that grew bigger each time he dragged a shoe out of the quagmire.

Trinder's feet were also so equipped. He was a tall, muscular, West Indian. His finely defined features were normally relaxed in a good-natured smile but not today. His right shoulder was weighed down by a portable Jensen spectrum analyser. After five hours slogging around the West Sussex countryside, it no longer felt very portable. Hanging from his other shoulder was a Husky field computer whose hard disk was loaded with detailed maps of the Pentworth area which they were currently investigating. His three months with the Radio Communications Agency was turning out to be the worst period of his degree course. The thought that it was nearly over and come August he would be taking up a promised job in Trinidad was the only thing that kept him going.

"This'll do," said Trinder, looking around for a dry spot to unload his gear for a brief respite and seeing nothing but yellow lake. They were a mile south of the sandstone bluff that Pentworth was built on, standing on the edge of the broad expanse of Pentworth Lake – a stretch of wetlands lake that had defied drainage attempts for 200 years. The symbols on the detailed maps in the Husky for this location were clumps of reeds, indicating a lake surrounded by marshland that normally covered about three square kilometres, now double that size owing to the storm. It was a noted beauty spot but there was nothing beautiful now about the yellowish, silt-coloured water. Nevertheless it had attracted a large number of herring gulls and little gulls in addition to the usual inhabitants of herons, and an assortment of waterfowl that included a few curlews, probing the shallows with their curious, downward curving bills – not caring about the colour of the water provided the feeding was good.

"Let's make it the last one," Rigsby suggested. "I've had enough for one day." He switched on his AOR scanner and punched the air band key. The scanner howled. "Christ – it's strong here." He held the DF loop above his head and turned it to null out the signal. It faded only slightly when he pointed it away from the swamp. The two men didn't need the hand-bearing compass to tell them that the squat and incredibly ugly Cellnet mobile telephone repeater mast a mile to the east was not the source of the rogue broadband emissions that had been screwing up the aircraft navigation beacon at Midhurst for the last twenty-four hours.

Trinder consulted the Husky and used its tracker ball to plot a line on a large-scale map from their present position to the centre of the swamp, where it formed a cocked-hat intersection with two previous lines plotted by the men during their investigation. Rigsby swept the area with his binoculars, paying close attention to clumps of reeds that might be camouflaging an aerial.

A portable telephone in Trinder's anorak pocket trilled. "That can only be Townsend again," the West Indian muttered. "Does that man like to give us hassle."

"He's got the National Air Traffic Service on his back," Rigsby commented.

Trinder grimaced and answered the call.

"So what's the latest?" Townsend demanded from the warmth and security of his Southampton office.

"It's definitely the Plague Swamp, George."

"The what?"

"Pentworth Lake," Trinder explained. "The locals call it the Plague Swamp. The bodies of Black Death victims from London and Chichester used to be dumped here. We've got three bearings from over the entire area and they all point to the centre of the swamp.

The Orange box at Henkley Down is whistle clean, and so is the Cellnet box. No spurious emissions from either of them."

"Where are you now? Give me your GR."

Trinder provided a grid reference and waited, holding the handset slightly away from his ear so that Rigsby could hear.

"Bloody radio amateurs up to their tricks," Townsend grumbled. "Do you know anything about that one in Pentworth High Street?"

"Bob Harding," said Trinder, feeling his feet sinking. "He runs the Pentworth Repair Shack. Yes – we've seen him. Rigsby here knows him slightly and says that what he's interested in planting isn't bugs. Also he's a top-flight government scientific consultant. Member of Pentworth Town Council. Hardly your average bug-planter."

"You told him to be circumspect about all this? The local plods don't want those UFO nutters back in the area."

"We told him," said Trinder patiently.

"What about the landowner? Maybe he knows something?"

Trinder consulted a list. "Ellen Duncan. Also a local councillor. Runs a herbalist's in North Street. Doesn't sound like a likely bug-planter either."

"Well, obviously some clever sod's planted one. So you lads be even cleverer and find it and fish it out."

"We're going to need a boat for this job, George. We're already up to our ankles in mud. They had fifty mill on Tuesday night. The water's the colour of shit."

"I'll cover your cleaning costs. At least take a look."

Rigsby took the telephone from his colleague. "This isn't the work of a radio amateur, George. Amateurs may indulge in jamming other amateurs but they don't risk having the RCA crawling all over them by going out of band and putting out broadband white noise right across airband navigation-beacon frequencies. More likely it was planted by a local to stop the UFO spotters from going home. They bought in a lot of trade on Wednesday and Thursday."

"Find the bug first and then we'll argue over who planted it later," Townsend retorted.

"It's not a bug, George. Bugs put out milliwatts of ERP and rely on their closeness to a repeater to jam its input frequency, and their batteries die after a few hours. This is something seriously large, with a large power supply to match if it's been transmitting for a day."

"And a large co-linear aerial sticking up to match which shouldn't be hard to find," Townsend snapped. Then he moderated his tone. "Just find it, please, lads. It's buggering up aircraft DME in the

Pentworth quadrant, or something like that. I've promised that it'll be located and disabled by nightfall."

Rigsby ended the call and returned the telephone to Trinder. "All they're worried about is their bloody distance-measuring equipment," he grumbled. "Airline pilots have forgotten how to navigate without masses of ground gear."

The West Indian tried to muster a grin. He gazed across the yellow water. "Maybe there was a Silent Vulcan UFO after all, George. Sitting on the bottom of the lake, and the RF they're splatting is them phoning home."

"What? On 105 meg?"

"It's as good a frequency as any. It would go to the stars."

Rigsby glumly surveyed Pentworth Lake and thought that the locals had got it right: it looked more like a swamp. He pointed. "Maybe there's an aerial in that clump of reeds. Be the best place to disguise it. Come on." He took several glugging steps and sank up to his knees. He tried to lift his leg but transferring all his weight to one foot caused him to sink even deeper. "Oh – fuck it. I'm stuck. Give me a hand. Go that side – it looks firmer."

Trinder avoided following Rigsby's footsteps and squelched in a semicircle to grab his colleague's outstretched hand, and he too sank to his knees. Despite being the lighter of the two men, he found himself sinking faster. His feet pumped frantically in the glutinous ooze, releasing sluggish bubbles of marsh gas that erupted through the cold, clay-coloured water that was closing around his thighs.

"We're going to have to get rid of all this clobber," Rigsby panted, sweating profusely despite the icy cold of the gunk that was inexorably claiming him. "Chuck it where we were just standing."

Trinder expressed doubts about subjecting their expensive equipment to such treatment.

"Fuck that. It'll be up to our waists soon if we don't get rid of it." With that Rigsby tried to release his haversack harness but he suddenly sank up to his groin. The shock of the cold, yellow mud groping his balls made him gasp but didn't stop him swearing. "Oh, shit, fuck and damnation." He tugged the binoculars from around his neck and lobbed them to firmer ground.

Trinder was normally a quiet, methodical man, not given to extremes of emotion except at cricket matches when the West Indies were getting hammered. He released the spectrum analyser's buckle and managed swing the heavy instrument by its strap so that it fell near Rigsby's binoculars. Losing the ten-kilo burden made matters worse because the recoil from his exertion quickened his sinking.

Until now both men had thought that solving their difficulties was merely a matter of floundering their way back to firmer ground, but the mud was closing around them like a straitjacket, and the water soaking into their clothes made movement virtually impossible. Pumping their legs merely tended to create a vacuum beneath their feet so that atmospheric pressure pushed them deeper.

"Fall backwards!" Trinder gasped. "Maybe we can swim through it!"

Rigsby was too preoccupied trying to release his harness to pay any attention. His fingers fought blindly through the cold and mud in search of the buckle that had slipped to his side. Suddenly what little support the ooze provided beneath his feet was gone and he was up to his neck and screaming in terror. Trinder fell forward and grabbed Rigsby's collar. Pushing his colleague's head above the surface resulted in his own head going under. He swallowed the sand-particle-charged water: it clogged his throat and windpipe. He managed to get his head above the surface, choked, gagged, and went under again, taking Rigsby with him.

The swamp closed over the two men, shutting off Rigsby's screams of panic. There was no returning to the surface; no frantic cries or waving of arms – the merciless swamp allowed no encores. Lost from the sight of their wildfowl audience, the two men flailed blindly at each other like drunks in a slow-motion movie, but the viscosity of the mud was such that the struggles of the Plague Swamp's latest victims were not recorded on the surface, although grubs and larvae churned up by their death throes attracted the attentions of the curlews.

Three

D avid Weir watched with avid interest as Charlie Crittenden added another old aluminium saucepan to the semi-molten mass in the iron cauldron.

"Step it up a bit, Gus, me boy," Charlie ordered his youngest son. Dad was a lumbering, amiable giant of a man, and his two boys – both in their twenties – were turning out much the same.

Gus, who was working the lever connected to the antique leather bellows, increased his cranking. The saucepan collapsed slowly into the liquid like a sinking ship. His older brother, Carl, stood by, ready to take over from Gus when he tired but the younger lad kept up his vigorous pumping so that the searing charcoal, banked around the cauldron, pulsed red and white like a breathing monster.

The heat became more intense, forcing David to take another step back, although Charlie didn't seem to notice as he used a shovel to skim the accumulating dross from the surface of the molten aluminium. Ruth Crittenden was leaning against the huge rear wheel of the Charles Burrell fifty-kilowatt showman's engine, ready to help her husband with the pouring of the aluminium. The other curious onlooker was Titan – a towering, eighteen-hand Suffolk punch that weighed over a tonne and was one of the largest shire horses in West Sussex, and certainly the most inquisitive. Titan hated missing out on anything; no stable door survived his abiding curiosity.

What Charlie Crittenden was about to attempt in the farmyard was something that David would not have considered possible, but nothing was impossible for the resourceful gypsy and his family.

The giant steam road loco traction engine, a neglected, rust-encrusted relic of a bygone age, was David's latest acquisition for the museum. Its name was Brenda, according to an engraved brass plate. It had been built in 1929 by Charles Burrell & Son of Thetford as a mobile power station capable of generating the electricity needs of a large travelling fair. In its day it had powered not only bumper cars, dippers, whips, carousels and all the other amusements of the traditional fair, but also the hundreds of coloured lights that festooned the rides. With a plentiful supply of coal, coke or charcoal, and a willing team to keep the behemoth's firebox roaring, Brenda could even meet the power needs of a large village. But no longer; in 1951 one of its metre-diameter cast-iron front wheel rims had broken. The monster had been abandoned as not worth repairing to be replaced by a modern, truck-mounted diesel generator that needed little tending other than filling its fuel tank and pressing a starter button. The old showman's engine had been allowed to rot in the corner of a Sussex field.

Charlie Crittenden had recommended purchase and had assured David that he could knock up a replacement for the broken front wheel.

"Be in ally – not cast iron," Charlie had said. "Be just as strong and no one will know when it's painted up and the original spokes are riveted back on." And he had brushed aside David's doubts about making a copy of the massive rim.

Charlie's age-old technique was deceptively simple yet required great skill in execution. He and his sons had dug a trench, filled it with dampened green sand, and used the broken wheel's segments as a pattern to form a sand mould for the new casting. A little sand sculpting to tidy the form when the broken segments had been lifted clear and the mould was ready.

"Like cope and drag casting," Charlie muttered, glancing up at the sky and mopping his forehead. "Haven't done this in years."

It was late afternoon. Charlie and his two sons had been working since first light and now they were almost ready for the final and most crucial stage of the operation.

The last piece of scrap aluminium from what had been a large pile was lowered carefully into the nearly brimming cauldron.

"How do you know that you've right amount of ally in the pot, Charlie?" David asked.

Charlie grinned. "Easy, Mr Weir. Dropped the bits of the broken wheel in a tank of water and marked the amount the level went up. Took it out and dropped scrap ally in the tank until the level matched. Plus a bit for losses and luck."

David remained silent. Charlie Crittenden had had no schooling; he could barely write his own name, and yet he had an intuitive understanding of the physical world that many of David's educated friends lacked. It was the same with all the members of Charlie's family.

The Crittendens were travellers who moved around southern England in search of seasonal farm work and customers for their remarkable repertoire of skills. They were cartwrights, wheelwrights, farriers, blacksmiths, charcoal-burners, trug makers. They could layer hedges that no animal larger than a rabbit could get through. They could turn a stand of hazel or ash saplings into sheep hurdles, or trench in bundles of brushwood as mole drains that could keep a field healthy for forty years. They could build and repair barns as they had done for David Weir's museum. They were a repository of all the skills that had created England and the English countryside, and much of its wealth.

Overall, the only traditional English skill that the Crittendens lacked was paying taxes.

David had made the entire family and their caravans welcome two years previously when they had arrived to help restore old agricultural implements, and they had stayed, glad of the regular work he offered and the chance to be free of official harassment other than school attendance officers interested in the youngest members of the family. Like many travelling families, the Crittendens had attendance officers like farm dogs had fleas.

It was Charlie's skills and love of the past that had turned the rural museum into a practical business. Apart from the restoration of horse-drawn implements, he would tackle anything, but this particular job was the most daunting task so far.

Gus pumped even harder, sending charcoal sparks spiralling into the sullen sky. Charlie pulled on a pair of goggles and watched the cauldron carefully. He skimmed more dross to reveal the aluminium's molten surface, gleaming like mercury. He stirred the hellish liquid and watched it run, smoking and spitting, off the shovel.

Titan tossed his great head. David grabbed his snaffle bridle and backed him away.

"Reckon that's it, lads. Now you get back, Mr Weir . . . And that bleedin' great lump of cat's meat. Right back . . . OK, lads – get that kit on."

Gus stopped pumping. He and Carl pulled on ancient welding helmets and gauntlets, and waited expectantly.

"Now listen," said Charlie seriously. "You all know the drill. If I can't hold her, I'll yell out before letting go and you all leg it like fuck. We can always start again tomorrow if we screw up, but you can't grow new feet. You all with me?"

The boys and Ruth understood.

Charlie crossed himself and spat on his hands. "Right – let's get started." He picked up a T-handle that was about three metres long and hooked it on to a handle near the cauldron's lip. He braced himself, feet planted firmly apart, his banana-size fingers clasping the T-handle. Ruth Crittenden stood behind him and got a good grip on her husband's leather belt.

"OK – go!" he ordered.

Gus used a long-handled rake to knock the banked charcoal from around one side of the giant iron pot. The unleashed heat sprang upon them like a wild animal, forcing David and Titan even further back.

"Now the block, Carl!"

Gus moved clear when Carl knocked a supporting concrete block from under the brimming pot. The veins on Charlie's bare forearms knotted as he took the strain. His solid strength and bulk won the day; degree by degree, he allowed the cauldron to tip away from him. The first splatters of molten aluminium hit the vitrified clay culvert pipe that was to guide the molten metal into the open mould. Charlie let the smoke clear and started pouring. His control was excellent: a shining silver river flowed steadily along the culvert and into the mould. Clouds of vapour rose from the damp sand but it held its shape as the molten aluminium flowed into the form.

Charlie allowed the lightened pot to tilt right over so that the last dribble puddled itself into the main mass, and the job was done. They gathered around the trench, staring down at their handiwork, unmindful of the intense heat. Escaping air popped from the liquid wheel like eruptions in a volcanic mud pool.

"Nice," breathed Charlie. "Really nice. No rippling. Be lots of little blow-holes – always is with ally, but they don't matter none."

"How long will it take to set?" David asked.

"Initial set'll be about thirty minutes. Then we'll be able to scrape some of the sand away – see if it's flowed proper all round. Be a bugger if we have to do it again."

"Thanks, Charlie. I'll be in the office." David handed Titan's reins to Carl and returned to his farm office over the museum's front entrance. A fax was waiting for him. He read it through and called a local number with some trepidation. Ellen Duncan was a passionate woman in every respect.

"Ellen? David. Sorry to call the shop number but—"

"What does another call matter? The phone's been going non-stop. You've heard about the two UFO prats who disappeared in my lake?"

"I caught it on the news. What's the latest?"

"Not enough light now. The proper search starts tomorrow."

"Anyway, m'dear – the last quote is in. Sussex Institute of Art and Design can do the complete tabloid for a shade under twenty kay. That's a full-size replica of the cave in glass fibre complete with the paintings, three figures, and concealed lighting."

There was a groan of dismay at the other end. "Can you afford it?"

"No."

"But, David, the Vallon-Pont-d'Arc cave is the most important discovery of the decade. The oldest cave paintings in Europe! Thirty-one thousand years old!"

"I know that as well as you, Ellen," said David quietly. "And I'm as disappointed as you. We'll just have to think of something a little less grand. Maybe just a section of wall – the one with the mammoth painting?"

"Our plan was to give visitors an idea of what it was like to actually be in the cave and see Palaeolithic artists at work!" Ellen retorted angrily.

David was tempted to point out that it was Ellen's plan, but wisely remained silent.

"Jesus Christ!" she continued. "Why do all these discoveries have to be in France? Twenty-four of them! And what have we got in England? Bugger all!"

"Let's discuss it over dinner tomorrow night."

Ellen calmed down. "As you're being such a miserable skinflint, I shall insist on you taking me somewhere ruinously expensive."

"There's a new Chinese restaurant in Midhurst."

"Just so long as they don't expect me to eat with those ludicrous chopstick things. Any culture that fails to recognise the superiority and efficiency of knives and forks over stupid bits of wood is not to be trusted. That's why their food looks as if it's already been eaten – they can't cut it up."

David laughed. He had once been in Ellen's shop when a customer had asked for a book on feng shui and Ellen had exploded with: "Buy a copy of the building regulations from the Stationery Office! A people so stupid that they've built over twenty million houses on the flood plains of rivers can't teach us anything about building safe and secure homes." And anyone who referred to herbal remedies as alternative medicine was likely to end up in need of it. Ellen's view was that the pharmaceutical industry, with its synthesising of ancient cures such as aspirin, was the real provider of alternative medicine.

He promised to pick Ellen up at eight and added: "Oh – one thing,

Ellen. That programme about the Byno dig is on The Learning Zone tonight. Three a.m."

"You set your video and I'll set mine," Ellen replied tartly. "That way we should manage one decent recording between us."

Charlie Crittenden chose that moment to shamble into the office. David finished the call without telling Ellen how much he adored her. He looked up enquiringly.

The traveller jerked his thumb at the window where his boys could be seen clearing up. His wife was already at work on the showman's engine with a chipping hammer, cleaning off decades of rust and scale from around the firebox door. "Perfect, Mr Weir. Absolutely bleeding perfect."

David beamed. "Well done, Charlie."

"Still be hot in the morning. Best let it cool slow so it don't twist." Charlie grinned and nodded to the monstrous showman's engine. "We'll drill the spoke rivet holes tomorrow and fit the spokes, Mr Weir. The Plus Gas has freed the pistons and valve gear, so we'll have that old road loco there fired up and running at low pressure in a week. Be nice to know that she's working before we set to prettying her up."

David was pleased; if Charlie Crittenden said that the showman's engine would be running in a week, then it would be so.

It was as well for David Weir's peace of mind that he had no idea of the important role that the huge machine would play in the momentous events that lay ahead.

Four

It was the menacing hiss of a snake that woke Ellen Duncan.

She didn't scream or dive under the bedclothes – nothing so unseemly. She lay perfectly still, listening intently while willing her heartbeat to slow from its Gatling hammering of 180 that was threatening to burst through her ribcage.

Don't be silly, she chided herself, it was a cat. Not Thomas, though, because she couldn't move her feet; her pet was a crushing presence on the bed, obeying the immutable law that states that a sleeping cat on a duvet trebles in weight.

There it was again. A sustained hiss – too long for a snake's hiss, and certainly not a cat. Half a million years' evolution had gone into the development of the cat's hiss – it was a brilliant piece of impersonation – and evolution had got it right because snakes rarely hissed for more than two or three seconds when expressing displeasure, nor did cats. This hiss lasted at least ten seconds.

The strange noise stopped. She stared up at the yellow glow of Pentworth's North Street's lights suffusing the low ceiling of her tiny bedroom over her shop, wondering if she had dreamed it. And there it was again, this time followed by a metallic rattling noise.

Ellen did not regard herself as imbued with great courage, but she was fiercely protective towards her little shop; the realisation that someone was trying to break in and so damage her beautifully restored Victorian front filled her with a rage that drove out all thought of personal safety. Without even stopping to consider why anyone would wish to break into a herbalist's, she yanked her feet from under Thomas, dashed to the window, and threw up the sash.

The two youths were street-wise; they were swathed from head to foot in black, including their balaclava helmets, and ran off soundlessly in opposite directions, taking long, unhurried, soundless strides, and were gone by the time Ellen had unlocked the shop's side door and rushed barefoot into the silent, deserted street. Her sharp sense of smell detected a faint, sickly taint of cellulose paint on the cold night air.

"Bastards!" she spat venomously, standing in the middle of the road and staring in the direction that the tallest youth had taken. "Fucking bastards!"

"That sort of behaviour can get you into trouble, Miss Duncan. Prominent Town Councillor charged with insulting behaviour. It wouldn't look too good in the papers."

Ellen wheeled around and gaped at the ghostly figure of a tall man who had emerged from behind a car parked against the towering wall of Pentworth House on the opposite side of the road. He was wearing a white tracksuit and white trainers. Even his sweat-soaked headband was white. His tall, muscular figure was picked out in stripes of orange and yellow reflective tape and there were chevrons of the stuff on his chest and legs. He looked like a Technicolor bar code.

"Who are you?" she blurted, feeling frightened and vulnerable in her inadequate nightdress.

The man in white joined her in the middle of the street but she recognised the expressionless, wide-set eyes and gaunt features without having to look at the offered warrant card. "Oh – Sergeant Malone." She relaxed and smiled in nervous relief. "Aren't you a little early? I thought our meeting was at ten?"

"I was jogging my weary way home when suddenly my cosy little world is turned upside-down by delectable ladies rushing about the town in skimpy night attire," Malone replied drolly.

Ellen wasn't sure how to react to that. "Well . . . I'll never complain again about the police not being around when they're needed."

Detective Sergeant Mike Malone returned her smile while taking in the full-breasted outline of Ellen's body against the glare of fluorescent lights from an estate agent's window.

During a stint as the sector's Crime Prevention Officer in his uniformed days, he had visited Ellen several times and had often wondered what she was hiding under her white coat – now he knew, and was impressed, particularly by her dishevelled tumble of rich, dark tresses that fell about her shoulders.

"I was about to nab them when you frightened them off," he said. "We had an informant." He tapped a mobile telephone clipped to his waistband. "I was on my way home and got diverted."

Certainly being diverted now, he thought. *Thirty-seven? Thirty-nine? At least five years older than me. What is it about older women that fills me with these uncontrolled lusts?*

Ellen glanced at the distant darkened octagonal tower of Hill House that reared above the town like a derelict lighthouse. "Cathy Price," she snorted. "Well – the nosy little madam has her uses."

"Can't say who it was," Malone replied.

"So why didn't you chase after them?" Ellen enquired reprovingly, trying to not to sound ungrateful. "You're kitted out for running."

"No point, Miss Duncan." Malone indicated the reflective stripes on his tracksuit. "Decked out like this, they'd have no trouble losing me, and I hate getting lost."

Ellen couldn't help smiling despite the strange circumstances. Uncertain what to say or do next, she shifted her weight from one foot to the other; the tarmac was cold and gritty. "Well," she said at length, "at least they didn't manage to break in. Brad Jackson and one of his mates, I bet. I caught that little bastard shoplifting last year. If I ever get my hands on—"

"It wasn't Brad Jackson," Malone interrupted. "They were both too tall. And they weren't trying to break in."

For the first time since rushing into the street Ellen looked at her shopfront. 'Earthforce' was sign-written in a semicircle of scrolled Victorian lettering on each window. Inside each arc, in smaller letters, was *Ellen Duncan – Herbalist* with her telephone number underneath. But now there was an addition: below the telephone number, written in the vivid yet stylishly ugly overlapping font favoured by skilled aerosol graffiti artists, was what appeared to be a four-digit telephone extension number.

"EX2218?" the police officer mused. "I'm sure I would've noticed if you had over two thousand phone extensions in your shop, Miss—" He broke off when he saw the sudden terror in Ellen Duncan's eyes. For an instant her face contorted as if a frenzied demon had seized control of her features.

"I—" she began. But she never completed the sentence. Malone darted nimbly forward and caught her around the waist as her legs buckled. He was fit and strong, and had no trouble scooping her into his arms, his hand went inadvertently under the nightdress, causing it ride up in the process.

"I'm OK," said Ellen weakly, struggling ineffectually to tug the errant nightdress around her thighs.

"Delayed reaction," said Malone cheerfully, pushing the shop's side door open with his hip. Carrying Ellen up the narrow stairs was out of the question so he entered the shop. The combined aroma of hundreds of herbs assailed him – a pleasant, evocative scent that stirred childhood memories of autumn meadows warmed by Indian summers. He shifted his grip so that his fingers were pressed against the side of her breast, and opened the counter flap with his knee. He carried her into the shop's back room, catching her nightie on the door handle and yanking it even higher.

"Please put me down, Mr Malone."

"Lights?"

Ellen turned on the lights and kept up her protests until Malone lowered her into the swivel chair at her desk in such a way that her nightdress rode up once again, this time affording him a tantalising glimpse of pubic hair, dark and inviting, before his mortified patient thrust the garment between her knees and clamped them securely together. The action caused a dark, cold-puckered aureole to appear briefly before she clutched a hand to her neck. She was about to speak but started trembling. Malone gripped her hands tightly.

"Don't say anything," he advised, noting her deathly pallor and wondering if he ought to call a doctor. "Just keep still, keep quiet, and breathe deeply."

Ellen did as she was told while Malone filled an electric kettle at the sink and switched it on. He glanced around the workroom-cum-office. Compared with the shop's floor-to-ceiling rosewood cubby holes and tiny drawers – reminiscent of a bygone age – the room was businesslike and modern. Along one wall was a wide stainless-steel worktop that served as a bench for several commercial coffee grinders that Ellen used for milling dried roots. There was also a small industrial kiln and even a teabag and sachet-sealing machine. Dominating the tools on a wall rack was a wicked-looking ebony-handled knife. Adjoining the door leading to an outer still room was a mail-order packing table with various sizes of Jiffy bags stacked neatly in racks together with a giant roll of brown paper, gaffer-tape dispensers, electronic scales, and a franking machine.

The chair he had sat Ellen in served a small workstation with a desktop PC, a laser printer, and a facsimile machine. Virtually all the wall space around the workstation consisted of shelves piled high with locally printed booklets written and published by Ellen Duncan.

One area of wall by the workstation was occupied by large colour glossies of her and David Weir at their Palaeolithic dig on land that the farmer rented from Ellen. The discovery the previous year of the forty-thousand-year-old flint-mine camp had been a local sensation. One picture showed Ellen proudly holding a huge, bifacially-worked axe head.

Although the room was warm from the kiln that switched itself on and off every few seconds, Malone knew about shock, and was sensitive enough to guess at Ellen's concern about the revealing nature of her nightdress. He raced upstairs without consulting her, told the beginnings of an erection that it wasn't wanted, and returned with her duvet, still warm and with her body scent clinging to it. He placed it across her shoulders and tucked it around her, which earned him a grateful smile.

"You're very kind, Mr Malone."

"Brave is the word, Miss Duncan. There's a ferocious black cat the size of a panther upstairs which tried to declare your duvet an occupied zone." His humour was rewarded by an even wider smile although the fear he had seen in her eyes was still there.

"Thomas wouldn't hurt you – he likes visitors."

"But could he eat a whole one, I ask myself?"

The old joke prompted a nervous laugh from Ellen despite the terror churning in her stomach. Thomas slunk under the desk in case the commotion had resulted in a tin of Felix being accidentally opened.

"Your kettle's slow," Malone remarked, eyeing the big black cat warily as it investigated its empty feeding bowl and regarded him with baleful yellow eyes. Strangers whipping a warm duvet from under Thomas met with feline disapproval.

"It is if you fill it right up."

"Not guilty, ma'am. Since I've started living alone, I've learned to be careful with electricity."

The kettle began a muted singing.

"Divorced?" asked Ellen.

"A year. My ex's mortgage and my digs to keep up. Maintenance on two children always means a lot of month left at the end of the money."

"Promotion?"

"I'd have to transfer out of this sector first."

Concentrating on small talk took Ellen's mind off the graffiti. "Inspector Harvey Evans. He's the Sector Inspector, isn't he?"

"He certainly is."

"Surely he'd recommend you, wouldn't he?"

"I can recommend a new kettle, Miss Duncan."

Ellen smiled at the warning tone but was not put off. "I've not seen you in his morris men side."

"I'd be surprised if you had."

"He's transformed the Pentworth Morris Men since he took over as their squire," said Ellen reprovingly. "Doing away with the fluttering handkerchiefs and bringing in those sword and staff dances has made them so much more macho. They raised over five kay last year."

"They practise mostly on Sundays," said Malone casually. "A day reserved for my kids."

Ellen sensed the reluctance behind the admission. It was obvious that Malone was a private man who disliked talking about himself. "Forgive me for prying, Mr Malone. I'm a nosy old biddy."

The electric kettle interrupted Malone's reply with its shrilling. He followed Ellen's directions and used yellow teabags bearing her Earthforce logo to make two mugs of curiously scented tea.

He drew up a stool, sat opposite her, and sipped cautiously. The brew had an unexpected invigorating taste. He regarded it with mock suspicion. "Nothing illegal, I hope, Miss Duncan?"

"Ginseng – and a few additions of my own. Just a temporary pick-me-up." Ellen closed her eyes and allowed the powered root decoction of the ancient remedy to go to work on her nervous system.

"I suppose that number must be a tag of some sort," said Malone, sounding offhand but watching Ellen carefully.

"Tag?" Ellen opened her eyes.

"A graffiti artist's signature. They sometimes spray them first in case they're chased off before they've finished. It warns their buddies that the site is spoken for. Funny sort of tag, though – EX2218."

"Yes – of course – a tag. I'll get it cleaned off first thing . . ." She hesitated. "Any more news about the UFO nutters that disappeared in my lake this afternoon?"

Anxious to change the subject, thought Malone. *Nor does she ask me who I think our artist friends were. On the other hand, she's the owner of Pentworth Lake, therefore it's natural that the disappearance of the two Trade and Industry inspectors on her land would be preying on her mind.* Malone liked to think matters over before speaking. "Still no sign of them when I left the station," he remarked. "A couple of plods borrowed from Whisky-Charlie posted down there for the night. They're not happy. Actually, those two weren't ufologists. They were from the Radio Communications Agency in Southampton."

"So what on earth were they doing?"

"Investigating a source of radio transmissions that were interfering with the VOR aircraft beacon at Midhurst."

"Broadcasting from the middle of my lake?"

Malone shrugged and took another sip of the potent tea. "Apparently."

"Since when?"

"Since Thursday. It'll come out now. The *Mid-Sussex Gazette* has got hold of the story."

"That'll bring the UFO nutters back by the coachload. Not that I'm complaining. They nearly cleaned out my stock, and there's not a stick of stressed-pine furniture to be had in the town now."

The policeman grinned. "The transmissions stopped just after the men disappeared."

"And they'll reappear," said Ellen emphatically, reaching down to stroke Thomas, who was trying to sneer Malone to death.

Malone looked at her speculatively. "Even if they're loaded with equipment and sucked down into quicksand?"

"There's no such thing as quicksand as a material, Mr Malone. There's sand and there's water. Mix them together in roughly equal proportions by volume and you have what people call quicksand. You can float in it much easier than you can in water because it's denser, you can even swim in it but it takes some doing."

"You ought to have that bog fenced, Miss Duncan."

"It's not a bog – it's a lake that can become a swamp under certain conditions."

"So what's the difference between a bog and a swamp?"

"A bog is mainly decayed vegetation with a high water content. All nitrogen and virtually no oxygen. Swamps are mineral particles in suspension – sand and clay. Pentworth Lake only becomes a swamp when exceptionally heavy rains cause an upwelling – such as we had on Tuesday night."

"It's called a swamp on some of our old maps," said Malone. "Black Death bodies were dumped in it. And some locals call it the Plague Swamp."

"Not in my hearing, they don't."

"It ought to be fenced."

Ellen shook her head. "I'd have the Ramblers' Association after me, the Council for the Preservation of Rural England, West Sussex Council, and God knows who else. That common is stitched up with covenants, which is why my parents and their parents before them have been stuck with it. I thought I had a buyer a couple of years ago but it fell through. Just as well, after last year's find. Even the Pentworth worm-drowning club has fishing rights for the next fifty-odd years. So, the land I don't need for my herbs, I rent to David Weir for his sheep. Which is all the low-lying parts are good for in the summer."

"Your Stone Age find is fenced. Chainlink and razor wire."

Ellen pulled a face. "I hate it. Temporary planning permission until we've completed the dig. It was that or souvenir hunters stripping the site, so the council sanctioned the fence."

"Certainly was a lucky find."

Ellen drained her tea and stood, pulling the duvet modestly around herself. "I'm fine now, Mr Malone. Thank you so much for your help – I really am most grateful, but I think I ought to catch up on my sleep."

Malone accepted the dismissal. He confirmed his arrangement to meet Ellen at ten the following morning by Pentworth Lake, exchanged good nights, and set off for home, running with long, easy strides close to the wall of Pentworth House.

Once out of sight of Ellen Duncan's shop he slowed and stopped, thinking hard. The strange tea had certainly spiked his exhaustion, even though he had been on duty for ten hours. He felt he could face anything – even the self-styled Divine Sentinel himself: Father Adrian Roscoe, founder and leader of the Bodian Brethren, and Lord of Pentworth Manor. There was no time like now.

He turned back towards Pentworth and loped quickly and silently along the hushed street with its shoulder-to-shoulder antique shops.

Pentworth House was a late-eighteenth-century ancestral pile whose total lack of architectural importance was redeemed by its collection of Turners and its 400 rolling acres of deer park and farmland. But when the great maritime painter's works were moved to the new national museum, the tourists had melted away so the National Trust were happy for Adrian Roscoe to take it off their hands as a mesne lord for twenty years at a nominal rent, with a purchase option, providing the house, farm and deer park were maintained in good order. In ten years Roscoe had revitalised the estate. He built a dairy and a large bakery, bought in an experienced manager and went into quality ice cream and bread production aimed at the top end of the market.

Pentworth House's five-metre-high wall that Malone was skirting was incredibly ugly; a mixture of granite, bargate stone and black chert. Its dark, forbidding presence gave Pentworth the brooding atmosphere of a prison town. It occupied the northern side of North Street, shouldering Pentworth brusquely to one side, so that the town's true centre was Market Square, about 100 metres to the south of Pentworth House's front entrance – two huge, brutal elm doors that looked like lock gates.

Malone approached the Videofone porter. Heat-activated security lights bathed him. A closed-circuit TV camera mounted over the gates whined softly in the stillness as it panned to keep him framed. A doorbell wasn't necessary.

While waiting, savouring the rich smells from the bakery that hung over the town at night, he wondered if he was being a little peremptory in visiting the Bodian Brethren HQ at such an hour. But among Mike Malone's many responsibilities in this desperately under-manned sector of Sussex Police's Western Division was a requirement to maintain a watching brief on Adrian Roscoe and his followers. Nothing overt – very low key. After a spate of mass suicides in France and America, Home Office directives on the matter of weird cults showed a degree of paranoia. A lesser consideration was that as mesne lord of Pentworth Manor, Roscoe had a seat on the Town Council.

"Good evening," said a well-educated woman's voice from the speaker grille. "I'm Helen, tonight's duty sentinel. Please state your business."

Malone held his warrant card up to the camera lens and identified himself. "There's been an incident in North Street. Nothing serious but I'd like a word with you, please. You may have seen something."

"But of course," said the voice. "Please come in."

Always 100 per cent co-operation with the police, Malone reflected as a solenoid lock on a side door buzzed. Two minutes later he was shown by a minor sentinel into a small office off the spacious, oak-panelled hall, where the duty sentinel was sitting behind a reception desk. An array of closed-circuit monitors confronted her; on the wall was the inevitable framed print of Johann Bode, the eighteenth-century astronomer after whom the Bodian Brethren were named.

The girl looked up and smiled as Malone showed her his warrant card again. A new recruit, he thought; blonde as far as he could judge from the wisp of hair that had escaped from under her close-fitting hood. That and her white monklike gown gave her an ageless quality, but he guessed around nineteen; Adrian Roscoe liked them young. Not too young, of course – never under eighteen. Adrian Roscoe was always meticulously careful where the law was concerned.

"How can we help, Officer?"

Nice voice. Educated. Roscoe put the bright ones in the front office and on administration – the dumb ones went in his bed. Sometimes several at a time if the rumours were true.

"Sorry to trouble you at this hour, miss, but there's been an incident of vandalism in North Street. Ellen Duncan's herbal shop. I wondered if you had seen anything."

"Our cameras don't see along North Street, Officer."

Malone glanced at the monitors and noticed that all six pictures were slightly shrunken with a black band around the edges.

"The camera on the roof flagpole has a three-hundred-degree pan and tilt head, and the best power zoom money can buy," he observed. "I advised on its overhaul when I was CPO. The system's old, but reliable. There's not much it can't see."

The girl met his gaze without flinching. "It wasn't trained on North Street at the time."

Malone grinned. Such composure was always a challenge. "At what time? Did I say anything about when?"

The girl matched his smile but he had rocked her a little. "I haven't touched any of the controls since I came on duty at ten."

"The main gate camera moved when I rolled up just now," said Malone casually, knowing full well why but using it to further discomfort his victim.

"That one locks automatically on to a source of body heat."

"Ah, yes – of course – I'd forgotten."

Malone noticed that she had moved her left hand to her lap. He had also advised on the location of the alarm push button. Wired to the Divine Adrian's bedroom and alarming him right now, with any luck.

"I believe a couple of your inmates were roaming the town a while back. They may have seen something. I'd like to talk to them, please."

"No one has been out of the house tonight."

"I think you're wrong there, Helen."

Malone's trained eye noted that his unexpected familiarity had further unsettled the girl but her composure remained good. Nevertheless, a crack had appeared and every good crack deserved a wedge.

"I would've seen them," she replied.

"How? You haven't shifted the cameras, remember. Anyway – we're talking about the last hour. It won't take me long to roll back the logging tapes a couple of hours and fast-forward through them."

"It would be more convenient in the morning, Officer."

Malone leaned confidingly across the desk. "Look, Helen. I've got an appointment first thing. I'd like to clear this up now. And please don't tell me that all your inmates are tucked up in bed. I happen to know there are always nine in your funny chapel praying for the solar system's salvation. One for each planet. Right?"

"The Solar Temple is *not* a 'funny chapel', Officer," said the girl primly. "Furthermore—"

"Good evening, Mr Roscoe." Malone's sudden interruption was spoken without him turning around. Then he turned to confront a gaunt, forbidding, white-gowned presence and a pair of eyes of such a compelling ultraviolet blue that the police officer was convinced could be achieved only by special contact lenses.

The self-styled Father Adrian Roscoe, leader of the Bodian Brethren, smiled engagingly at the police officer. Those who heard him speak for the first time were always surprised by his rich, resonate voice, which was at odds with his slight build. It was a famous voice that had featured in over a thousand American television commercials; ten years earlier, Roscoe had been Britain's first voice-over multi-millionaire. "You must have eyes in the back of your head, Sergeant Malone."

No. Just damn good ones in the front of it. Sharp enough to see a reflection in this lovely girl's eyes.

"I have indeed, sir," said Malone.

Father Roscoe gave an easy chuckle as they shook hands. There was genuine friendliness in his whole demeanour, his grip and even the remarkable blue eyes conveyed warmth, but they never blinked – ever.

"Good evening, Sergeant Malone. Forgive two small corrections. Firstly, as you are well aware, our brother and sister sentinels are *not* inmates, as you choose to call them. We have a happy kibbutzim community here; sentinels are free to leave at any time if they so wish."

Which keeps the press off your back, thought Malone.

"Secondly, there are always *ten* solar sentinels at prayer in the temple. The belt of asteroids between Mars and Jupiter is the remnants of the fifth planet from the sun. It aroused the wrath of God and so he destroyed it and all its peoples. We pray for the salvation of their souls, and, through the intensity of continuous prayer, we are also beseeching God not to exact the same fearful but well-deserved retribution upon this sin-wracked earth."

"Well, it certainly seems to be working, Mr Roscoe," Malone observed. "We're talking to each other in this world and not the next."

The flippant remark caused a little of the friendliness to fade from the intense gaze. "It is customary to address me as *Father*

Roscoe. I believe Inspector Evans has already spoken to you on this matter."

The sudden chilling, slight as it was, induced a strange sensation of foreboding in Malone. He had met Roscoe on several occasions and could well understand the strange influence he exerted over susceptible young people. Crossing him took courage.

"Perhaps I'd better just stick to 'sir'," Malone offered. He was hardly a good Catholic, but he was buggered if he was going to accord this creep the same title as Father Kendrick of St Dominic's. Nor did he flinch away from that hypnotic, compelling gaze. Mike Malone could stare down an opal-eyed mummified Egyptian cat, but it took some doing with Adrian Roscoe.

The older man shrugged. "As you wish. So what's the problem, Sergeant?"

Malone outlined the incident in North Street.

"Ellen Duncan? Ah, yes – the herbalist. The woman with the large black cat . . . And you saw the two men outside this woman's shop?"

"Youths. Very clearly, sir." Not strictly a lie because Malone had seen them – although not their faces, which had been masked by their balaclavas.

"And what makes you think they're from here?"

"They were city-wise. They used teamwork. They weren't your average can-kicking, gum-chomping, brain-dead Pentworth yobs."

"And yet they indulged in mindless aerosol vandalism," said Roscoe pointedly.

"Maybe it wasn't so mindless, Mr Roscoe. Any idea what EX2218 means?"

Roscoe gave the question several moments' thought – several moments too long. It was a typical acting cliché that Malone recognised immediately. "I'm afraid not, Sergeant."

Liar! If you really didn't know you would've said so straight off and not indulged in a pretend pause.

"Well, it certainly scared Miss Duncan."

"Then it would be more sensible to ask her." Roscoe paused for a moment and then came an unexpected climb down. "Of course, it's perfectly possible that the two you saw were our more recent novitiates. As you know, we rescue many from the streets of Chichester, Brighton, Littlehampton, Bognor . . . Drug addicts . . . Beggars . . . Drop-outs . . . They're all God's children, destined to carry out God's work. Unhappily, it takes a while for some of them to shake off their ungodly ways."

He beamed suddenly. A gnarled, almost emaciated hand reached out from the folds of his gown and took Malone by the elbow. "However, if you say you've actually seen them, then you'd better come and pick them out."

File under heading: bluff, called, thought Malone, kicking himself for not anticipating the climb down; Roscoe always cooperated 100 per cent with the police. He turned to the girl, who appeared to have shown no interest in the conversation. "Just a small point, Helen. Get those monitors adjusted. The pictures are about twenty per cent too small."

"It's an old system," said Roscoe.

"Still a damn good system, though," Malone countered. "Get Bob Harding to take a look at it."

Roscoe led Malone across the main hall, beneath a huge, glittering crystal chandelier. He passed a security card through a swipe reader and opened the double oak-panelled doors to what had once been the stately home's banqueting hall. The results that had been achieved with the clever use of drapes patterned with gothic arches were dramatic. The huge tapestries, hung from ceiling to floor, completely covered the minstrels' gallery. They made the hall narrower and thus exaggerated its height, giving the impression of being in a cathedral. The northern end was almost completely hidden by a giant, flower-garlanded portrait of Johann Bode with hidden lights creating a halo around the old astronomer-mathematician's head, illuminating his venerable features in a milky, ethereal glow. But the centre piece of the Solar Temple of the Bodian Brethren was the floor – totally black on to which an overhead planetarium projector threw images of the planets with the sun in the precise centre. The image of each planet was correctly proportioned: Jupiter, huge and menacing with its giant red spot glowing like a baleful eye; Venus, a featureless haze of light; Mars, with its reddish rills and dormant volcanoes. The asteroid belt was depicted as a sparkling dust ring of glittering points of light. And, most glorious of all: Earth – a blue-green iridescent disc swathed in the spirals of delicate white lace of its weather systems. The overall effect of the hall was like being inside a giant, luminous orrery.

Outside the orbit of Pluto was a circle of ten white-gowned figures, sitting cross-legged on the floor. They were perfectly still, hands folded in laps, cowls pushed back, heads bowed in silent mediation.

"Help yourself," Roscoe invited. Even when whispering, his voice lost none of its sonorous qualities. "Walk around the outside, but

please don't go inside the circle. Each sentinel has focused his
or her entire consciousness on their assigned planet. A break in
their concentration, for even a second, could be disastrous. And
if they're not among them, then I'll assemble all the others in the
lecture room."

Feeling slightly foolish, and rather wishing that he hadn't pushed
his bluff so hard, Malone approached the circle of silent meditators
and regarded them in turn. Damned hard judging their height and
build under those gowns, but he could see enough to eliminate four
of them right away, plus the stupid kid with the tattooed face.

He walked slowly around the outside of the circle. None of
them gave the slightest indication that they were aware of his
presence – each pair of eyes remained fixed in a hard stare at
their designated planet.

Malone completed a circuit of the floor and was about to admit
defeat when he caught a faint whiff of acrylic paint. He had
patched enough rust holes in his old Escort to know the smell
well, and how difficult it was to get rid once the paint particles got into hair and clothing. He stared down at the nearest youth, who had his back to him. The brilliant glow of the
sun's image in the centre of the circle highlighted tiny beads
of sweat on his temple. He had been exerting himself recently.
The white sole edging of an Adidas trainer poked out from under
the gown of another youth to his left. Malone touched each one
on the shoulder for a couple of seconds. One gave a noticeable start at the contact. With that, the policeman returned to
Roscoe's side.

"Those two," he muttered.

Roscoe placed a bony finger to his lips and the two men returned
to the entrance hall.

"Frank and George," said Roscoe regretfully. "They were saved
on our last London mission. I will ensure that they face up to their
responsibilities. Criminal damage? Well, I dare say they've done
worse."

"I can't speak for Miss Duncan, but if the graffiti is removed
pronto, she'll probably drop the matter."

Roscoe nodded. "I will send them around to the woman's shop
first thing."

There was nothing in Roscoe's tone to suggest hostility towards
Ellen Duncan, but that was the second time he had referred to
her as 'the woman'; it made Malone wonder what she had done
to annoy him. "I don't think that would be such a good idea, Mr

Roscoe. They've already given her a bad fright. Perhaps a cleaning company?"

"Yes – of course – good thinking, Sergeant. I'll attend to it in the morning."

Malone thanked Roscoe and apologised for disturbing him.

"Not at all, Mr Malone. We like to maintain our good working relationship with the police. Your Inspector Evans is an excellent man. His Pentworth Morris Men raise such a lot for charity, as I'm sure you know."

"I do know," said Malone evenly.

"They put on a show here last month. I don't recall seeing your face—"

"I was probably on duty. Good night, Mr Roscoe."

Malone paused as he was crossing the courtyard and used his mobile phone to leave a message on Ellen Duncan's answering machine to say that a local resident had been disturbed to hear about the graffiti on her shopfront and that a cleaning firm would remove it immediately.

He was returning the phone to its waist clip when the main gates swung open and he was temporarily blinded by the headlights of a giant Winnebago camper. As it trundled past and headed towards the rear of Pentworth House, Malone caught a glimpse of Nelson Faraday at the wheel. The Londoner was an unlikely lieutenant for Roscoe, but if you want to get the measure of a man, take a look at his friends.

Faraday was thirty-five, a sadist. Very tall, lantern-jawed. A dress sense as sharp as his shiv. A permanent scowl, and a lot of previous that was wasn't permanent because of the Spent Convictions Act. Faraday hadn't pimped or beaten up or raped a prostitute for ten years – no Schedule 1 offences – so the law said he was clean. Leopard and spots were two words that crossed Malone's mind as he watched the vehicle's tail lights disappear.

The big white camper, emblazoned with a picture of Johann Bode and a logo that showed a divine mailed fist smashing a planet, was Roscoe's mobile temple to take the word to the masses, provided they were huddled or downtrodden and preferably old enough to have been written off by despairing parents who would be unlikely to come searching for their errant offspring.

It was used several times a year when Roscoe craved new blood because too many devoted disciples were proving less than devoted when it came to praying in the Solar Temple, working long hours on Pentworth House's highly productive farm, or making ice cream or baking bread, and decided that begging, prostitution, or flogging the *Big Issue* on street corners was an easier deal.

The camper would set off from Pentworth House, with Faraday driving, and be later sighted in the sleazy areas of Brighton or Southampton. Inside the camper were hot showers, warm beds, a galley that doled out not Salvation Army soup but junk food on a grand scale: fried chicken quarters, hamburgers, kebabs, and french fries by the tonne – natural bait for the young and hungry. And while they queued, they would be regaled by a dazzling, professionally produced video shown on a giant projection screen with a superb sound system that used clips from recent big-budget science-fiction movies interspersed with an unblinking Adrian Roscoe preaching the message of his Bodian Brethren.

His compelling eyes and commanding voice made it impossible for all but the strongest-willed to turn away. He used his formidable oratory skills to deliver a seductively simple message that preached purity of prayer as being more important than purity of body. Better still, he told a story: a gripping story of great civilizations across the galaxy who had abandoned God and became locked in terrible battles – of mighty star-roaming cruisers crewed by demons and witches from which even the angels fled in panic.

One such civilisation had risen on what had been the fifth planet of the solar system. Over a period of a thousand millennia the people had forgotten their origins and had become omnipotent. They were so powerful that they believed that their collective entity was God . . . Until God, after repeated warnings which they heeded not, struck them down by smashing their planet to thousands of asteroids. They were, Roscoe proclaimed, guilty of the ultimate presumption deserving the ultimate punishment.

Raising bony, clenched fists above his head he declared that mankind, on the third planet from the sun, was embarking on the same disastrous course. But it wasn't too late because God had given us a warning by revealing to Johann Bode the terrible punishment he had meted out to the fifth planet. The revelation had been in the form of a fabulous, yet simple, mathematical formula that anyone could understand, that gave the positions of all the planets of the solar system. The 'law' stated that there should be a fifth planet between the orbits of Mars and Jupiter, but there was no fifth planet – merely a belt of asteroids, space rubble whose mass added up to what had been a fair-sized planet, circling the sun where a planet should be.

But had message of Bode's law been heeded? Roscoe trumpeted. Had the world of eighteenth-century astronomers recognised it as the word of God? No! Satan and his forces of witchcraft had intervened by ensuring that the scientists would prostitute the divine word for their own ends. Bode's law predicted a seventh planet so the scientists used the law to search for it, and they found Uranus – exactly where the law said it would be. Glory for the astronomers. Victory to the devil and his acolytes of witchcraft. Then the astronomers found Neptune and Pluto, *and still* they refused to accept Bode's law as God's warning.

"But we can accept it!" Roscoe thundered, his rich voice booming from speakers without a ripple of distortion. "We can warmly embrace it in the resolution of our prayer and in our steadfast rejection of Satan and his disciples of darkness and witchcraft. We seek not only God's forgiveness but also his intervention. We seek his help and guidance so that his terrible wrath, which destroyed the fifth planet, will never be needed against Earth. And we seek his forgiveness, not for our sins, but for the forgiveness of others so that all Mankind will survive. The purity of our bodies is of no consequence to God! All that matters is the purity of our prayers and our implacable opposition to Satan and his witches!" Malone, who had once followed the camper, reflected that Roscoe's message had everything: science; hi-tech star wars; astronomy; astrology; and an almost total absence of any complex theology and doctrine. Roscoe's cult was sufficiently outlandish to stand apart from the established religions. Its greatest attraction was its simplicity. It was an easily understood cult shorn of all dogma. All it demanded was prayer for the salvation of others, and the fervent rejection of Satan and all his works, although the cult's concepts of the devil and his acolytes were firmly rooted in medieval Christian beliefs.

Roscoe was particularly fond of proclaiming that Man's sex drive was the gift of God and that even Christ in his teachings had shown little interest in the so-called sins of adulterers and fornicators.

Above all, the doctrine of the Bodian Brethren tapped deep into a growing need for simplicity; and its basic underlying message was unique in modern cults, and indeed in the monotheistic religions.

Purity of prayer is more important than purity of body!

In other words he did not require his followers to adopt a monklike existence: they could go on boozing, snorting up, and fucking their brains out. Roscoe included. Of course, what clinched the matter as far as the young were concerned was that Roscoe preached that life was God's gift and was meant to be enjoyed to the full. That gift included an appreciation of music – all music – the louder, the better.

The side door swung shut behind Malone. Relieved to be clear of the brooding gates of Pentworth House and its strange occupants, he broke into a jog, gradually building up his pace for his three-kilometre run home.

A watcher followed the fluorescent-striped figure's long, easy strides along the darkened streets. It was the crablike device that had followed Vikki the previous afternoon but it was now equipped for operating where there were likely to be more people about. It waited under a parked truck until Malone was a safe distance away, gently flexing the pump muscles in its eight legs to stimulate the flow of coolant through its joints. The fluid maintained its body temperature to as near ambient temperature as possible, thus making it difficult to see in the infrared segment of the spectrum. The system was one in its formidable stealth armoury.

Once its quarry was several paces ahead, it moved off in silent pursuit, unaware that it had competition in the surveillance stakes.

Five

Cathy Price's home was an excellent location for her to spend many hours keeping Pentworth under close observation. Her office-cum-bedroom at the top of the octagonal tower of Hill House, a rambling Edwardian folly inherited from her mother, was the highest point in Pentworth, with stunning views of the town and the surrounding countryside from its eight windows. A window cleaner called once a week to ensure that the optically flat panes were always spotless so that nothing interfered with the images she saw through her 110mm Vixen refractor telescope, mounted on the arm of her electric wheelchair.

At thirty-two, Cathy was mentally and physically in good shape, with an exhibitionistic pride in a body fine-tuned each day by three hours' vigorous exercising on various machines in her living room one floor below. Mondays – pumping iron; Tuesdays – the rowing machine; Wednesdays – furious pedalling on an exercise bicycle; Thursdays – back to the weights. A relentless regime that had become her master – not only because the alkaloids released into her bloodstream during these bouts of frenzied activity gave her powerful orgasms, which was reason enough, but mainly because she was terrified that her body would atrophy if she didn't drive it to its extremes.

Her pony had thrown her at the age of ten and left her without any sense of balance. The stirrup bones in her middle ears that sensed the position of the body were fine, but the part of the brain that maintains balance by sending a continuous stream of signals to the leg, thigh and foot muscles had been permanently damaged by the fall. As a result Cathy was 100 per cent fit and 100 per cent disabled. She could slide into and drive an ordinary car – although the ordinariness of her restored 1960 E-type Jaguar was questionable; she could move from chair to chair; sit up; use her exercise machines; and even make energetic love – always in a frenzied manner as if she feared that even that ability would be taken from her. In short, she could do everything that most able-bodied people can do, but she

44

had great difficulty standing or walking. Hours of physiotherapy as a teenager had failed to persuade other parts of her brain to take over the function of maintaining balance.

Driven by her indomitable spirit and a burning desire never to be dependent on anyone, she had taken a degree in graphic arts at Kingston University. Following the necessity of moving her mother to a residential home, she had raised a mortgage on the house, used the money to buy a turnkey Macintosh computer system, and had set herself up in business designing catalogues and brochures for the ever-expanding junk mail industry. Her work had started inauspiciously enough seven years before with the production of stylish menus for pubs and restaurants in Surrey and West Sussex.

Which was how she had met Josh.

He had tracked her down – determined to discover the creator of such innovative nightclub fliers – for recruitment into the graphic design department of his advertising agency.

Josh had changed her, and her life.

Before him she had been a virgin – self-effacing and painfully shy in the presence of men, largely as a result of her disability – although assertive enough on the phone where business was concerned. The telephone was a great equaliser. Her only interests other than her work had been cooking in her neat little kitchen with its low worktops.

But after Josh she was a different woman. With his infectious fun attitude to sex, he had treated her as normal in every respect, making no concessions nor patronising her in any way. Married, with two children and a devastating streak of honesty, he had told Cathy that he wanted her for three things: sex, sex, and more sex. A candour she warmly embraced and which set the tone of their tempestuous weekly encounters. He was a skilled, rampant lucifer match that had plunged lustily into her tinder box and set her on fire, releasing a lifetime's latent inhibitions. It was an article of faith with Josh that fucking shouldn't start until his partner had come at least five times. He joked that to achieve this he had grown a six-inch tongue and learned to breathe through his ears.

Now Cathy was no longer interested in cooking; she was just cooking.

But Josh had done more than eroticise Cathy; thanks to him she was on the way to becoming a rich woman, and Josh the UK's first virtual Internet Webcam pimp.

The Connectrix Quickcam perched on top of her computer monitor took a picture of her desk with the bed in the background. The miniature TV camera, a little larger than a golf ball, had been Josh's idea after a weekend's fun and games with a Sony camcorder. The Quickcam was a computer-linked electronic camera set to take a picture every ten minutes. It was totally silent in operation but its associated software obligingly generated a click through the Mac's speakers so that she knew when a picture had been taken. It took the Mac a few milliseconds to process the image into a JPEG file and complete the operation by dialling up her Internet server in France through a GSM mobile phone that was used for no other purpose. A further twenty seconds was all it took to despatch the image via the Mac's high-speed modem. The process was repeated automatically six times an hour, twenty-four hours a day for the benefit of the CathyCam Web site on the Internet and the 150,000-plus CathyCam subscribers around the world who paid one euro per month to access the site any time they wished to see the latest picture. After six months Cathy had learned to ignore the camera when working. And she always kept a coat draped across the back of the wheelchair. To her many thousands of admirers she was a healthy, grey-eyed blonde with an air of sweet innocence despite being an outrageous exhibitionist on occasions, without a hint of a serious disability.

Most of the time she was out of shot because her work station was wide and the Quickcam's field of vision was narrow, or simply working. But her fans were imbued with that Job-like patience of all true voyeurs. They rarely complained, and were content to wait for that tantalising glimpse of a nipple, or even more if she was in the mood. To aid them she always slept with a bedside light on so that could appreciate her habit of kicking her duvet off the bed when asleep.

Strange . . . They had more hardcore Webporn at their fingertips than they could ever hope to see if they sat at their computers for a hundred years, and yet they logged into the relatively innocuous, low-resolution CathyCam Web site by the thousand, particularly now that her site was being publicised by several unofficial free-access Web pages that had popped up devoted to the 'Best of CathyCam'.

Right now the object of the sex fantasies and masturbatory aid of over 150,000 fans was out of shot, sitting at a north-facing window, peering through the eyepiece of the huge Vixen telescope, admiring the promising lunchbox jiggle of Mike Malone's genitals under his sweat-shrunk tracksuit as he jogged towards her along Pentworth High Street.

The Quickcam snapped a picture of the unoccupied double bed.

The slate roof of the Crown public house in Market Square obscured Malone momentarily, and then he was back in view, the street lights sheening his face with yellow sweat. Closer now, his balls bouncing merrily under his tracksuit. And then he was lost to sight when he swung on to the Chichester Road and wouldn't be visible for another five minutes.

Cathy spun her wheelchair around and brought the telescope to bear on Ellen Duncan's herbal shop again. It had been an hour since she had seen two figures behaving suspiciously with aerosol paint cans and had reported them to the police. A pity that the shop was at the wrong angle for her to see what the little swine had drawn but an early morning drive would solve that.

Time for bed but first a quick look at the recreation ground pavilion about 500 metres away. The little wooden building beside the bowling green, with its veranda benches sheltered from the wind, was often used for nocturnal activity. It was the town's unofficial youth club. Only last week, with the moon in its first quarter, she had seen Sarah Gale, skirt hitched around her waist, panties pulled to one side, sitting astride Robbie Hammond and indulging in advanced power lap dancing, the pale light on her pumping buttocks providing an interesting comparison with the real moon.

The moon was obscured tonight but Cathy's eye was self-trained to interpret shadows. She looked for movement. People in a darkened car or on a park bench never kept absolutely still. A slight turn of the head, a hand encircling a neck would be enough for her brain to translate the patches of dark and darker into definite shapes. The flare of a match or cigarette lighter was always a bonus and sometimes enabled her to identify those whom she was observing.

But the park was deserted, as were the huddled streets of the silent little town whose night-time patterns of light and shadow were imprinted on her memory; the slightest change was always worthy of investigation. But tonight the street lights seemed fractionally dimmer. Humidity, no doubt – it was warmer than usual for March.

There were no interesting lit windows other than Pentworth's regular crop of insomniacs. She could see a light from Bob Harding's circular repair workshop-observatory at the back of his High Street shop spilling on to his neat lawn and his not so neat collection of satellite dishes and amateur radio antennae. She knew the scientist-engineer's habits well, particularly since last summer when he had acquired a new wife over half his age. That was when he starting shutting up shop at four p.m. instead of five p.m. One hot afternoon, with the Hardings' bedroom's lace curtains being whipped open by a breeze, she had caught a number of interesting glimpses that suggested that Bob Harding wasn't all talk when it came to horizontal aerobics.

During the nights he worked on his repairs, every two hours the light would come on in the flat over the shop when he made himself a cup of coffee. She wondered why he didn't fix up a percolator in the workshop to save all that traipsing – he always had a few on sale in his shop as uncollected repairs.

The workshop light went out. Cathy looked closely and saw a split appear in the workshop's roof. It was a clear night apart from a bank of cloud obscuring the moon, so it looked as though Bob was going to indulge in some star-gazing – one of his many interests. He had once confided in her that amateur astronomy was an obvious hobby for an insomniac. She had a standing invitation to visit his workshop on a clear night and take a look through his 200mm Newtonian telescope. He had ground the mirrors himself. Bob Harding was fifty-eight – likeable, tall, stooping, good-looking, and an outrageous flirt that his new wife seemed to accept. Cathy had no doubt that the instrument he was really interested in her getting to grips with didn't have mirrors. It might be an interesting diversion take up his offer some time. She was always in favour of adding new beaux to her string . . .

Cathy roved the eyepiece. There were a few lights to the south where the police were keeping watch over the old Plague Swamp where two men had disappeared the previous day, but they were too far away and too indistinct to be of interest.

Mike Malone came into view again. The safety stripes on his tracksuit made him easy to follow, this time with his back to her as he neared the outskirts of the town and the end of the street lighting.

Did anyone ever tell you that you've got a tasty arse, Mike Malone?

She was about to unship the telescope from its mounting socket in the arm of her wheelchair when she saw a sudden blur of movement – something small and low that seemed to be following the police officer. A cat?

Unlikely. Apart from their occasional swearing contests, and choir practice sessions, cats were largely secretive creatures that avoided people when going about their mysterious nocturnal affairs.

Careful adjustment of the telescope's knurled focusing wheel failed to sharpen the image; changing to the 9mm eyepiece would give more magnification but would cost too much in lost light. The deep field wide-angle eyepiece stayed in place as she tracked the curious creature that seemed to be following Malone at a distance of about twenty metres. It had no discernible edges, but she got the distinct impression of a crab or giant spider. The word 'Spyder' popped into her mind and lodged there. Certainly it seemed to be spying, and then her suspicions were confirmed.

Malone slowed, and it slowed. He must have heard something because he suddenly stopped and spun around. But the thing was incredibly quick. It seemed to have anticipated his actions such was its speed when it darted under a hedge before he had a chance to complete his turn.

Cathy kept her attention and the telescope focused very precisely on the exact spot where the spyder had disappeared. She adjusted the instrument's knurled wheel with micrometer precision.

God damn this flare from street lights!

The Vixen's fluorite objective lens was among the best in the world, but it was designed to cope with shining pinpoints of main sequence stars light-years away – not 300-watt quartz iodine street lamps right on the periphery of its field. She opened her eye as wide as possible and pressed it even closer to the eyepiece but all she could make out beneath the hedge was a confusing pattern of grey and darker grey streaks and bars. And then her brain flipped as it sometimes does when viewing an optical illusion and she realised that she was actually seeing the spyder. Its outline had hardened now that it was perfectly still.

She counted at least eight legs, possibly more. They had a metallic look about them but she couldn't be certain.

Mike Malone appeared to have seen nothing. After a final glance around he resumed his homeward jog and, once again, the spyder's outline softened to a blur as it followed him. The apparent awkwardness of its articulated leg movements, although its forward motion was smooth enough, confirmed Cathy's hunch that the thing was mechanical.

How big?

Hard to say. About the size of Yorkshire terrier. Maybe a little bigger. Probably some kid having a bit of fun with a radio-controlled toy. Bloody expensive toy, though.

And then the runner and his mysterious follower were lost permanently to sight around a bend in the lane.

Six

Cathy was right and wrong about the spyder. It was mechanical but it was no toy. Her choice of a name was excellent because its primary function at the moment was exactly that – a mobile observation instrument, designed to send information on its surroundings back to the swamp that Pentworth Lake had become.

To minimise the risk of detection the refractive index of its outer skin was close to that of air, thus making it difficult to see in the visible-light spectrum. That Cathy had seen it was a credit to her eyesight and her telescope's crystal lens, but what she had really seen was mostly the fine film of condensation that the spyder had collected during its foray.

With the telescope unshipped and laid it across a settee, Cathy locked the wheelchair's wheels and used it as a support while she got undressed for bed. She had little trouble standing provided as she had something to hang on to; long practice had made her adept at dressing and undressing with one hand.

Once in her shortie nightie, she adjusted her blonde wig and did her usual abandoned flop on to the bed and into the Quickcam's field of vision. Sometimes the camera caught her in mid-flop and the resulting beaver JPEG image would be echoed around the world on the Internet by jubilant fans.

One of her most dedicated fans was a psychiatrist in California who liked to study Cathy when she was asleep and send her long e-mails containing an analysis of her changing positions. She owed him a reply to his last outpouring so she grabbed her white comms board and wrote on it in bold Chinagraph letters:

THIS A PICTURE FOR RAFFLES IN CA. BIG SPECIAL KISSES!

The stilted wording was deliberate, to perpetuate the widespread belief that 'Cathy' was French and that her room was in France.

After that it was only matter of holding the board up with her legs slightly apart and waiting for the Quickcam to click.

Seven

M ike Malone's trainers were soft and silent, and his hearing good. There it was again: a faint scrabbling noise as though something metallic were following him.

He stopped jogging abruptly and spun around, his eyes probing the shadows along the narrow lane's hedgerows, his breathing shallow to give his ears a chance.

Nothing.

But he knew there was something. It could be an injured animal – a dog, most likely – and what he had heard was the scratch of its claws on the road.

He called out in a friendly, coaxing voice, but no animal emerged from the shadows.

When he resumed running he heard the strange sound again but maintained his pace because he had a plan. A little way ahead the lane became a narrow cutting with the bank on each side buttressed by steep retaining walls. There was no cover so he stood a good chance of seeing the poor beast and sending in a description. A wandering, injured animal, its senses dulled by pain, was a danger to road users. He might even be able to catch it if he were quick enough.

He reached the cutting and kept going, his keen ears picked up the curious metallic scratching again. The change of acoustics told him when creature was enclosed by the retaining walls. Good timing was essential, and Malone's was excellent: without giving a warning by slowing down, he suddenly wheeled around and charged.

The spyder's makers had provided their surveillance machine with certain instincts and assigned them priorities. Curiosity was the primary instinct simply because the spyder was an observation instrument, although it had other facilities. Indeed, its powers of observation were remarkable. It could 'see' right across the spectrum from radio emissions to visible light and far beyond to the delicate rhythms of organic brains . . . Such thought patterns could be transmitted or recorded. Provided it was close enough to its quarry.

Self-preservation came second.

But those priorities could be changed according to circumstances. When the spyder saw its quarry spin around and come racing towards it, its self-preservation programming became dominant. To say it was undecided for a few milliseconds would be to give a false impression of its capabilities. The speed at which Malone came at it was not really the problem: the rapidity of the spyder's own cognitive processes were such that it perceived Malone moving towards it as if in slow motion – a foot lifted and brought down, the slow compression of the trainer's sole and heel as it absorbed Malone's weight . . .

Several options had to be analysed. Turning and running was the obvious one but the spyder possessed mass and hence inertia. Although its eight legs equipped it admirably for moving over almost any terrain, it had already noted problems with acceleration and deceleration on this present hard surface which, at this point, continued upwards on either side of it. It performed several hundred calculations which included its probable climbing rate if it attempted to scale the lane's retaining walls.

Now that the being coming towards it was closer, it picked up a confused picture of itself as seen from its quarry's point of view. There were no fantasies for it to mirror back as a distraction. For that system to work, the subject had to be receptive.

The other trainer hit the road . . .

The spyder measured the acceleration of the being coming towards it against the time it would take to deploy its soft pads. They gave better grip but they reduced its acceleration and ground speed.

In the time it took Malone's muscles to contract for his next great stride, the spyder had analysed several hundred more options and followed them along as many branching probability paths. They tapered down like an inverted pyramid to one course of action.

The spyder had never been required to use its flight capability. Atmospheric flight meant displacing air and that meant making a considerably amount of noise which conflicted with its primary purpose of observing without being observed. Flight also consumed a great deal of power. The spyder's creators possessed considerable ingenuity, but, like all life throughout the universe, they were bound by the immutable laws of the universe. They could not perform miracles. But what happened next seemed pretty miraculous to Malone.

His surmise when he saw the spyder's ghostly outline more clearly than before coincided with Cathy Price's conclusion: that the thing was a kid's toy of some sort. Well – it was going to be confiscated and the owner subjected to a stern verballing when he or she tried to reclaim it. A thing like that roaming the countryside could easily frighten people. He was within four strides of the spyder when its upper shell snapped open into four segments like a neatly peeled orange. Three strides to go and the umbrella-like segments started spinning like a helicopter's rotors.

Bloody hell! This is no toy!

Two strides . . .

It emitted a shrill whistle as the double contra-rotating rotor tips reached the speed of sound. In that instant he realised that it was going to escape so he threw himself forward, hands outstretched, in a flying rugby tackle. He fell heavily, bruising his elbows painfully on the hard asphalt, and his clutching fingers closed on

God damn it to hell!

Nothing.

The thing had done the impossible in such a short time and leapt straight up into the night sky. Malone felt a powerful downwash rom its rotors on his face as he stared up but it climbed so fast that it had vanished by the time he could focus his eyes. He followed its progress with his ears for several seconds as the whine was absorbed into the night. So far as he could judge, it did not change course but continued climbing vertically until it could no longer be heard.

The harsh cry of a nightjar robbed the night of its silence.

Malone climbed to feet, brushed himself down, and stood in the middle of the lane rubbing his elbows. His first thought was to report the incident but stayed his hand when he reached for his mobile telephone.

Report what? That you were chased across West Sussex by a mechanical glass crab that took off like a V2 when you tried to catch it?

Just the sort of thing Sector Inspector Harvey Evans would love him to report.

"A flying crab, Malone? Are you sure one of its pincers wasn't a pink trunk? And maybe two of its legs weren't tusks?"

Christ – he'd be handing the old bugger a loaded gun.

Malone broke into a slow jog. He could think more clearly when running. Had he imagined it? After all, the crablike spider thing had been almost impossible to see properly, which might suggest that it had been a product of a weary imagination not bothered about details. He weighed up the factors. Firstly, he was tired – not just tired now, but fall-on-the-bed-without-undressing tired; secondly, he had been running, and everyone knew that hallucinations queued up in the wings under such circumstances. And if one was also as hungry as he was, then they queue-jumped.

On the plus side he hadn't been drinking.

His pace slowed.

Or had he?

He decided there and then to find out exactly what Ellen Duncan put in her home-made teabags.

Eight

Ellen Duncan woke two hours before dawn with that sudden wide-awake feeling that told her that going back to sleep was unlikely. The sinister graffiti sprayed on her shop window had been an insidious nagging and gnawing when she had finally fallen asleep, and it was there when she woke. The only consolation was that Sergeant Malone had not known the evil meaning of EX2218.

But someone else might so she ought to do something about it before daylight.

She relinquished the portion of her bed that Thomas grudgingly permitted her to occupy, pulled on her dressing gown and rummaged in her junk cupboard under the kitchen sink. The colour of the half-empty tin of Woolworth's emulsion paint didn't matter. Several brush strokes across the odious message were enough to obliterate it.

Feeling much better, she cleaned up, made herself an ordinary mug of tea, and padded into her tiny living room over the still room at the rear that faced south-east to the downs. There were no curtains because she loved to see down the slopes leading to Pentworth Lake at all times. Often she would sit in her ancient rocking chair facing the lead-latticed window and try to picture the scene as it must have been 40,000 years ago.

The cold, desiccating winds blowing off the huge northern ice sheet had made it impossible for the great pre-ice-age forests of Europe to re-establish during the warming period of 40,000 years ago except in pockets and valleys. But sedges and grasses flourished. Forests are slow-growing, slow to renew, their woody product providing little nourishment for wild life. Grasses are fast-growing and, in those prehistoric days, the continent-wide, treeless plains and steppes of Europe supported vast grazing herds of game the like of which the world had never seen before. Bison; antelope; giant reindeer-like megaloceros; woolly rhinoceros; small, fleet-footed horses that were preyed upon by cave lions and sabre-tooth tigers; and, largest of them all, the mighty woolly mammoth – all following annual migratory patterns, using the short, hot summers to build up fat that would sustain them through the bitter winters.

Into this harsh yet plentiful world had come a tiny handful of a remarkable people.

Cro-Magnon.

Where they came from was unknown. They were lighter, smaller-boned, and with smaller brains than their more sturdy Neanderthaler contemporaries. They were taller and more slender, which meant that their bodies were not so well adapted as those of the Neanderthalers at conserving heat. To look at their remains one could be forgiven for thinking that the Neanderthalers were better equipped for survival.

But Cro-Magnon Man's brain was more efficient in one vital respect: imagination. When presented with a problem they could see a likely solution in their minds and were prepared to experiment and innovate to solve that problem.

The short, heavy, flint-tipped stabbing spear of the Neanderthalers was a case in point. It was fine for dispatching an animal already brought down by a trap or pitfall, but why not make it smaller and lighter so that it could be thrown, thus saving the labour of digging pitfalls? And there was the huge advantage of not only being able to change tactics if stampeding animals veered away from pitfalls, but being able kill many animals during a stampede and not just one or two per pitfall.

The efficiency of Cro-Magnon hunting techniques was not fully appreciated until the discovery at Solutre in France of the remains of over 10,000 horses at a single settlement. Their simple method had been to stampede entire herds of onagers over a precipice.

Ellen ached for a time machine to take her back to the ending of the last ice age. She wanted to see those strange but unique men and women at first hand. They were the recent ancestors of modern man – the throw of the evolutionary dice that had been a triumph after the quarter of a million year failure of the Neanderthalers. Had the Cro-Magnons really hunted the Neanderthalers to extinction or had the older race been doomed by their failure to adapt and innovate?

The Cro-Magnons had learned how to cure skins and had invented thong-stitching so that they could make warm, close-fitting clothes that enabled them to follow the great herds north as the mighty ice cap retreated. The Neanderthalers, it was thought, had merely wrapped and knotted themselves into furs as best they could. To them the ice was the great enemy, whereas the Cro-Magnon had made it their ally.

The lack of caves on the broad steppes was a problem for the

Neanderthalers; they had to follow the herds, yet without shelter they would perish, and did perish. The Cro-Magnons solved the problem by building their own caves. They set up tepee-like circles of mammoth tusks and covered them with hide, often sinking the structure quite deep into the ground and covering it with earth as protection against the glacial-chilled blasts of the long winters which they spent, snug and secure, making new weapons, clothes and babies. Their deep-freezer for storing winter supplies was the outdoors, with their food caches protected against scavengers under huge rock cairns. The remains of one such cache had been discovered in deep mud at Ellen's dig and was now at Manchester University for preservation and analysis.

The volunteers helping with the excavation had also uncovered one of the greatest inventions of the Cro-Magnons: the forced-draught hearth. It was little more than a trench in the floor of their hide tents that was bridged with flat stones and sealed with packed earth. The duct led from the central hearth to the outside with its opening facing the freezing prevailing wind and so provided a constant supply of air for the high temperatures needed to use bone as a fuel in regions where wood was scarce. It was a huge leap which laid the foundations of ceramics and metallurgy, and gave Europe its early technological lead.

But for Ellen it was not their greatest achievement.

She was more fortunate than many in her passionate interest in palaeontology because she had actually dug artefacts out of the ground with her bare hands and held them. On one occasion last summer her careful brushing had exposed the halves of a flint knife: long and delicate and so thin that, when cleaned, light shone through its razor-sharp edge. But the flint-knapper had made a mistake with his bone hammer and broken the virtually finished blade. An archaeologist from the Weald and Downland Museum had even been able to point out the incorrect spawling blow that had led to the breakage. It was sobering to think that she was the first to hold the two halves of the broken tool since the flint knapper had thrown them down in disgust all those centuries ago. She had repaired it with superglue and used it as a letter knife.

But flint tools were common. What Ellen craved was the one discovery that had eluded British palaeontologists: a significant art find. There had been no discoveries in the British Isles to equal the magnificent cave paintings of Lascaux and Chauvet in France. She and David Weir had visited them the previous year and had been enthralled by the vivid, beautifully painted scenes of bison, horses, antelope and all the other great herds that had roamed the fertile plains of prehistoric Europe.

Ellen had been more captivated than David. Looking at the paintings at first hand, and not reproductions in books, had turned her interest into a burning passion. Her aching desire to know more about these strange people who were her ancestors gnawed at her reason. She wanted to see them at work; at play: above all she wanted to see them working on their marvellous paintings and try to quantify the mighty intellectual leap involved in their realisation that what they saw before them in bright sunlight could be carried in their remarkable minds and reproduced on cave walls deep in the earth where the sun never shone.

But a time machine wasn't possible, so Ellen assuaged her craving for information by collecting books on the subject. Over 200 now filled the pine bookcases in her living room. Apart from the large books containing reproductions of Palaeolithic art discoveries around the world, on balance they were a disappointment – long on conjecture and short on facts. She suspected that many of the authors knew less about the subject than she did.

Running her eye over the collection reminded her that before going to bed she had heeded David's reminder and set her video recorder to tape a BBC Learning Zone programme about the discoveries at Byno in the Czech Republic. She wasn't going to get any sleep now so she might as well settle in her rocking chair and watch it.

The tape was unwatchable. The picture had horizontal tears across the middle, and the sound wow and fluttered badly. A couple of commercially recorded tapes bunged in the machine produced the same result.

Damn and blast! That meant that the video recorder was loused up. Hopefully David would have a decent copy of the programme.

She flicked to Channel 4. The elderly television's picture had shrunk; there was a black band around the edges. The other channels and test cards were the same.

A wonky video recorder *and* TV! Double damn and blast.

The television was old – well past its watch-by date – but she could ill afford a new one. Well – maybe if she played up to Bob Harding's cheerful flirting he would put both appliances at the top of his repair pile. He had supplied the video recorder in the first place and had repaired it several times.

"Pussy hairs," he had lectured her the last time, "belong on pussies – not in VCRs. Don't let that cat sleep on it any more. That'll be twenty quid with a fifty per cent discount if I get one of your lovely, dazzling smiles." Hard to believe that two days a week the outrageous yet likeable old flirt was a highly regarded government scientific consultant.

A flare of headlights across the fields caught her attention. About a mile distant were the lights of the police vehicle guarding the scene where the two men had disappeared. Before nightfall all the available fishing punts had been pressed into service. Local volunteer searchers had probed the depths with long rods in a futile attempt to find the swamp's latest victims. A new search with scuba divers was due to start work at first light. Ellen knew that they stood little chance of finding the two men but she had readily agreed to help. No one had such a detailed knowledge of the area as her.

She decided that she ought to cadge some bed space off Thomas and try to snatch a couple more hours' sleep. Today was Saturday. Always a busy day . . .

Really must get some sleep . . .

And so she did – right there in the rocking chair.

Nine

The spyder kept its flight as short as possible. It landed in a field and folded its rotors. It was as well for Malone that he had failed to catch it. The machine had learned enough that day about the human metabolism from Vikki Taylor to have manufactured in a matter of milliseconds an effective beta-blocker nerve gas that would have knocked Malone unconscious and left him with a granddaddy of a headache for several hours thereafter.

It was to Vikki Taylor that the spyder now turned its attention. It set off across the grass in the direction of the Taylors' house, the curious articulation of its legs converting to a smooth forward momentum.

The spyder's controllers had an abiding curiosity about all humans, but of all the pupils that had streamed out of St Catherine's the previous afternoon, Vikki Taylor had caught their special interest because the rhythms emanating from her brain were of a particular richness, strength and texture. There was another reason: in the visible-light part of the spectrum her body was externally symmetrical like all the others, but not in the infrared part of the spectrum.

The need for good balance and coordination on high-gravity planets capable of retaining an atmosphere dictates the symmetrical structure of higher life forms. Symmetry, in which each half of the body is a mirror image of the other half, is a universal characteristic. The blind watchmaker of evolution had determined that larger creatures that needed to move efficiently – to run, change direction, jump and climb – in order to survive, needed the equilibrium of a degree of symmetry although this requirement did not have to extend to the arrangement of internal organs.

So the spyder had followed Vikki from school, keeping close so that it could read the infinitesimally weak emanations of her brain rhythms which, compared with the others, were remarkably strong. Being able to get close enough at one point to amplify the girl's idle daydream into a vivid reality, thus distracting her long enough to remove a tiny blood and tissue sample from her leg, had proved an unexpected bonus.

Now, an hour before dawn, it had returned to fill gaps in the knowledge it had acquired, and was under her bedroom window, monitoring those rhythms to be certain that its quarry was in deep sleep.

A whiplike rod extended quickly upwards from its body case and a series of tiny barbs on the end of the rod got a good purchase on a first-floor window sill. The spyder climbed up the side of house by the simple expedient of winding in the whip. It repeated the process with the next floor, and three minutes after leaving the ground it was moving silently across the slate roof to the dormer window of Vikki's bedroom.

Its study of the structure of the glass in the sash window lasted no more than a few nanoseconds.

Chemically glass is a liquid, albeit a high-viscosity liquid; over the years it flows downward so that windowpanes gradually thicken at the bottom. The spyder selected an area of glass large enough for it to pass through and accelerated the ageing process so that the designated section of glass flowed like hot wax leaving a hole large enough for it to climb through and lower itself to the floor.

It moved to the bed where Vikki was asleep, curled into a foetal position with her duvet pulled snugly around her neck. It determined that the bedcovers would be transparent to its probes and extended a sensor, which it held above the sleeping girl and moved the length of her body. It repeated the operation with different heads on the sensor, at one point even unleashing a burst of low-level X-ray radiation.

The body scan was quick and thorough. Together with the information garnered that day from Vikki's blood and tissue samples, the spyder's makers now had more information on the human race than humans themselves.

The mapping of the human genome – the unravelling of the billions of bonds in the DNA molecule's double helix – is mankind's most ambitious coordinated biological research programme, involving many thousands of research workers in universities scattered across the globe. Conservative estimates put completion of the mighty task, if it ever could be called completed, around the mid-twenty-first century.

Unravelling the human genetic code was a seventy-year project for mankind that the spyder's makers accomplished in as many seconds. Vikki stirred and turned on to her back, her handless left arm now draped over the side of the bed above the spyder.

The spyder had already noted the wrist's damaged bone and tissue, which answered the question about the girl's asymmetric form in the infrared, but it was required to provide more detailed information. That the wrist's carpal bones and tendons in the carpal tunnel had been terminated and fused into a single mass with no attempt at repair or regeneration answered several more questions, as did the examination of Vikki's artificial hand in its box on her dressing table. Without opening the box, the spyder probed the hand's structure, internal mechanism, and materials. There was yet one more question to be answered. It returned to Vikki, positioned a sensor above her head, and started searching.

Ten

Jack and Anne Taylor's first overseas holiday in the four years since Vikki's birth turned into a disaster hardly before it had began. Their flight from Gatwick to Alicante was delayed eight hours and it was after midnight when their coach finally pulled up outside the ageing El Alamo apartment block near Calpe's Fossa-Levante Beach on the Costa Blanca. It was all Jack and Anne could afford in those days.

"These are your apartment's keys," said the embarrassed courier as the sullen coach driver yanked their cases out of the bay and dumped them on the forecourt. "Apartment 4B. That's apartment B on the fourth floor."

"But you're coming up to make sure everything's OK?" Jack Taylor protested.

"I'm awfully sorry, but the driver might leave without me," said the courier apologetically. "We've got six couples to drop off at Javia. The main electric power switch is on the wall by the door as you go in. The water and gas should be on – you should be fine."

The driver crashed into gear and the coach started moving. The courier gave them a parting wave as he hopped aboard. Vikki started wailing. She was tired, hungry, and wanted the familiar surroundings of her bedroom. Anne scooped her up and carried the lightest case into the block's deserted lobby while Jack struggled with the larger cases. The lift was typical of Spain's 1960s-built apartment blocks: a tiny car barely large enough for four adults, with a hinged outer door that had to be propped open with a bag while it was loaded. Anne entered the lift first and put Vikki down so she could help Jack stack the cases. Once all three and their belongings were crowded in and the outer door closed, Jack pushed the button for the fourth floor.

Time would never blot out the memory of Vikki's terrible scream of agony when the lift started moving. The couple had never encountered a lift without an inner door. Anne's cry of terror when she saw her daughter's hand being dragged into the gap between the lift's floor and the side of the lift shaft as the car started rising was lost in the sheer volume of Vikki's scream. Jack's horrified glance took in everything as Anne fell to her knees beside her stricken daughter. Priceless seconds were lost as he struggled with the unfamiliar control panel to stop the lift. It jerked to a halt and he threw himself dementedly against the door in a futile attempt to spring it open, but the lift had risen two metres; the safety interlocks and the floor above held the outer door closed.

The next two hours passed in a nightmare montage of sounds and images. English voices in the lobby; Jack pleading with them not to try to move the lift, shouting above Vikki's terrible screams; the blood pooling across the floor; the sudden silence when Vikki mercifully fainted; the blood; Anne's handkerchief as a makeshift tourniquet; Spanish voices; arguments; a crash overhead as the roof panel was ripped off and an engineer adding to the crush in the lift; the blood; the suitcases being passed up to make room for a doctor and a nurse; the blood; Anne refusing to leave Vikki; the blue flare and crackle of cutting equipment slicing into the door; Vikki being carried unconscious to an ambulance that disappeared into the night, sirens howling despite the hour, with Jack and Anne following in a Guardia Civil car.

It was exactly four hours after the terrible accident that a surgeon in the general hospital at Denia told Anne and Jack that Vikki was out of danger. He normally spoke good English but exhaustion had him reverting to Spanish as he tried to explain that the damage had been too severe and it had been too late to save their daughter's left hand.

Eleven

The spyder didn't get the full story but the fleeting images it had dredged from the depths of Vikki's subconscious were enough.

It would never be known if the feelings of those who controlled the spyder towards this girl who had provided them with so much eagerly sought information were those of sympathy, but a decision was taken although they could not have foreseen the terrible consequences for Vikki it would have.

The spyder became still as an analysis program was set in motion to isolate and replicate those parts of Vikki's genetic code that determined the configuration of her missing left hand. Building the picture took a little over three seconds. The rest was routine. The operation was completed with the aid of a gas laser beam only a few photons in diameter that performed in much the same manner as a hypodermic syringe. The complex neural and hormone triggers that flowed into Vikki's brain and nervous system included stem cell-division stimulants that had ceased functioning because their job was done when she was in her mother's womb. Aiding them were thousands of nano-machines – mechanisms so small that they could be seen only under an electron microscope. Not that they ever would be seen; when their task of triggering dormant self-replicating molecules was complete they would be absorbed into Vikki's body.

The spyder's work was done. It left the room, reverse-engineered the hole it had made in the bedroom window, and made its way back to Pentworth Lake. Slowly, because its energy cells were seriously depleted.

Vikki slept on without stirring.

Twelve

Bob Harding was a Fellow of the Royal Society and therefore the most over-qualified electrical repairman in the country. He was in a sombre mood when he finished repairing the clock radio. The deaths of the two DTI inspectors had affected him badly. Rigsby had been a radio amateur whom he had 'worked' on several occasions, but what made it worse was the thought that he had probably been the last person the two men had spoken to when they had visited him in his shop the previous afternoon to track down the problem of the illegal transmissions.

The two inspectors had declared that Bob's station was clean but they wanted to know if he had sold any electronic or transmitting gear that could be used for the purpose, or whether he knew of anyone in the area who would be likely to set up a pirate beacon.

If only he'd suggested that they see Ellen Duncan before visiting Pentworth Lake. The area had become a swamp after a storm on several occasions. Ellen would've warned them of the dangers.

He tied a customer identification label to the radio, shoved it to one side on his cluttered work bench, and switched on his VHF transceiver, still tuned to the Midhurst VOR beacon, to checked that the transmissions hadn't started again. All was well – the data from the beacon was loud and clear.

The howl of white noise, which had caused the hand on the signal strength meter to fly across the scale and hit the stop, had been too powerful to be from anything but a large installation; the DTI men must've been mistaken about the source as being the lake. On the other hand, they knew their business and had been equipped with some serious DF 'fox-hunting' gear.

He switched the set off and pulled a window blind aside. A reasonably clear night, so he might be able to get that longed-for group photograph of Jupiter, Uranus and Neptune. It would be another 200 years or so before the three planets were favourably aligned again, so if he didn't get the picture this year, he never would. He pressed the button that opened the roof panels and derived an engineer's sense of satisfaction as the petals that formed the domed roof of his workshop slid smoothly open, powered by a scrap vacuum-cleaner motor. Bob Harding, a tall, stooping, permanently round-shouldered man, was a perfectionist which was why, ten years before at the age of forty-eight, he had thrown up a full-time career as a government scientific adviser, and turned down the chance of becoming the University of Surrey's youngest pro-chancellor. For Robert Harding the perfect life was one that allowed him to indulge in his interests of astronomy and electronics and get away from the heavy particles of city air which played hell with his asthma.

He had achieved this with two well-paid days per week in London as a consultant to several government committees that included the British Association for the Advancement of Science, and the rest of the time playing amateur astronomer and repairing electronic gadgets in the cleaner air of the country.

He had drifted into repair work as a result of fixing friends' TVs. The shop hardly paid its way, but what the hell; he made enough for a comfortable living, enjoyed his work, and most of his customers were his friends. He was co-opted on to the Town Council when an uncontested seat fell vacant, and now he had a loving wife, Suzi, who had enough tricks up her divine sleeve to turn all his bachelor fantasies into realities. Not tonight though – it was her 'week off', therefore this week was his night-time hobbies week: such as planet watching, playing amateur radio, or messing about with the various satellite receivers that were connected to a small battery of televisions mounted on steel racking around a third of his circular workshop.

He swung around on his swivel chair to confront his Newtonian telescope, bolted to its equatorial mounting post in the centre of the workshop. The instrument was his great pride. Building it had taken many hours, but that was before he had met and married his beloved Suzi, a lovely twenty-year-old brunette and a former student at a college where he had lectured part time. Both had been disappointed by the lack of a scandal that their marriage had provoked – they had expected better of Pentworth.

He looked through the eyepiece on the side of the tube and swore softly at the heavy film of condensation that covered the primary mirror. Damned storm! Fifty millimetres of rain in twenty-four hours and a driving south-westerly that had searched out every weakness in the roof. He had spent most of that day and the day before drying everything out, too concerned about his customers' repair work to worry about his own equipment. He considered cleaning the mirror, but his hygrometer was clocking 80 per cent relative humidity which meant that the mirror would be sure to cloud over again with the roof open. No Jupiter-watching tonight.

Harding coddled his telescope. He didn't even have a kettle in the workshop because it fogged the mirror. He closed the motorised roof and wondered what to do next.

It was coming up to the hour. Time for *Sky News*. Maybe a mention about the two inspectors. To his surprise the satellite TV picture had sparklies – flashes of white light across the screen – a sure indication of a weak signal. He flicked through all the Astra analogue channels: SAT1, Pro-7, QVC – the signal strength was down on every one, and most of the digital channels were too weak for the picture to lock up.

A check on the antenna connections showed that everything was as it should be. That meant water in the LNB. Damned storm!

He grabbed a torch and went into the back garden. His fixed Astra dishes were mounted on stubby poles and were easily accessible. The low-noise blocks were protected by several layers of cling film. Everything was dry underneath and the alignment of both dishes was also OK.

He returned to the workshop, switched to his steerable dish and was astonished to discover that the signal from the Eutelsat Hotbird was also down by at least five decibels. Hotbird blasted a powerful signal across most of Europe. It had a solid footprint. Atmospheric pressure was extremely high at 1030 millibars – that had to be a record, but it wouldn't account for the weak TV reception.

It was the shrunken picture on an old Philips valve TV set that he kept for fast tuning into terrestrial TV DX from Europe that fingered the problem. The transformer power supplies in old TVs could not compensate for reduced voltages like modern sets. He checked the mains voltage with a multimeter, snatched up his telephone, and called Southern Electric's HQ in Basingstoke. A recorded announcement quoting another phone number eventually got him through to a duty engineer after he'd persuaded an intermediary that he knew what he was talking about.

"Two hundred volts!" the engineer echoed in astonishment when Harding had explained the problem.

"Two hundred point six volts RMS to be precise," said Harding. "That's on two properly calibrated multimeters. And the peak-to-peak voltage tallies. You seem to have lost nearly forty volts somewhere."

"Hold on please, sir."

Harding held on for several minutes and was on the point of hanging up, thinking he'd been forgotten, when the engineer came back. "Pentworth is supplied through an unmanned sub-station at Henkley Down. We're not getting any incorrect readings from it so it could be a fault on your local domestic voltage step-down trannie. There's a couple of spurs feeding Pentworth High Street. It could be storm damage that's only just shown up. Thanks for informing us, sir – we'll look into it."

Harding finished the call, locked the workshop and returned to the flat over the shop, moving quietly to avoid disturbing Suzi. He filled the kettle to make coffee and was surprised at the low water pressure. Normally the jet from the mono-bloc mixer tap was enough to splatter water all over the place if it was turned half on, but tonight all the tap could manage was a meagre stream. That meant yet another burst main somewhere.

Trouble comes in twos, thought Harding, placing the kettle quietly on the gas ring. First the electricity – now the water.

He was wrong: trouble could come in threes, fours and even fives. He stared in astonishment at the insipid gas flame and double-checked to make sure he had turned the control full on. He removed the ring from the hob and flushed it under the hot water tap. A few flakes of scale came out but otherwise the burner was clean. He tried again but the ring of flames was still yellowish-blue and gutless. All four rings were the same so it couldn't be that all four supply jets were suddenly blocked.

Bob Harding had to wait longer than usual for the kettle to boil and had time to reflect on the strange things that were happening in Pentworth.

Thirteen

H unger woke Vikki as the first flush of dawn stole across her bedroom ceiling. These were no ordinary early morning pangs triggered by the smells of coffee and toast that could be ignored by turning over and calling up another dream about Dario, but an insistent craving like phantom hands tying her stomach in knots.

She was up, down the stairs, and into kitchen before she was fully awake. She hadn't even bothered to slip her hand on; she didn't need two hands to rip open a fresh loaf and cram two slices of bread into her mouth. It was thick-sliced white bread that Vikki normally disliked except as toast, but this time the taste of the supermarket pap was bliss. She started stuffing another slice into her mouth and realised that she'd never swallow it without a drink.

She never drank milk. She loathed milk. Skimmed; semi-skimmed; full cream – it was all disgusting. Freshly squeezed orange juice was her favourite breakfast drink. The half-litre carton of Pentworth House Jersey full cream in the refrigerator didn't stand a chance. It was seized, its tab ripped off, and its contents squeezed down her throat. Its violation completed by her crushing it flat to extract the last drop. And then two more slices of bread bonded together by a thick mortar of peanut butter. The contents of an opened carton of semi-skimmed helped that little dessert down.

She felt good. The buzz of elation she was experiencing was so loud and insistent that she could almost hear it. Her whole being was tingling. And then she caught sight of herself in the kitchen mirror: peanut butter and breadcrumbs smeared around her mouth, and a milk-soaked nightie clinging to her breasts.

She cleaned herself and the kitchen quickly and returned to bed, wondering how she was going to explain the missing milk to her mother. Pentworth House milk was expensive. The sensation of heady euphoria made sleep impossible, she experienced the sensation of left fingers and was even able to wriggle them.

Gosh – phantom fingers. How long since I last felt those? Must be years. Be a busy day in the shop. Must get some sleep. Must. Must. Must.

She willed herself to doze off for a few minutes and then was suddenly wide awake again.

Ravenously hungry.

Fourteen

The insistent ringing of the front door bell woke Ellen with what would have been a respectable guilty start had she been capable of using her neck muscles. Looking at her watch – *8:00 a.m. Oh shit* – involved holding her wrist before her eyes rather than risk moving her head. The sun hurt her eyes.

Falling asleep in a chair: damn, blast, and buggeration – that meant she was going to feel like hell all day. She stumbled, rick-necked and leaden-limbed down the stairs, and opened the door.

Vikki Taylor had turned up for her Saturday job. Infuriatingly pretty and button-neat in a short pleated skirt and silk blouse, clutching her bicycle. The morning light making a sheen of halos around her long blonde hair. Her green eyes beacon-bright and alert. Ellen hated her.

"Good morning, Miss Duncan. You look a fright."

Ellen hated her even more. "You're an hour early."

"You phoned Mum asking me to be early, Miss Duncan."

"So I did. Why the hell can't you be unreliable like the last girl?"

"The overtime will be useful."

"Overtime? Coming in early is undertime."

"If it's time over my agreed hours then it's overtime," said Vikki spiritedly. She looked at Ellen in concern. "Are you all right, Miss Duncan?"

"No," said Ellen sourly, leading the way into the workroom at the back of the shop. "I am far from all right. I fell asleep in my chair. You can have half a dozen grudging apologies in advance for all the abuse I'll be giving you today."

Vikki wheeled her bicycle into the back garden and returned a minute later. "You go and get some proper sleep, Miss Duncan. I can manage the shop and do the orders."

Ellen had flopped into her chair at the workstation. "I've got to go and see the police down at the lake about those two men."

"It was on the news last night," said Vikki, holding the electric

73

kettle under the tap and waiting for it to fill. "It's terrible. UFO watchers, were they?"

"Looking for the UFO in my lake or something," Ellen replied, marvelling at the way Vikki's new hand could support the weight of a filling kettle.

Vikki gave an involuntary shudder. "I wouldn't go near the Plague Swamp for anything after heavy rain."

"Its proper name is Pentworth Lake. No wonder I couldn't flog it."

"Water pressure's low. You'd think it was mid-summer. What happened to the shop window?"

Ellen had no wish to discuss the matter. "Some graffiti yobboes used it for practice."

"What did they draw? It's been painted over."

"Vikki, angel. Do me a big favour. Make the tea and don't let's talk for at least five years."

The schoolgirl had been working for Ellen Duncan for two months and was proving an excellent Saturday employee. She could process the week's mail orders quickly and efficiently, and had a pleasing manner in the shop and on the telephone. The earliest lesson she had learned was reading Ellen's danger signals although she had long realised that most of her employer's starchy cuffs came straight from the irony board. She busied herself with address labels and Jiffy bags at the packing table.

"For Christ's sake!" Ellen exploded. "Where the hell's that tea? You must've over-filled the kettle."

Vikki glanced at the electric kettle that was only just beginning to sing. "I didn't, Miss Duncan. It was the same at home. The coffee took an age to boil."

Thomas jumped on Ellen's lap to register loud complaints about the non-appearance of his breakfast. She shoved him off, pulled herself up, and went upstairs, swearing at Thomas's attempts to trip her up. She returned an hour later wearing jeans, a shapeless pullover, a more relaxed expression, and still swearing at Thomas although not so vehemently. A long soak in the bath and she was feeling marginally more human. She owed Vikki an apology because the electric kettle in the kitchen upstairs had also taken a long time to boil and the bath's gas heater had been slow filling. The girl had opened the shop and was dealing with a difficult customer on the telephone. Ellen listened in for a few moments and took over the call.

"That's right, Mrs Greaves. I stock aromatherapy snake oils in the shop but there're not in my mail order catalogue or on my Web site. The catalogue is a personal thing – tried and tested remedies – traditional herbal remedies that work and many new ones that have been thoroughly tested. It doesn't include voodoo dolls, copper bangles, smelly therapy oils or any other pseudo-scientific claptrap rubbish that seem to appeal to so many nerd-brained sad loonies these days. The self-service section of my shop is full of useless but harmless proprietary-branded quackery – if that's what people want, then they can pick it up for themselves, but it doesn't go in my catalogue, or receive advice on its use. I'm sorry we can't be of assistance. Try looking under witch doctors in Yellow Pages."

Ellen hung up and grinned at Vikki. "I feel better now. One advantage of living in a loony, politically correct world is that good, old-fashioned downright rudeness can now be passed off as integrity. Right – I've got to go and see the law." She pulled on an ancient donkey jacket and stuffed her feet into a well-worn pair of green wellingtons. "I'll be back about noon. Nice morning so I'll walk. Call me on my mobile if you have any problems. And don't let Thomas con you into letting him sleep on the kiln. Sure you can manage?"

Vikki nodded happily; she loved being left in charge. "There's a telephone message from a Sergeant Malone to say that a local resident will arrange for the shopfront to be cleaned."

"Really?"

Vikki caught the warning look in her employer's eye and added quickly: "I've downloaded the overnight e-mail. A stack of orders have come in for the cat and dog allergy treatment. At least twenty from America. Fifty-eight altogether."

"All for full-course packs?"

"Yes."

Ellen bent over the computer and checked her stock levels. "Bugger. We've only got enough quercetin for twenty packs and none made up. OK, Vikki – make up the full number of three-day packs and put all the customers down for free post follow-ups. There's a macro somewhere for printing explanation slips. I'll put an order in for more of the stuff . . . Christ – we're going to need at least another three kilos. Better make it six – it seems to be taking off."

Vikki wriggled her right hand into a disposable glove and lifted a sealed bin on to the packing table. She felt her left hand shift a little in its snug suction fit on her wrist. Odd – the bin wasn't that heavy. "What is quercetin made of, Miss Duncan?"

Ellen paused at the door. "One of the few things I can't grow here in sufficient quantity and it wouldn't be worthwhile if I could. Buckwheat."

"How does it work?" Vikki had an eager, enquiring mind and liked to know about the various herbs and herbal products she handled. But this time she had a specific reason for asking. She had tried to make the question sound casual but her omission of the customary 'Miss Duncan' betrayed her.

Ellen gave the girl an enquiring look but she was intent on weighing out sachet portions of the greyish powder. "Do you know what allergies are, Vikki?"

"When your body reacts badly to some things?"

"Roughly – yes. Allergies occur when your immune system mistakes harmless substances for dangerous invaders and responds accordingly. With cats, most people react to *Felis domesticus* allergen one, a glycoprotein that cats secrete through their skin, hair, and saliva. It gets spread all over the house. The particles are charged, so they stick easily to just about everything. Quercetin works well with hay fever, and cats and dogs, it seems. A dose between meals stabilises the nasal membrane mast cells that release histamine. That's what gives you those allergy symptoms, running nose, sore throat, and so on. The first drug company to isolate and synthesise it will make a fortune. Now tell me why you asked."

"I always like to ask, Miss Duncan."

"I know you do, Vikki. But this time I gave you an unusually detailed answer. I could almost hear your eyes glazing over. So what's the real reason?"

Vikki hesitated. She was unable to meet her employer's eye but her innate honesty led to her blurting out: "I just wondered if any of the materials I handle might effect me in some way."

"It's more likely that you'd *affect* them, Vikki. That's why you have to wear the gloves – sorry – glove. Do you really think I would allow you to handle anything dangerous?"

"No, Miss Duncan." Flat, monotone response. The girl could be infuriating at times.

"You're not growing a third breast, or a – or anything . . . er – masculine?"

No trace of a smile to banish Vikki's serious expression. She merely shook her head.

Ellen sat in her swivel chair. "So what then?"

"I woke up really early ravenously hungry this morning and ate about ten slices of bread."

Ellen didn't laugh. "You're worried about a larder raid?"

"My mother went ape."

"You're still growing, Vikki. You don't grow evenly but in fits and starts. You put on a spurt and your brain sends out signals for more of this, or more of that. Larder raids are literally a part of growing up." Ellen paused and looked speculatively at the girl. "There's something else, isn't there?"

"No, Miss Duncan."

"You might as well tell me, Vikki, because I shall worm it out of you one way or the other. Look at me!"

Vikki looked up, worry clouding her green eyes as the memories of her Dario daydream came flooding back. "I had a bad trip yesterday, Miss Duncan."

The older woman's first thought was the town's Green Dragon soft drink disco where, if the rumours were true, pretty girls like Vikki were plied with Ecstasy tablets by hopeful studs.

"What exactly do you mean by 'trip'? Hallucinations?"

"Well, yes – sort of."

"I'm listening."

Vikki outlined her strange encounter the previous day with the Zulu warrior. She omitted the sexual details but Ellen sensed the girl's embarrassment when she had to answer a few questions. The older woman decided not to push her – the sexual fantasies of a healthy young girl were not for parading or scrutiny outside her peer group.

"And all this happened in broad daylight when you were wheeling your bike?"

Vikki nodded. The feeling of euphoria that had marked the start of her day was gone. Tears pricked the corners of her eyes.

"Well, I can promise you that you weren't hallucinating."

A tear escaped and coursed down Vikki's cheek. *Oh, God – she really is frightened.*

Ellen stood and put a comforting arm around the girl's shoulders. "Listen, Vikki. What you experienced was nothing to worry about. At your age your hormones are still way out of kilter. They're tugging your emotions this way and that. You were walking along a route that you've used hundreds of times – you don't have to think about it because you know every rut and stone. Your mind drifts to your Zulu poster and that sets off your daydream. That's all it was – a good, old-fashioned daydream. We joke about them when we're older, forgetting just how powerful and disturbing they can be."

Vikki shook her head. "It was more than a daydream, Miss Duncan. I found myself knowing things about the Zulus that I'd never been taught."

"About their sexual practices?"

The girl coloured slightly. "Yes. I looked them up in Dad's *All God's Children* CD encyclopaedia last night. Everything in the daydream was right."

Ellen straightened. "So obviously you've looked them up before and forgotten about it."

"No!" Vikki's tone was uncharacteristically vehement. "I've never looked up anything like that before. And even if I had, I would've remembered those sort of things. I know I would've."

Guilt and denial at work here, thought Ellen. "It doesn't need a positive effort on your part, Vikki. You heard something years ago – a TV narration or a talk on the radio. Little snippets that have lodged in your mind without you knowing they were there. Then you have this daydream and they all drop into place and become alive – like a door suddenly opening on a room you didn't know was there. The brain's like that. It could even have been something you heard when you were in your pram."

Vikki respected Ellen's knowledge, and what the older woman said made some sort of sense. It was a valued straw. "Yes – I suppose so."

"No supposing about it."

"There's something else, Miss Duncan. Please don't laugh at me but I think I saw something that looked like a mechanical crab just after the daydream."

Ellen didn't laugh but she did ask for more details.

"It moved very quickly," Vikki explained. "I didn't get a good look at it, not really. But it looked real enough. Like a clock-work crab."

"Well – if it was right after your daydream, it was probably your brain unwinding. A hard week at school? Lots of home-work?"

Vikki nodded. "I'm taking ten GCSEs."

Ellen grinned. "I'd be seeing formations of flying pink elephants if I were swotting for ten GCSEs."

The schoolgirl managed a weak smile. Ellen's practical down-to-earth common sense had a greater effect than the older woman guessed.

"Was your Zulu good-looking?"

"Oh, yes."

"And well equipped, no doubt." Ellen gave the girl a playful nudge. "Well next time he pops up – pun intended – send him along to me."

This time Ellen was rewarded with a broad, grateful smile.

Fifteen

What a bloody time for the clutch to play up!

Mike Malone swore roundly, stood on the brakes, and hooked his unmarked Escort behind the Southern Electric maintenance van that was labouring up Duncton Hill. The last overtaking opportunity northbound on the A285 between the South Downs and Pentworth would be gone after the next bend so he dropped into second and made another attempt. The same thing happened again: the engine revs surged ahead of his road speed as he pulled out – a sure indication of a slipping clutch. A diagnosis confirmed by the pungent smell of burning clutch-plate liner sucked through the heater. There was nothing for it but to tuck in behind the van, nurse the ailing Escort as best he could, and try to be patient – something Malone wasn't noted for, particularly as the van seemed to be having much the same trouble. It had slowed to a crawl; the black smoke it was spewing from its exhaust smelt worse than the clutch. The driver kept tight to the verge and waved him on but all Malone could do was flash his lights and hope that the driver understood.

Strange that an unladen two-year-old vehicle in good condition should be having similar problems with the hill. Another mile or so to the top – maybe he'd be able to get past going downhill.

No such luck.

The bloody clutch even slipped going *downhill*! And what was really bizarre was that jamming the pedal to the floor to disengage it made bugger all difference: there was a strange resistance clawing at the car similar to the dragging effect of driving through shallow flooding. The van driver banged his palm impatiently on the outside of his door, urging his labouring steed to keep going. A colleague driving a Southern Electric cherry-picker in the opposite direction was also having a struggle. He made a circular gesture with his finger pointing to his head.

I know how you feel, matey. If it wasn't March, I'd think the bloody road was melting.

The bewildered expressions of all drivers coming in the opposite

80

direction suggested that the trouble wasn't confined to a few vehicles. This was a big, bold ten on the weird scale. It had to be some new road surface that Highways had come up with. And yet this was the same road he drove on nearly every day; there hadn't been any resurfacing work on this stretch for a year.

He found that the clutch slip wasn't nearly so bad if he kept his speed down. At 25 m.p.h. the rev counter needle gave a correct reading for his speed in top gear. But trying to go faster sent the engine revs up but not the road speed. Nothing for it but to drop well back from the smoking van, tease the Escort along in top at 20–25, and ignore the high-pitched rattle of the engine's valves pinking their stems off.

Malone was three miles from Pentworth when the strange effect suddenly ceased and the Escort surged forward. The car behaved perfectly. Snick into second, gun the engine, and he sailed effortlessly past the van, which was also picking up speed. He gave the driver a friendly wave as he swept past. He would be five minutes late for his appointment with Cathy Price, and after that he was due at Pentworth Lake to see Ellen Duncan and the search team. Thinking about her – in particular, the warmth of her body against him when he had carried her into her shop last night – took his mind off the recent strange behaviour of the car for a few moments. But what had just happened was too extraordinary to banish for long. Maybe he had imagined it?

But the lingering taint of burnt clutch-plate liner told otherwise.

Sixteen

The rear of Ellen's terraced shop and flat was in such contrast to its narrow, north-facing frontage, overshadowed by the high prison-like wall surrounding Pentworth House, that visitors shown the garden were invariably overwhelmed by the magnificent vista spread out before them. It was as if the row of drab little Victorian shops had deliberately huddled themselves together to shut out the splendours that would otherwise be visible from North Street.

Her garden where it joined the house was the same width as her shop, but her plot was wedge-shaped, widening rapidly as the land fell steeply away from her two greenhouses in a series of slopes and terraces from the sandstone escarpment that Pentworth was built on.

Following the death of her mother ten years before, Ellen had decided to turn the shop into a real herbalist's in which she was assured of fresh supplies by raising her own crops wherever possible. Five years' back-breaking work clearing the scrubby woodland had resulted in a seemingly wild environment in which a huge variety of herbs and wild flowers flourished in an apparent random fashion. But they had been planted with great care, taking advantage of the well-drained, south-facing slopes, to ensure that they were provided with the right conditions of soil, and sun or shade.

On this surprisingly warm Saturday morning in March, four days after the storm, and following a week of hard frosts, she was pleased to see how well many of her less hardy crops had withstood the winter. Even a small stand of the Mediterranean borage, protected from the south-westerly prevailing wind by a dry sandstone wall that she had built, had come through well. In addition to ginseng, the tea that Mike Malone had made the night before contained a tisane of borage that would have given his nervous system a sharp adrenalin hit.

Ellen walked on, picking her way carefully down a well-trodden, steep path beside a swollen stream, one of many that discharged into Pentworth Lake, now a dazzling sheet of filigreed silver that covered the entire flood plain, dotted with the white flecks of herring gulls. On the far side she could see the police car and another two vehicles that had joined it. Two divers in wetsuits were manoeuvring a Zodiac inflatable boat into the middle of the lake.

She paused occasionally, taking stock, her quick eye missing nothing. Her attempt to root mistletoe cuttings into an old apple tree that she had spared for the purpose had not been a success. Just as well really: the efficacy of the herb's viscotoxins as an anti-cancer drug was a contentious issue, although her reasons for wanting a fresh supply was for her choline-based high blood pressure remedy – a well-known cure; she had no wish to be drawn into the mistletoe-cancer debate.

Her fennel was doing well, some new growth relishing the unseasonal warmth; the scurvy grass was a mistake – it was taking over. There was now enough to treat every case of acne in the south of England. Her little crop of heartsease wasn't thriving despite being native to Europe. There was enough to keep Dawn Linegar's epilepsy in check but Ellen would've preferred more.

She reached an outcrop of weathered chalk erratic where the stream swung east on a new course that David Weir had dug with his Kubota. The miniature digger had done a good job of diverting the stream away from a chainlink fence enclosure and along the contour of the rise before being allowed to tumble into the lake. The chalk line was bounded by a sheep-proof lay-ered hedge, and an evil-smelling ginkgo (maidenhair) tree which marked the end of her cultivated area and the edge of the land that she rented to David Weir. The ginkgo, prized by Chinese herbalists, was a survivor of the Jurassic Age. It stood guard over her crops because no deer or rabbit would risk having its olfactory system jammed by its prodigious pong which could turn a peaceful ramblers' hike into a panic-stricken stampede. The nuts were delicious when cooked, and provided a range of herbal remedies.

Further down the slope was the ugly chainlink enclosure, topped with a coil of razor wire, guarding a parcel of land about thirty metres square. This was the 'dig'.

The discovery had come about the previous year when she had braved the ginkgo's appalling stink and set to work with a pickaxe to break up the hard pan of Weald clay at the foot of the chalk face, intending to enlarge the stream into a small pond at this point, and had found the remains of the flint-miners' camp – a bed of flint chippings nearly half a metre deep. More artefacts had come to light as the site was cleared under the direction of the Weald and Downland Museum.

Carbon-14 dating of ash and animal bones had established the camp as being over 40,000 years old and it was therefore regarded as a major find. Excavation work had stopped in November and would resume the following month provided she and David could recruit enough volunteers for the painstaking work in close proximity to the putrefying dead-camel smell of the ginkgo tree. Luckily the prevailing wind kept the stench reasonably at bay most days.

Ellen reached the fence and stared through the wire at the dig. Strange how her elation of last year was now gone; she wasn't particularly looking forward to the coming season's work. She knew what they would find: more flint chippings, more bone hammers, more undecorated antler knife handles. Never a trace of art or ornamentation. Not so much as a solitary decorated bead had turned up in the carefully sieved spoil.

Maybe the miners of prehistory who had worked here were too preoccupied with the grim business of survival to make carvings; maybe they didn't have the talent, inclination or time. Yet they had knapped wonderfully artistic axe heads. No . . . that was wrong. She looked on them as artistic because they were so beautifully symmetrical and polished. But their elegant symmetry was for balance so that they could be swung accurately when bound to a long handle, and the polish prevented them from jamming. Was craftsmanship art? Or was art any embellishment, no matter how crude, that signified imagination and the leisure time to apply it?

David's theory was that leisure time was the first attribute of wealth and that the production of ornamentation was intended as visible evidence of that wealth. The more intricate the ornamentation, the greater the wealth.

She looked around at the landscape, wondering why her Cro-Magnon flint miners hadn't concerned themselves with art when they had lived at a time that marked the flowering of Palaeolithic art across Europe.

Her gaze took in the great sandstone scarp at the eastern end of her land. The flat platform of rock protruding from a wooded hillside was a noted observation point. It was known locally as the Temple of the Winds and had been one of Alfred, Lord Tennyson's favourite spots on his walks from his nearby home. It was easy to believe that the scowling gargoyle face that rain and wind had carved into the great outcrop was that of a legendary god that ruled the sky, the earth, and the eternal winds. On hot days it was a place that Ellen liked to visit for solitary sunbathing – a place where she felt as one with and in close harmony with nature. Very close sometimes, as Harvey Evans had discovered last summer when had come on her unawares when flying his microlight aircraft. But the demands made on her time by the dig and her growing business meant that such opportunities were rare now.

With one backward glance at the fence, she swung over a stile, scattering some of David's Southdown sheep, and tramped around the perimeter of the lake's flood margin towards the little group of vehicles surrounded by long streamers of fluttering police barrier tape.

Now that she was closer, the lake had lost its silvery sheen and taken on a yellowish silt hue. In its centre was a solitary diver sitting in the Zodiac inflatable. She was not pleased to see that Asquith Prescott's Range Rover had joined the party. Prescott had been made Chairman of Pentworth Town Council, not on the grounds of merit but on the Buggins' turn principle. The landowner was standing by his vehicle, talking to Inspector Harvey Evans. Both men broke off what looked like the beginnings of an argument when they saw her approach.

A small, crablike creature followed her at a safe distance, darting silently along the bottom of the hedgerow, keeping in the shadows and undergrowth to minimize the risk of detection.

Seventeen

M ike Malone usually enjoyed the company of women, but Cathy Price was deliberately trying to unsettle him with frequent crossing and uncrossing of her admittedly very attractive legs.

You've picked a wrong one in me for your game-play tactics, sister.

He perched on the edge of Cathy Price's settee and concentrated on stirring his coffee. He recalled her as a somewhat reserved young woman who had once sought his advice on her burglar system about two years back. He didn't allow his eyes as much as a momentary flicker in the direction of his host's undoubted charms. But he did glance around at the exercise equipment that looked out of place in the octagonal living room. The cycling machine was no ordinary piece of domestic kit, but a substantial stainless-steel affair. Expensive – built to withstand robust commercial gymnasium usage. She had been making serious money recently.

"You have some nice equipment, Miss Price."

The grey eyes watched him speculatively.

So do you, Mike Malone.

"Thank you, Mike. Do you mind if I call you Mike? I like to keep in shape."

Malone did mind but said nothing. He wondered why her dark hair was so close-cropped. The 1960s Audrey Hepburn urchin style was popular again but it didn't suit her. She was sitting in a high-wing armchair, a teasing, amused half-smile playing at the corners of her mouth. Hard to credit that she was disabled. There was no sign of a wheelchair, but there was an oddball radio remote-control box on the coffee table. Presumably her wheels could be summoned when needed.

"You seem to be better organized than on my last visit, Miss Price – electric front-door lock. A lift. All mod cons." The coffee was good. She had made it before he arrived. He poured himself a second cup from the vacuum jug without asking.

86

"Is this a social call or business, Mike?"

"Business. I want to thank you for your call last night."

"Did you catch them?"

"Let's say that the damage to Miss Duncan's shopfront will be repaired at no cost or inconvenience to her."

"It's been painted over," said Cathy. "What was underneath?"

"You've been out?"

"I had a delivery to make."

"So you got dressed this morning, went out, and changed back into a nightdress and silk dressing gown for my visit?"

"I often slip out in my nightie and dressing gown first thing," said Cathy, as though she had read Malone's thoughts. "I love thrashing my Jag along winding country lanes at illegal speeds. Heater and stereo going full blast. There's something tremendously sexual about it, especially in an E-type." She laughed. "Deep down I'm a bit of a rebel. No – not so deep down, really." As if to emphasise the point, she crossed her legs yet again to expose more thigh and was disappointed that her guest did not lower his gaze. Cathy's sexuality was a means to an end – she enjoyed exercising power over creatures physically stronger than her. Before her accident she had often tormented her stallion by riding him near the stables set aside for brood mares. The power of denial and reward. "So what did those two oiks spray on Ellen Duncan's window?"

Malone told her. Her reaction was too prompt to be a lie.

"EX2218?" she echoed, genuinely surprised. "What does that mean?"

"I was hoping that you might tell me, Miss Price."

"Didn't Ellen know?"

"She didn't say."

"EX2218," Cathy repeated slowly. "No . . . Oh I know! How about an elixir number from her list of home-brewed medicines?" She laughed and added: "An E-number that got on the wrong side of a customer?"

Malone was impressed: it was a good suggestion and could explain Ellen Duncan's refusal to discuss the matter.

"Not that it's likely," Cathy continued. "She's a good herbalist – certainly helped me out recently with an embarrassing little problem."

Malone rarely allowed himself to be led in conversation and ignored the bait. He rose, crossed to the window, and looked down at Pentworth. "A stunning view," he remarked.

"It's even better from my bedroom upstairs, Mike. You'd be amazed at what you can see. With or without my telescope."

Her feeble attempts at game-play using facile sexual innuendoes were beginning to annoy Malone. He decided that he'd teach her a little lesson in real gamesmanship before the interview was over. It was unlikely that she had a tape recorder rolling and he didn't much care if she had. He regarded her impassively. "Did you see anything else of interest last night, Miss Price?"

"No."

"You saw me, surely?"

"When you were jogging? I certainly did. I've seen you several times. Your tracksuit looks uncomfortably tight. And please don't call me Shirley."

It was funny in Airplane, *sister.*

"Did you follow me? With your telescope, that is?"

"Yes."

"And you saw nothing unusual?"

"Other than an interesting jiggle?"

Malone's face was stone.

Cathy gestured impatiently. "Damn – I'm sorry, Mike – I get these silly, playful moods. Consider my wrists slapped . . ." She hesitated. "Yes – I did see something strange . . . But you'd only laugh."

"I rarely laugh, Miss Price."

Cathy could believe him. "It was like a kid's toy. A sort of crablike device – I called it a spyder. Spelt S-P-Y. It seemed to fit. It was very hard to see – and it was following you. I thought I was imagining it at first – I'd had a long day – and then you seemed to see it, too."

Cross out Ellen Duncan's tea.

"Yes," said Malone slowly. "I did see it briefly."

"Was it a toy?"

"It must've been. Did you see where it came from?"

"No."

"Or where it went to?"

"No." She added, "Perhaps there really was a UFO on Tuesday night. Maybe it was something they left behind."

There was a silence as Malone stared into the middle distance, his hostess apparently forgotten. She regarded him, puzzled by his unexpected absent-mindedness. He suddenly shook his head as if clearing unwelcome thoughts.

"I'm sorry, Miss Price—"

"Oh, please call me Cathy."

"I was miles away."

Come on, sister. Now you ask me what I was thinking.
"What were you thinking?"
Bingo!
Malone moved from the window and stood looking down at her. A dismissive wave of his hand, and his embarrassed, self-effacing smile was just right. "Oh – I couldn't tell you that."
"Yes, you can."
"You'll be angry."
"Who says?"
"Promise you won't be angry?"
"Cross my heart, et cetera."
Too easy!
"Well," said Malone with disarming affability, "having been treated to frequent glimpses of your pubes during the last ten minutes, I couldn't help wondering what it would be like to run my tongue up and down your clitoris."
The grey eyes widened in shocked disbelief, but for only an instant. The silence in the room was total.
Then Cathy threw back her head and laughed. "My God – I walked right into that. Touché, Mike – I really asked for it. I do apologise, and I think our policeman are marvellous."
Malone felt he could forgive her much for such a generous reaction to his trap unless it was an attempt to gain control.
Cathy smiled mischievously up at him and allowed her knees to part slightly. "As a public-spirited citizen, I always believe in helping the police with their enquiries."
"I think," said Malone carefully, "that I have as much information as I need, and more than I want."
It was a blunt rejection that kept control with him. As expected, her expression became icy. She snapped her legs together. "A pleasure meeting you, Mr Malone. You will forgive me if I don't see you to the door."
Five minutes later, as Malone was driving to his appointment with Ellen at Pentworth Lake, he reflected that perhaps he had been hard on Cathy Price. But he had no regrets; she had tried to manipulate him and that he could never accept no matter how enticing the reward.

Eighteen

V ikki felt her hand's wrist socket lose its suction. She dropped the large Jiffy bag she had been holding open, and managed to push the hand more firmly into place before it fell off. It was a normal daily occurrence, usually cured by a few quick presses of the hidden vacuum pump beneath the hand's artificial skin. But this time she heard the faint hiss of air leaking past the wrist seal when she worked the pump. It wasn't necessary to press the escape valve to release the vacuum; the hand slipped off on to the packing table of its own accord. She examined its wrist socket. The soft, moulded inner contours with their film of lanolin were in perfect condition, but there was something wrong with her wrist – she hated calling it a stump, such a brutal word. A lump was protruding from the tough layers of skin that had been built up over the severed carpal bones in a series of operations.

Vikki examined the growth with mounting dismay. It was quite firm, only about eight millimetres long and the same width but it was enough to interfere with the suction bond, and she was certain it hadn't been there when she had washed. She dreaded problems with her wrist. Last month a rash of blisters had meant the temporary use of her old, claw-like jointless prosthetic hand with an uncomfortable arm harness to hold it in place that meant having to wear long-sleeved blouses.

The Taylors' family physician, Dr Millicent Vaughan, had told Vikki to call her at any time on her home number if she had problems with her wrist. Normally Vikki hated making a fuss but the growth was so worrying that she picked up the telephone, called Millicent Vaughan and luckily caught her just before she was leaving to go shopping. It was a bad line. Vicki had to repeat her profuse apologies about bothering the doctor on a Saturday.

"Where are you now, Vikki?"

"I'm looking after Ellen Duncan's Earthforce shop. I really am sorry to—"

"That's on my shopping list," said Millicent briskly. "I'm low on oil of rosemary. Stop fretting. I'll be with you in fifteen minutes. What the devil's the matter with the phones? This is the third bad line this morning." Vikki returned to her work and was completing an order when the old-fashioned shop bell jangled.

Millicent Vaughan was a stern-looking, greying, gaunt woman whose kindly nature towards her genuine patients was belied by her forbidding appearance. She knew that Vikki would not have called her, particularly on a Saturday, unless she was desperately concerned.

In the shop's backroom she examined the strange growth and was at a loss. It certainly wasn't a blister as Vikki thought. The skin covering the lump looked new and healthy. She pressed it gently and took her finger away. The pressure-whitened area turned pink immediately. Whatever it was, it had a good blood supply.

"I can feel you touching it!" Vikki suddenly exclaimed.

Millicent was incredulous. The whole area of skin over the stump was nerveless. Skin could renew itself, but not nerves. "Look away, Vikki, and tell me when you can feel my touch."

Vikki turned her head and was unable to feel any contact around the stump until the doctor touched the growth. It was a very light touch.

"It tickles, Doctor."

The doctor was puzzled and repeated the experiment to be certain. She pressed her fingertip more firmly against the curious lump and fancied she could feel five tiny nodes at the tip that were slightly harder than the new skin.

"What do you think, Doctor?"

The doctor meet the troubled green eyes. She was always frank with her patients. "To be honest, Vikki, I'm not sure what to think. But it certainly doesn't look malignant – the skin's much too healthy. It could be your hormone factory stirring up some bone growth. Does it stop you wearing your hand?"

"No – there's a lot of give in the lining, but I have to pump a bit harder for it to stay on." Vikki hesitated. "I think it's grown a bit in the last half-hour."

"I think that's you becoming a little bit obsessive, young lady."

"I suppose so."

Millicent considered for a moment. "Can you come and see me at Monday evening's surgery?"

"Yes – of course."

"Good. I will have had a chance to consult with Dr Reynolds by then." She gathered up her shopping bags and gave Vikki a reassuring smile before turning to leave. "And don't you go worrying, Vikki – it looks like a little unwanted bone growth. Perfectly harmless. I'll see you on Monday evening. God bless."

Millicent was lost in thought as she made her way to the shops. Regeneration of nerves? That was impossible – there must have been intact nerves in that patch of skin in the first place. But the growth? And the five hard nodes beneath the skin? Now where the devil had she seen that before?

She spotted a patient who was certain to waylay her with an account of a trifling ailment and dodged into an antique shop.

"Ah, Dr Vaughan," said the manager, beaming. "What a stroke of luck. I've been meaning to see you about these blinding headaches I've been getting."

Nineteen

"It can't be fenced," said Ellen emphatically. She swept her hand around the expanse of flooded wetlands of Pentworth Lake. "Wooden posts would rot away in no time – the water's acid – and concrete posts would sink."

"And it's designated as an area of outstanding natural beauty," Asquith Prescott boomed in a voice that was the result of generations of breeding to ensure it could be heard across restaurants.

"An area of outstanding natural danger," Harvey Evans observed sourly. The police inspector was a stocky, powerfully built man, five years from retirement, whose rising rank and weight made him look shorter than the regulation height for police officers. He and Prescott were dressed in casual wear for their customary Saturday morning round of golf. "Thank God those radio transmissions have stopped. But if they start again, we'll the Silent Vulcan UFO hunters back and then we'll *have* to do something about this lake."

The three watched the two police constables haul on the ropes to guide the Zodiac dinghy into a new position. The first diver was seated in the boat, now fully kitted out in wetsuit and aqualung, watching his colleague's bubble tracks, ready to go to his aid. Normally they would be in the water together but they had decided not to stir up the silt any more than it was already.

"You'll be resuming work on your dig soon, Ellen?" said Prescott conversationally.

"Another month, *Mr* Prescott," Ellen replied. The emphasis on the 'Mister' was to discourage the landowner's familiarity. A wasted effort, of course. Underneath his colourful silk waistcoats, flat caps and tweed suits, the flamboyant, ambitious Asquith Prescott, Chairman of Pentworth Town Council, and the biggest landowner and baby-kisser in the district, wore an ego-filled, thought-tight armour suit of vanity and political cunning that allowed no room for points of view other than his own.

The year before, at one of the fund-raising balls organised by his wife, Prescott had stalked Ellen with the deadly stealth of a

93

marshmallow steamroller and had cornered her in his library. As a mark of his regard for her, he had breathed whisky fumes in her face, plunged an uninvited hand down the front of her evening dress, and shoved the other between her thighs. Ellen's protests and struggles had had little effect until she had delivered a knee to the groin. It wasn't an accurate goolie-crusher, nor was its message clear. Prescott had staggered backwards with: "Ah – time of the month, eh, Ellen? Should've said. Not fair getting you excited like that. Quite understand. Quite understand." And he had shambled off to find a less biologically challenged victim.

Since then Ellen had given the Prescott balls a wide berth. She never liked having to wear evening dresses anyway. Also her integrity ensured that the few quiet words she had had the previous month about his behaviour to the chairman of the association's selection committee were believed. Ellen wasn't the only complainant. The result was that Asquith Prescott's name on the constituency's short list of parliamentary candidates got short shrift and fell off.

"DS Malone should be here by now," Evans grumbled. "He'd have some ideas on protecting this place. Something's got to be done, Miss Duncan."

"It's only dangerous after exceptionally heavy rain, Mr Evans. And Mr Malone had a late night. He very kindly sorted out some trouble I had with vandals early this morning after he'd gone off duty."

"Damn it," Prescott muttered, looking at his mobile phone. "Service keeps dropping out. I need to speak to my manager."

"Try mine." Ellen delved into the depths of her donkey jacket and offered her handset to Prescott. The service faded as soon as he got through. "Odd both services being on the blink," she commented.

Mike Malone's blue Escort arrived. He paused as he was walking past the divers' pickup truck and seemed to be sniffing before joining the group. Evans brushed aside his apologies for being late and introduced him to Prescott.

"I thought Miss Duncan owned this lake?" said Malone, eyeing Prescott dispassionately.

"As Chairman of the Town Council, I'm naturally concerned that two men should disappear on my patch," said Prescott pompously.

"You mean you wouldn't be concerned if you weren't the chairman, sir?"

"*And* I'm a member of the District Council, of course. Have been for ten years."

"And a trustee on the board of several local charities, I believe," Malone added respectfully.

"Not forgetting my chairmanship of the Board of Governors of Pentworth Primary School," Prescott rejoined, pleased that this nonentity was showing due respect. "So I have an interest in the safety of our children."

"We are most fortunate indeed to have you here, sir."

Ellen struggled to maintain a straight face.

"Mr Prescott and I always play golf on Saturday mornings," said Evans huffily. Two minutes on the scene and already Malone was trying to tread on egos, although Prescott was too full of himself to realise when the piss was being taken. Then it was Evans' turn.

"Golf?" Malone queried. "I thought that your morris men and your model aeroplane took up all your spare time, Mr Evans?" Malone's face was expressionless yet Ellen was sure that he gave her a surreptitious, conspiratorial wink.

"There's no sign of the missing men, Sergeant," said Evans pointedly.

Malone glanced at the divers and constables. "That I'd guessed, Mr Evans."

"They will return—" Ellen began but was interrupted by a shout from the diver. She had intended to say that the missing men would return to the surface.

They all moved on to squelchy ground and watched the constables hauling in the dinghy. The first diver was hanging on to his colleague who had hooked an arm over the side of the Zodiac. Once in shallow water he managed to stand with difficulty. His wetsuit was streaked with silt and sand, and compressed air was hissing explosively from the demand valve's exhaust in his full face mask. He grabbed the long pole that a policeman in waders held out for him and staggered out of the water, the quicksand almost pulling his flippers off as he lifted them out of the water. The weight belt fell with a dull thud on the ground and one of the policemen took the weight of his aqualung as the diver twisted the harness's quick release buckle. "That has got to be the most disgusting muck I've ever dived in," he declared, sitting down and shutting off the cylinder valves on the aqualung's silt-smothered mixer manifold. The hissing stopped. He inspected the face mask and shook out a thick syrup of sand and water. "Look at that – muck stopping the reg's diaphragm from working." He looked up at the gathering. "Sorry, Mr Evans, but I can't possibly allow any diving in that stuff. What the hell is this bloody lake anyway? It's got no discernible bottom. A bloody great area of quicksand. It just gets thicker and thicker." He looked at the depth gauge on his wrist. "Ten metres I managed."

"I'm surprised you managed to go that deep," said Ellen.

The diver started sponging the worst of the silt off his wetsuit. "Just how deep is it, anyway?"

"No one knows," said Ellen. "The Pentworth Society did a survey about five years ago using drain-cleaning rods as a probe. They got as far as a hundred metres, ran out of rods and had to give up."

"Over three hundred feet," Evans commented.

"Well over three hundred feet," Ellen replied. "But a bed does form during long dry spells when the silt has a chance to settle. It becomes quite firm and safe. People go swimming in hot spells. What happens is that the lake's fed by subterranean springs that cause an upwelling, particularly after heavy rains." She gestured to the hills. "There's a huge run-off from the South Downs. It's the upwelling that creates the swamp conditions – when the sand and water become mixed in roughly equal proportions."

"Which is all quicksand is," Malone commented. "Sand and water. Nothing special. Right, Miss Duncan?"

"Nothing special!" Evans exclaimed. "Two men drowned in it yesterday!"

"They could've just as easily have drowned in clear water," Ellen countered. "More easily, in fact. In quicksand you're more buoyant than in water. It's about twice the density of water therefore you're pushed up by a correspondingly greater force – just as the high salinity of the Dead Sea makes you so buoyant that it's impossible to sink."

"You needed twice the normal amount of lead on your weightbelt," observed the first diver who was stowing the diving gear in the pickup.

"That's true," agreed the second diver.

Prescott put an arm around Ellen's waist. "Ah . . . But what this little lady is forgetting is that quicksand sucks you down. Nasty stuff, Ellen. The council will have to consider some sort of outer fencing option. Expensive, but we must think of the children."

It looked as though in covering Prescott's hand with her own hand that Ellen was responding to the landowner's friendly gesture. In fact she was sinking her nails into the back of his wrist with all the strength she could muster. Prescott took the hint and released her – slowly so that no one would notice anything, but Malone, who missed nothing, saw the red marks before Prescott thrust his hand casually in his pocket. His estimation of Ellen went up another point.

"It's something I've never forgotten, Mr Prescott," said Ellen innocently. "I never forget the important things."

"Ah . . ."

"Because I've never learned such garbage in the first place. When sand and water are mixed together it becomes a thixotropic fluid – it possesses shear thickening. When you deform such a liquid the viscosity actually increases with the deformation rate. It's the opposite of what happens in most fluids, which tend to be shear thinning – such as non-drip emulsion paint. So, if you're stuck in quicksand, to avoid submerging, you need to move very carefully. Any upward motion has to be made slowly, and any downward motion made quickly. In theory, Mr Prescott, if you fell into a swamp and, as likely as not, there was no mad rush to pull you out, by keeping calm you should be able to climb out. And if you ever need to entertain your grandchildren at parties instead of indulging in other activities, all you have to do is mix cornstarch and water. It makes a hell of a thixotropic fluid."

A hard look came into Prescott's eyes as he stared at Ellen. His hand still smarting from her nails, her hostile tone and veiled hints confirmed his suspicions as to who had sabotaged his ambition of becoming the local member of parliament. Ellen turned pointedly away and helped the divers stow their gear in the pickup.

"All very interesting but it doesn't solve our immediate problem," said Harvey Evans.

Malone made an excuse and joined Ellen at the pickup just as the Zodiac was being secured. "You lads had a spot of clutch trouble?" he asked.

The second diver looked surprised. "Can you smell it?"

"Burnt Ferrodo linings. Know the smell anywhere."

"It started playing up a couple of miles south of Northchapel. No go in her for about a mile, and then it cleared up."

"Odd," said Malone. "I had clutch trouble south of Pentworth, and you had clutch trouble north of Pentworth."

"All these hills," said Ellen.

"We were on the flat," the first diver remarked, checking that the Zodiac's ropes were secure.

There was a flash of crimson waistcoat as Asquith Prescott got into his Range Rover. The look he gave Ellen before driving off was as cold as a ferryman's penny.

"Looks as if your dislike of the gentlemen has finally sunk in," Malone observed quietly.

"Your perception always astonishes me, Mr Malone."

"There's a lot to perceive, Miss Duncan."

Harvey Evans stumped over. "Bang goes my morning golf," he grumbled. "Any ideas on this mess, Malone?"

"Short term – I think we'll have to keep a watching brief for at least another forty-eight hours, sir. Long term . . . I was going to suggest that Miss Duncan gives a talk to the local schools about the dangers of this lake, but that might be counter-productive – we'd have a hundreds of kids swarming down here to learn about thixotropic fluids."

"It's only dangerous under certain conditions," Ellen added.

"Like now?" said Evans.

"Like now," Ellen agreed.

"I'll give it some careful thought over the weekend, Mr Evans," Malone promised.

Evans grunted, levered his stocky figure behind the wheel of his car and started the engine. "Nice day for a spot of flying but I'd better get some sort of duty rota sorted. Damned nuisance. Grown men getting themselves drowned on my patch." He suddenly thought of something. "Have you considered that position, Sergeant?"

"I have indeed, sir, and must respectfully decline. I don't think my ex will want to change our Sunday agreement for access to my kids."

"Understood. Good day to you, Miss Duncan. Thank you for coming." Malone was accorded a grunt and Harvey Evans drove off.

"My turn to do some perceiving," said Ellen. "Inspector Evans is keen for you to join the Pentworth Morris Men side?"

"Spot on, Miss Duncan."

"Your refusal is not a politically sound decision if you want to transfer out of this division."

Malone grinned. "You're not thinking laterally. He'll want me off his sector in the hope that my replacement will be more compliant – if he could get a replacement. But don't get him wrong – he's a decent man who's kept morale high, and he's a good organiser."

"He plays golf with Asquith Prescott."

"Someone has to."

Ellen smiled. "Thank you for arranging to have my shopfront cleaned up."

"Tell me about this place. How is it possible to have a lake in the middle of southern England and no one knows how deep it is?"

Ellen gazed across her lake. "This was karst country. Where acidic surface water leached down into the limestone and dissolved it away over thousands of years. If there's overlying stratum of more durable rock such as granite, you end up with a labyrinth of caverns such you have in Cheddar Gorge. But this part of southern England doesn't have much igneous rock. So, huge caverns formed underground and eventually the land collapsed. You end up with sink holes and swallow holes all over the place. That's karst, Mr Malone."

Ellen paused as she gazed across the glittering yellow lake, as always, trying to picture what this place must have like before recorded history.

"Water cascades in," she continued. "Maybe for centuries. The water brings silt and loess with it, and, given a few more thousand years you end up with this . . . An innocent-looking and rather beautiful lake. Well – beautiful when the bottom silt isn't stirred up." She frowned at the expanse of mustard-coloured water. "But I've never seen it as bad as this – not even after the floods of three years ago. The discoloration and agitation wasn't anything like this. Something's very different this time."

Twenty

The shop bell jangled.

Vikki swallowed down the last of her sandwich, hunger having driven her to an early start on her packed lunch, shooed Thomas off the kiln, and went into the shop to attend the customer. The tall, Dracula-like figure at the counter was a surprise – he reminded her of the mysterious cloaked silhouette in the Sandiman Sherry advertisements. He was clad in beautifully tooled black leather from his turn-topped Cavalier boots to his hand-stitched trilby. Even his crimson-lined cloak, fastened with a gold chain at his neck, was fashioned from stretched and worked hide. It hung from his shoulders with the symmetric precision of a folded ink blot. With heels that added five centimetres to his already considerable height, Nelson Faraday was an impressive figure.

"Yes, sir?"

He gave an almost imperceptible start when he shifted his gaze from Vikki's breasts to her face, but recovered quickly. "Can I speak to the woman that owns this place, please."

The voice and lean, hard features disconcerted and yet captivated Vikki. She could imagine him doing all manner of swashbuckling things – such as dangling from a helicopter to deliver boxes of chocolate to lovelorn damsels imprisoned in ivory towers. He was a man who knew how to exert power. Vikki prided herself on her ability to handle the self-conscious pimply youths who haunted the Green Dragon. She could always keep command of a situation, particularly when they got too adventurous with their hands during pulls, but this was a man who expected and got his own way as a matter of course. She felt that he wasn't merely stripping her naked with his brooding eyes, but forcing her to undress for him, slowly, and making her fold her clothes neatly.

"I'm very sorry, sir, but Miss Duncan is unavailable at the moment."

"When will the woman be in?"

"I'm not sure, sir. Can I take a message?"

"Tell her that a cleaning company will be along on Monday morning to do her shopfront."

The way he referred to her employer irritated Vikki but she was careful not to show it. "Certainly, sir."

He regarded her thoughtfully, making no attempt to conceal his interest in the swell of her breasts. "I'm Nelson Faraday." He smiled unexpectedly and held out his hand.

Vikki took it with her right hand but he didn't let go after they had shaken. She tried to establish some sort of control. "Haven't I seen you driving a big camper through the town?"

He ignored the question and asked what her name was.

"Vikki . . . Vikki Taylor." She was angry with herself for answering so promptly.

He stroked her hand. "St Catherine's?"

Vikki steeled herself to say nothing but his hard gaze extorted a nod.

"Well, Vikki – we're having one of our weekend raves at the House . . ." He jerked his thumb in the direction of the wall on the opposite side of the street. "Starting tonight – finishing tomorrow night. Tempus Fugit will be doing a gig at two a.m."

The news that the fabulous new band would be performing locally caused Vikki to forget her imprisoned hand. "Here? In Pentworth?"

"How old are you?"

None of your bloody business!

"Fifteen."

He released her hand, unzipped a pocket, and laid two gilt-edged invitations on the counter. "A pen please, Vikki. These have to be endorsed."

Intrigued, she gave him a pen. He signed both cards and pushed them across the counter. "Make yourself look eighteen-plus. And your friend. Don't forget the message for the owner of this place." He gave the surprised girl a friendly smile, turned away on his stylish heels, and left the shop without a backward glance.

It was some moments before Vikki could bring herself to pick up the prized invitations. She returned to the packing table and stared down at the cards. Pentworth House's weekend parties were well known in the area although locals rarely received invitations, and certainly no one under eighteen. And she had *two*! They had bar codes on the back. Security at Pentworth House was strict; none of the local youths had ever succeeded in gate-crashing their events. She picked up the telephone, called a local number and asked for

101

Sarah. The line was faint. She had to repeat her request to Mrs Gale several times.

"Hallo, Sarah. Vikki."

The line was terrible. "Who?"

"I'll redial!" Vikki yelled. The result of the second attempt was no better. "Listen, Sarah! Can you hear me?"

"Just about."

"What are we doing tonight?"

"Green Dragon, I suppose. The usual non-vocalised Saturday night house and garage bang-bang crap tonight. Why?"

"I've got a better idea. How about the House party? I've got two invites."

"What a fucking awful line!" Sarah shouted. "No, I'm not swearing, Mum!" Despite the poor line Vikki could hear the normal hullabaloo of the permanent state of war that existed between all the members of the Gale household. Mother screaming at her lover, Sarah screaming at everyone to be quiet, and baby Simon screaming at no one in particular. The Gales were one big snappy family. "Hold the phone close," Sarah yelled. "It sounded like you said something about two invites for the House party."

"I have!"

"Bugger off! *For fuck's sake, Mum – I'm not swearing!*"

"I tell you I have! And they've got Tempus Fugit playing at two a.m.!"

"Hey – cool! How'd you get them?"

Vikki described the visitor.

"Hey, man! Nelson Faraday! Isn't he well cool? Ten on the F scale. Are you at the shop?"

"Yes!"

The line got worse.

"Fuck. This is hopeless. They can all hear every word. I'll be round in fifteen minutes!"

Sarah lived nearby and made it in ten minutes. There were no customers, thus the two girls were able to hatch a parental-suspicion-proof plot without interruption.

In his room in Pentworth House, Nelson Faraday was also making plans for that night. He sprawled on the bed and relaxed while two girls pulled his boots off and generally tended to his needs. One unwrapped a cigar and put it his mouth; the other lit it. He lay back and inhaled contentedly, an arm around each girl, a breast cupped in each hand under their T-shirts, absent-mindedly rolling a nipple in and out between each thumb and index finger. Thinking about Vikki was enough to cause the stirrings of an erection without the girls' administrations. His thoughts dwelt on her with suppressed savagery. He liked having two or more girls at the same time, but not tonight. Tonight was going to be different.

Roscoe could go and take a flying fuck at his stupid rules about no one under eighteen. Tonight it was going to be just one girl. A sweet, virginal fifteen-year-old Catholic girl, the dead spit of the bitch that had shopped him and his mates when he was twelve – his first brush with the law. Fucking hell – none of them had been able to get it up so they had used a Coke bottle on the stupid, hysterical cow. Should've used it sideways. No Coke bottle tonight, though.

Not tonight, my little Vikki – for you the real thing. Not only will I have your blood and cozzie juice smeared all over my cock when I've finished with you, but I'll have you begging for more.

Twenty-One

Ellen's near sleepless night and lack of breakfast caught up with her as she was returning to her shop. She had passed the dig enclosure and was near the top of the bluff when her legs decided that enough was enough. The steep slope overlooking Pentworth Lake was as pleasant a place as any to rest so she sank gratefully to the ground, wriggled out of her donkey jacket, and used it as a cushion for her back against an outcrop of limestone.

The sun was pleasantly warm; high above, a skylark was celebrating the arrival of spring with its clear song, riding on a thermal of warm air rising from the Temple of the Winds. To her right the stream that David had rerouted tumbled contentedly down its series of waterfalls. It had widened during the winter and now looked quite natural. A few moments were spent indulging in her favourite pastime of imagining what this area must have looked like when it was a Palaeolithic flint miners' camp. Weathered, rounded hills? Probably – it was an ancient landscape even then. Her eyes closed. A few minutes doze wouldn't hurt. The pang of guilt at leaving Vikki alone in the shop didn't last – the girl loved being left in charge. She was probably allowing Thomas to sleep on the kiln.

Later Ellen would go over those moments again and again in a futile attempt to pinpoint the exact moment when she had fallen asleep.

If, indeed, she had fallen asleep . . .

The song of the skylark faded and it was suddenly very hot – extraordinarily hot – and there was a strange, menacing roar of water above the incessant buzz of insects. She sat upright, started yanking her pullover over her head and froze, her elbows twisted at an awkward angle and her expression of astonishment framed by the rough, homespun wool.

The familiar outline of the distant South Downs was no more. In place of the soft, rounded contours was a sawtooth line of harsh escarpments, chalk outcrops, ragged tors, and a sun beating down from a sky so clear and blue that it looked wrong. But it wasn't the sky that skewered Ellen's attention: below her was a scene so unreal that she rose to her feet without realising it and stared, awe-struck, at the spectacle. To the west was a broad, swift-flowing yellow river. The raging waters piled up against a steep ravine and changed course, eastward – charging rapids in front of her plunging into a yawning, crater-like chasm that was at least a kilometre across where Pentworth Lake should have been. The spectacular waterfall was the cause of the roaring noise that had woken her. The mighty cascade fell in apparent slow motion out of sight below the rim of the chasm, creating a permanent halo of iridescent rainbow colours hovering over the scene in that impossible light.

Timeless moments passed as Ellen drank in the wondrous spectacle. She knew she was asleep. She knew that this was a dream. She didn't want to pinch herself or close her eyes for an instant, or make any move for fear that she would wake up. Suddenly reality was a feared enemy that would take this miracle away from her. It was imperative to fix every detail of the scene in her mind because the process of waking was a merciless memory-wiping function that swept through the brain's hippocampus, deleting short-term dream images because they weren't considered essential for survival. She moved her eyes slowly, terrified to allow her gaze to flit about lest the delicate patterns of light and sound that were the very substance of this marvel became confused and blurred.

The almost total lack of trees, except in hollows and valleys where they grew in profusion, hinted at a latent vitality that was just waiting for the right conditions. The yellowing, wind-desiccated grasses covered a plain whose contours bore a faint resemblance to the plain she knew so well, but it was impossible to be certain for there were none of the familiar reference markers of hedgerows and field systems; nature had marked this landscape – not Man.

She lowered her gaze to where the dig enclosure should be and her breath caught in her throat when she saw the flint mine as it had once been: a broad, crescent-shaped gash caused by centuries of bone and flint picks gnawing and gouging deep into the chalk where the precious nodules of the waxy-sheened, high-quality floor-stone chert were to be found. The working was about 200 metres wide and strewn with chalk and flint chippings, and there were even mammoth knee bones set into the ground as anvils.

Eddies of a strengthening north wind spilled over the sandstone bluff behind her and struck with icy coldness on her back, and yet her chest was hot and sticky from the solar radiation that her dark pullover was absorbing. With the wind came a low moaning sound from behind. She turned very slowly, still terrified that movement would banish these wonders, and saw something that caused the freezing wind to spasm in her throat.

It was the Temple of the Winds.

But the great sandstone outcrop was far larger than it should be and the features of the scowling gargoyle were sharper and more pronounced. The rising slope from which the great slab projected was bare of trees. And that wasn't all, for standing on the slab plateau was a huge, trumpet-like structure, breaking the bluff's once-wooded northern skyline where North Street with its slate-roofed huddled terraces ought to be.

A tentative step up the slope.

Nothing happened. The sun and wind were conflicting swords of hot and cold.

Two more steps. The freezing eddies stung her cheeks. The dreamscape remained sharp and clear – providing a flood of vivid details that no dream could ever match. This was a real world! And with that heady realisation she found herself scrambling up the steep slope, her rubber boots crunching the freeze-dried sedge grass, the cold sucking the warmth greedily from her fingers when she grasped tufts of the stuff to maintain her momentum. She reached the brow and the searing cold of the north wind burned her throat dry. How could the wind be so cold and yet the sun so hot? Low or zero humidity had to be the answer. Humidity so low that the wind sucked the moisture from her throat.

Glaciers!

They would be two days' march to the north, perhaps only a day to the margins of the mighty ice sheet that covered the whole of Northern Europe. It was the glaciers that had sucked the wind dry and so created these freeze-dried steppes.

It was information to be carefully recorded against the treachery of waking but right now her interest was in the strange trumpet contraption. The easier route she had followed up the slope had taken her away from the Temple of the Winds. She broke into a run, her wellingtons clumping along what would become, centuries in the future, the long back gardens of the south side of North Street. To her joy, there was a zigzag track leading up to the Temple of the Winds – not the rough, narrow track she was familiar with, but almost a hewn roadway, wide and clear of loose rocks. She raced up the steep, snaking track and emerged breathless on to the plateau.

The squat stone marker obelisk that identified distant landmarks for the benefit of ramblers was no more. In its place stood the strange, horn-like contraption.

Close to, the extraordinary structure was bigger than she had realised. The framework of thong-lashed hazel saplings stood nearly three times her height. The entire structure had been fashioned with great skill. It was mounted on two larger poles with hewed ends in the manner of sledge runners. These in turn were anchored down by sturdy notched stakes driven deep into cracks in the sandstone. Ellen stooped and saw that the runners were worn suggesting that the thing was intended to be moveable.

She turned her attention to the huge, rectangular horn made from chamois or goat hides – all beautifully worked and cured to an even colour and texture, and stitched together and cross-braced with smaller saplings to form what looked to Ellen like a gigantic foghorn. She stared into the contraption's gaping maw and pondered its purpose as the hide panels cracked and flexed in the freezing gusts.

Some sort of appeasement to a wind god?

She dismissed the notion. Why go to the trouble of making it transportable?

It was when the wind abated for a few moments that she thought she heard voices coming from the horn. She leaned right into the opening, caught a snatch of laughter before the icy gusts from the north smothered the sounds, driving them back into the horn's depths.

She moved back a few paces to get a clearer overall picture and saw that the horn's throat wasn't merely ragged tails of hide as she had first supposed, but that the leathern ends were stitched together to form a narrow duct. She went closer and nearly trod on the delicate intestine that had been stretched over internal hoops at intervals to keep it open. The intestinal ducting, about the diameter of her thigh, was almost the same colour as the sedge grass so it wasn't surprising that she hadn't noticed it at first. But what manner of animal had an intestine this size?

There was only one possible answer: one that was both illogical and yet crazily logical: the woolly mammoth.

And then the purpose of the horn struck her:

A ventilator! A giant scoop to catch the wind and take it . . . Take it where? A forge? A kiln?

There was only one way to find out. Hardly able to contain her excitement, Ellen set off, down the track, and slithering and slipping down the steep hillside, following the snaking duct. At one point she came on a new section of gleaming white intestine that was sufficiently translucent for her to peer at the internal wooden hoops that maintained the ducting's shape. It was obviously a recent repair. A discarded section solved the problem of how the makers had managed to manipulate the hoops into position. The hoops were pre-shaped lengths of hazel with key-notched ends. The sandstone-smoothed sticks were passed along inside the intestine until they were in the right position and bent around and the ends snapped sideways together like oversize shower curtain rings.

Dear God – these people are clever.

What people?

The people at the end of this ducting! People who know laughter!

She resumed her scramble down the hillside, finally half falling on to a narrow path where the intestine ducting followed the track's contour and disappeared behind the debris of a small landslide. Escaping air hissing from a small leak this far from the great wind horn indicated just how efficient the remarkable system was. Ellen could smell wood smoke. Some fifty metres beyond the landslide was something she had hardly dared hope she would ever see, but there it was.

A cave!

The smoke was eddying from the opening into which the intestine ducting disappeared. Heedless of possible danger, Ellen quickened her pace. The low opening was in a steep part of the bank, almost a small cliff, and the area around the entrance was carpeted with flat stones set flush into the soil – she supposed to prevent the ground turning into a quagmire in the summer. Ellen hesitated, caution triumphing over courage and curiosity, but not for long. She was about to enter the cave but froze when the figure of a man emerged from the smoke. For timeless seconds the two stared at other in mutual astonishment. The man was naked apart from a hide breech clout. He was slightly built, shorter than Ellen. His lean arms were streaked with dyes, particularly red ochre, which was also caked into his lank hair and straggling grey beard. Hanging from a thong around his neck was a curved tooth as long as a forefinger. But it was his eyes that held Ellen. Brown, wide-set, with a brooding intelligence that seemed to be absorbing every detail of the apparition before him. To Ellen his gaze was that of an observant artist.

She held her hands out to show that they were empty and took a step towards him. Fear clouded his gaze. He muttered something, clutched the tooth, and backed towards the cave so that he was framed by the smoke.

"Please," said Ellen, speaking quietly but her hammering heart making her voice unsteady. "I won't hurt you."

Her words decided the man. He uttered a cry and disappeared into the smoke. She went to follow him, ducking down to enter the cave but was driven back, coughing and spluttering, by dense white clouds of wood smoke that came billowing out of the cave with renewed vigour to engulf her. At first she thought that she would be able withstand the fumes – she just *had* to enter the cave. She tried again but this time was forced to run back a few paces along the bank, keeping her head low and tugging the pullover across her mouth. Eventually her bursting lungs forced her to take a deep breath. The acrid smoke scalded into her throat and eyes like an enraged wasp swarm. She fell to her knees, blinded, choking and sobbing, and then was frantically waving her arms in a futile attempt to drive back the suffocating cloud.

The south-westerly did a more efficient job.

The smoke rolled away. She greedily hoovered down lungfuls of clean, smoke-free air while wiping her eyes on her pullover. Eventually her breathing and sobbing steadied and she could hear the song of the skylark, now joined by the shrill scream of a distant chainsaw.

She opened her eyes and everything was as it should be: the stream; the glitter of Pentworth Lake; the rolling downs under a greyish-blue sky; David's sheep, and a ribbon of snarled-up traffic far to the south on the Chichester road. The land immediately around her was as it had always been, and had lost the angular harshness of her vision. The weathered, scowling face of the Temple of the Winds was as she had always known it. Her anger and disappointment at the abrupt ending of the strange daydream was tempered by the thought that come what may, she had to pinpoint the exact position of the cave's entrance.

I was right here and the cave's entrance was there – west – not twenty metres from where I stopped running.

She kept her eyes fixed on the side of the slope where she believed the cave had been, not daring to even look down at the uneven ground as she went forward, and stopped only when she was at what she was convinced was the precise spot. Without moving, she searched the bank for a clue – a discoloration of the grass – anything to confirm that she had the right spot. But there was nothing. All she had to go on was her gut feeling, and she was even unsure of that now.

She knelt and made a small marker cairn of pebbles and uprooted clods of grass before she dared leave the place. Her donkey jacket was about 100 metres away where she had left it. To reach it meant wading across the stream but it was shallow and she took a quick drink, the water spilling through her shaking fingers. She pulled her telephone from the pocket. The bar graph was showing an abnormally weak signal from the repeater but it ought to be enough. She called up David Weir's mobile number from the handset's memory but paused before pressing the send button.

What on earth could she say? That she had been transported back perhaps 40,000 years in a daydream so vivid, so detailed, that it just had to be true? David would laugh and tease her. She recalled her advice earlier that morning to Vikki about daydreams and wondered . . . Perhaps this weird experience had sprung from something she had read? God knows – she had enough books on palaeontology. But not one of them mentioned wind-trap horns or anything remotely like them.

She stabbed the button, and had to call twice more before getting a proper connection.

"David. It's Ellen. Listen." She broke off to clear her throat – the smoke was still stinging.

"Sounds like you need a drink, m'dear. What's the problem?"

"I'm just above the dig. Listen, David – I need you and the Kubota and strong arms with picks and shovels up here as soon as possible."

"Oh my God. What have you found now, Ellen?"

Channel break-up obliterated most of Ellen's reply. "Please, David, *please*! Get that mini-digger and Charlie and a few of his lads up here ASAP and I'll shower you with sexual favours tonight that'll have you crawling up the wall."

"But you always do have me crawling up the wall, m'dear."

"Then I'll have you hanging from the ceiling!" Ellen retorted.

David made a mock panting noise. "Not the gymslip and black stockings!"

"And the hockey stick!" Ellen shot back, trying not to laugh.

"Good heavens – I'm on my way! Thirty minutes. Norwich is the appropriate expression, is it not?"

"Idiot!"

Pleased that David hadn't wanted explanations, Ellen crammed the handset in her pocket and took the shortest route up the slope towards home. The effort forced her to concentrate and so the doubts came muscling back like a gang of unruly skinheads trying to get past a nightclub bouncer. It *had* to be a daydream, and her imagination had supplied all the details. God knows – she had spent enough hours trying to visualise what it had been like in this broad valley 40,000 years ago.

Forty thousand years!

Spelling it out in her mind brought the figure into sharp focus.

Think about that figure, Ellen!

More than 35,000 years before the rise of the shepherd kings of Egypt and the building of the pyramids. About the same period of time before the invention of writing in Sumeria. The whole of recorded history had yet to be written. Three hundred and fifty centuries – *centuries!* – before Abram set out from Ur! And you think you heard the voices and laughter of the people of that time, that you have looked upon their creations in wood and leather, and even met one of their artists? Wouldn't it be sensible to imagine something more conventionally insane – that you're Napoleon, or his mistress maybe? That way you wouldn't get yourself sectioned under the Mental Health Act for anything like as long. Twenty years binned and you'd be fine.

She was so preoccupied with her sudden depression and her decision to phone David to call the whole thing off, that she didn't realise she was home. Vikki had heard the back door and came to meet her. The girl looked alarmed as she took in the dishevelled figure: dark hair awry, face covered in sweat-streaked soot smuts.

"Are you all right, Miss Duncan?"

Ellen stared listlessly at the girl and beyond her at the shop's stillroom. She'd lose it all, of course. Everything.

"Miss Duncan?" Vikki moved forward, thinking for a moment that her employer was about to faint. She paused and smiled. "Oh dear. I think I guess what's happened."

"You can?" Ellen looked at the girl in surprise.

"The same thing that happened last month. You started a bonfire and it got out of control."

The incongruity of the statement restored Ellen's tongue and temper. "Now why on earth should you think anything so bloody stupid? I may make mistakes, young lady, but rarely twice."

Vikki wrinkled her nose. "But you stink of bonfire."

Ellen's eyes glazed with shock as the girl's words sank in. "I do?" She sniffed cautiously at her pullover. "Yes – I do, don't I?"

The girl smiled, pleased to have won a point. "You certainly do, Miss Duncan. You should see your face. It must be in your hair. Your clothes. Everything—" She broke off in surprise as Ellen suddenly flung her arms around her.

"Vikki!" Ellen declared laughingly, her eyes now shining. "I think you're the most wonderful creature on God's earth!"

Before the bemused girl could respond, Ellen had pushed past her and was rummaging frantically through the workstation's drawers.

"Camera. Where the hell did I put the digital camera?"

"Middle left, Miss Duncan."

"I never keep it in there – yes – it's here. How can I ever find anything if you keep putting things back in the right place? Those aerial photographs that Harvey Evans took last year from his microlight?"

"That box file."

It continued in that vein until Ellen had a Sainsbury's carrier stuffed with an Olympus digital camera, a torch, drawing implements, and a set of aerial photographs of her land.

"Vikki – can I ask a huge, impossible favour and get you to mind the shop for another two or three hours, please?"

"That's fine, Miss Duncan. I could stay on till closing time if you wish."

"You're a sweet, wonderful angel, Vikki."

"Even angels deserve time and a half, Miss Duncan."

"I know one that doesn't. Yes – all right."

"And there's the extra hour I did this morning."

Ellen was too impatient to be away to explode with wrath. "OK. OK. Right. I'm off. Hope you don't get too rushed."

Vikki was about to assure Ellen that she didn't mind being busy but her employer had gone, leaving the girl wondering what it was that Ellen had discovered. She sniffed her blouse where Ellen had hugged her and detected the lingering scent of wood smoke . . .

From a fire that had been lit 40,000 years ago.

Twenty-Two

M ike Malone's wide-set eyes and penetrating gaze made Bob Harding feel decidedly uncomfortable. He shuffled some papers on the bench in his workshop. "I did a bit of digging as soon as I got your call, Mr Malone. I tried accessing the Net, but I couldn't get a clean connection."

"It was very good of you to look into it right away, Mr Harding."

"It *was* Johann Bode you wanted information on? Not the Bodian berks at the House? It was such a God-awful line . . ."

"Just Bode, please."

Harding chuckled. "Just as well. I don't have anything on the Bodian lot. Bunch of loonies, if you ask me. Fancy founding a religion based on the findings of an old fraud like Bode. But they do make fantastic ice cream and bake fabulous bread."

Malone opened his notebook. He rarely used it but this time it would be useful to keep Harding's opinions and the facts clearly separate. "So tell me about Johann Bode," he invited.

"Got it here somewhere," said Harding looking through the papers. "Yes – Johann Elert Bode. Born Germany 1747. Died 1826. A self-educated mathematical genius. He became director of the Berlin Academy Observatory when he was thirty-nine. Normally a job given to old fogies on the Buggins' turn principle, but Johann had been publishing brilliant star catalogues since his early twenties and had an international reputation. He made a fuss and landed the job." Harding gestured to some shelves bowing under the weight of several large tomes. "I've got some old reprints of his. Damn good they are, too."

Malone studied Harding's Newtonian telescope for some moments before turning his gaze on its owner. "So why was he a fraud?"

"They all were, Mr Malone – all those eighteenth- and nineteenth-century prodigies – always nicking each other's ideas. It was Johann Titius who did the spadework on Bode's law, which is why it's called Titius-Bode's law today."

"So what exactly is this law?"

Harding laughed. "It's not really a law, Mr Malone. Not one that fits into any pattern of astrophysics. It's a shaky formula for predicting the distances of the planets from the sun. It's dead simple to understand – must be, because his Divine Pratness, Adrian Roscoe, hasn't had much trouble selling it to all the deadbeats and dropouts he's lured up to the House. Sorry if I'm teaching grandmother and all that, but do you know what an Astronomical Unit is?"

"No idea," Malone confessed. "Something big, I expect."

"Actually, it's quite small. An AU is the earth's distance from the sun – 1 AU equals about 150 million kilometres. With me?"

Malone confirmed that he was.

"The Bodian mob think it's a holy unit because it was determined by God," said Harding. He took a blank sheet of paper and wrote the following numbers in bold characters using a marker pen:

3   6   12   24   48   96   192   384   768

He stopped and looked expectantly at the police officer. "That string of numbers was Bode's starting point. See their relationship?"

"Each number is a doubling of the previous number."

"Spot on. Next Bode added four to each number like so, and we have . . ."

4   7   10   16   28   52   100   196   388   772

"And then he divided each number by ten. Shift the decimal point one place and we have . . ."

0.4   0.7   1   1.6   2.8   5.2   10   19.6   38.8   77.2

Harding underlined the last row of numbers with the marker pen. "Bode believed that those numbers were the distance of each planet in the solar system from the sun in Astronomical Units. I'll show you . . ." He added the following table to the sheet:

Planet	Actual distance from sun (AU)	Bode's law distance (AU)
Mercury	0.39	0.4
Venus	0.72	0.7
Earth	1	1
Mars	1.52	1.6
Asteroid Belt	2.8	2.8
Jupiter	5.2	5.2
Saturn	9.6	10
Uranus	19	19.6
Neptune	30	38.8
Pluto	39.4	77.2

"Interesting," Malone commented. "But it doesn't seem work too well in the case of Pluto."

"Pluto's a weird planet," Harding replied. "It wasn't discovered until 1930. Its orbit isn't concentric, and it's not even in the plane of the ecliptic like the other planets. Many astronomers now believe that it's a captured body that wasn't part of the solar system to begin with. Or it may have been a moon of Neptune.

"Of course, when Bode published his law, the scientific establishment tore him to shreds. A totally arbitrary law governing the distance of the planets from the sun didn't make sense, and still doesn't. His law predicted a planet after Saturn and there wasn't one. Then Uranus was discovered in 1781 by Sir William Herschel at a distance of 19 AUs from the sun – exactly where Bode said it would be.

"Bode's enemies went into their corner, and came out fighting, pointing out that there wasn't a planet between Mars and Jupiter. They were shafted in 1801 when the first of thousands of asteroids was found in what is now known as the asteroid belt . . . At the exact distance from the sun that Bode predicted."

"The planet smashed by the wrath of God," Malone commented.

"If you believe nutters like Adrian Roscoe," said Harding. "He sometimes turns up at council meetings. Good talker. Hypnotic. But as loony as a lemming."

There was a few moments silence as both men contemplated the strange table before them.

Malone toyed with his notebook. "What do you believe, Mr Harding?"

"I'm an atheist, Mr Malone. I don't believe in a divine force. Like most scientists, I think that Bode's law is nothing more than a coincidence. The asteroid belt may have been a planet in the making that never made it."

"Extraordinary coincidence, though."

"A coincidence," Harding insisted. "It has to be."

"Am I right in thinking that no other planetary systems have been discovered?"

Harding found it easier to avoid Malone's gaze. "You certainly are, Mr Malone. No hard and fast evidence as yet. All the nearest stars are being researched. The Hubble orbital telescope has found what could be a planet around a star some four hundred and fifty light-years away. And it may be that Barnard's Star, which is only a few light-years away, has an invisible companion." He smiled. "If there are astronomers on planets out there, they've probably came to the same conclusion about our sun. That the solar system consists of the sun and a dark companion – Jupiter."

"What if Bode's law is found to apply to other planetary systems?"

"Then I'd take a leaf out of Blaise Pascal's book. I'd buy me a Bible and start studying it to hedge my bets."

The police officer folded the Bode's law table into his notebook, and thanked his host.

"Any news on the electricity fault?" Harding asked as he showed Malone through the repair shop to the front door. "The voltage was still down a couple of hours ago."

"I don't think so. Lots of Southern Electric vans rushing about."

"It must be the knock-on effect from a burst water main. It seems to have affected everything," Harding grumbled. "Luckily we've got the bottled gas cooker out of our camper otherwise we'd have to start cooking Sunday lunch today. And most of my customers with Astra systems are getting sparkly pictures. All moaning like hell because there's a decent film on the Movie Channel tonight. Now there's a real mystery for you to solve. I'm sure it can't be due to the weird high pressure we're getting."

He unlocked the door and hesitated. "There is something else you ought to know, Mr Malone. I'm not saying that Bode's law isn't a coincidence, you understand, but the damnable thing about it is that it also works for the moons of the planets."

Twenty-Three

To Ellen's delight, a close scrutiny of Harvey Evans' aerial survey photographs while she was waiting for David Weir showed the grass covering the cave site on the hillside as being a slightly different hue from the surroundings. On the other hand it was much the same as the mottling of the grass all over the site but, with luck, it would be enough to sell the idea to David.

She heard the sound of a small petrol engine and jumped to her feet. A movement out of the corner of her eye. She wheeled in time to catch a brief glimpse of a crablike device disappear down the slope.

What the hell was that?

She stared at the spot where it had disappeared, in half a mind to go after it, but the slope was dangerously steep at that point.

Vikki said something about a sort of mechanical crab. That young lady's daydreams are catching.

A loud whistle shifted her attention. David had finally appeared, riding his Kubota, climbing the narrow track from the lake. The machine's articulated arm with its digging bucket was tucked in sideways. Ellen was too relieved at seeing him to be annoyed that he was alone. David saw her frantic waving of her donkey jacket and altered course to take the higher path alongside the stream. The track-laying miniature digger was a sure-footed beast on uneven ground. With its narrow, slit-trench bucket, the little Japanese machine, not much bigger than a ride-on mower, was ideal for digging new drain trenches and cutting ditches in Sussex's heavy Weald clay. It had paid for itself in weekend rentals to do-it-yourselfers for scratching out the footings of extensions and patios.

He drew up alongside Ellen and stopped. There was an eager light in her eyes which he had last seen when she had dug out a flint axe head with her bare hands.

"Where're the others?" Ellen demanded.

"It's Saturday. Where are all of the Crittendens on a Saturday after they've been paid? Boozed out of their skulls. Young and old. What's all this about, Ellen?"

"David – I think I've found the site of a cave!" David slid off the Kubota's seat and wrinkled his nose. "Smells like you also found a perfume rep to unload some samples on you. If you're going to wear that stuff tonight, then I'm going to feign a headache. You smell worse than that dreadful ginkgo tree – like a warthogs' graveyard."

"Where do you get your wonderful chat-up lines from, David?"

"Same place you get your wonderful perfumes from, m'dear." He put an arm around Ellen's waist and gave her an affectionate hug. "OK – so show me."

Ellen gave him the photograph and pointed out the discoloration. As expected, he was unimpressed and voiced a number of objections.

"This isn't cave country, Ellen. What limestone has been washed out has been replaced by silt and sand which is now solid sandstone."

Ellen pointed to her little cairn marker by the bank. "*Please*, David. Dig."

"What angle?"

"Straight into the bank. Levelish and down at a slight angle."

"Nothing like a precise job spec."

"Dig, please, David."

"The bank might collapse."

Ellen seized a shovel from the digger's tool rack and brandished it menacingly. "David, my love, light of my life, my little swede-bashing dreamboat, if you don't start digging I'm going to chop your cock off and splatter your miserable balls all over this valley."

Realising that he'd have no peace until she had been proved wrong and that she might just carry out her threat, David started the Kubota's engine. He manoeuvred the machine into position and worked the row of hydraulic control levers so that the bucket cut out a neat metre square of turf in strips which Ellen moved clear of the site.

The first bucketful dumped to one side was yellowish loam and clay. David said nothing but continued working methodically, cutting into the opening and not going deeper until the first bucket depth was clear. Half a metre into the bank and he was dumping heavy blue clay that stuck to the bucket and had to be dislodged by Ellen with the shovel. It slowed them down. At the end of thirty minutes they had a huge, sticky pile of spoil to show for their efforts and a square hole, now a metre deep, that tunnelled at an angle into the bank.

The bucket grated on rocks. David stopped digging to poke at the large stones. "Bits of sandstone, chalk, flint, and that lump looks like granite . . . Ellen – we're getting erratics. What we're digging into is probably an old landslide. We could be weeks—"

"I shall pickle it and keep it in a jar on my desk. The refractive index of formaldehyde will make it look bigger than it is. You'd like that, wouldn't you?"

David mopped his face with a handkerchief and decided that it might be unwise to complain about the warmth. He continued digging. Eventually he was working virtually blind, with the digger's arm fully extended, reaching two metres into the tunnel. "I can't go much deeper, Ellen. We're going to have to widen the opening to get the Kub in further —Bloody hell . . ."

"What's up?" Ellen's eyes were suddenly alight with hope. David rarely swore.

"There's nothing there . . ." said David wonderingly. He waggled a lever. "No resistance. The bucket's broken through."

Ellen gave a little dance of impatience as David backed the Kubota away. As soon as the bucket was clear she wriggled into the tunnel with the torch, ignoring David's suggestion that they ought to shore up the roof first.

"Hallo! Hallo!" she called.

"Hallooo!" David answered in a spectral voice.

"Shut up. And leave my arse alone."

"Sorry, m'dear. I yielded to temptation."

"You'll be yielding to a black eye in a minute." Ellen emerged backwards, her hair and face streaked with clay but too excited to care.

"Anyone at home?" David asked.

Ellen's eyes were shining. "It's a cave, all right! I couldn't get the torch in position but it was a bit echoey when I shouted. You'll need to cut to the left and up a bit."

This time David worked with some enthusiasm, reaching the bucket deep into the opening and dragging out spoil. When he had done all he could, Ellen crawled in with the shovel, dislodging rocks and small boulders, and rolling them out of the way with gusto.

David was no coward but he reckoned that what Ellen did next took guts: she seized the torch and crawled straight into the opening at the end of the short tunnel. He peered after her but saw only a flash of light.

"Come on, David!" Ellen's voice was cracking with excitement. "There's just enough height to stand."

"There might be . . . something in there."

"I'll look after you. Come on!"

David wriggled along the tunnel and through the opening. Ellen helped him to his feet. The torchlight flashed on bright points of garnet and silicates that were sprinkled across the rockface like star dust. They were in a narrow triangular chamber formed by huge slabs of fractured stratum.

David was about to express disappointment when Ellen's torch picked out a darker triangle that led into a narrow passage. She directed the beam down and David saw the unmistakable mark of Man: flat stones skilfully tessellated to form a floor.

"It's exactly how I saw – visualised it!" breathed Ellen. She moved forward and told David to keep to one side because she had seen footprints. The passage was at least ten metres long, rock-strewn which made for hard going, yet surprisingly dry considering that it was near a stream and lay beneath tonnes of sticky, wet Weald clay. David was about to suggest that they go back and fetch better lights when their voices suddenly acquired a noticeable echo, and the torch's beam plunged into nothingness. Ellen swung the light, screamed, and dropped the torch.

In the half-second before darkness engulfed them they both saw the huge, wide-eyed, salivating creature that was charging straight at them.

Twenty-Four

B en Watson watched Mike Malone's tracksuited figure pound past the snarled-up traffic crawling up Duncton Hill and veer into his lay-by. He placed a glass of orange juice on the counter of his mobile snack bar. Malone was hardly sweating yet he downed the drink in one gulp.

"And another, please, Ben. Throat's parched."

Ben refilled the glass. "Fumes from that lot, Mr Malone," he said sourly, nodding at the crawling traffic. "Buggered my trade, it has."

"Certainly buggered my day," Malone replied.

"Any idea what's behind it?"

Malone smiled. "You're asking *me* for info, Ben?" He became serious. "No one knows. Some bright spark thought it might someone playing around with a radiation device that swamps ignition coils. But drivers of diesel vehicles have been reporting the same problem, and light aircraft have been affected – so that's that idea knocked on the head. Anyway, every bloody road in and out of Pentworth is affected. Last I heard when I left the nick was that a garbled fax had come through from the AA's BIS Room at Basingstoke saying that they'd had over twenty reports of burnt-out clutches in this area today, and what the hell was going on."

"Lot of Electricity and Water vans running around like chickens with their heads cut off," Ben observed.

"And British Telecom," Malone added. "And British Gas have been going spare. Pressure's so low they're convinced that there must be a major leak somewhere that they can't find. They're thinking of cutting the area off altogether. Latest theory is that a burst main has caused problems with the electric and gas supplies but no one knows where."

Ben jerked a thumb at a portable TV. "Given up on the Pompey-Aldershot match. Lousy picture. Usually works well here, too. Runs off me battery. Radio's the same."

"It's been put down to the exceptionally high atmospheric pressure, Ben. 1060 millibars. *That* is high. A record."

"Bloody weird," said Ben, who thought a millibar was a chocolate snack. "Hot too. Not like March, is it?"

Malone finished his drink and paid his bill. "March is the month for madness. Looks like our cosy little world is falling apart, Ben."

"It's a curse on us for our sinful ways, Mr Malone."

Normally Ben's information was reliable but Malone doubted the credibility of this latest pearl. He adjusted his sweatband. "There'll be a curse on me if I'm late for my daughter's school concert this evening. Be seeing you."

Twenty-Five

The sharpness of the startling image on Ellen's computer monitor was a credit to the makers of her digital camera and its built-in flash because her hands had been trembling when she had started taking pictures in the cave.

The strands of reddish wool, hanging like a huge, shaggy blanket from the great beast, looked so realistic that she imagined that she could reach out and touch them. The second picture, with David standing beside the Palaeolithic mural, gave a better indication of the woolly mammoth's size. It stood about four metres to its withers. The artists had exploited a natural protrusion in the rock face to give the great beast's head a startling three-dimensional quality, which was why she had screamed. The huge head was lowered, as if about to charge, inflicting terrible injuries on the diminutive figures of its human tormentors in the foreground. The creature's tusks were truly formidable: they swept outwards and then inwards, the tips crossing each other. So accurate was the giant wall painting that the chipped and damaged state of the ancient ivories was clearly apparent. Their purpose was not for weapons – the mammoths had had no enemies other than Man and warmth – but for breaking up the ice that covered the sedge grasses of the northern steppes. The creature had been blinded by volleys of absurdly small throwing spears that clung to it like porcupine quills.

Ellen clicked on the next thumbnail image and experienced an almost sexual thrill when the picture exploded to full screen. This was a detail of the group of hunters, some clutching discharged spear-throwers – the forerunner of the bow and arrow. Others, including women, were ready to rush in with loaded spear-throwers.

It was quiet now. The shop was closed and Vikki had been sent off with a substantial bonus. Ellen had had a bath, not as hot as she would've liked because the gas pressure was down, and now was feeling relaxed and content, and going through the pictures for the twentieth time. Her cave would become world famous, for it was the world's only example of a life-size mammoth painting.

She looked up as David came padding bootless through the back door. He kicked off his mud-caked jeans, pulled his T-shirt over his head and flopped tiredly into a chair in just his underpants.

"Done," he said. "Just beat the light. All the spoil taken away in the dumper. I cut an old sheep hurdle to fit into the opening and put the turf back. Fed the sheep around the site so that they've churned up the Kubota marks. They don't seem to mind the appalling stink from that wretched tree of yours." He fell silent, watching the changing images on the computer monitor and asked Ellen to stop at a picture that showed Lowry-like figures driving a rhinoceros into a corral trap. They had found six such hunting scenes in the cave.

"Amazing," said David shaking his head. "They had discovered perspective."

"How do you mean?"

"They knew that painting figures higher up, and smaller and fainter made them appear further away . . . I took another look before closing up."

Ellen smiled without taking her eyes off the screen. "I don't blame you."

"A close look – a really close look with a halogen lantern and a magnifying glass. None of the paint strokes are continuous – they may look like straight lines but they're broken up by thousands of tiny erosion gaps and crystalline formations. All the scenes are like that."

"Meaning?"

"Meaning that the paintings are genuine," said David wearily. "That's something a forger could never reproduce. And all those bones scattered about. They look like cave bear remains. Several of them – probably trapped by the landslide. Where would a forger get such remains?"

Ellen turned and looked sharply at him. "Was there ever any doubt?"

David hesitated, not trusting Ellen's temper but feeling bound to tell the truth. "The way you knew exactly where the opening was? Yes – of course there was doubt. Forgive me, Ellen, but knowing how keen you were to make such a discovery . . . Well – I thought . . ."

Ellen was too happy to be angry. She sidled on to David's knee and kissed him. "You're forgiven, you old sceptic. Let's not go out tonight. Let's get you cleaned up and have an early night."

He smiled wanly. "I might just fall asleep on you."

"I'll even forgive you that as well."

"This town's never going to be the same again," said David with a hint of sadness. "There is something that's bothering me about the mammoth painting, Ellen. Light. You'd need good light to get such even colouring over such a big area. You couldn't possibly get enough light from animal-fat wick lamps, and the smoke from torches would've asphyxiated them."

Ellen smiled and kissed him again, tracing the contour of his broken nose with the tip of her tongue. "Remember that bone needle you found last year and how we all wondered how they could've possibly bored the hole without breaking through the sides because the needle was so slender?"

David chuckled. "There was that student who said that maybe Erich von Däniken was right and that machines had been given to them by space visitors."

"The willingness of loonies to deny the ingenuity of Mankind," said Ellen contemptuously. "The answer was so bloody obvious that none of us could see it; they took a nice chunky bone, bored and shaped the hole first, and then rubbed the bone down to a fine needle around the hole."

"So?"

"The obvious always eludes us." Ellen made a rough sketch of the windtrap horn and its mammoth intestine ducting, explaining its method of construction. "They position the horn so that it's pointing into the prevailing wind and pipe the draught into the cave to where they're working. It provides the artists with plenty of fresh air and drives out the smoke from their torches at the same time."

David studied the sketch and shook his head wonderingly. "That's got to be it. Bless me if they didn't invent air-conditioning."

Ellen nodded. "It's a logical development of the forced-draught hearth. Those people gave Europe a technological and cultural superiority which it has never lost."

Twenty-Six

S arah Gale was a tall, gawky, worldly wise bottle-blonde brunette of fifteen who had been a not unwilling participant in underage sex on many occasions since she was twelve with the exception of the first time – one of her mother's more brutish lovers.

She sprawled on her bed, an awkward tangle of arms and legs, like a broken bicycle, looking enviously at Vikki, a ring-pull lager can resting on her ring-pull navel. "Christ, Vikki. It looks better on you than it would ever look on me in a million years, but not with those stupid panties. Big black knickers – white mini – not a good idea."

There was no full-length mirror in Sarah's friendly tip of a bedroom, which was just as well otherwise Vikki would've been even more mortified at the shortness of the dress that Sarah was lending her.

"I could go home and get some white panties," she ventured.

"Or go without."

"Sarah!"

Sarah laughed, she always took a perverse delight in shocking her friend. "For fuck's sake cheer up, Vikki. What's the matter with you? We're going to a fabulous party and you're being a miserable tosspot."

Vikki fiddled nervously with her hand. It was something she rarely did and it didn't escape her friend's notice. "I'm sorry, Sarah. I'm not sure I want to go now."

"After all those porkies we told your mother? I know. Those knickers." Sarah bounced off the bed, rummaged in a drunken chipboard wardrobe, and tossed a pair of white thong panties to Vikki. "It's OK – I've never worn them. A naff Christmas present. A set of seven from Mum's latest. Cheeky sod wanted me to try them all on in front of him."

Vikki held up the tiny garment. It had *Sunday* embroidered on what little there was of the front. "Sarah – really – I could never wear this."

"Why not?"

"It's indecent."

"Actually those bum-floss tangas aren't as bad as they look – they pull up tight over the hips and stay put. Try them. Oh, don't be such a blanket, Vikki. Go on – at least try them."

Eventually Vikki was persuaded to surrender the draught-excluding security of her elasticated panties and step into Sarah's offering. Once hitched into place the garment felt about as comfortable as a wire cheese-cutter but Sarah brushed aside her friend's protests about the unsuitability of underwear that hardly existed and tended to disappear.

"For fuck's sake stop worrying, Vikki. Wearing those means that you've got to learn to behave ladylike. Bend from the knees if you drop something."

Vikki stared at her friend and managed a smile. Sarah talking about ladylike behaviour was like Hermann Goering discussing urban renewal in Coventry. "Sarah – have you got a dress with pockets? So I can take the weight off my wrist without making it obvious?"

Sarah was more sensitive than her brash manner suggested. She slid across the bed and put her arms around her friend. "What's up, Viks? The old plastic pinkies don't usually give you gyp."

"It's not just that . . . There'll be strangers there . . . We know all the boys at the Green Dragon and we know how to handle them."

"Specially Robbie Hammond. He's got a lot to handle."

"Please be serious, Sarah."

Sarah looked thoughtfully at Vikki. "Maybe you're right. How about long skirts tonight? I've got plenty – and some with pockets. There's one that would look fabulous with your blouse."

Vikki brightened.

There was the sound of the front door opening and closing followed by someone stumbling on the stairs, a splutter of giggling and heavy treads outside Sarah's door. The sound effects moved into the adjoining bedroom and degenerated into loud moans and a repeated two-word exhortation from Sarah's mother urging her lover to do her what he seemed to be doing anyway.

Sarah glanced at her watch. "Midnight," she said disapprovingly, as though sex was something she had invented. "You can set your watch by them. They'll be dead to the world in half an hour."

"You're sure it'll be all right in the morning?"

"So long as I'm back by eight to get Simon up and fed. They don't stir till about ten on Sundays. Anyway, we'll burn that bridge when we come to it. Come on – let's dress to kill."

An hour later, with heavy snores having replaced the sounds of patent infringement from the neighbouring bedroom, the two girls sneaked out of the darkened house and set off at a brisk pace through the gloomy streets of a depressing social housing estate. The night was so mild that they didn't need jackets. Both had pinned their hair up to make them look older. Vikki walked with her arms folded – the classic teeny-trot that she usually avoided but it helped support her hand. The lump was even larger now and the hand needed frequent pumps to maintain suction. She was desperately worried about getting through the night without a humiliating disaster. But this concern was almost swamped by hunger pangs which had returned to torment her.

"Bloody street lighting," Sarah grumbled. "Gets worse every year. Look at 'em – dim as dishwater."

"It's something to do with the electricity and gas problems they've been having today," Vikki replied. "Listen, Sarah – can we stick together tonight? Not let anyone separate us. Please."

"That'll cramp my style. I fancied double-clicking my mouse on Nelson Faraday."

Vikki had been thinking of the same person but not in the same favourable light as her friend. She remembered the way he had stared so openly at her breasts, and shivered.

A battered Escort full of hopeful, loudmouthed studlets sidled up to the girls and kept pace with them.

"Hey, Sarah. Howya doin', girl? Fancy the Bognor chippy?"

It was a polite enough Lad Culture enquiry from the driver that received an equally polite Lad Culture, "Fuck off, shitface," reply from Sarah.

"Aw, Sarah. And to think you're right at top of my girls to screw list."

"Yeah – well if you do and I get to find out about it, I shall be really mad."

The ancient Escort shot off in a temper, its passengers laughing and catcalling at the driver's expense, leaving their aspirations behind in a cloud of blue smoke from worn pistons.

The girls walked on in silence other than the clop of their heavy heels echoing off shopfronts. They quietened their footsteps when passing Ellen Duncan's Earthforce shop, and Vikki walked on the nearside with her head bowed, just in case Ellen chose that moment to look out of her bedroom window.

"SAS!" Sarah breathed as they neared the open gates of Pentworth House.

The black-helmeted, black-uniformed men were not members of the Special Air Service Regiment although the large SAS letters on their bomber jackets gave that impression and were the subject of a pending lawsuit being brought by the Ministry of Defence. They were well-trained heavies whose intelligence had run to muscle, employed by the Southern Area Security Company. There were thirty of them out of their cages tonight – a small private army – quartering the grounds of Pentworth House, all in touch with each other via their earphone and throat mike Motorola Handie-Com radios. They were on private land therefore they went about armed with weapons that were barely legal. That night several youths who had scaled the wall had encountered the terror of temporary blindness caused by the SAS's medium-power pointer lasers and handheld strobe blasters. The security men took no prisoners; the hapless youths were beaten up and thrown out. The limited pay of these guardians of lawlessness and disorder was compensated by the promise of unlimited pussy. The two who took Vikki's and Sarah's invitations had not had that promise fulfilled as yet and looked the girls over speculatively before allowing them through.

"Too skinny," said one as the girls were escorted into the house. "But her friend's got nice tits."

"Over eighteen?"

"No way."

The company that had fixed up the sound and lighting gear in Pentworth House's former ballroom had done a good job adjusting their power supplies to compensate for the reduced mains voltage. The skull-jarring beat and flashing strobes that greeted the girls would've sapped the will to live of most but they were used to it.

"Must get something to eat!" Vikki yelled in Sarah's ear. "I'm starving!"

"Not again!"

Groping their way around the tables that surrounded the packed dance floor gave them a chance to orientate themselves. There were as many drinking and laughing in groups at the tables as dancing. None of the revellers appeared to be over thirty and their clothes ranged from fancy dress and stylish evening attire to – in the case of a line of girls gyrating on a stage – no clothes at all other than head-to-toe changing patterns of livid-hued projected light painting. A near-naked man jumped on to the stage, a prodigious bulge threatening to burst the seams of his leather dance pouch as he seized a girl to him. She unsnapped a buckle which allowed his imprisoned erection to rush off in all directions.

"Wow! Some party!" Sarah shouted.

They found several seriously ravaged but still well-stocked buffet tables at the far end of the ballroom where it was just about possible to talk. Nearby was a dais on which a beaming, white-gowned Father Adrian Roscoe and his close acolytes were seated at a long table, looking down on the proceedings with evident approval. Nelson Faraday was in the group, in sullen glower mode until he spotted Vikki. On the wall behind them hung a huge picture of Johann Bode, whose expression was less approving. They all rose to applaud and cheer on the girl who, having exposed her partner's erection, was now on her knees before him, doing her best to hide it. His thrusts were in perfect time with the insidious beat from the giant speakers.

"Jesus!" Sarah yelled. "A tonsil-hockey tournament!"

Rather than comment on Sarah's picturesque observation, Vikki started stuffing herself with vol-au-vents without bothering with a plate. She would've preferred the Pentworth Bakery French bread spread with lashing of butter or garlic mayonnaise but that would've meant using two hands. Sarah loaded a cardboard plate with slices of roast turkey and steered her friend to an empty table. She grabbed two glasses of champagne from a passing waitress.

Vikki was experiencing the same sensation of euphoria and well-being when she had raided the refrigerator the previous morning. She downed her glass in one gulp. "Please, Sarah – do me a favour and get a plate of that bread and loads of butter. It would be difficult for me."

Sarah was surprised. Vikki always coped with her disability and never asked for help, and she had never known her eat so much. "After all those sarnies you wolfed at my place?" And with her belief in always getting to the point added: "Hey, Viks – not in the club, are we?"

"No I'm bloody not! Just get me some food, please! Lots of that French bread!"

"Swearing, too. Not like our Vikki. They say being pregnant changes your personality." With that Sarah fled to the buffet.

Vikki gulped down Sarah's drink – she would've preferred milk – and tried not to look at the goings-on on the stage, but the roars of laughter and clapping that greeted the inevitable outcome of the girl's administrations thwarted her intention and reminded her all too vividly her of her daydream with Dario. A sudden flush of wetness added to the discomfort of her cheese-cutter, bum-floss tanga.

Sarah returned with a mountainous pile of bread and butter that was intended as a joke. But Vikki started tucking in one-handed without comment. Sarah neatly heisted two more glasses of champagne and watched the girl on the stage smearing herself so that her breasts glistened under the strobes.

"I missed the climax," she said regretfully.

"Vikki, my darling! You came! How wonderful!"

It was Nelson Faraday with four statuesque blondes in attendance. He was no longer the sullen, hungry-eyed panther that Vikki had met in Ellen's shop, but was all charm, and with a smile as wide and as genuine as a factory-made Tudor bed. He enveloped Vikki in his huge black cloak like a giant bat and kissed her. By the time she had got over the shock of realising that he was naked under the cloak other than his boots, he and the four smiling blondes had pulled up chairs. Their leader was the tallest, wearing a lace-up red vinyl bodysuit, as tight as she was, breasts spilling over the top, thick sensual lips that shone with wetness. Her name was Helga, Austrian. Vikki was uncomfortably aware of large brown eyes that seemed to be devouring her.

"So you enjoyed the little impromptu show, Sarah?" asked Faraday after the introductions.

Sarah laughed and sipped her wine. "He looked good from here."

"Would you like to meet him?"

"Oh – he wouldn't be much use now."

Faraday grinned. "I wouldn't be too sure." He stood, keeping his cloak drawn around him. "Theta – introduce Sarah to Steve and his friends . . ." He turned and smiled down at the girls. "I have to go now. See you later, Vikki – duty calls. Glad you came." He turned and disappeared into the throng.

The girl called Theta took Sarah's hand and steered her into the melee on the dance floor. Vikki wasn't too concerned at being left – not in the company of girls. She exchanged small talk and laughs with Helga – the only one of the threesome who spoke English – and drank two more glasses of champagne. She was enjoying herself and she had given her hand extra surreptitious pumps to ensure it stayed in place even though her wrist was beginning to ache. She needed to visit the toilet but it could wait.

Helga was telling a laboured joke when there was a crash as a neighbouring table collapsed. Vikki saw a laughing girl disappear under a swirl of eager males and looked around in some apprehension. The stage show had been bad enough but now the party was beginning to get out of hand.

"Have you seen around the house, Vikki?" asked Helga.

Vikki said that she hadn't, adding that she wouldn't mind finding a loo.

"But it is so magnificent."

The girl's dress was ripped off and her breasts appeared, winking white and blue in the strobes. Her laughter changed to shrieks when champagne was poured over her and several eager tongues went to work licking it up.

Helga rose and took Vikki's arm. "Perhaps it would be a good idea to have a little look around before the band perform. It will all be better behaved then, yes?"

It seemed like a sensible suggestion so Vikki allowed herself to be shepherded through a side door and into a long passage. The floor rocked and spun which made her realise that maybe she had had a little too much to drink, but the other two girls were at her side.

Helga pushed a heavy door open, it was padded with green hide on the inside. Vikki was ushered into a spacious room dominated by huge divan bed covered with a crimson spread into which was worked a picture of Johann Bode.

"This used to be the small library,' said Helga. "It has a very beautiful panelled ceiling. You must look." Before Vikki could comment she was turned around and given a gentle push. The bed caught at the back of her knees and she overbalanced, flopping backwards. She was about to laughingly apologise when the girls were upon like lionesses at a kill. Helga ripped her blouse open with a single slash and yanked her bra up. She heard her skirt ripping and was about to scream when a hand was clapped over her mouth.

"Scream all you like, little sister," breathed Helga in her ear. "It won't make any difference." And then the girl crushed Vikki's breasts hard together and fastened her lips greedily on her nipples, moving from one to the other like a frenzied lamprey. Strong hands grabbed her flailing legs and forced them back. A pillow was rammed under her buttocks.

"Let the slut scream if she wants to."

It was Nelson Faraday's voice.

Helga took her hand away and Vikki did just that when she saw his hard eyes staring down at her. His cloak was thrown over his shoulders and he was kneeling between her spread legs. She drew breath for a second scream but it was curdled to a terrified whimper by a stinging slap across the face.

"Save it until you're getting something to scream about!" Faraday snarled. And then his venom was directed at Helga who was pulling Vikki's tanga aside. "Leave it, you fucking dike – she yours when I'm done."

Vikki's desperation and terror led strength to her frantic squirms but they were of little use – the laughing girls pinning her down were strong.

Faraday looked down and smiled at his victim's panties. "Just enough to get in the way." He gestured to one the girls. She produced a flick knife, cut deftly through the tanga's side cords with two upward jerks and yanked it clear. Faraday stared hard into Vikki's eyes, feeding on the fear he saw there especially when he slipped a long, bony forefinger into her and found the hoped-for obstruction. The clasping spasms helped build his erection without the help of the girl with the flick knife, whom he pushed roughly aside. "Nice, Vikki – nice. All present and correct. No need to bag up if I'm first, eh?"

He grinned down and parted her, rocking back and forth so that the underside of his upturned penis rasped over her clitoris without penetrating her. Vikki sobbed in panic and fought to bring her hysteria under control.

It's no use fighting! It's no use fighting!

She relaxed a little and felt a lessening of the pressure that the girls were using to hold her down as they watched with fascination what Faraday was doing.

He saw Vikki's head flop back and gave a sickly grin. "You like that, don't you, Vikki? They always do . . ." His tone became wheedling. He kept rocking. "Come on, Vikki – tell me you like it."

Nod! For God's sake nod!

She nodded and Faraday's face twisted in sudden maniacal rage and the hatred he had nursed over years spewed like a broken sewer. "Bitch! Fucking bitch! You not here to fucking enjoy it! You're here for pain!"

He drew back with the intention of plunging home. Vikki closed her eyes and squeezed. The golden stream hit his penis and sprayed in all directions, showering the girls and Faraday. They squealed in alarm and drew back but too late to escape a soaking. Faraday gave a bellow of rage just as Vikki gave a sudden powerful heave and managed to yank her left arm free. She lashed out at Faraday's face.

"Bitch!"

He grabbed at her hand and then he and all three girls were screaming. It was bad enough seeing Vikki's hand come off while getting drenched in urine, but what really freaked them was the baby's fist, clenched and pink, and growing from the end of her stump.

And then all the lights went out.

Twenty-Seven

Cathy Price was the first to encounter the force wall in its finished state.

She was heading south in her E-type, accelerating hard, nearing the end of the built-up zone, when the street and shop lights went out. She flicked to main beam and wound up Dire Straits to maximum volume. The outage added to her foul temper. If the power hadn't been restored by her return she would have the devil of a job opening the electric garage door manually. Not having the lift working wasn't too bad – her stairs had two handrails – but she hated leaving her precious Jaguar in the drive. Brad Jackson and his gang of envious baseball-capped, three-stripe tracksuited street rats took a perverse delight in key-scoring nice cars or dropping a smouldering cigarette butt on a fabric roof. The delinquent and his two followers came from the families of former travellers that owned smallholdings at Fittleworth.

The reason for Cathy's rage had been an acrimonious e-mail row with Josh. He had accused her of sending corrupted pictures, saying she must've messed about with the software settings for the Quickcam TV camera. He said that there had been shoal of moans from CathyCam subscribers that day. What would've been a snitch of a snatch shot had dissolved into garbage halfway down the image. Also she must've tampered with her computer's modem initialising software because her e-mails and crudded JPEG images were taking an age to get through to the server. Another thing – a new subscriber lived dangerously near at Northchapel. Had Cathy's exhibitionism led to her tipping off a local? If so, kiss goodbye to her income because if the authorities got wind that her pictures were coming from a UK site, they'd have the Obscene Publications Squad and Christ knows who else jumping all over them like fleas on a hedgehog.

Her fury at Josh's accusations and the threat that he would be too busy sorting out subscriber whinges to visit her the next day made her jam her foot to the floor. The E-type's flattened phallic bonnet seemed to leap up as the torque powered through the car's chassis.

A full moon broke through the cloud, illuminating this straight stretch of the old Roman road to Chichester. She dropped into second to negotiate the sharp, ninety-degree left-hander at Seaford College, and snicked straight into top. The needle passed 100 m.p.h. and kept climbing. She didn't see the police sign warning of a suspect road surface ahead.

The thundering Jaguar was five kilometres south of Pentworth, wind screaming dementedly at the soft roof, notching 150 m.p.h., burning half a litre of petrol a minute, the insidious beat of 'Private Investigations' just about winning the noise war, when the impossible happened: the car was clawed to a straight-line standstill like a fighter hitting a carrier's deck and catching on the arrestor wires. At the same time the moon and stars, and the wavy profile of the South Downs went out. A blanket of total and terrifying blackness reared up before Cathy, swallowing the light from the headlights and enveloping the Jaguar. Her first thought was that her foot must have slipped off the throttle on to the brake pedal but that wasn't the case. Despite being unable to see anything ahead, she gunned the engine. The tyres spun, screaming their treads off, spewing Catherine wheel dervishes of smoke, but the car went nowhere.

More baffled and shaken than frightened, she killed the stereo and was about to urge the car forward when she realised that it *was* moving. Backwards. Tyres skittering and juddering, the body shaking, wanting to go one way and being forced to go the wrong way.

She had the presence of mind to snick into reverse. This time everything was OK: the engine revved, the clutch bit, the tyres spun, and the E-type screeched backwards like a cat off an Aga. She stopped, looked forwards, and everything was as it should be: bright moon, stars, the Downs. All perfectly normal.

Or was it?

She stared hard straight ahead. The moonlight picked out ferns, saplings, grass . . . But no road! Ten metres ahead the A285 came an abrupt end. The asphalted surface abutted a shallow bank with larger trees a few metres beyond. Had she not been stopped she would now be dead.

Her first thought was that she had taken a wrong turning and had run into a clever system for stopping the car, but this was definitely the main road that she knew so well.

Cathy tried to recall a news report she'd half-heard on local radio that day. Something about mysterious road surface problems causing clutch burnouts. But that was at midday. Surely the trouble had been fixed by now? And if not, was it possible that they'd go to the trouble of ripping up the road so that absolutely nothing remained? And even put grass back?

No! And yet something weird had stopped the Jag. Like running into a wall of mattresses. At least the car seemed undamaged, thank God – headlights burning bright and straight.

She dropped into first and trickled the car forward. The moon and stars darkened. The resistance felt like she was driving on melting tar. More throttle. The moon and stars blacked out and, as before, no matter how much power she poured into the smoke-spewing rear wheels, the Jaguar was forced inexorably backwards.

She turned the car around and headed back. OK, then – the Pulborough Road, east out of the town. More twisty but it would get her to the A272 east-west trunk for a blast towards Portsmouth. If Cathy couldn't get sex then speed was a nearly as good substitute. The trouble with Pentworth that it was further from a motorway than any other town in England.

A confusion of vehicles leaving a party at the House. A long blast on her horn – sod the built-up area speed restriction – and she roared past them and turned east on to the A283. Five kilometres outside Pentworth, the same thing happened again: the Jaguar ran smack into an invisible marshmallow mountain and was forced backwards. It was the same story on the northbound leg of the A283 towards Northchapel and Chiddingfold but this time Cathy hit the brakes when she saw the long tailback of rear lights ahead and didn't try to pass them. Fuming at the uselessness of West Sussex Council's Highways Department, she returned to a home in which nothing worked. By the time she had pulled herself up the stairs to her room with the aid of a key ring torch gripped between her teeth, she had mentally composed a blistering letter to Southern Electric which she couldn't write, of course, because the Macintosh was a big, silent, useless lump of plastics and silicon.

She couldn't even make herself coffee. There was nothing for it but to go to bed, which she did, and try to sleep, but first things first. The batteries in her vibrator expired when she had one cloud level to go. In fury she flung the device across her darkened bedroom and there was an expensive shattering sound. It was the Mac's monitor tube imploding. A bad day for Cathy Price and it wasn't over yet.

Twenty-Eight

In the confusion that followed the bedroom being plunged into darkness, Nelson Faraday lashed out blindly and hit Helga. The girl swore and launched herself at her assailant, thinking it was Vikki. Despite her terror Vikki had the presence of mind to roll sideways off the divan. She had lost her shoes and her hand but that couldn't be helped now. She crawled around the edge of the room, bumping into furniture until her groping fingers encountered a door that she prayed wasn't a wardrobe. She scrambled to her feet, yanked the door open, and staggered into the passage, desperately trying to orientate herself in the darkness. She ran towards the shouts and the sounds. With people she felt she would be safe from Nelson Faraday but foremost in her mind was to find Sarah and get out of this terrible place. Headlights of parked vehicles outside came on, throwing blinding beams through the windows. The fire alarm system had sensed the loss of power and was drawing on its batteries to keep its sirens howling, adding to the confusion. Vikki found the ballroom. There had been a panic. One of the buffet tables had been overturned, food and paper plates scattered across the floor. The debris included broken glass, as Vikki discovered. The sharp pain cleared the last vestiges of her panic and she saw with dismay that her left foot was bleeding. No time to worry about that, or that her bra was broken and hanging loose outside the torn remnants of her blouse, and that her panties were gone. At the far end of the ballroom the last of the guests were leaving in response to the shouted orders of two SAS men.

Vikki hobbled across the dance floor with the intention of joining the exodus, certain that Sarah would be waiting outside, but the security men had spotted her. They had been on inside duty and therefore not wearing helmets, but their figures were thick with body armour under their riot gear. Their heads were close-shaven. A reversing car outside briefly caught their gleaming eyes before it drove off. They eyed Vikki like hungry hyenas that had cut out a wounded antelope from the main herd.

"It's OK, miss – no fire. No need to panic. Just a power cut that set the alarms off." It was the one on the left who had spoken. His voice sounded kindly.

"My friend will be waiting for me." Vikki made to move past them but hesitated when they stood their ground. The ballroom was empty now.

The one who hadn't spoken played his torch on her. Mortified by her nakedness, Vikki clapped her right arm across her breasts but kept her left forearm plunged firmly in the pocket of her shredded skirt, not realising until it was too late just how exposed she was and how her failure to completely cover herself conveyed the wrong impression to the heavies.

"I do believe we're getting a come-on," said the torchbearer affably. "A genuine blonde, too. Not many of them around."

"She's scared, Gav."

"Scared we won't measure up? No worries on that score, darling." The torchbearer laughed and moved purposefully towards Vikki.

She stepped back. Instead of surrendering to panic, her mind raced like an engine without a load, assessing chances, sizing up distances.

"Now come on, sweetheart. Looks like you've been giving it to someone. So what about the workers?"

The SAS man made a sudden move towards her. Vikki stumbled back. A bottle skittering from under her heel caused her to lose her balance. She put out her right hand to save herself and her fingers closed around the neck of the bottle as she hit the floor. It may not have been the same bottle but it didn't matter – it was full, had weight, and was a weapon. There was a sudden commotion from the back of the ballroom. Then Nelson Faraday was shouting: "There she is! Get the bitch!"

Vikki jumped to her feet and saw a flash of crimson in the shadows as Helga circled around to the SAS men. Vikki charged, ignoring the pain in her cut foot, uttering a piercing scream as she raced forward. The torchbearer saw the demented, near-naked apparition coming straight at him and was undecided – the bottle worried him.

"Get her!" yelled Helga, racing to put herself between Vikki and the exit.

The SAS men were too slow, little match for the adrenalin being pumped into the girl's bloodstream. One ended up with a strip of blouse in his hands to show for his effort. Suddenly Helga was in front of Vikki, reaching for her. Vikki swung her right arm. Her poor grip on the neck of the bottle was fortunate, for it flew from her fingers and caught Helga a glancing blow on the temple. She plunged on without looking back. The crowd in the courtyard were drunk and laughing – they would be of little use in protecting her from Nelson Faraday, who was certain to be following her. They parted in surprise as Vikki plunged into their midst. Whistles and catcalls followed her out of the main gate.

After 200 metres running barefoot, exhaustion and the throbbing pain in her foot overrode her terror and forced her to slow. She risked a backward glance. No street lighting. No lit-up shopfronts, but an ethereal moonlight making ghostly shadows filled with batlike figures coming after her. She ran on, no clear plan in mind other than to put distance between herself and the terrors of Pentworth House. Even in semi-darkness, Ellen Duncan's herbal shop was a beckoning haven. Sobbing with relief she pounded frantically on the side door and yelled through the letterbox. A window opened upstairs.

"Miss Duncan! Please! Please! Help me! It's Vikki!"

"Vikki? Vikki! Oh my God!"

A flash of a torch on the stairs. The door opened, and Vikki collapsed, sobbing, into the arms of an astonished Ellen Duncan.

Twenty-Nine

To say that Cathy Price's crazy early morning drive in her E-type had given the spyder problems would be to imbue what was essentially a machine with emotions.

Following the completion of the force wall that night, the spyder had been required to maintain a watch and determine what effect it might have on the first person to come into contact with it. For this sortie it had been provided with additional energy cells that permitted extended flight. From a height of 400 metres above Pentworth it had seen the Jaguar heading south, and set off in pursuit.

The speed of the ground vehicle defeated it. By the time it reached the location where the vehicle had its first encounter with the force wall, the driver had turned around and was heading east at a speed that the spyder could not match. Its maximum speed had been determined as a compromise between reasonable energy consumption and need. Its makers had long known about Murphy's law, although they had a different name for it. It was, it seemed, a law that permeated the entire universe.

The spyder judged that the vehicle's driver was unharmed but it was required to be certain. It returned to 400 metres and tracked the thermal wake left by the vehicle back to its source. A house with a tower structure and adequate grounds where it settled down to wait. After all, the vehicle wasn't going anywhere and the probability was high that it would return.

Its analysis was rewarded twenty minutes later when the Jaguar returned. It was undamaged but the behaviour of its driver warranted careful consideration. Some difficulty in walking was noted. Support was required for every step. Self-inflicted intoxication was considered and rejected immediately: the driver would not have had such excellent control over its vehicle had its nervous system been temporarily impaired.

The unanswered questions were enough for the spyder to drop on to the roof of Hill House and wait for that now familiar flattening of the cerebral rhythms that told it when its quarry was asleep.

141

It was a long wait because the target was unusually agitated but eventually sleep came. Gaining access through the bedroom window was simply a matter of ageing the glass until it flowed – the same method it had used on Vikki's bedroom window – and lowering itself to the floor. A little more energy was required to match the refractive index of its outer case to the stretch of moonlit carpet between itself and the bed. It noted the position of hundreds of slivers of glass, glinting in the moonlight, and avoided them as it moved cautiously towards its objective. The foot hanging over the side of the bed would make things easier.

Five minutes later the spyder's work was complete. Some damage to the neural network controlling balance was subjected to close scrutiny, but it was found to be old and easily repairable. In all respects the driver of the vehicle had not been harmed by its encounter with the force wall. It started towards the window, moving cautiously to avoid treading on the fragments of glass.

A chill draught brought Cathy to instant wakefulness. She knew immediately that something was wrong because she never slept with a window open. She was on her knees, and shouting, "Who's there!" as loudly as she could.

The spyder froze but Cathy's eyes, self-trained by many hours at the eyepiece of her telescope, spotted the distortion of moonlight against the background of glass splinters scattered across the carpet. She seized her only weapon, half a glass of apple juice on her bedside table, and flung it. It had been a night for throwing things in her bedroom.

The spyder reared up and spat a jet of gas in her face.

In the half-second before she lost consciousness Cathy saw the juice-smothered outline of a crablike creature surrounded by glistening shards of glass.

The spyder left the bedroom the way it had entered and restored the windowpane. A short flight across the darkened town took it to Pentworth Lake. It landed in the exact centre without disturbing the yellowish, moonlit water, and sank out of sight.

Its makers decided that their eyes and ears on the outside world had been compromised. There had now been two uncomfortably close encounters. The spyder's work was largely complete, therefore it would not be used again for some time.

Thirty

David Weir climbed the stairs and entered Ellen Duncan's tiny second bedroom where she was watching over Vikki, now tucked into the little divan bed. The candlelight caught the sudden stab of fear in the girl's eyes when the door opened but she relaxed when she saw who it was. Ellen leaned forward and stroked her hair away from her face. "It's all right, Vikki – it's only David."

"Fax line and shop line both out," David reported, setting down the candle he was carrying. "Your mobile's dead and so's mine. No gas or no mains water – the power cut must be widespread to have knocked out pumping stations and the mobile phone masts. I found your camping Gaz stove. Full bottle, luckily. It's in the kitchen." He smiled down at the bed. "Hallo, m'dear. How are you feeling now?"

"She'll feel a lot better after a hot drink," said Ellen quietly. She kissed Vikki on the forehead. "David and I are going to make some tea, Vikki. We won't be a minute."

"Please don't tell my mother, Miss Duncan."

"Vikki – I really think we should."

"But she won't be worried, really. She thinks I'm staying with a friend – Sarah Gale. *Please* don't tell her."

"Well – the phones aren't working. David came here in his dump truck, which doesn't have lights, and I don't have a car, so we won't be doing anything just yet."

In the kitchen Ellen tried to fill a camping kettle from the cold water tap, realised her mistake and used the hot water tap.

"That's tank water," warned David. "You'd better boil it thoroughly."

"I think she's lost her artificial hand," said Ellen, keeping her voice low. "She wouldn't let me change her out of that skirt – she kept her left hand jammed tightly in the pocket all the time."

"Poor kid."

"One wonders what else she's lost but she doesn't want to talk about it. Her doctor's Milly Vaughan but she doesn't want to see her. But I think she should. How do you feel about going around and knocking her up?"

"Milly would pump me full of strychnine," David protested. "The Hippocratic oath doesn't cover people banging on her door at night."

"Not with a real emergency, she wouldn't."

There was a tentative knocking at the shop door. David went to answer it. It was Sarah – immensely relieved at having discovered Vikki's whereabouts.

"We were at a party at the House during the power cut," she explained to David and Ellen in the kitchen. "The alarms went off and some stupid cu— idiot yelled something about a fire. I couldn't find Vikki so I thought she was outside. Then she came rushing out and didn't hear me. Just went haring off, going like the wind, her clothes all torn. I thought she'd gone to my place but she hadn't. Then I thought—"

"Sarah!" Vikki cried out.

"Can I see her?"

Ellen gestured. "Room opposite."

Ellen followed Sarah into the little bedroom. The two girls were embracing and sobbing in relief, exchanging garbled sentences. The older woman noticed that Vikki used only her right arm to hold her friend.

Thirty-One

Bob Harding considered that sending a police car to his shop at four twenty a.m., blue lights strobing the night and alarming Suzi, was either mistaken identity or an over-reaction to an unpaid parking fine. A power cut. He had to grope around for a torch before stumbling downstairs and unbolting.

"We're extremely sorry to disturb you, Mr Harding," said Harvey Evans. "But we need your advice on an urgent matter."

Fifteen minutes later Harding was at the police's southern road block, pressing his fingers against the yielding, invisible wall, and was utterly baffled. Not only by the bizarre resistance but by the fact that the road ended suddenly just beyond the resistance.

He moved to where a headlight beam was better positioned, clenched his fist, and punched. It was like hitting a cushion. He noticed the slight blackening around his fist as the strange force pushed back. Whatever it was wasn't entirely invisible.

"We can try it with a car if you wish, sir," said Evans.

"Yes, please."

This time the blackening effect was more pronounced as the Peugeot nosed forward, and became almost opaque in the area around the shuddering car as its wheels spun on the road. Eventually the car was forced back. The driver stopped the engine and looked expectantly at Evans.

"Again, sir?"

"That'll be enough," the police officer replied. He took Harding to one side. "I believe I'm what might be defined as an authorised person within the meanings of the Official Secrets Act, Mr Harding?"

"I think that's likely," Harding agreed cautiously.

"I also believe that you're an adviser on several government scientific committees?"

"That's true."

"Then perhaps you'd be good enough to tell me what all this is about?"

Harding watched a policeman leaning against the force wall, arms outstretched so that he looked certain to fall. "You say it's all around the town?"

The police officer shone his lamp on a map spread out on a car's bonnet. He pointed. "A three-mile radius around Pentworth Lake. I haven't the manpower to have checked all the footpaths and tracks yet, but it seems that the town's completely cut off. No electricity, no gas, no water, telephones – radio and TV. Everything. Even the roads stop."

There was a silence.

"Well, it explains everything and yet it explains nothing," said Harding at length.

"I beg your pardon, sir?"

"Perhaps not quite everything." Harding pointed at the moon and stars. "Light's getting through it."

Evans' tone hardened. "So what is it, Mr Harding? Some sort of experiment that's gone wrong?"

Harding met the police officer's gaze. "I don't know, Mr Evans. I simply have absolutely no idea."

Thirty-Two

Dr Millicent Vaughan's reputation for waspishness was largely undeserved. When necessary she was a model of kindness and understanding. Her smile in the candlelight was warm and comforting and did much to ease Vikki's embarrassment at having to answer her questions.

"You're sure about that, Vikki? No penetration?"

The girl nodded.

"And he didn't eja— he didn't come on you or in you?"

"No, Doctor."

Dr Vaughan nodded. This was a case of sexual assault and not rape, therefore there was no point in subjecting the wretched girl to an internal examination; she had been through enough that night. She had already made a note of the bruising on Vikki's legs but she knew enough about police work to know that bruises of this nature were not good evidence.

"Well, Vikki. I've given you a jab for that cut on your foot. I'm not going to disturb the dressing because I know Ellen would've done a good job. That leaves only one thing. Your left hand."

"It's all right, Doctor."

"Then why have you been hiding it? Vikki, I'm not stupid. Ever since I arrived you've been careful to keep your left hand hidden. What about that growth you showed me this afternoon?"

"It's all right now, Doctor – really."

"You mean the growth's gone?"

"Well . . . Sort of."

The fear in the girl's eyes reinforced Millicent's determination. "In that case, you'd better show me, Vikki. I won't leave until you have."

Vikki gave a little sob and withdrew her left arm slowly from the depths of the bed covers.

The doctor could only marvel at British Aerospace's workmanship; in the soft light of the flickering candle, the hand looked perfect.

147

Her tone softened. "You'll have to take it off, Vikki. I can't look at your—"

"I can't," Vikki whispered, panic catching in her throat. "It's grown into a real one. Look." She concentrated hard and succeeded in waggling two fingers. Millicent sat frozen into silence. It was some seconds before she could speak. "Do that again," she said very quietly.

Vikki complied but it seemed to take an effort.

Again a long silence. The girl's fear-filled green eyes were staring fixedly at her.

"Can you make a fist?"

Vikki did so but drawing the fingers and thumb closed took several seconds.

The doctor held Vikki's left hand and ran her fingertips over the wrist and knuckles. She opened the palm and touched each perfect finger in turn. She had examined the girl's stump on countless occasions over the years. She knew every misshapen contour of the aftermath of that terrible accident in Spain all those years ago. And now she was holding a perfect hand. She took Vikki's other hand and held them side by side. Despite her inner turmoil and confusion she noticed that the patterning of freckles on the back of both hands was identical.

"It started last night," said Vikki in a small voice. "And it just kept on growing and growing." She broke off, tears filling her eyes. "It's horrible, Doctor. Some sort of horrible, horrible . . ." She searched for the right word and then choked it out: "Miracle."

All Millicent's agnostic and humanist principles rebelled at such a conclusion. She opened her mouth to speak but was unable to form words. She was holding the irrefutable evidence of something terrible or something wonderful and she didn't know which.

"Why do you say horrible, Vikki?"

"Because it's useless! I can't do anything with it. I won't be able to wear my proper hand any more and I'll be helpless!" Vikki leaned forward, convulsed with sobs.

"Vikki . . . Vikki – listen to me. Why do you say you can't do anything with it?"

"Because I can't!" The answer was spat out with uncharacteristic vehemence.

"Have you tried?"

"Yes!"

The doctor decided that her black bag might be too big and placed her handbag on the bed.

"Try picking that up, Vikki." She had to repeat the request. Eventually the girl wiped away her tears and moved her left hand hesitantly towards the handbag. Her fingers hovered over the handle and made uncertain movements that clasped at air, like a baby learning to pick up a toy brick.

"You see?"

"Try again, Vikki. Concentrate hard."

This time Vikki succeeded in knocking the bag over. Millicent stood it up again. "And again, Vikki!"

"I can't . . ."

"You can. Now do it!"

Somehow Vikki managed to exert more control and hooked her thumb and forefinger around the handle. She looked from the doctor to the handbag in wonder, the despair fading from her eyes.

"Lift it, Vikki . . . Lift it!"

Vikki lifted the handbag off the bed. Tears welled up in her eyes that were suddenly alight and alive. "It works, Doctor!"

"Of course it works . . . Have you ever seen a baby trying to pick things up? The way it has to learn what movements work and what movements don't work? Well, you've got to go through that process, Vikki. Providence or some such has given you a new hand and now you have to learn how to use it."

"Providence? You mean God?"

"Well . . . Whatever. You're a Catholic, Vikki – you tell me."

Thomas jumped on to the bed, gave the doctor a scornful, yellow-eyed look, and rubbed himself against Vikki. She smiled for the first time in a long while and returned the favour, using her new hand for an awkward stroke that the black cat accepted. She even managed to curl the fingers to scratch him under the chin. Thomas responded with loud purrs and insistent head butts that broadened Vikki's smile. The therapeutic powers of pets never ceased to surprise Millicent. The big, friendly cat was an unwitting healer even if it did start demanding more than its fair share of space on Ellen's spare bed.

"But . . . I don't want anyone else to know about it, Doctor – not just yet – I need time."

"You can't hide it for long, Vikki . . . Wait a minute." The doctor searched in her handbag and produced some foundation cream that she rubbed on the hand to give it an even, unnatural texture. A final touch was a bandage around the wrist. "There – better?"

Vikki studied the effect of a slight clench, the default configuration of her artificial hand, and nodded.

There was the sound of a car drawing up outside. "That'll be your mother. Mr Weir borrowed my car to fetch her."

"You won't tell her, will you?"

"Not if you don't want me to. What about charges against that thug?"

"No!"

David Weir and Anne Taylor were being greeted by Ellen as Millicent came down the narrow stairs.

"Your daughter's fine, Mrs Taylor," she said briskly before Anne could speak. "Nothing untoward happened to her. She's come to no harm whatsoever other than a few cuts and bruises. Some delayed shock but that's wearing off. Sleep is all she needs now. Plenty of sleep."

"But—"

"My keys please, Mr Weir."

David handled over the car keys. "Is she—?"

"Sleep," the doctor repeated sternly, eyeing them all in turn. "Vikki is fine. Better than she has been for many years, in fact. I think it would be best if she was left alone. Doctor's orders which you will all obey without question. I've left a colleague up there in charge."

They stared at her in bewilderment.

"A large black cat. Doing a better job than I ever could. I'll call round at ten o'clock. Goodnight."

Millicent drove her car 200 metres and had to stop, such was her trembling. She pressed her head against the steering wheel.

For the first time in her life she felt a powerful need to visit a church.

Any church.

Thirty-Three

Nelson Faraday considered himself tough but not when it came to facing up to the wrath of the Divine Sentinel, Father Adrian Roscoe, founder and leader of the Bodian Brethren.

It was the eyes that sent a berserk food blender churning dementedly through Faraday's stomach – those ice-cold chips of cobalt isotopes that seared through him like twin thermic lances.

"Forty minutes!" Roscoe raged, pacing up and down his office. "Forty minutes without power! Forty minutes in which the duty sentinels abandoned the temple! Forty minutes without prayer! Forty minutes in which the temple and the Divine Johann Bode were wreathed in darkness! Forty minutes in which this planet lay helpless before Satan and his demons and witches!"

"There was a fire alarm—" began Faraday limply, wanting to look at the carpet but unable to tear his eyes away from that compelling gaze. Even the dim light of the solitary forty-watt desk lamp that lit the room was enough to make Roscoe's eyes burn relentlessly into his soul.

"Fire!" Roscoe thundered. "Fire! Of course there'll be a fire! A fire that will crisp your flesh on your bones if you've left the door ajar for Satan! We make a welcome for Satan and the Lord will surely and swiftly smash this planet!" He calmed down and sat in his chair, drumming his fingers on his desk while staring at the artificial hand. "It's your job to check the generator each day – to make sure it kicks in immediately when there's a power cut. When did you last check it?"

"This morning, Father."

"Liar! You were out most of the morning. I checked the log."

"I checked the jenny before I went out, Father." There was a hint of defiance in Faraday's voice but not enough to aggravate Roscoe more than he was already.

The cult leader picked up the hand. Faraday braced himself for another onslaught. "So how did this gatecrasher get in?"

"That's what I was about to ask her when the power failed, Father."

151

"In the guest bedroom?"

"It was away from the noise."

"And she hit Helga with the bottle when trying to escape?"

"It was a deliberate, unprovoked attack, Father."

"I shall get at the truth, Nelson." He held up the artificial hand. "This thing beats a glass slipper. The girl won't be hard to find. If I find that you've been lying . . ."

Faraday said nothing. No doubt Roscoe would go over the details with the girls but he was confident that they would stick to the story they had agreed and say nothing about the embryonic hand they had seen growing out of the girl's stump. That would be sure to start Roscoe raving, particularly if he found out that the girl worked for the hated witch, Ellen Duncan, but he was hardly likely to ask about something he didn't know about.

Roscoe looked at his watch. "Two hours the power's been off now. You'd better make sure the generator's tank's full. It looks like it's going to be a long one. Radio and TV stations down."

"I filled it just before you summoned me, Father."

Roscoe turned to his computer, forgetting for the moment that the machine was down. "We'd better log the assault on Helga and her injuries. Damn . . . Can we spare power for this thing?"

"I don't think so, Father. The temple needs the jenny's full output. Your desk lamp and the corridor lights take it close to overload. It'll be OK in daylight. We'll have to do half the milking by hand in the morning."

"Remind me to order a bigger generator on Monday."

Faraday was about to leave when there was the sound of a heavy vehicle entering the courtyard. Roscoe crossed the office and drew the curtain aside. He gave Faraday a puzzled look. "Southern Area Security's coach has returned. With all their men on board by the look of it. And some guests' cars. Now why do you suppose that is?"

Thirty-Four

B ob Harding was too intent on his work to take much notice of Cathy Price, who had poured herself into a catsuit and was down on her hands and knees picking out the last glass splinters from the Mac's broken monitor out of the pile of her bedroom carpet.

He checked a compass and an Ordnance Survey map on the table beside him, and swung Cathy's magnificent telescope to a new bearing. It was a bright, sunny morning with the humidity touching 80 per cent, which made it seem abnormally close and sticky for March. Apart from rising columns of smoke from barbecues, the air was reasonably clear. There was some wind movement – the smoke columns were drifting east towards Pentworth Lake.

Another check on the telescope's bearing so that it was pointing at Pratchetts Farm.

But there was nothing. Where there should be a huddle of barns and outhouses just beyond the line of the force wall, there was nothing but windswept downland. He focused the image carefully to get maximum sharpness.

"Cathy . . . Can you spare a moment, please."

Cathy levered herself into her swivel chair and gave a push with her foot so that it rolled into position on its castors.

Harding locked the pan and tilt head. "I've got it trained on where Pratchetts Farm should be. Take a look and tell me if you can see anything odd."

"Everything's odd," said Cathy sourly. "Roads stop. Paths stop. Not a whisper on the radio – AM and FM – all dead. Everything's stopped except this bloody hangover which I swear is getting worse." She peered through the eyepiece and adjusted the focus. "What am I supposed to— Oh . . . you mean that wavy effect?"

"Exactly."

"It's too slow to be heat distortion."

"That's what I thought. Mind if I remove the Porro prism?"

"Go ahead."

"An excellent instrument, Cathy. Normally I don't like refractors but this telescope is quite something."

"The only damned gadget I've got that doesn't need electricity."

Harding smiled. He removed the Porro prism and replaced the eyepiece. The device merely corrected the telescope's mirror image effect. Dispensing with it meant a few less lenses and prisms to add aberrations. He checked again and found no noticeable difference. "Weird," he muttered, making a pencil note on the map.

Cathy's reply was drowned by a police car travelling slowly by, a public address speaker mounted on its roof.

"Please do not use your toilets . . . The sewers are backing up . . . It is vital that you don't flush your toilets . . . The drains are flooding. Save your tank water for drinking . . . Please do not use your toilets . . ."

"So what the hell are we supposed to do?" Cathy demanded as the police car faded into the distance. "Dig a hole in the garden?"

"It might just come to that if this craziness goes on," Harding replied. He had finished his 360 degree survey of the surrounding countryside and was even more baffled than when he had started. At a radius of just over five kilometres from Pentworth Lake normality ceased. Inside the radius all was well: farms and outhouses, pubs, large houses, roads, cultivated fields – all as they should be. But beyond the periphery of the force wall, or whatever it was, nothing but a steppe-like landscape with some woodland in sheltered valleys; the patchwork of the ancient field systems that covered the South Downs was no more. There wasn't even the usual line of repeater and TV transmitter masts along the distant rim of the downs to the north and south.

He turned the telescope south to the foot of Duncton Hill where the A285 suddenly ended. The verges at the dead end were crammed with sightseers' cars like an illegal car boot sale. But the owners and their families were spread out in a line across the fields. Hazy dark patches appearing and disappearing showed where they were testing the force wall's strange repelling properties. In the early hours of that Sunday morning the police had tried to keep people away from the wall, but with the coming of daylight it had been impossible for the handful of hard-pressed police officers to patrol its thirty-kilometre perimeter, and besides, no one had come to any harm from contact with the thing. "You must feel like God sometimes up here," Harding remarked. "I had no idea you had such remarkable views."

"I don't feel like God now," muttered Cathy.

But you look like a goddess in that outfit, thought Harding.

"I had a lousy dream last night," Cathy continued. "A bad one. And now I've got a stinker of a headache, and I've not had my fix of morning coffee. Warm Coke from the fridge – yuck."

Harding reached down and took a vacuum flask from his rucksack. "Help yourself."

"Coffee?"

"Black and strong."

"Bob – you're wonderful!"

While his host was relishing her caffeine hit, Harding roamed the telescope over the town. "Good Lord – is that normal for this time on Sunday mornings? All those people pouring out of St Mary's?"

Cathy didn't need the telescope to see the unusually large congregation leaving the Anglican church. "No – I've never seen it like that before. And look at all the cars parked around St Dominic's."

"People are frightened," Harding commented. He turned the telescope north and stiffened. The view of Pentworth House's courtyard was mostly obscured by rooftops but through a gap he could see the white-gowned figure of Adrian Roscoe. He was standing on a rostrum, addressing an out of sight crowd, long, bony arms held up, hands outstretched in appeal. "Raving Roscoe seems to have an audience," he remarked.

Cathy looked through the telescope. "He's never done that before. Wonder what he's saying?" She tilted the instrument up.

Harding started stowing his things in the rucksack. "Thank you for your help, Cathy."

"I must've been notching a ton when I hit the Wall and yet I didn't come to any harm. Not a scratch on my Jag. It must be something to do with that Silent Vulcan UFO sighting on Tuesday night."

"There's about a hundred reports a year in the south of England."

"It's the first UFO I've ever seen. I don't miss much up here. Don't look so surprised. Check with the police. They should have my name on their log. I saw the same thing as the others said on the TV – a sort of shapeless object lit up by lightning flashes. Moving eastward."

"A plane heading into Gatwick," Harding suggested.

"That's what the police said. Except that planes have lights. This didn't have anything. If it hadn't been for the lightning I wouldn't've seen it." Cathy swung the telescope and focused it on the distant hills. Bleak – bare of hedges and boundary walls. "It's like looking at the past."

"What is?"

"The land beyond. Like it must've been thousands of years ago. Like we're looking back in time."

Harding paused and smiled. "It's a thought."

"You once told me that looking at the past was easy. That you just had to look up at the stars at night. The Milky Way is about fifty thousand years in the past. I often think about that on clear nights. Even the sun is some minutes in the past, you said."

"Eight minutes," said Harding hollowly, suddenly staring hard at Cathy.

"Is it something I said, Bob?"

Harding pulled himself together. "Sorry . . . You may just have hit on something." He hurriedly finished packing and pushed the vacuum flask across the table. "Yours. Drop it into the shop sometime. Thanks for all your help."

He was down the stairs and gone before Cathy could reply.

Outside Hill House, Harding pulled a Yaesu UHF handheld transceiver from his rucksack and selected a pre-arranged police channel. He listened to ensure that the frequency wasn't in use, pressed the PPT button and gave his amateur radio call sign.

"Go ahead, Golf Four."

"I've completed the survey and think I may have something."

"Wait, please." The channel went dead. No carrier. No longer having a repeater to amplify and retransmit messages meant direct handset to handset simplex communications like Citizens' Band radio with handsets on maximum power. The police didn't know when they would be able to recharge their batteries and were restricting radio communications to the absolute minimum.

The carrier came back. "Mr Evans asks if you can RV with DS Malone outside Pentworth House."

"Affirmative. I'm on my way. Ten minutes."

Harding started walking quickly. There was light traffic – the fumes which made him want to sneeze made worse by drivers stopping with their engines running while exchanging what scant information they had.

"Ah – Councillor Harding," someone called out. "What's happening? When will the power come back on?"

"I'm sorry – I know as much as you do." And he hurried on, feeling guilty. People were lost, seeking information, feeling betrayed because the only manifestation of authority had been a couple of police cars telling them not to flush their lavatories. In the absence of anything else, rumours were certain to flourish, but what outlandish rumour could match the bizarre impossibility that was surrounding Pentworth?

By the time Harding had reached the gates of Pentworth House,

Roscoe had disappeared but there was a queue out of the gates and extending along the wall. People were emerging from the courtyard, eating all manner of fried foods. Some standing around talking animatedly while spearing chicken nuggets or eating hot bread rolls straight from the bakery. Its ovens were fired by methane gas produced from cow dung. In the courtyard the source of this high-cholesterol fest was apparent: the Bodian Brethren's huge Winnebago, manned by a busy team of smiling young sentinels who were cooking and dishing out the food. They were not taking money. A girl in a sentinel gown was moving along the queue issuing leaflets, another was taking names and addresses on a clipboard. Several black-uniformed SAS men were strolling around the courtyard exchanging small-talk with members of the public. They looked less intimidating without their body armour.

"Have some fries, Councillor – they're good."

Harding wheeled around. Mike Malone, looking neat in grey slacks and an open-neck shirt, held out his bag of chips.

"What's going on, Mr Malone?"

"Hearts and minds, Mr Harding."

Harding took a chip. Malone was right – it was good. "You mean Roscoe's taking on the feeding of the entire area?"

"I think his supply of food will outlast his supply of bottled propane gas. He knocked up the manager of Freezerfare this morning and bought the supermarket's entire stock of frozen food at a knockdown price. It was all about to thaw anyway. One of Roscoe's pretty disciples told me that they've completely filled their ice cream delivery truck. Forty tonnes crammed in."

"Good God."

"That's what Roscoe was saying . . . So feast today and famine tomorrow. A shrewd move. A sign of leadership, control and authority. Mind you, if one of those thugs sets foot outside the courtyard, I might be tempted to show my authority by nicking him under the Public Order Act."

"You mean Roscoe preached his crackpot message to all these people and they listened to him?"

Malone regarded Harding dolefully. "No – he didn't. All he said was that the brethren were here to help. Wartime spirit. Mutual co-operation." He nodded to the girl with the clipboard. "She's collecting names and addresses of all those with children and babies. The brethren plan to start milk and bread deliveries tomorrow morning if the crisis continues."

"You're joking!"

Malone took a chip and offered the remainder to Harding. "They've got fifty head of Jerseys and they can't make their ice cream now. Don't underestimate Roscoe, Mr Harding. He judges well what people want and need. Right now they want action and leadership and bread rather than religious rhetoric and that's exactly what he's providing. I hear you've come up with something?"

"I need to visit the Wall."

"There's about thirty kilometres of it for the asking, Mr Harding. I'll give you a lift. I'd like to discuss something with you."

Malone's Escort, equipped with temporary police stickers on the doors and public address amplifier and speaker on the roof rack, was parked nearby within sight of Ellen's shop. The two men got in. Malone stared at the steady stream of people passing the parked car, all heading towards Pentworth House. Old women with shopping trucks, mothers pushing baby buggies, youths on bicycles.

"Word gets around," Harding remarked.

Ellen and two blondes emerged from the shop. The blondes exchanged kisses and goodbyes with Ellen and entered a Mini.

"Anne Taylor and her daughter, Victoria," Harding replied in answer to Malone's query. "Vikki works Saturdays for Ellen. As sweet a kid as you could ever wish to meet. And that's David Weir. He and Ellen seem to have an understanding, ever since their find."

"I know about it," said Malone expressionlessly, watching the newcomer and trying to suppress a sudden torch-like flare of jealousy.

Harding continued: "They're both on the Town Council but I expect you know that. Vikki looks like she's seen a ghost."

The Mini drove off. Ellen and David waved after it. They were about to enter the shop when David noticed the painted-over graffiti. He seemed to be commenting on it but Ellen took him by the arm. A fresh wave of pedestrians converged on Pentworth House.

"My God," Harding muttered. "Looks like the whole town's turning out."

The two men watched the lengthening queue for a few moments. Malone glanced at his passenger as he inserted the ignition key. "Do you realise that Roscoe's brethren represents the biggest organisation in Pentworth?"

"But surely there's . . ." Harding's voice trailed away as he thought.

"Who?" Malone prompted.

"Well – the police." Harding realised the inaccuracy of the statement before he completed the sentence.

"Eight officers, two WPCs, a couple of specials, four civilian part-time office staff. And that's due to be cut next month. Roscoe's got about fifty of his so-called sentinels actually working and living in Pentworth House, which gives him total control over them. Plus he's got a few full-time employees who manage the dairy, and about thirty security men."

"Thirty!"

"He booked them for a big party last night, now he's stuck with them. And about fifty guests." Malone paused and watched some youngsters walking towards them. They were chatting animatedly, clutching paper cones brimming with chips. One was reading the leaflet. He shook his head. "It's all changed."

Harding was getting impatient. He was anxious to visit the Wall. "What has?"

"A hundred years ago Pentworth was self-sufficient and self-governing, Mr Harding. The local farms fed the local populace, and the local populace provided labour and the machinery of local government: school boards; health; the police; the local council – even a gaol in those days when they were a charge on local rates. What's Pentworth Town Council responsible for now? Changing street light bulbs, painting benches, and a few other odd jobs that Chichester District Council can't be bothered with."

Harding smiled. "That's about the size of it, Mr Malone."

The police officer started the car and moved off. "Man's greatest invention isn't writing," he continued, "it's government – it predates writing by thousands of years. Over the past thirty years virtually the entire infrastructure of Pentworth's local government has been systematically destroyed. Real power is now with the District Council twenty miles away in Chichester. The hospital's gone – get a broken arm now and you have to go to Chichester. No welfare office; no public health office; the library hardly ever open now, when it used to be open six days a week; local registration of births, deaths and marriages – gone. The magistrates' court – gone. Even mundane things that local councils were good at, such as running a local bus service, a dance hall, and the municipal band – all finished. And it's the same all over the country: a successful system painstakingly built up over a thousand years, with mistakes made and lessons learned, destroyed in less than three decades – a victim of the current British obsession for fixing everything that isn't broken. The only working vestige of the Victorian era we have left is the Royal Mail, and the only reason we've still got that is because the politicians who wanted to fix it were warned off by Buckingham Palace."

"And your point is?"

"My point, Mr Harding," said Malone, heading north out of the town, "is that nature abhors a vacuum, and human nature abhors a power vacuum. Power vacuums are always filled, as we've just seen."

Harding chuckled. "You're quite a student of human nature, Sergeant. Even so, I think you're building a lot on Roscoe's initiative in setting up a hotdog stall."

"Invalidation."

"Pardon?"

"Your calling of Roscoe's Winnebago a hotdog stall. It means that you recognise the underlying truth of what I've said but are reluctant to accept it. It's called invalidation. The danger of invalidation is that it obscures real threats in untrained minds. Hindenberg referred to Hitler as 'that Austrian corporal' and millions thought the same. Invalidation is not a good thought process or tactic for recognising problems and therefore dealing with them."

Harding remained silent. A colleague on the Town Council had once said that Malone was odd. He was wrong. Harding thought about all the woolly-thinking politicians he had to deal with and wished they had a quarter of the reasoning ability of this remarkable police officer.

The Escort swung right off the main road and bumped along a farm track. Malone's guess that there would be few if any sightseers along this route turned out to be correct. The point where the unmade road yielded to wild country was deserted. The two men got out the car and approached the track's cut-off point with caution.

Close to, the aberration that Harding had first noticed wasn't so apparent but it was still there. Like the flickering of a television when looking slightly away from the screen, there was something not quite right about the image when using peripheral vision.

Harding reached out a hand and took a step forward. Immediately an area around his fingertips darkened.

"It's like a polarising effect. Damn – I wish I'd thought to bring a light meter."

"It'll still be here tomorrow," Malone replied drolly.

"You think so?"

"A safe bet."

Harding pressed his finger two centimetres into the resistance and held them in place. "Can't feel any— Yes, I can. A sort of tingling sensation. Getting stronger."

The darkening effect started even though the scientist had not pushed his finger any deeper.

"Ah – now it's pushing back – quite hard, too. It's beginning to hurt a bit." Harding pulled his hand away and noticed that his fingertip had turned white. He watched in close interest as the blood supply was restored and his finger regained its normal colour. "Bugger me . . ." he muttered.

"Not good," said Malone.

"What?"

"A proper scientist would say: 'Fascinating . . . Quite fascinating . . .' Not 'Bugger me.' And you should have a beautiful daughter for me to drool over."

Harding chuckled, found a stone, and tossed it at the wall. A brief splat of black and it bounced back as if it had hit a rubber sheet.

"And for your next trick, sir?"

"Come here and I'll show you." Harding unstrapped his wrist-watch. He gripped it between his fingertips and pushed it into the wall. The second hand stopped its busy swing around the chapter face, and started again when he moved it back. Malone tried the same thing with his watch. It had a digital display. The flashing colon stopped and the numerals indicating lapsed seconds froze on 15.

"Push it in harder," breathed Harding, his eyes gleaming with suppressed excitement.

Malone did so and the digits changed to 14 and then 13. When he pulled the watch out to rub his fingers, the digits jumped to 22 and the watch carried on running normally. The police officer was so intrigued that he repeated the experiment twice. He looked enquiring at Harding. "Strange," he murmured. "Isn't this where you say that we're up against strange forces that are totally beyond our understanding?"

"Well, I'll say that if it makes you feel better, Mr Malone. But I'd rather say that we're up against something that's possibly within our understanding, but beyond our ability."

"Sounds like a cop out."

"Pretty well."

"This thing has come between me and having my kids stay with me for the weekend, so I'd like to hear your cop out, sir."

Harding realised that he was beginning to like Malone. "It was Arthur C. Clarke who said that the products of a sufficiently advanced technology would seem like magic to a lesser technology.

Well – we can eliminate magic right away. This Wall – we might as well call it that – is economical with energy. The polarising effect is only apparent as and when and where it's needed."

"Like security lights that come on only when they detect body heat instead of burning all the time?"

Harding nodded. "Exactly. That tells us that the people who made, or formed, or built this Wall are up against the same conservation of energy laws, and the same design problems that confront any engineer." He gazed at the woodland beyond the track. "And if that is the past we're looking at, then Cathy Price was right."

"Cathy Price?" Malone was interested but careful to make his tone faintly dismissive.

"She put me on to the idea. I think the Wall's inner boundary is the beginning of a time wedge. A centimetre's penetration is one second in the past. Two centimetres, perhaps two seconds back into the past, and so on. A linear or exponential progression – I don't know, but that countryside looks like it predates Man. I'll know tonight when I've had a chance to look at the sky."

"How can time create a physical barrier?" Malone asked.

The scientist was lost in thought for few moments. "Now you're putting me into the realms of guesswork. Maybe time has entropy just like everything else in the universe. You try moving back in time and time pushes you back to into the present. The harder you push, the harder it repels." He extended his forefinger and watched the characteristic darkening around the tip. "Damned clever trick, though. You know, it's possible that there's someone not a metre from us on the other side of this Wall who's just as baffled as we are."

Malone touched his sleeve and pointed. Harding suppressed an expletive. Not thirty metres ahead, a giant deer had appeared in a clearing. It was bigger than a moose or elk, and its magnificent antlers had a spread of at least three metres. It moved to a convenient overhanging branch and began rubbing the huge rack back and forth as though it had an itch. Bits of chewed bark fell on to its reddish-grey haunches.

Malone suddenly clapped his hands and shouted. The huge creature continued rubbing its rack unconcernedly on the branch. Eventually it tired of the project and melted into the forest.

"What the hell was that?" Harding breathed.

It was Malone's turn to provide information. "Last year I gave my eldest daughter a big colour book on extinct creatures. She loves it so I had to buy another copy to keep in my flat for weekends. I have to go through it with her every time they visit. The sabre-tooth tiger, mammoth, the dodo. That was a megaloceros."

"When did it become extinct?"

"Can't remember exactly. About twenty thousand years ago. Clever special effects, don't you think? Projecting the past all around Pentworth."

"That's one way of looking at it."

"There *is* only one way of looking at it – the way we're meant to. I took my kids to the London Planetarium for their Christmas outing. They showed the 1999 total eclipse of the sun, and the night sky as it looked in Israel at the time of the birth of Christ. All done from a projector in the centre of the dome, just as Pentworth Lake is at the centre of this thing."

"Meaning that there *was* a UFO on Tuesday night after all and that it's now sitting in Pentworth Lake?"

"You're the scientist, Mr Harding. You tell me."

Harding was silent for some moments. He shook his head. "I don't know what to think, Mr Malone."

Malone jabbed at the Wall. "Maybe the ufologists will have better luck getting back in than we've had getting out. They were certainly determined enough. We'd better be getting back. I've got a lot to do."

They returned to the Escort. Malone was silent until they were on the main road. "There's a lot of radio gear in your workshop, Mr Harding. Can you use it while there's no power?"

"It's mostly amateur radio stuff – twelve-volt DC equipment. I've got a huge truck battery as my standby uninterruptible power supply. Why?"

"Do you have the capability of transmitting on broadcast bands?"

"I have. But I don't. It would be contrary to the conditions in my amateur radio licence."

"How about the FM band?"

"I've got a couple of old Spectrum Band II transmitters. Meant for community radio. I bought them at a junk sale."

"Working?"

"Yes."

"Frequency?"

"Eighty-seven point five. What's this leading up to, Sergeant?"

"Would one of them cover the whole of the area inside the Wall?"

"A five-kilometre radius? No trouble. If you're thinking what I think you're—"

"What's the first thing revolutionaries do in tinpot republics when they seize power?"

Harding was in no mood for games and made no answer.

"They grab the palace and the radio station. The Divine Adrian Roscoe's already got the palace. We have to beat him to the radio station."

Thirty-Five

Like many in outlying homes, the Taylors were better equipped than town dwellers to cope with the crisis. They relied on an LPG supply from a large tank in their garden for their central heating and cooking which had been refilled the previous week following heavy use during the hard winter. Also, not uncommonly, their water supply came from the original well, now capped, that served as a borehole. Without electricity for the automatic pump it was necessary to periodically crank an outside hand pump to force a supply of water through the filtration system to the header tank in the roof, but they had done it before during power cuts. Mains drainage consisted of a large fibreglass septic tank buried under the front garden, which meant that they were already in the habit of not flushing the toilet after taking a pee, and they used their washing machine sparingly with its discharge emptying into a soakaway.

While many in the town were having to go without, Anne and Vikki were able to sit down in the kitchen to hot coffee upon their return from Ellen Duncan's shop.

Vikki sipped her drink appreciatively, keeping her left hand out of sight on her lap. She avoided her mother's eye. The drive back from the town had been an agony of embarrassed silence.

"How are you feeling now?" said Anne at length.

Vikki smiled and glanced around the friendly kitchen, the shining copper pans that were never used, the strings of swollen Spanish onions hanging from an overhead rack. "Glad to be home."

"Is that all you've got to say?"

"I'm sorry, Mum."

"You've already said that about a million times."

"No – I'm not just saying it. I'm sorry deep down inside that I lied to you."

Anne sighed and shook her head. "That Sarah Gale – she put you up to that story? The girl's a slut. I don't know what you see in her."

"She's kind, Mum."

"I've heard a lot about her kind of kindness."

Vikki deemed it wise to say nothing.

"I only pray to God that you're telling the truth about nothing happening."

"I've told you the absolute truth, Mum. He started to try it on and then the lights went out and I managed to run away."

"After your clothes had been ripped to shreds."

"Someone grabbed at me while I was running." Vikki gave an inward shudder at the recollection of her flight from Pentworth House but was unable to choke back the sob that rose unbidden in her throat.

Anne rose and put her arms around her daughter. "My turn to say sorry. Milly Vaughan said you were OK. It's just . . . Oh well . . . All's well, et cetera, eh?" She kissed Vikki on the cheek and brushed away an errant strand of blonde hair.

Vikki nodded.

Anne sat and picked up her mug. "We'll forget all about it. But if there is something you want to tell me, tell me now and let's have done with it."

The girl looked at her mother. Large, troubled green eyes. "There is something . . . I lost my hand there . . ."

"Oh. Did Dave Weir go and get it, then?"

"No. It must still be there."

Anne stared at her daughter in bewilderment. "So you're wearing your spare? But I thought . . ."

Vikki stared down at her mug. "I'm not wearing anything, Mum . . . It's not my real hand . . ."

"Not your . . . ?"

"What I mean is that it *is* real . . ."

"What on earth are you talking about?"

Vikki clasped the mug with her left hand and picked it up. She now had reasonable control but not good enough yet to chance using the handle. She set it down again while Anne stared, speechless, the colour draining from her face. Then Vikki held up the hand and spread her fingers. She was fearful of her mother's reaction, and had wondered what would happen, but was not prepared for what happened next.

Anne screamed in terror and jumped up. The kitchen chair keeled over as she staggered backwards and grabbed the sink, her face contorted in abject horror. She crossed herself – something that Vikki had never seen her do outside a church.

"My God, child!" she screamed. "What have you done! *What have you done!*"

Frightened and confused by her mother's response, Vikki could only cry out, "What do you mean? I haven't done anything! It started growing yesterday!" She stood and thrust her left hand out of sight.

Anne clutched the edge of the sink. And then she was babbling, but with a terrible logic. "They've got a temple there! You did a deal!"

"Deal?" Vikki was now on the verge of tears. "I don't know what you mean!" She took a step towards her mother but Anne shrank back in terror. This was God's final punishment for that momentary lapse of motherly attention all those years ago. Her punishment was living through the ordeal of countless operations on Vikki's wrist, sitting with Jack in bleak antiseptic corridors, waiting for verdicts. Taking Vikki to specialists who had prodded and probed and said little but their accusing eyes speaking unspoken thoughts. And now this – the culmination of all that torment – the most hideous punishment of all: her daughter's abandoning of God in favour of something too terrible to even think about.

Vikki took another step towards this wide-eyed, terrified woman who was now a stranger. "Mum . . . please!"

Anne's hand scrabbled blindly at the draining board. She snatched up a knife. "Don't come near me!"

Vikki froze. Her thoughts a maddened kaleidoscope of terror in the eye of a hurricane of despair.

"Mum . . ."

"You made a pact! You're not my Vikki! You're vermin! Vermin from hell! A witch!"

Her mother's words cut like a whip. Coming after twenty-four hours of torment and agonising terror, they were enough to snap what little was left of the girl's otherwise remarkable resilience. Her mind went blank and her reason imploded to a nothingness save for a sudden and terrible resolution. She yanked a drawer open and seized a meat cleaver.

"If that's what you think then I'll get rid of it!" she screamed.

She laid her left wrist on the table and raised the cleaver high above her head.

Thirty-Six

"One thing," said Malone, as he dropped Bob Harding off at his shop. "You said that you had two of those Spectrum transmitters?"

"Yes. Why?"

"It might be an idea to keep quiet about the second one."

Harding was puzzled. "Why?"

"The best aces are always the ones up your sleeve, Mr Harding."

The scientist grinned. "You're an odd character, Malone, but I'll keep mum if it makes you feel better."

Malone thanked him and drove to the police station to report to Inspector Harvey Evans. The Sector Inspector had been on duty for fourteen hours and it showed. His face was haggard from lack of sleep. He waved the sergeant to a chair.

"Damned strange not having phones ringing all the time. OK – fire away." He listened intently to Malone's account of the visit to the Wall with Harding.

"So he thinks it's here to stay?"

"I got that impression, too. Whatever put it there didn't intend it to be a five-minute wonder. Mr Harding also thinks that it's a completely enclosing sphere with Pentworth Lake in the exact centre according to his survey."

Evans turned his chair and studied a wall map. The acetate overlay was grease-pencil marked with a series of short arcs around Pentworth. They could be joined to form a circle. "Well – we all thought it was a dome, but a sphere?"

"Which is why the gas, water and telephones are cut. They're all underground."

There was a silence apart from the pecking of a typewriter that someone had rescued from the basement.

"For an advanced intelligence, or whatever they are, they're not very well informed," Evans remarked at length. "Obviously they've not done much reading or watching movies. They've not gone around in fearsome flying machines incinerating everything they see. They've just ignored us."

Malone thought about the crablike machine that he and Cathy Price had seen and decided to remain silent on the matter for the time being. "Mr Harding is also concerned about the air quality. Carbon build-up from car exhausts and barbecues. Sulphur from diesels."

"The petrol and diesel problem will solve itself," said Evans, consulting a handwritten document. "The Jet filling station say that they haven't got a hand pump. Air pollution is on the list of problems to be looked at tomorrow. We've only got so many hours of daylight."

"We could deal with it today," said Malone. "I've seen Asquith Prescott." Not strictly a lie because he had – the previous day at Pentworth Lake. "Would you think it a good idea if he made a broadcast this evening in his capacity as chairman of the Town Council?"

Evans considered the question; it was hardly a police matter. "Well . . ."

"He could include an appeal to everyone not use their cars unless it was absolutely essential, and ask people to combine forces with neighbours for communal cooking. And anything else we'd like put across in the interim."

"Certainly an idea," said Evans thoughtfully. "Yes – a good one, but a small point, Sergeant: what would he use for a radio station?"

"Robert Harding has got a battery-powered Band II FM transmitter. He can have it working in time for an eighteen hundred hours bulletin."

"Well, it sounds a damn sight more efficient than wasting petrol with response cars going around with PA gear."

"We'll need them to publicise the time and frequency, sir. Eighty-seven point five at six o'clock. I'll get that organised. You look beat, if you don't mind me saying."

Evans smiled. "Not at all, Sergeant. Smart of Asquith. People are used to getting their news fix at that time."

"That's what I thought," said Malone, moving to the door.

"You know," mused Evans, "not that I'm saying anything against Asquith Prescott, you understand, but it surprises me – him coming up with such a bright idea. In fact, I've a shrewd suspicion that . . ."

But Malone had gone, leaving his superior officer counting his blessings that he had at least one officer on his tiny force who was prepared to use his initiative.

Malone left the police station and drove to Asquith Prescott's house – a fine Tudor mansion that fronted the main farm – where he found the farmer trying to help his manager get a hand-operated milking machine into working order. In the manager's office Malone wasted no time in getting straight to the point in terms that appealed to Prescott's vanity.

"Inspector Evans thinks it would be an excellent idea if, in your capacity as Chairman of Pentworth Town Council, you made a broadcast to the people of Pentworth at six o'clock this evening, sir. A Churchillian rallying speech. Wartime spirit. Need for co-operation and mutual support – that sort of thing. Councillor Bob Harding is fixing up his workshop as your broadcast studio."

Prescott's florid features sagged in alarm. "You mean that this thing might go on?"

"It's better to assume the worst and be wrong than to assume the best and not be right, sir. Old Chinese proverb."

"Is it? Yes, but—"

With remarkable timing, aided largely by Malone pressing the PPT key on the radio in his pocket and sending three bursts of blank carrier, a response car cruised by at that moment, its driver armed with a loudhailer.

"Please tune in your radios this evening at six o'clock to eighty-seven point five FM when Asquith Prescott, Chairman of Pentworth Town Council, will broadcast an address on the present crisis. That's eighty-seven point five FM at six p.m. . . . If you have a neighbour without a battery radio, please invite them to listen to this important broadcast with you." The repeated message faded into the distance.

"It's being well publicised, sir. People will listen to you because they're looking for leadership. They need the sort of positive leadership that only you can provide."

"Yes – of course. But dammit, it's nearly four . . . I haven't got time to write a speech."

"That's being taken care of, sir. Your time is much too important. A speech writer has been appointed to you. Churchill had one."

"He did?"

"So did Margaret Thatcher. Great leaders always have their own speech writers, sir. Naturally, you can add your own touches to breathe life into it. If you could be at Bob Harding's place at five fifty to go over it."

"Yes – of course. Hang on, though – that will only give me ten min—"

"If you'll excuse me, sir. I have to rush. Several urgent calls before it gets dark. Five fifty at Councillor Harding's shop. Good day, sir."

Malone drove straight to see Harding. The scientist was in his workshop, headphones clamped over ears and reciting 'Mary Had a Little Lamb' into a desk microphone that was connected to a transmitter not much larger than a car radio.

"Both sets are working fine," he reported, removing the headphones. "This one has slightly cleaner audio of the two, but there's nothing much in it. Just been testing it into a dummy load. Good audio quality, and I've got the deviation set up just right. I'm shoving the signal through a ten-watt linear so that it'll be strong everywhere."

"And the spare set's hidden?"

"In the best place – amongst all my junk."

"Prescott will be here at ten to six," said Malone glancing out of the window. The sun was still bright. "Do you have a mechanical typewriter I could use, sir?"

Harding chuckled. "I've got about ten uncollected repairs. I've a feeling that they're going to be worth something now."

"And some paper, please, and a desk by a window."

"Yes – of course. But it's hardly a good time to start that novel you've been putting off, is it?"

Malone gave a thin smile. "I'm not going to write a novel, Mr Harding."

Thirty-Seven

"No!" screamed Anne, and she threw herself across the kitchen just as Vikki swung the cleaver down. But the wicked blade snagged on the overhead onion strings. Such was the girl's demented strength that she ripped the rack from its ceiling Rawlplugs and sent a salvo of giant Spanish onions cannonballing across the kitchen, bouncing off walls and clattering across the Aga. The rack crashed to the floor just as Anne made a frantic grab for Vikki's hand. That the cleaver had become briefly entangled did little to lessen the force of Vikki's swing but it was deflected with the result that the heavy blade splintered into the pine table with such force that it sank deep into the stout planking, missing Vikki's outstretched wrist by a centimetre. She sobbed in anguish and tried to lever the cleaver free, frantically working it back and forth, but her mother was upon her. They crashed to the floor – a flail of entangled blonde hair and thrashing limbs.

"Vikki, my darling! I'm so sorry! I'm so sorry!"

Then mother and daughter were in each other's arms, embracing in a mutual flood of tears. Anne's hysterical sobbing make it impossible for her to blurt out coherent sentences. "How could I have said . . . Oh, Vikki – my darling . . . Precious . . . Please forgive me . . . Please . . ."

"Mum . . ."

"Such a wicked thing I said . . ."

"You were frightened. Just as I was . . ."

"Vikki . . . Vikki . . ." Anne clung to her daughter and yet she was alone in a vacuum of misery and guilt. She had been the cause of it so very nearly happening again. Her anguish brought on renewed sobs.

Vikki cradled her mother's face in her hands and smiled through her tears. "Please don't cry, Mum. I do understand – really I do."

The miracle of Vikki's loving touch stilled Anne's torment. Two wonderfully perfect, comforting hands, two warm caressing palms, ten tenderly stroking fingers, long and perfect. She stared at her daughter, took those wonderful hands in her own, and looked at them in turn before pressing them against her face again. She closed her eyes and felt the warmth of an angel touching her, soothing away the years of guilt – banishing the agony of a decade of recriminations and stopping baying packs of a new and equally terrifying guilt that would have snarled and snapped at her reason until the end of her days, and would have surely ripped her soul from her body and condemned her to eternal damnation. How could she have thought that this wonder she was holding now, that was holding her, was anything other than the work of God?

Thirty-Eight

"**D**inner will be served in one hour," David announced, entering his small living room. He dropped into an armchair and admired the outline of Ellen's figure. She was standing at the window, enjoying the last of the setting sun while watching the Crittendens at work on 'Brenda'. The light made fascinating highlights in her rich, dark hair. "Roast chicken – strangled by my own hand . . ."

"Please, David!"

"New potatoes – first of the year – grown in the greenhouse. Baked parsnips – just lifted. And gravy granules just arrived on the gravy train."

Ellen laughed. "Do they always work on Sunday?"

"Bisto granules work every day of the week."

"Charlie and his family!"

"Oh, they never worry about time. They're working because it's still daylight, because they enjoy it, because they love steam engines, and because they're sober. Charlie's dad owned a beast like 'Brenda', which is why he's so keen to get her running."

David joined Ellen at the window. Together they watched Charlie Crittenden position the new wheel for the showman's engine on the monster's front axle and yell at his sons for the toolbox. The entire family were swarming over the machine, even Grandpa Crittenden was hard at work, vigorously working a long-handled wire brush back and forth through the boiler tubes, producing clouds of powdery rust. Charlie's wife was using wire soap pads on brass pipes so that any leaks would be clean for brazing. In the process she was restoring a shine that the venerable pipework hadn't known for nearly half a century.

"Charlie says there's less wrong with the thing than he thought. He reckons if I can spare some anthracite beans from the greenhouse boiler, he'll have it at running at low pressure by Wednesday . . . You know – it might come in useful if the dynamo's OK and this crazy situation goes on. In her day 'Brenda' could generate enough power to run a village."

"And enough sulphur and smoke to asphyxiate a village." Ellen paused and added quietly, "I think it will continue."

She and David had visited the Wall that afternoon and had marvelled at its strange resistance properties. They had chatted to others and were surprised at how widespread was the belief that there were some sort of alien creatures hiding in the unknown depths of Pentworth Lake. One of them was an earnest young man – one of the original ufologist invasion. He had stayed on when his colleagues had tired of the hunt and gone home. He had assured Ellen and David that there was a galactic war in progress and that there was a scout ship in Pentworth Lake that had surrounded itself with a shield as protection against enemy scout ships.

"If there are aliens or whatever in your swamp—"

"Lake!"

"Then you ought to charge them rent."

"I can't joke about it, Dave. I think the damned thing's permanent."

"Maybe you're right," David replied, looking at his watch. "We'll know one way or the other what our beloved chairman thinks in a few minutes."

Ellen snorted and leaned contentedly against him when he put his arm around her. "Smells good. I'm starving. I've not eaten all day."

"You had your chance at lunchtime. Freebie chips from Adrian Roscoe."

David didn't see the hardening of Ellen's expression. "I have to watch my weight – fried food is not a good idea."

"This from someone who can scoff doorstep bacon sarnies when digging and whose idea of a balanced diet is how much Camembert she can perch on a cream cracker."

"I wish we could have gone to see the cave today."

"Tomorrow."

"David . . ."

"Hmm?"

"Supposing this . . . This crisis goes on for ever? The world will never know about my discovery."

The light was failing. The Crittendens started cleaning and stowing their tools.

"Funny, really," mused David. "If it does go on for a long time, Charlie and his family will notice the least. They haven't got much use for electricity. I offered to lay it on to their caravans but they weren't interested. They cook with oil or gas or whatever they can

175

steal. Their day is geared to the hours of daylight. They're up as soon it's light, work till they drop, and go to bed early. They're happy living in the past." He looked at his watch. "Time to hear what the asinine Asquith has to say."

Ellen grimaced. "He'll drone on for hours and never get to the point."

"He's not that bad, Ellen."

"I liken him to a mud-dwelling estuary creature with just enough brain cells to perceive a dim sense of panic twice a day when the tide goes out."

They sat down. David switched on a portable radio and tuned across the FM band. "Amazing," he muttered. "Stone dead silence."

The tuner hit on a pilot tone. A minute later the tone faded and Bob Harding's voice was heard. He announced the first broadcast of Radio Pentworth and introduced Asquith Prescott.

"Good evening, ladies and gentlemen," Prescott began. "I doubt if there is anyone in the Pentworth area who isn't aware of the extraordinary fate that has overtaken our community. As from last night we have been enclosed by a seemingly impenetrable and invisible dome, six miles in diameter and effectively imprisoning some six thousand of us within an area of thirty square miles, with many suffering the anguish of separation from loved ones."

Ellen's dislike of the man coloured her judgement; although boorish, Prescott was an experienced speaker with an easy, informal and brisk, businesslike delivery that inspired confidence and carried authority. His usage of miles instead of kilometres conveyed an affinity for the security of the past.

"We are lucky in having the services of Councillor Robert Harding, who is a senior government adviser on scientific matters. It's thanks to him that I am able to talk to you now. He has examined the Wall and has confirmed what many of you have suspected all along – that it is definitely not of earthly origin. It is also certain that the centre of the dome is Pentworth Lake. It is to the credit of the good sense of the people of Pentworth that there has been no panic. Whoever these creatures or beings are, or what their purpose is in coming here, or how long they intend to stay, we can only guess. But at least we know from the design of their amazing force wall that they mean us no harm. But the loss of all our public utilities and our total isolation is causing massive problems for all of us.

"But our immediate concern is our air quality. It has got steadily worse today, therefore, even if the dome lasts only a day or so, we must deal with the problem now. In the interests of us all, particularly our children, do not use your cars, or motorbikes, or any form of combustion engine unless it is *absolutely essential*. Only emergency vehicles are exempt. The same goes for barbecues and bonfires: a total voluntary ban until we have more information from our advisers. Clean air must be our first priority."

Prescott spoke for a further three minutes in which he urged those with bottled or LPG gas, or methane digesters, to form communal cooking groups for those without – such gases gave off very little carbon and sulphur; those with good boreholes to provide an outside tap for others to use. He urged utmost economy with water in household tanks and on no account were lavatories on main drainage to be flushed. In all he covered a further five interim emergency measures, including a request for all food shops to sell only perishable stock, and concluded with:

"If the crisis continues we will call on everyone to set up voluntary groups to deal with day-to-day and long-term problems. The British have always been good at rising to challenges such as these which I am laying before you. Our best qualities shine in adversity. Father Adrian Roscoe and his Bodian Brethren have already responded by providing free cooked lunches today and will do so again tomorrow at Pentworth House between midday and two p.m. They will also be making a start on deliveries of fresh bread and milk tomorrow morning. Initial priority will be given to families with children. With such public-spiritedness and your fortitude and willingness to make sacrifices, I am confident that we will overcome all our problems.

"Thank you for listening to me. I will talk to you again at the same time tomorrow. Goodnight and God bless you all."

Harding came on. "That was Asquith Prescott, Chairman of Pentworth Town Council. If the crisis continues, there will be an informal extraordinary meeting of the Town Council at Mr Prescott's house at ten tomorrow morning. All Town Councillors and District Councillors are urged to do their utmost to attend. There will be further bulletins on this frequency tomorrow at noon and six p.m. Radio Pentworth is closing down now. Good night. Please switch off your radio now."

The carrier continued for a few seconds and dropped.

"Well," said David, jabbing the radio's power key and looking at his watch. "Believe it or not but Prescott spoke for less than five minutes. Why can't he do that in committee?"

"He was impressive," Ellen grudgingly admitted.

"More than that, he carried weight and authority. That little piece is going to help a lot of people sleep easier tonight. Right – I'd better see about dinner." He paused at the door. "It'll have to be a candlelit dinner. Probably just as well with my cooking."

"David – did anyone ever call you a great romantic? If so, they were lying."

"And no TV. So afterwards it's either looking at my old family photos with a torch, or an early night."

"Which would you prefer, Don Juan?"

"I'll go and look for the albums and a torch."

Ellen threw a cushion at him.

Thirty-Nine

Prescott stacked the three pages of his typewritten speech and looked at Malone and Harding in turn. The battery light that Harding had rigged in the workshop caught his self-satisfied expression.

"How did I do, gentlemen?"

"Not one fluff, sir," said Malone, maintaining a blank expression to conceal his surprise at Prescott's smooth, authoritative delivery.

Harding was more forthcoming. "You were excellent, Asquith. The best I've ever heard you."

Prescott nodded and steepled his fingers. Reading the speech seemed to have changed his whole demeanour. He was more assured, confident. "Having a good speech helped. My compliments to whoever wrote it, Mr Malone."

"I'll see that they're passed on, sir."

"I'd like to hear the tape, please."

Harding rewound a battery-powered cassette. The three men listened to the replay.

"Mmm . . ." said Prescott when it was over. "I don't like puffing up that madman, Roscoe, but you were right, Mr Malone. The way it comes across makes it sound as if we initiated his efforts."

"Why did you change the venue for the council meeting from the Town Hall to your house, sir?" asked Malone, half-suspecting what the answer would be.

"In a word – control," said Prescott curtly. "As it's to be an extraordinary meeting, I can hold it where I like. I want people to speak freely and I want to invite more than just local councillors. We're going to need the input from a lot of talented people if we're to see ourselves through this mess. People who may not be used to council procedure. I don't want their ideas inhibited by packed public benches. Holding the meeting at my house means that I can exclude the public and make it more relaxed and informal. Does that answer your question?"

"Thank you, sir," said Malone, deriving no satisfaction from having been right.

Prescott stood. He even seemed to have gained in physical stature. "Right. Well done getting all this fixed up, Bob. Radio is going to be our most powerful asset. Keeping people informed. Absolutely vital to ensure their willing co-operation." He glanced at his watch. "I'd better be going. It'll take me a good hour to get home."

"An hour?" Harding queried.

"I walked," Prescott replied. "If the bit about pollution hadn't been included in the speech, I would've insisted on it going in. I'm certain to run into a lot of people on my way home. They will see me setting an example. To say one thing and be seen doing another would undermine my authority."

Harding rose to show Prescott out.

"One thing, Mr Malone," said Prescott, pausing at the door. "If Inspector Evans can spare you, I'd like you to attend the council meeting. Perhaps you'll write me an even better speech for tomorrow evening's broadcast?"

When he was alone Malone wondered about Prescott's unsuspected hidden depths. It seemed that he had misjudged the man.

And that worried him.

Forty

One man who was not pleased with Asquith Prescott's broadcast was Adrian Roscoe. He summoned Claire Lake to his office. An intelligent girl. Good family. Well educated and a good organiser, which was why he had put her in charge of the milk-distribution scheme.

"Did you see a tall man in the courtyard at lunchtime, Claire? Brown, wide-set eyes. Grey slacks. Athletic-looking." His tone was kindly. His quarrel wasn't with her.

"Yes, Father. He gave me a couple of names and addresses. Neighbours of his with children."

Malone!

"And he asked you questions, I expect?"

"Well – yes." The girl looked worried and fingered her clipboard nervously. She had considered the man attractive. "I'm sorry, Father – did I do wrong in talking to him?"

Roscoe smiled reassuringly. "Of course not, Claire. But I expect he asked a lot of questions?"

"Yes – in a friendly sort of way."

"And you answered them in friendly sort of way. Well – that's good, Claire. We need to spread the word. God's word should never be hidden if we are to triumph over his enemies."

"Yes, Father."

"How are the distribution plans going?"

"Very well, Father. We've just done a dummy loading-up of one of the phaetons. The ponies will have no trouble no pulling a load of about five hundred half-litre cartons."

Roscoe nodded. Pentworth House had two of the lightweight pony-drawn open carriages. They were used to take visitors on tours of the park. They had been popular and profitable.

"My big worry is that we'll run out of cartons by Wednesday," Claire continued. "I did think of asking people to return them but we'd run into horrible sterilising problems. If the divine curse

181

continues, we'll have to resort to delivery direct from churns into people's jugs as they did in the olden days."

"The curse will continue, Claire, until we root out and destroy the evil that has brought God's wrath down upon us. But you're doing an excellent job. You have God's blessing, for he is watching over us to see how we bear up under the burden he has placed upon us."

Claire smiled happily. Six months before she had tried to commit suicide after losing a baby and being abandoned by her husband, whom she had loved passionately – the only man she had ever slept with. Joining the brethren had given her a new-found self-respect – it was the best thing she had ever done.

"There is something, Father. The lost property from the party – the artificial hand. Quite by chance I think I've found the owner." She paused and consulted her clipboard. "Yes – one of the helpful ladies I spoke to at lunchtime is a teacher at St Catherine's. A Mrs Simmons. She gave me several names and addresses. She mentioned a girl in her year who had a terrible accident about ten years ago and lost her left hand."

"I don't think the owner is a schoolgirl, Claire."

"But the hand does look like it was made for a young girl, Father. The name I have is Victoria Taylor. Stewards Cottage. They're down for half a litre because the girl is under sixteen. She's fifteen. I could find out if the hand is hers and give it to her if it is."

A fifteen-year-old schoolgirl! Damn Faraday to eternal hell fires!

"Father?"

"Yes – that's an excellent idea, Claire. Any other information?"

"Mrs Simmons said that the girl works in the Earthforce herbal shop on Saturdays."

Roscoe was an accomplished actor and gave no outward sign of the rage and hatred that churned his soul. It all fitted: Faraday had gone out on Saturday morning. He had gone to the accursed witch's shop and given her apprentice an invitation to the party. It was an omen, of course – the way the witch kept crossing his path – God's way of pointing her out to him – showing his servant that which had to be destroyed. He smiled benignly at Claire and rose to kiss her on the forehead – his blessing.

"Thank you, Claire. And now perhaps you'd kindly find Sentinel Nelson, please, and tell him that I'd like to see him."

Forty-One

The seeing was wonderful.

Harding peered through the eyepiece of his telescope and marvelled at the night sky as he tracked the ecliptic plane to locate Jupiter. No light pollution from street lights; no distant flare of Midhurst's lights to the west. The humidity was higher than he would've preferred but there was no cloud.

He straightened and set the telescope's azimuth and elevation vernier scales to centre Polaris – the Pole Star or North Star. There was no need to check the time because Polaris was always in the same place. Polaris was a second-magnitude star, 680 light-years distant, and almost dead above the Earth's North Pole axis so that in the course of a twenty-four-hour period the heavens appeared to rotate around it. It was a celestial hub whose reliable, stationary presence had helped trigger the explosion of great voyages of exploration in the Middle Ages, and the rapid expansion of trade in the northern hemisphere while the southern hemisphere, without a similar reliable star, had largely stagnated.

And it was gone.

Harding checked the telescope's settings. Elevation – 42.3 degrees; azimuth – 358.9 degrees; declination: 89 degrees 13 minutes – almost 90 degrees, which was straight up in relation to the equator.

Nothing.

He searched the heavens with the next best instrument to his telescope – the naked eye. Polaris was in the constellation Ursa Major. The pattern of stars looked like a serving ladle, hence its more common name of the Little Dipper. Polaris itself was at the extreme end of ladle's handle. He located the Little Dipper and was astonished to see that the entire constellation was offset several degrees from its usual position and that it was rotated through 180 degrees so that Polaris was actually the furthest star in the Little Dipper from celestial north.

Harding realised that his gut feelings were correct, and that Malone's comparison with the London Planetarium showing pictures of the night sky as it appeared in the past was a very close analogy to this strange phenomenon he was now witnessing.

The Earth is rotating on its axis like a spinning top, and like a spinning top, it precesses or wobbles. The wobble has a period of 26,000 years. It is this wobble which causes Polaris to drift away over the centuries from true north and drift back again.

After taking measurements with the telescope to establish Polaris's new position, Harding set to work with the Skyglobe planetarium program on his laptop computer. It took him a few minutes to come up with an answer. Or rather several answers, each one correct at intervals and half intervals of 26,000 years either side of the present.

The answer he favoured was the one that said the night sky he was seeing was as it would have appeared 40,000 years ago.

Forty-Two

Vikki dropped her watch on the grass, took a deep breath, and dived into the new swimming pool. The cold punched the breath from her body but she didn't care. It was a glorious morning and she would be able to spend a few minutes soaking up the sun to dry her costume. The two men who had finished filling the pool yesterday had warned that it would soon become unusable without electricity to run the filtration and bromine treatment equipment. So she had decided to enjoy it while she could.

She had always loved swimming but now there was a special joy in being able to drive her lithe body through the water using equal power in both hands. She did a fast crawl, marvelling at her amazing increase in speed. Getting used to her new hand had come easier than she dared hope. She rolled over in the shallow end and propelled herself with seemingly little effort to the deep end using a back stroke.

A blue sky above; a mother who loved her; a mother she loved; two wonderful hands. She felt a special joy coursing through her body – the joy of one who had been singled out by God to experience a wonderful miracle. Just one dark cloud: she wondered when she would see her beloved father again. But the sombre moment passed quickly and then she was off again, splashing the water to a bubbling foam by frenzied thrashing of her arms and legs, revelling in the sheer joyful exuberance of being whole and being young.

The cold eventually overcame her heady exaltation. She grasped the handrails with both hands, pulled herself up the ladder and felt a renewed surge of joy at having two hands to take her weight.

"Victoria Taylor?"

Vikki snatched up her bath towel and spun around to meet a pair of bright blue, smiling eyes belonging to a pretty girl dressed in the short white skirt and short red smock of a Pentworth House dairy-maid. She was carrying a basket containing half-litre milk cartons. The Pentworth House Dairy logo on her breast brought back the terrors of her ordeal.

"Oh, I'm sorry – did I make you jump?"

Vikki tugged the towel around her shoulders and hid her hands. She returned the girl's smile. "A bit."

"I'm sorry. I did call out. I thought you heard me. Anyway, hallo. I'm Claire Lake from Pentworth House Dairy. We're delivering milk. You probably heard about it on the radio yesterday evening?"

"Yes – we did."

"You're down for half a litre."

"We've got some Long Life."

"Fresh full-cream milk from our Jersey herd. Don't worry – it's free." Claire smiled and held out a carton.

Vikki snaked her right hand from the towel's folds and took it, thanking the girl.

"Are you Victoria Taylor?"

"No one calls me Victoria. It's always Vikki."

Claire looked puzzled. "But you are Victoria Taylor?"

"Yes – of course."

"Oh . . . This is yours, then." Claire pulled aside a cloth in her basket and held out Vikki's artificial hand. "You lost it at the party. All that panic when the alarms went off – it was a bit chaotic, wasn't it?"

Again Vikki's right hand emerged from the security of the towel. She stammered her thanks.

Claire's smile was unwavering. "Glad it's found its home. See you tomorrow . . . Vikki. We've a lot of calls to make. Bye." She reached the front entrance and turned to look back but Vikki was nowhere to be seen.

"Young lady!"

It was an old woman leaning on a stick who had called out from the front gate of a nearby row of cottages. A large Siamese cat was sitting on the gatepost beside her. Both were watching her with interest.

"Yes?" asked Claire politely.

"I'd like some of that milk, please."

"I don't think you're on our list." Claire smiled engagingly. "I don't mean to be rude but I'm sure you're over sixteen."

"I am, but he isn't." The woman jabbed a gnarled finger at the cat. "And I like it in my tea, I do. Can't stand that powdered muck. Nor can he."

"I'm really sorry, Mrs . . . ?"

"Johnson."

"Mrs Johnson, but the milk is for children." She stroked the cat who arched his back and purred loudly. "But he is beautiful. What's his name?"

"Hitler."

"Hitler?"

"Himmler," the old woman grumbled. "Never can remember . . . Little sod, he is. Specially if he hasn't had his milk. Gives me hell, he does."

Himmler regarded Claire sleepily with eyes the colour of the sky. He had scented Jersey full-cream milk and was prepared to kill.

"Not mine, he isn't. Belongs to the Taylors, I think, but he takes it out on me if he don't get fed."

Claire had an idea. She half lifted a carton from her basket and seemed undecided. Mrs Johnson's eyes glittered greedily.

"The Taylors have a daughter. Vikki." Claire made the enquiry sound casual.

"That's right."

"Tall, slender; long, blonde hair? Green eyes?"

"That's her. Why?"

"We have to make sure the milk goes to the right place. Vikki has one hand. Is that right?"

"Course it's right! Got it torn off in an accident when she was four – poor little mite. Has to wear a horrible plastic thing."

"Well – maybe we can stretch a point this time."

The carton was snatched from Claire's hand. Mrs Johnson muttered a hurried "thank you" and tried to beat Himmler through the front door but wasn't quick enough.

Forty-Three

Cathy Price had always been able to stand for short periods in much the same way that a coin can be stood on edge. Simple activities such as cleaning her teeth – tasks that could be carried out without significant changes in her centre of gravity – were possible, but she needed to have the security of grab handles close to hand. For this reason her bathroom was fitted with plenty of handles at strategic points.

Thirty seconds under the icy cold shower was as much as she could bear. She backed out of the shower cabinet, her hair and eyes still running with unrinsed shampoo, and groped blindly for a towel. It wasn't in its normal place. She remembered she had left it hanging on the door and took a step towards the door. She reached for a grab handle, and missed. Normally she would've stumbled but this time, to her astonishment, she actually managed to take three steps and reach the door, steady herself, and snatch the towel.

She sat on her linen bin, wiped her eyes, and contemplated the distance from the shower to the door.

Not possible, she told herself. Dear God, I'm having some bad dreams lately.

But you don't have dreams, good or bad, when you're wide awake and your skin is stinging in protest at being under a freezing shower. She pulled on her dressing gown and felt in the pocket for the radio remote control to bring her wheelchair nearer. The machine started towards her, its motor purring sluggishly, and stopped.

Cathy stabbed the remote control but the wheelchair refused to budge.

Damn! It hasn't been charged for two nights. Now what do I do?

She hated crawling. Measuring the distance between herself and the wheelchair with a practised eye, she decided that a good lurch would enable her reach it. Once seated she could propel it manually. Nuisance not having power but at least she'd be mobile again.

The wheelchair's flat battery meant that its automatic parking brake had failed to engage. The thing rolled out of her clutches when she staggered towards it but instead of falling over she somehow remained standing in an awkward posture that normally would have meant a certain fall.

I'm standing! My God! I'm actually standing!

A moment later Cathy discovered that she could do more than merely stand.

She could walk.

Forty-Four

The change in Asquith Prescott was a surprise to most of the fourteen men and women seated at the long table in his Regency-furnished dining room. The usual flamboyant waistcoat had been replaced by a sober short-sleeved white safari suit. He sat at the head of the long table, arms folded, his normally bland, florid features now set in a stern glower that was directed at the Town Clerk. Diana Sheldon felt decidedly uncomfortable. Hitherto Asquith Prescott had always been malleable.

"You heard my broadcast yesterday evening, Town Clerk?"

"Yes, Mr Chairman."

"And yet you came here by car. Everyone else arrived on foot, or on a bicycle, or in a trap. You came by car."

"But I had so many papers to bring. The files—"

"I made it abundantly clear that it was to be an informal meeting," said Prescott mildly. He pointed to a blackboard. "That's the agenda, Town Clerk. No mention of reading and approving minutes or wading through reports and correspondence. We have urgent business to transact and do not have the time to mess about with your bits of paper. If you were pelted with stones as you came through the town, then all I can say is that you're lucky they weren't bricks. Is that right, Inspector Evans?"

For this meeting the senior police officer was wearing his uniform. "There have been a number of incidents of bricks thrown at vehicles," he said cautiously, not happy with this set-up.

"But generally the response to my appeal has been ninety-nine per cent?"

The statement was unnecessary; before the meeting had started there had been much comment about the almost total lack of motor vehicles that morning.

"It's been a remarkable response," Evans replied. He caught Malone's eye. It annoyed him that Prescott had invited a junior officer to attend.

"Self policing is effective policing," Prescott observed. "It seems that I already have the support of the people."

"I would be grateful of some police protection when I drive home," said Diana Sheldon. She was a self-effacing, nervous woman of fifty-five, deeply embarrassed at being the focus of attention. As a practising solicitor, she hated appearing in court, which was why she had upset her father by leaving the family's law firm and taking on the job of Town Clerk.

"You won't be driving home, Town Clerk. I'm sure someone will drop you off in their trap."

"But—"

"As a local government officer you have a clear duty to set an example just as everyone else has," said Prescott curtly. "Your car will be looked after but you will not be driving it. It has already been disabled."

Rather than burst into tears in front of everyone, Diana made a stammered apology, gathered up her belongings, and dashed from the room.

"To business," said Prescott briskly.

Ellen was about to raise a point of order but was beaten to it by Dan Baldock, a pig-headed pig farmer who made it his business to argue with everything. Not so much because he disliked Prescott, but because he was naturally argumentative. He was a small, greying, sour-faced man. It grieved him that his candour ensured that he was better liked than his belligerent manner warranted. He had been made Deputy Chairman very much against his wishes.

"Point of order, Mr Chairman," he said. "Can we continue without the Town Clerk?"

"I was about to move suspension of standing orders, Councillor," Prescott replied. "We need contributions from everyone. Proposer and seconder, please. Only councillors can vote."

The motion went through on a solid show of hands with Dan Baldock's objections being overruled by Prescott.

"We don't have a law officer present," Ellen whispered to David. "This can't be legal."

"You tell 'em, m'dear."

Ellen decided to remain silent although she was certain that Prescott, who knew Diana Sheldon's sensitive nature, had deliberately provoked her into leaving.

Prescott placed a cassette tape recorder on the table and started it recording. "A one-hour tape," he said. "That's as long as we need. My wife will type a transcript and copies will be made

191

public. I'd like to extend a warm welcome to Inspector Harvey Evans, Sussex Police's Pentworth Sector Inspector; Gerald Young, a sanitation engineer, and Dr Millicent Vaughan, head of the largest group practice in the area. Detective Sergeant Mike Malone is here as my aide."

Malone's impassive expression gave no indication of his dislike of the surprise post.

"That's the agenda on the blackboard, ladies and gentlemen. Let's get started. An apology for absence has been received from Councillor Father Adrian Roscoe. I have a proposal to make concerning our policy towards this crisis and I'd like to hear your views.

"We don't know how long the crisis will last although Councillor Harding has some views on the matter which we will hear later. What I propose is that this meeting concerns itself with short-term essential matters to get us through the next seven days. If the crisis persists, then we will hold another meeting a week from today to deal with the medium-term problems to get us through another month. If the crisis persists for thirty days from today, then we will hold a key meeting to decide policy to take us through a year. Let us pray that it won't come to that, but with this approach we establish clear objectives right from the outset. This way we do a few things at a time properly, rather than try to tackle everything at once. Any comments before we vote?"

The majority of those seated at the table were looking at Prescott in admiration mixed with surprise. They had never seen their Chairman being so assertive. Even Ellen had to admit to herself that he was showing an astonishing degree of common sense, and Dan Baldock, who regarded Prescott as something that pigs kept under their tails, looked quite taken aback.

"An excellent policy, Mr Chairman," said a councillor with almost reverence.

Again, the vote was solid. Ellen raised her hand in favour, telling herself that she was there to represent people's interests and that her personal prejudices were irrelevant.

"Thank you. We start with a report from Councillor Robert Harding on the nature of the force wall and his evaluation of the crisis facing us."

The tall, stooping figure rose, obliging those sitting near him to twist their necks. Prescott said that he could sit and ruled that all meetings would be conducted sitting.

Using the psychological advantage of being in his own home to establish a few innocuous precedents, thought Malone. Paving the way for more serious ones later. Interesting.

Harding spoke quickly from notes, briefly outlining what everyone now knew about the force wall and moving on to his findings the previous night.

"So you think that the sun and moon and stars we're seeing is some sort of generated image from forty thousand years ago?" Prescott queried.

"That's my analysis, Mr Chairman. The sun's power wasn't significantly different forty thousand years ago from what it is today. An hour ago I measured it at five hundred watts per square metre. High for the morning at this time of year but that's due to the lack of clouds. It's pushing the relative humidity up to eighty per cent which is making it feel muggy."

"Brought on my tomatoes a week in the last two days," said Gavin Hobson, a market grower and a staunch advocate of organic growing.

"The Wall is definitely *not* the product of human technology," Harding continued. "Of that there is no doubt. That leaves extraterrestrial technology. It would seem that the claims of those that they saw an object in the sky last Tuesday may have been accurate after all. The ufologists who scoured the area on Wednesday and Thursday looking for this so-called Silent Vulcan didn't find anything because they didn't investigate Pentworth Lake, which is the geographic centre of the Wall. An excellent choice of hiding place for a flying saucer, spacecraft, Silent Vulcan – call it what you will. We can send probes to the planets and submersibles to the greatest depths of the oceans, but we do not have the instruments to probe very deep swamps." He paused. "I took some readings first thing this morning with a small gravimeter. There's a definite anomaly in the centre of the lake."

"How deep, Councillor?" asked Prescott.

"Unfortunately my gravimeter doesn't give range."

"What's more to the point, where are the buggers *from*?" Baldock demanded.

The scientist glanced uneasily at Prescott. "That would take us into the realms of supposition, which is hardly the purpose of this meeting."

Prescott saw how all eyes were turned eagerly to the speaker. "Go ahead, Councillor Harding," he said. "Five minutes."

Nice control, thought Malone. Judging the mood of others well. A latent hunger for power bludgeoning its way out of the boorish nature of Asquith Prescott and asserting itself in a surprising degree of political acumen. The creep had started crawling with his broadcast.

At the beginning of the meeting he had been learning to walk; now he was striding. If the pattern continued, he would soon be trampling. He castigated himself for misjudging Prescott so.

"We know enough about the solar system to rule out all the planets," said Harding. "That leaves our galaxy – the Milky Way. Our nearest star is Proxima Centauri. A type M red-dwarf flare star whose light takes four point three years to reach us – just over one parsec. For the sake of argument let us assume that Centauri has a planetary system and that's where our visitors are from. We know that they can't be from anywhere nearer, and the probability is that they're from somewhere a good deal further away. Certain characteristics of the Wall – we now know from a check on the sewers and an old lead mine that it's actually a sphere – indicate that our visitors are not in possession of the sort of super-advanced technology as favoured by most science-fiction writers. It is advanced enough – but from what I've observed, I doubt if they're much more than three hundred years ahead of us."

"My God – it's enough."

Harding smiled at the observation. "Certainly enough to give us serious problems. I'm going to make another supposition and give our visitors' spacecraft a capability of one fifth of the speed of light – around sixty thousand kilometres per second. Allowing for periods of acceleration and deceleration, the journey from Centauri to Earth would take them about twenty-two years. A round trip of forty-four years. An awesome time-span but within the realms of possibility for a survey expedition by a determined people with enquiring minds." He paused. "The scientist in me rebels at all this stretching of a theory but I've started it so I'll continue. I believe that our visitors had problems with their spacecraft when they went into orbit around the Earth. Rather than remain in orbit and risk detection and possible destruction by us, they searched for a haven. Where better than a deep swamp? And as an added safeguard, they threw up an enclosing protective sphere around themselves. They then broadcast for help – they certainly generated a lot of broadband radio noise around 100 megahertz on Thursday and Friday, which led to the drowning of two Radio Communications Agency investigators. The visitors' SOS is now on its way to Centauri and will reach it in four years and four months. Assuming that HQ can launch a rescue mission right away, we can expect to be reluctant hosts to our visitors for the next twenty-seven years. On the other hand, they may be from the heart of our galaxy in which case they, and we, will have to wait many thousands of years."

The silence that followed was broken by David Weir. "But surely, Bob, they wouldn't send a survey mission without some sort of backup?"

"Why not?" Harding countered. "None of the Apollo manned missions to the moon had a backup Saturn rocket standing by. And there never has been a second shuttle at the ready in case a flight gets into trouble. Once you have a working technology, the temptation is to get on and use it within the parameters of acceptable risk otherwise nothing would ever be done for the first time. It may be that this mission by our visitors is the culmination of many years of sending unmanned probes. We've certainly had enough sightings of UFOs over the last half-century. If they've learned anything about us, one can hardly blame them for surrounding themselves with a protective sphere having made a forced landing."

"Load of bollocks," Dan Baldock muttered.

Prescott regarded him icily. "I beg your pardon, Councillor?"

"I said, a load of bollocks."

"It would be appreciated if you could moderate your language."

"All right, then – a load of crap." He glared at Bob Harding. "How do you know the little buggers aren't from Mars? If they are, they could be gone next week."

"The evidence from unmanned landers and orbital probes indicates that there is no life on Mars," said Harding. "The same goes for all the planets in the solar sys—"

"What about *in* Mars? Maybe they went underground hundreds of years ago? Absence of evidence is not evidence of absence."

Malone was impressed. Baldock's comment demonstrated a capacity for logical thought, and it had caught Harding wrong-footed. The scientist had opened his mouth to speak and changed his mind. Malone guessed that Dan Baldock often scored good points – that one was a lulu.

"There would be evidence on the surface of Mars," Harding ventured at length, knowing that he sounded lame.

The pig farmer snorted. "We see what they want us to see – like that weird countryside beyond the Wall."

Harding turned to Prescott. "Mr Chairman – it's a safe assumption that if there is intelligent life on Mars, they would have made contact with us years ago. Mars is in our own backyard and there hasn't been as much as a whisper of response over the years to the Americans' SETI broadcasts. I hardly think that we would've been ignored."

"Those buggers in the Plague Swamp have ignored us," Baldock retorted.

"That's true," Prescott commented.

"It's called 'Pentworth Lake'," reminded Ellen, eyeing Baldock, who merely grinned back at her.

"Mr Chairman. May I speak, please?" asked Malone.

"Go ahead, Mr Malone," said Prescott.

All eyes swivelled around to the police officer.

"They haven't ignored us," said Malone. "I was jogging home late on Friday night when a strange machine followed me. It was like a mechanical crab – very hard to see, as if it were made of glass – but I definitely saw it quite clearly at one point."

David felt Ellen suddenly stiffen. He looked enquiringly at her but she was staring fixedly at Malone.

"This is extraordinary!" Harding exclaimed. "But how can you be sure it came from our visitors?"

"I tried to catch it, and the thing turned into an electric helicopter and vanished. It went straight up. I thought it was some sort of kids' toy at first, but no toy can do that. It looked heavy and would've needed a lot more power than we know how to pack into a battery."

"You never reported it," Harvey Evans observed.

"I'm reporting it now, Mr Evans." Malone looked around the table, his brooding, wide-set eyes settling briefly on everyone in turn. He continued, "It was some hours before the Wall appeared. I didn't altogether believe it myself and doubted if anyone else would. As luck would have it, I found out the following morning that Miss Catherine Price of Hill House had also seen it through her telescope when it was following me. She called it a spyder. An apt name. I got a distinct impression that it was spying on me."

"I've seen it, too, Mr Chairman," said Ellen abruptly.

There was a stir of surprise.

"Go ahead, Councillor Duncan."

"It was after I'd seen you and Inspector Evans by the lake on Saturday morning. It was only a glimpse. I thought I'd imagined it at the time. Also Vikki Taylor who works for me on Saturday mornings has seen it. She told me that she'd seen a crablike thing after school on Friday afternoon. Just very briefly."

Dr Millicent Vaughan regarded Ellen with interest.

Harding started firing eager questions but Prescott cut him short. "I think it would be best, Councillor, if I ask Mr Malone to collect full statements from all the witnesses and report back, otherwise we'll be here all day. If you've finished, Councillor Harding. Next item on the agenda is drinking water."

196

Gerald Young, the sanitation engineer, reported that most people on mains supply would have at least another three days' supply of water in their domestic tanks provided they had heeded the Chairman's warning about economy. He and a colleague had examined the town's concrete water tower, disused since 1965. It was structurally sound but needed cleaning and lining with sheet polythene. Filling could be accomplished by running a diesel pump from the original artesian well. The water table was high. The work would take ten volunteers one day. Prescott gave permission for a diesel pump to be run for no more than ten hours in the first instance.

Sanitation: the chairman would include an appeal in his evening broadcast for those with cesspits and septic tanks to share their facilities. There was evidence that this was already happening.

Food: the town had an estimated ten days' supply in shops and larders. A census would be organised to determine exactly how much EU grain was held in farm silos and what the main-crop vegetable-storage situation was. Thanks to the Bodian Brethren, much frozen food had been saved and the sentinels had undertaken to deliver milk and step up bread production. Permission was granted for Pentworth House to run its generator for their milking machines.

"I've actually arranged to send Father Adrian Roscoe several of my Guernseys because we can't cope," Prescott concluded. "His acreage is under-grazed. Detective Sergeant Malone – unless Inspector Evans has objections, I would be most grateful if you would be so kind as to draft all the points we've covered for inclusion in my broadcast this evening."

"No objections, Mr Chairman," said Evans uneasily.

Prescott beamed at Malone with eyes that said: *Shafted, eh, Mr Malone?* "Excellent – we've got through everything. No more points? I declare the meeting clo—"

"One point please, Mr Chairman."

Prescott looked enquiringly at Ellen.

"I move that the venue of the next meeting be back at the council chamber. It difficult for many of us to get here. The Town Hall would be much more convenient."

"Well," said Prescott expansively. "The only reason for holding it in private is that I thought the Town Hall might be inundated. I didn't wish to overstretch Inspector Evans' limited resources. But, as we've all seen this morning, public co-operation has been remarkable. So yes – we'll hold the next meeting in the chamber as normal. Thank you, ladies and gentlemen. The meeting is closed."

People started to rise and sat again when Prescott continued speaking. "Inspector Evans is staying for lunch. In the communal spirit we're encouraging, you're all invited to stay on."

Everyone professed to having much to do.

"I'm going to open my shop," said Ellen. "Business as usual."

"That's the spirit, Ellen," said Prescott, beaming. "We won't let the buggers get us down, eh?"

Ellen and David said their goodbyes outside in the bright sunlight and boarded David's black-lacquered pony-drawn trap – lovingly restored by Charlie Crittenden's boys during the winter. "Patronising bastard," she muttered as they turned on to the road and set off at a smart pace.

"I'm astonished at the change in him," said David. "He exuded confidence."

"Power," said Ellen savagely. "That's all he's interested in. Did you see the way his eyes lit up when Bob Harding talked about us being trapped for thousands of years? He sees himself as the founder of a new dynasty."

David laughed and touched the pony's flank with the whip. It increased its pace. "Thirty square miles? Some dynasty."

"Big enough for a city-state."

"Ellen – listen. OK – so he's a power-grubbing little toad. But what do his motives matter so long as he does a good job? And on this morning's showing, he's certainly doing that. He's got people co-operating with him, eating out of his hand. That's what we need." He gestured at the road ahead. It was deserted apart from a cyclist in the distance. "Not a car in sight. When did we last see that on the A285 on a fine day?"

He breathed deeply. The air smelt good and the pony seemed keen to go faster. "This beats driving. Don't have to concentrate and you can see over hedges. Hey – you know what, m'dear? This is rather fun. Tell me about this mechanical crab you saw."

Forty-Five

H arding had put on a pair of rusty cycle clips and was studying the sky intently when Millicent buttonholed him in Prescott's drive.

"That bicycle looks decidedly unsafe, Bob."

Harding chuckled. The old upright Raleigh had earned him a good deal of ribbing when he had arrived on it but he had taken it in good heart. "Oh, it is, Milly. It is. But the roads are suddenly so much safer. You could make a middle-aged man very happy by accepting a lift on his cross-bar." His attention returned to the sky.

"It's a lady's bicycle."

"I can improvise a cross-bar."

"I think I'd rather walk. And you're well past middle age – how many people do you know who are a hundred and twenty?"

"Cruel, Milly. Cruel."

"I was interested in what you said about our visitors being at least three hundred years ahead of us."

"Pure theorising based on good but scant evidence," Harding replied absently, sky watching again. "There seem to be clouds forming."

"But definitely well ahead of us?"

"There's no doubt about that. They're here where we come from, but we're not there where they come from."

"And they'd also be three hundred years ahead of us in medical research."

"It's a sobering thought, but yes."

"How long before we create self-replicating molecules, Bob?"

The question surprised the scientist. He lost interest in the sky. "Artificial tissue growth? The medical profession's dream. Being able to grow new body parts."

"That would be one thing," said Millicent cautiously, thinking how astute the scientist was – he was almost reading her thoughts.

"Well – it's been just around the corner for ten years. But so has controlled nuclear fusion. I'd say fifty years. Definitely within a hundred years. But foretelling the future is hazardous. I was taken to the Festival of Britain as a kiddiwink. In the Dome of Discovery we were told that by the end of the twentieth century we'd be living in houses that looked like golf balls on stilts. Here we are in the twenty-first century, living in brick houses with tiled roofs built the same way that the Romans built them."

They started walking, Harding wheeling his antique bicycle. He kept glancing up.

"There's so much we could learn from the visitors," said Millicent wistfully.

"They might even have a cure for cancer," said Harding. "But we don't even know if they're a carbon-based lifeform. Although I'd be prepared to bet that they are."

"Well . . . I'm sorry to have kept you, Bob. Do be careful on that thing."

Harding laughed. "I shall stand on the edge of the Plague Swamp and yell for help if anything untoward happens to me or my bits. Good day, Milly." He mounted the bicycle and wobbled towards the town, his safety not enhanced by his tendency to show a greater interest in the sky than the road.

Millicent Vaughan's thoughts as she walked home were that Vikki Taylor would not have yelled for help. Or had she done so unwittingly?

Forty-Six

"You were hard on Diana Sheldon, Asquith," said Harvey Evans, pouring himself some more whisky.

Prescott smiled wolfishly. "She will receive a private apology, and a grovelling public apology at the next meeting followed by a fulsome eulogy about her work and how her services are indispensable. After that she'll do anything I say. Otherwise she can always resign and go back to family's law firm."

The two men were sitting at a garden table on Prescott's lawn having enjoyed a heavy lunch. Through an open downstairs window the landowner's wife could be seen, cutting old-fashioned Gestetner stencils on a typewriter, headphones over her ears.

"What did you think of Bob Harding's appraisal?" asked Prescott.

"Extremely well put."

"He toned it down a little at my request. He didn't favour the model of our visitors coming from our nearest star. Too convenient. He considered that the centre of the galaxy was more likely."

"Meaning that it's possible that this situation could drag on indefinitely?"

"Precisely, Harvey. Precisely." Prescott sipped his Scotch. "What's the firearm situation at Pentworth Police Station?"

"I'm sorry, Asquith, but that's something I'm not prepared to discuss."

"Of course, Harvey – forgive me for asking. But one cannot help but conjecture about the number of firearms in the community."

"Very little now. The last amnesty just after the new law came in produced a small crop – mostly rusty old firing pieces."

"There was that sub-machine gun two or three days ago," said Prescott. "Quite unbelievable."

Evans smiled. Two days previously the lead story on local radio had been the woman who had wandered into Pentworth police station carrying two Sainsbury's shopping bags. One contained a heavily greased British Army Sterling sub-machine gun, and other was burdened with two loaded magazines. She had moved into a house in Northchapel that had been standing empty for fifteen years and had found the cache rolled up in an old carpet in the loft.

"Unbelievable," Evans agreed.

"Shotguns are a different matter, of course."

"They are indeed," Evans replied. Prescott's questions sounded conversational but the policeman didn't like the turn the discussion had taken.

"You have the permit records here?"

"We have a log. That's no secret. As you well know, we have to carry out periodic checks on storage security. But I can't tell you how many."

"Well, I've got four," Prescott observed. "Assuming every farmer and grower has one, that could be well over a hundred."

Evans made no reply.

"This situation creates an interesting dilemma," Prescott continued. "After my little broadcast last night, I called on Diana Sheldon and asked her about the legal situation here. She was surprisingly forthcoming. As she sees it, Pentworth is what she called 'beyond jurisdiction'. Under the present circumstances it is beyond the enforcement of the monarch's writ. In other words, we're temporarily not part of the United Kingdom. Of course, when the crisis is over, it would revert to its former status. She cannot see any other course of action open to the Lord Chancellor other than to issue retrospective ratification of all reasonable actions taken by a democratically elected emergency government where such actions were in the interests of the populace as a whole. Are you following me?"

"Perfectly," said Evans stiffly, feeling that he was getting the measure of the man. "What you're saying is that the police should be placed under your control."

"Not *my* control, Harvey, the control of the Pentworth Emergency Council – a democratically elected body. Nothing revolutionary about that. It's the way the police has always been controlled."

Evans mopped his face. He was hot and uncomfortable, his uniform tight because he had put on weight recently. Last time he had flown his microlight it had needed half the length of his paddock to unstick. It irritated him that Prescott looked cool and relaxed. He decided then that there was absolutely no way that Prescott was going to gain control of the police but he didn't want a confrontation now. "It will need thinking about. There's no need to change anything just yet."

"Not just yet," Prescott agreed.

"You ought to talk to Judge Hooper. Find out what he thinks of the legal situation."

"A good point," Prescott replied. "My immediate concern is that this honeymoon period with the people won't last if the crisis continues, as I'm sure it will. Within a month or so we'll need a much enlarged and much tougher police force – one that will be called upon to enforce a number of unpopular measures."

"*If* the crisis persists."

"I have a feeling in my bones that it will. Perhaps for as long as a thousand years."

"Hitler wanted his Third Reich to last a thousand years," Evans observed pointedly. "It didn't last one and a half decades."

"Precisely, Harvey. For us to survive means that we're going to have to be a lot tougher than Hitler."

Forty-Seven

"What do you think?" Suzi asked her husband.

Harding examined the four-metre-diameter satellite TV dish that his wife had covered with aluminium baking foil. The dish, minus its electronics but with three support arms meeting at the focal point, was mounted on a frame that wasn't fixed down. He had bought the thing the year before with the idea of using it to receive Band C satellite TV transmissions but it had proved too big and cumbersome to be practical, and besides, the neighbours had complained. He had considered sinking it flush into the lawn as an ornamental pond but had never found the time.

"Excellent, darling," he exclaimed.

"Devil of a job getting it to stick down smooth."

"Where did you get the foil from? The shops aren't supposed to sell non-perishable goods."

"Diana Sheldon obtained it on a Town Hall requisition note."

"Well, it certainly looks the business," said Harding. Let's get it in position."

They manoeuvred the dish until Harding was satisfied that it was pointing at the sun. He climbed a step stool. Suzi passed him a full black-enamelled whistling kettle which he hooked on to one of the LNB support arms so that it was hanging in the dish's focal point.

"How long?" asked Suzi.

"I've really no idea. But it must be receiving about three thousand watts."

A few moments later Suzi said: "This reminds me of the saying about a watched kettle."

"Give it time."

At that moment the kettle started a faint singing. A minute later it was rumbling, and then steam was screaming through its whistle.

Harding was delighted. "Go and fetch the teapot, darling – we might as well make use of it."

Forty-Eight

"But, darling," Anne pleaded, "you must go to school. It's reopening on Wednesday."

Vikki played with the tablecloth, unconsciously twisting the corner only with her right hand. Ever since the Pentworth House milkmaid had seen her climbing out the pool using both hands, she had virtually stopped using her left hand. It now lay out of sight on her lap, its usual position when it had been artificial.

"I need more time, Mum."

Anne sighed. "You'll have to face up to it sooner rather than later, Vikki."

"Well, I'd rather it was later. Please, Mum – just give me time."

"What about Saturday morning? What did Ellen's note say?"

"She still wants me to go in. She wants me to help with some drying work in the greenhouses. I'd like to go so long as I'm not left alone in the shop."

"Can you manage?"

"Well, I've managed before with my real hand!"

"Vikki – that *is* your real hand."

"Miss Duncan usually leaves me by myself in the greenhouses. She won't notice. But they will at school."

"You could wear gloves all the time. They'd never say anything. You told me that they never stare."

"They might," said Vikki sulkily. "I don't want to go back."

Anne sighed. She didn't know what else to suggest. Vikki had been withdrawn and difficult ever since the incident with the milk delivery girl. It was like the two hellish years of her puberty all over again. Then she had an idea.

"Would you like Sarah to come and stay with us for a few days?"

Vikki's eyes lit up immediately. It was something she had never dared suggest because of her mother's reservations about Sarah's morals. "I'd love that, Mum!" She jumped up and flung her arms around Anne.

"She could have the spare room," Anne suggested.

"No. No. We could squeeze another bed in my room! Oh, Mum – you're wonderful." Anne laughingly disengaged herself and reached automatically for the telephone, stopping herself with a gesture of irritation. Her hand was still going to the light switch when entering a room. Habits of a lifetime died hard. "I'll go and see her. It's another lovely day so the walk won't hurt."

"I'll come with you."

"No," said Anne firmly. "You'll do that essay. If you're going to skive off school then you'll spend the daylight hours working."

Anne's other reason for going alone was that she wanted an opportunity for a serious talk with Sarah.

Forty-Nine

O f the several action groups set up by Prescott – he preferred to call them task forces – the one to deal with the water problem produced the fastest results. Under the direction of Gerald Young, a team of volunteers sweated in the hot confines of the water tower to clean and line it. On Tuesday they broke open a Southern Water store and installed standpipes at several locations around the town. With the water tower filled and a daily schedule agreed with the Town Hall for use of a diesel pump to keep the tower primed, a limited drinking water supply for the town was back on stream from standpipes by Wednesday evening.

Prescott's broadcast that evening included an apology to those living on the outskirts and in rural areas for the lack of a supply. The Water Task Force had only a limited supply of standpipes and what resources there were had to be used for the benefit of the greatest number.

It was on the following day that Pentworth experienced its foretaste of things to come.

A pickup driver and a helper with Town Hall authorisation to use the vehicle because they were collecting water for a village faced a barrage of abuse over the time they were taking to fill a cargo of water containers.

"The farms have got boreholes!" someone shouted. "They're taking our water!"

The scene degenerated into scuffles which the police broke up. Other than bruised egos, no one was hurt but Harvey Evans read a report of the incident with deep misgivings. It was a minor disturbance that required the presence of four police officers; for forty minutes the rest of the community had been without police cover on response.

Prescott didn't mention the matter on his evening broadcast but he did point out that, on balance, rural dwellers were more fortunate than their town counterparts.

"But it would be wrong," he told his listeners, "to assume that those not living in the town must be living on farms. There are many remote houses and small communities whose needs must be considered."

On Wednesday the schools reopened with parents required to provide packed lunches for their children.

On Thursday the Sanitation Task Force, with fifty volunteers, opened the first public toilets on Sandy Green near the town centre. The cubicles consisted of a neat row of twenty small garden sheds, each one fitted with a flushing lavatory supplied from a common header tank mounted on scaffold poles. Press-fit plastic soil pipe fittings purchased from a plumbers' merchant's using promissory notes issued by the Town Hall made for an easy and quick installation. Discharge was into a covered cesspit that had been dug out by a JCB from a local plant hire company. The toilets were free but users had to provide their own paper. A rota of attendants to provide twenty-four-hour cover was drawn up. Two more sites had been surveyed and were planned for the following day.

The majority of the populace had now visited the Wall and had experienced its strange powers at first hand. The growing feeling was that it might be in place for some time and there was much grief at the prospect of separation from loved ones. But, overall, morale was remarkably high, boosted to a considerable extent by the buzz of activity orchestrated by the Town Hall and Prescott's repeated calls for volunteers larded with his 'Your community needs you' and his reading out each evening of the day's achievements. Long-term unemployed who had lost much of their self-respect were shaken out of their lethargy when a spade was thrust in their hands and they were invited to join in the camaraderie of the working parties.

The continuing warm weather helped.

Fifty

Cathy had often undertaken graphic design work for Pentworth Town Council but this job was the most extraordinary order of all. She was sitting in her wheelchair and staring at her two visitors in some astonishment, her worries momentarily forgotten. They were Diana Sheldon and Vernon Kelly, a lean, serious young man whom Cathy knew slightly because he was the chief accountant at her bank.

"Money!" Cathy exclaimed, looking up from the rough design she had been given. "You want me to design and print money!"

"Work vouchers," the Town Clerk corrected. "We need them urgently."

"Is this anything to with shops not being able sell non-perishable goods?"

"That was to stop panic buying," said the banker smoothly. "We need something like that design in denominations of five, ten, twenty, and fifty Euros, Miss Price. Mr Prescott had an urgent meeting with representatives from the banks this morning. I've been nominated Chairman of the Financial Working Party. In view of the present – ah – difficult situation we find ourselves in, all existing banknotes and accounts are frozen. All debits and credits have been suspended until further notice."

"The banks have decided that the only way to deal with the situation is to stop the banking clock until the crisis is over," said Diana.

Cathy grinned. She liked the Town Clerk. "Did they have much choice?"

Vernon Kelly's worried expression deepened. "Not really. As from now, the only valid currency will be work vouchers, but coins will still be allowed."

"Should you be telling me this, Mr Kelly?"

"It'll be on the midday news."

"Who will be issuing these vouchers?"

"The Emergency Council," Vernon Kelly replied. "If you look at the wording—"

"I always thought banks could issue banknotes if they wished?"

"The work vouchers will be more like bonds rather than cash although they can be used as such," said Diana. "We'll be issuing them in lieu of payment for public work and community service undertaken by individuals, and for pension payments. Initially, the only way of obtaining them will be by working, apart from those issued to the sick and the elderly. After that they'll pass into circulation as currency. They'll be redeemable at their face value in euros when the crisis is over."

"Provided central government or the EU foot the bill?" said Cathy mischievously. "No wonder the banks didn't want to issue them."

Vernon Kelly seemed keen to change the subject. "Miss Price, do you have a stock of unusual or distinctive paper that the council can purchase from you?"

Cathy indicated her stock cabinet. She was tempted to stand and walk but her new-found ability was causing her great misery by proving inconsistent; she was terrified of falling over and making a spectacle of herself. "There are about forty reams of hundred-gram linen-based paper in there. I bought it from a specialist supplier in Spain. A menu job for a hotel chain. Expensive. I don't suppose it'll be needed now."

The banker found the paper and examined one of the large A1-size sheets, running his fingernail over the surface. The heavy cream-laid paper had an unusual texture. "This will be excellent, Miss Price. Tough and durable – just what we need. There must be quarter of a tonne of it here."

"What happened to your monitor?" Diana asked.

"It got broken," said Cathy laconically. "I've got a spare."

"We should be able to get a hundred and twenty vouchers on each sheet," Vernon Kelly commented. "Do you have enough laser printer toner to print an initial five reams, Miss Price?"

"Plenty if the background design is simplified a bit. But there is one thing I haven't got."

"What's that?"

"Electricity."

"Oh, that's all right," said Diana. "We've got a mobile generator outside. It won't take my helpers a minute to connect it up. Shall we get started?"

Ten minutes later Cathy was intent on producing the basic voucher design on her Macintosh's computer screen. Normally she disliked having customers watching her work but her visitors insisted on staying in the room. But she was pleased to have her system up and running again, and her audience were content to rely on her expertise – they didn't make a nuisance of themselves by demanding endless experiments with different fonts. The 'promise to pay the bearer' was accomplished in an Old English font and looked authoritative. It took her about thirty minutes to create a master design, with colour changes for the different denominations, that they were happy with.

"If you could make the serial number panel just a little larger, please," Diana requested. "We'll be hand stamping them with a numbering machine."

Cathy obliged and clicked the mouse to flow the design for the five-euro denomination vouchers into a ready-made boilerplate that duplicated the voucher 150 times. A quick tidy up of margins, and a test print on to ordinary paper. The visitors pronounced themselves happy with the sixth trial sheet that rolled out of big laser printer and dropped into its collection bin. Vernon Kelly loaded the first half-ream of the textured paper into the feed hopper while Diana tore up the test sheets and put them in a large envelope. With everything ready, the print run began.

"This really is an excellent printer, Miss Price," said Vernon Kelly a few minutes later. He had removed a sheet from the collection bin and was examining the rows and columns of coloured vouchers.

"It ought to be. It cost enough."

"Is there another like it in Pentworth? One that can manage this sort of resolution and colouring?"

Cathy shook her head. "This is the only one, Mr Kelly. Some colour photocopiers might do a good job but no one will be able to match that paper."

Diana produced a numbering machine and stamped consecutive serial numbers on the first sheet. "Good – it takes stamping ink very well. Perhaps you'd make out the bill please, Miss Price. Put down all the paper, please – we'll be taking it all with us, of course."

Cathy wrote out an itemised bill while Diana used the paper trimmer to slice the first sheet into individual vouchers. She checked Cathy's figures, counted out the total in the freshly printed vouchers and handed them over. "Thank you, Miss Price. We may need you again if the crisis continues, but let us hope not."

The visitors left two hours later, taking their electricity and paper with them. Cathy watched their van moving off and wished she'd thought of asking if she could drive it to the end of the road. God – how she missed the feel of cold vinyl beneath her thighs and a steering wheel in her hands. She stood at the window for some moments, staring down at her beloved E-type, wondering if she would ever be allowed to drive it again. But it was no use dwelling on it; at least it was good to be making money again.

Fifty-One

A nne Taylor tightened the last jubilee clip that secured the input hose to the ancient central-heating radiator. It had taken her, with Vikki's and Sarah's help, an hour to drag the huge piece of ironmongery out of the garage, stand it in the middle of the lawn where it received full sun, and flush it clean. She stood back and glanced across the garden at the two girls by the kitchen door. Getting Sarah to stay with them had been a good move: it had shaken Vikki out of her lethargy, and Anne had learned to appreciate Sarah's good qualities, although her earthy sense of humour could be a little trying. But the little trollop was disarmingly honest, and Anne had come to understand why Vikki valued her friendship.

"OK – ready!" Anne called out.

Vikki and Sarah started cranking the outdoor pump. The makeshift feeder pipe – a length of garden hose that snaked across the lawn to the radiator – stiffened. Anne adjusted her sweatband, stooped and listened to water gurgling into the radiator.

"It's filling!" she announced. "Keep pumping. This thing probably holds about twenty gallons."

"Litres, mum! No one uses gallons any more."

"I don't give a toss if my bath is filled with gallons or litres so long as they're hot," Anne retorted.

The two girls pumped energetically for another five minutes. A meagre dribble of water eventually trickled from the return hose into a zinc bath that was even older than the radiator. Jack Taylor's reluctance to throw anything away because it might come in useful was coming in useful even though the bath had a small leak – hence Anne's decision that they should bathe outside.

"It's coming through, Mum!"

"Is it hot?"

Vikki held her left hand in the thin stream of rust-coloured water trickling from the return pipe. "Just a bit warm!"

Sarah sucked in her breath. "I saw him first. He's mine," she announced quietly.

Vikki followed her friend's gaze and turned around as Malone jogged up the drive to them. He was wearing white shorts and a sweat-clinging T-shirt. He stopped and surveyed them, breathing easily. It seemed to Sarah that his wide-set eyes were swallowing them up. Her inclination was to do the same to him but not with her eyes.

"Good morning, ladies. I'm looking for Victoria Taylor."

"Can I help?" Anne asked, approaching. "I'm Vikki's mother."

Malone produced his warrant card and introduced himself. He smiled at Vikki. "I saw you both outside Ellen Duncan's shop on Sunday, and I don't need to be much of a detective to deduce that you must be Victoria."

Anne looked worried. "What have you done, Vikki?"

"She hasn't done anything, Mrs Taylor. I called at St Catherine's but the form mistress said that she'd been away."

"She's been ill," said Anne severely. "But she's going back tomorrow."

"Mum . . ."

"Tomorrow," Anne repeated firmly. "What do you want with her, Mr Malone?"

The police officer looked thoughtfully at Vikki. She stared boldly back at him, hands behind her back, like a defiant schoolgirl bracing herself for a showdown with a teacher.

"Well, Vikki – it seems that you're one of four witnesses who saw a crablike device around the time the crisis started. It's possible that it was some sort of manifestation of the UFO that may or may not be in the Plague Swamp. All very speculative, of course, but I've been given the job of collecting statements."

The girl's relief was obvious. "Oh, that. It was only a glimpse."

Anne gestured to a picnic table and benches near the radiator. "She told us about it. You'd better make yourselves comfortable. We've got some tea in a thermos jug, Mr Malone."

A few minutes later Malone was drinking a mug of stewed tea and wishing he wasn't while watching Vikki produce a rough sketch of the spyder. Her left hand stayed out of sight under the bench.

"How many legs, Vikki?"

"I didn't see it close enough for that. And it was for only about a second."

"Looks like a crab," was Sarah's contribution, pressing her thigh against Malone as she leaned forward.

"It was no crab," said Malone. He took the sketch and glanced through the notes Vikki had dictated. "Is there anything else you want to add? It doesn't matter how unimportant it may seem."

"Well . . . I was daydreaming at the time. Does that matter, do you think?"

Malone pocketed his notebook and the sketch. "Probably not." He rose. "Best be on my way. Thank you for your hospitality, Mrs Taylor."

Anne looked up from the kitchen door where she was holding the radiator's outlet hose. "That's all right, Mr Malone. Dammit – I don't think this idea is going to work."

"It might be an idea to paint the radiator black, Mrs Taylor. Black absorbs the sun's heat more efficiently than white." With that, Malone thanked Vikki, said his goodbyes, and jogged down the drive.

"Wow," Sarah murmured appreciatively. "He's a ten."

"Do you think he noticed anything?" Vikki asked anxiously.

"What about?"

"My left hand, stupid! I was using it when he turned up. He's sure to have noticed."

"Naw . . . You're barking up a dead horse. Typical thick plod. I was giving him the come-on while you were talking and he never noticed a thing."

The radiator gave a sudden belch followed by an ominous gurgling rumble. Anne directed the hose into the zinc bath and gave a whoop of triumph: the water spraying from the nozzle was scalding hot.

Fifty-Two

Early on Friday morning, an hour before dawn, something happened that Harding had been worrying about.

It rained.

He heard the light drumming and rose without waking Suzi. Tonight there was no light ground fog as there had been for last two nights as a result of the high humidity and falling night time temperatures. With the sun's ground evaporation raising the humidity to such exceptional levels, he knew that rain was inevitable but it was a huge relief when it finally came. On several occasions during the last four days he had tramped towards the Pentworth Lake, estimating the daily drop in the volume of water flowing in the streams. More particularly he been watching the sky, noting the movement of smoke from the few licensed fires, to assess the convection currents within the dome. The smoke had always swung towards Pentworth Lake, where the dome was its highest, and then had been borne upwards. Sometimes the moisture-laden currents had surrendered their warmth to colder air, causing sparse clouds to appear briefly, spreading outwards – displaced by the rising air. He knew that the moisture had to go somewhere. Each day there had been more clouds.

It was only a matter of time.

And now it was raining.

He stood in the middle of his lawn in his pyjamas, enjoying the sensation of the warm, soft splashes while holding up a sterilised flask to catch a sample. He returned to the kitchen and used a swimming pool test kit to measure the sample's pH. The mauve it turned matched the colour chart for a pH of 7.5, meaning that the rainwater was neutral – neither acid nor alkaline. Nor did it leave a deposit when he dried a drop on a slide. He tasted the flask's contents – nothing like tastebuds to confirm a scientific finding.

It was the purest water to have fallen on Pentworth for many years and its effect would be profound.

Fifty-Three

"All this talk of UFOs and mechanical crabs is nothing but a crude smokescreen, Asquith," said Roscoe, staring across the candlelit table at his guest. He threw down the duplicated witness reports in contempt.

"There were several witnesses who saw something lit up by lightning flashes just before the storm broke. They were reliable—" Prescott began but Roscoe interrupted with a snort of contempt.

"The police said that it was an aircraft going into Gatwick."

"And there're the four witnesses who claim to have seen a mechanical crablike device, Adrian." Prescott fiddled with his brandy balloon stem to avoid Roscoe's cobalt-blue eyes which looked even more intimidating by candlelight. The two men were in the dining room of Roscoe's modest private apartment on the top floor of Pentworth House.

"Witnesses! Mechanical crabs!" Roscoe snapped scathingly. He picked up the reports. "The Duncan woman – a glimpse of something. The same for her apprentice, this Victoria Taylor. Malone says he saw something in the dark when he'd been running. He doesn't say that he had been on duty for fourteen hours!"

"Fourteen hours?" Prescott queried. "How do you know?"

"Ask him!" Roscoe snapped. "I went to the trouble of finding out. And as for the Price woman – something she saw through her telescope, through glass, at night, at a distance of half a mile. What sort of evidence is that? And what is it that they all claim to have seen? A fleeting glimpse of something that sounds like a kid's radio-controlled toy."

"There is the evidence of the Wall."

Roscoe leaned forward, elbows on the table, the sleeves of his gown fell back to reveal his long, bony arms. He stared fixedly at Prescott, willing his guest to look up and succeeded. "Yes – now that *is* evidence, Asquith. Evidence of God's work. A divine curse. We have been isolated as a punishment for permitting His enemies to practice their evil within our midst. There have

217

been diabolical perversions going on. Of that I have irrefutable evidence."

"I don't follow you."

"The four witnesses who said they saw this crab. What do they all have in common?"

Prescott tried to focus his mind on the problem.

"Where is the centre of the Wall?" Roscoe demanded.

"Pentworth Lake."

"Who owns it?"

"Ellen Duncan."

"Exactly," said Roscoe. "That the centre of the Wall's circle is on land owned by the Duncan woman is His way of pointing her out to us. Consider the facts: Malone is a friend of hers. He used his off-duty time to come around here making wild accusations on her behalf. Catherine Price is a regular customer, and the Victoria Taylor girl works for her as an apprentice in her witchcraft obscenities."

"Oh, really, Adrian. The Taylors are a decent family. Jack Taylor bought a couple of cottages from me. The girl lost her hand in an accident in Spain when she was a toddler. Cathy Price does design work and printing – she did an excellent job of printing the work vouchers. And Ellen Duncan is a herbalist – nothing more."

"I seem to recollect you once telling me that you suspected the Duncan woman of being behind your being dropped as a parliamentary candidate."

Prescott remembered the incident at Pentworth Lake when his suspicion had crystallised into a certainty. "Well . . . Yes."

Roscoe's fist came down on the table. "She's a witch and I can prove it! The longer we procrastinate in dealing with her, the more terrible will be the wrath of the Almighty!" He tugged an old-fashioned bell pull and returned his gaze to Prescott, his anger seemingly gone. He smiled. "I forgot to congratulate you on your excellent work during these difficult days, Asquith."

Prescott gave a disparaging wave. "Merely been doing my duty. Your own contribution has been remarkable. Your girls seem to have the milk and bread distribution down to a fine art." He chuckled. "I think their uniforms have gladdened a few hearts in the mornings now that you're delivering to the elderly. Only wish I were old enough to qualify."

The two men laughed but there was no humour in Roscoe's eyes. The ice-blue chips remained cold and calculating. "I'm considering stepping up bread production in the next two or three days, Asquith. With your approval, of course."

Prescott helped himself to another brandy. "Of course. How much grain are you sitting on?"

"Four hundred tonnes. And you?"

"A thousand," said Prescott, hiccuping. "Rented some silos on Greg Jonquil's Farm. Four thousand tonnes in the area altogether. No shortage of grain." He raised his glass. "Here's to the EU's Common Agricultural Policy and their cheques for looking after their grain . . . What will you do? Build more ovens?"

"We already have them. Disused. From the days when the estate baked all the bread for several miles around. We have more than enough methane from the pigs. We've even adapted our generators to run off it."

Prescott nodded. "Rather wish I'd thought to install digesters. Damned useful . . ."

"With the party guests that didn't get away and the security men, I now have over sixty extra mouths to feed. But there's plenty of work for them all. The fine weather's helped. Grass is coming on early and fast."

Roscoe was about to say something but the door opened and Theta entered carrying a camcorder. She was wearing a provocative, low-cut cotton dress. Prescott's eyes dwelt on the sway of her breasts as she placed the camcorder on the table. His conversation had ceased each time she had appeared to serve the two men. She gave Prescott a dazzling smile and withdrew.

"Damn pretty girl, Adrian."

"An accomplished masseuse," Roscoe observed, pouring his guest some more brandy. He swung out the camcorder's large LCD monitor screen and started the tape. "Tell me what you make of that, Asquith." He turned the device around.

The colour picture stood out sharp and clear in the dimly lit room. It showed Vikki and Sarah playing table tennis in the Taylors' garden. Out-of-focus foliage around the edge of the frame indicated that the shot had been taken surreptitiously.

"Looks like my old cottages . . . Yes – that's Vikki Taylor. Don't know who the other girl is."

"The Taylor girl didn't go back to school when it reopened," said Roscoe, looking up at the ceiling as though he realised just how distracting his gaze could be. "Look carefully and you'll see why."

"Can't see anything—" Prescott broke off and stared at the picture as it zoomed in on Vikki and panned several times from hand to hand before loosening to a medium shot. "Good God!" he muttered. "She's got two hands!"

"Precisely."

"But . . . But . . . Well – it's amazing what they can do with artif—"

"Keep watching!" Roscoe cut in, this time studying his guest carefully. Even by candlelight it was possible to discern the paling of his Prescott's expression when the picture showed Vikki jumping to catch a wide serve with her left hand. By way of celebration she bounced the ball on the table using each hand in turn like a table tennis bat.

"My God . . . It's not possible. There must be some mistake. That can't be Vikki Taylor!"

Roscoe rewound the tape. He plugged an earphone into a socket on the camcorder and offered it to Prescott who pressed it into his ear. Roscoe restarted the tape.

"It's fantastic, Vikki!" Sarah cried in the closing shot. "It's a wonderful hand! So perfectly, wonderfully fantastic! Now you've got it, you've got to start using it more!"

Roscoe stopped the tape. Prescott continued staring at the camcorder's blank screen.

"Point one," said Roscoe carefully. "That, as anyone can see, is *not* an artificial hand. Point two: the other girl's words make it clear that the hand is new. Point three: Victoria Taylor works for the Duncan woman – she's her apprentice."

Prescott shook his head disbelievingly. "Seems extraordinary," he muttered.

Roscoe rose, tugged the bell pull and removed some press cuttings from a sideboard drawer which he placed before his guest and sat down, arms folded, his intense blue eyes cold, cold.

"It's her!" said Prescott when he saw the photograph of Ellen Duncan. He read quickly through the columns. "Good heavens – I don't believe it . . ."

"Quite definitely a witch, wouldn't you say, Asquith?"

"Was it in our local papers? I don't recall—"

"Why should it be? A report on a case before a coroner's court in Yorkshire. It didn't even make the nationals. The question is, what do we do about her and her blasphemies?"

The door opened and Theta entered again. This time Prescott was too engrossed in the Ellen Duncan story to respond to her presence until she moved behind him and began gently massaging his shoulders. He took his attention off the press cuttings and closed his eyes. "Oh yes . . . That's good . . . She is good, Adrian."

Roscoe smiled and nodded his approval to the girl. "Thirty

minutes' treatment by Theta is the ideal end to a hectic day. Something you deserve, Asquith. Why don't you try it?"

Theta pulled Prescott to his feet and urged him towards the door. "Well," he said uncertainly. The girl took his arm and put it around her waist so that his hand was almost cupping her breast.

"I'll say goodnight now, Asquith. Theta will look after you. And thank you for your company. In view of this . . ." he gestured to the cuttings and the camcorder. "Perhaps you now understand why I won't attend the meeting. For me to be in the same room as a living blasphemy . . ."

"Yes – of course." But Prescott wasn't taking much notice of his host as he allowed himself to be guided to the door. His hand had shifted and a plump, hard nipple was thrusting enticingly between his fingers.

The moment he was alone, Roscoe produced a Handie-Com transceiver from a deep pocket in his gown.

"Nelson receiving?"

"Copy, Father."

"They're on their way."

"We're all set, Father."

"Don't let me down."

Faraday promised that the pictures would be perfect.

Fifty-Four

Prescott kept his word. In front of the entire Emergency Council, gathered in the Town Hall chamber for their second full meeting, he apologised to Diana and went on to praise her for the way she had organised her staff and recruited volunteers. He stated that thanks to the Town Clerk's hard work Pentworth was well on the way to having an effective administrative system. Diana stammered a grateful acceptance and subsided into her seat, touched and confused.

Malone wondered if there was anything between them. Diana Sheldon was unmarried, in her mid-fifties. A shy, retiring woman. Greying, slim, attractive although she didn't make the best of herself. Her lack of confidence made her vulnerable and therefore likely to be an eager and easily flattered victim of overtures from Asquith Prescott.

Well done, Prescott, thought Malone. *You've got the crowd outside on your side and your civil service's chief executive worshipping you.*

Before the meeting a small but eager group was waiting outside the Town Hall to meet Prescott. They had shaken his hand, taken care of his horse, told him what a fine fellow he was and what a wonderful job he was doing. And Prescott had revelled in the adulation, clapping people on the back, his booming laugh making horses skittish, and his florid features flushed pink with pleasure.

Malone turned his attention to Ellen Duncan. He was sitting at the far end of the table beside Harvey Evans, under orders from his superior not to speak unless spoken to. There was little for him to do so he contented himself with admiring Ellen's profile. She sensed his attention and looked up but he made no attempt to avoid eye contact. Ellen was the first to look away but Malone felt no sense of victory – not with this woman. He cursed himself for his childish game play and studied the meeting's lengthy and detailed agenda. Pentworth was bracing itself for a long crisis. The second Sunday without him seeing his two daughters had come and gone, leaving a dull ache which was certain to get worse.

"Right," said Prescott when the preliminaries were out of the way. "Before we get started, I have a brief statement to make. There's been criticism directed at me from some quarters because the work voucher scheme was introduced so quickly without reference to the council. It was my decision following a meeting with a deputation from the banks. They felt that speed was essential to introduce a non-inflationary scheme that would have the joint effect of financing our immediate work requirements and prevent panic buying. That's why I ordered shops to remain shut and authorised the printing and distribution of the vouchers. Early indications are that the scheme is a success. Panic buying has been nipped in the bud and we've had hardly any problems recruiting labour. The idea came from the banks but responsibility for its promulgation was mine. If there's a proposer and seconder and two assenters for my resignation, I will do so here and now, and re-stand for election."

Prescott's unexpected statement caught Ellen off guard and neatly sabotaged her own plans for a censure motion. To get four to oppose Prescott before a vote was cast would be impossible. It was essential for a vote to take place because a few raised hands encouraged others to follow suite. David would second but, judging by the alarmed expressions around the table and comments of warm support Prescott was receiving, two assenters would not be forthcoming.

Prescott glanced confidently at everyone in turn. "So I continue as chairman. Are we all agreed?"

A shrewd operator would single out Ellen Duncan's approval, thought Malone.

"Councillor Duncan?" Prescott enquired.

"No objections, Mr Chairman," said Ellen stonily.

By God, he's learning fast, thought Malone.

"Minute that, please, Town Clerk. Unanimous rejection of my offer to resign."

Malone reflected that not only was Asquith Prescott learning the art of political shafting with remarkable speed, but he was practising it with commendable skill.

"Excellent," Prescott beamed at the gathering. "First item. Air quality. Councillor Harding."

The government scientist summarised the readings from the monitoring site run by Pentworth Sixth Form College. The sharp rise in carbon dioxide, sulphur and carbon monoxide levels experienced after the start of the crisis had been checked and was falling. "But the present strict controls on CO_2 emissions must remain in place until we have a clearer idea of their effect on our atmosphere," he stressed. "We must continue to limit the use of fires, particularly wood fires, but we don't have to ban them altogether. Don't run away with the idea that carbon dioxide is a poison – it's not, it's a vital part of the carbon cycle. Plants need to absorb CO_2 in order to release oxygen. The danger is that an excess of the stuff is poisonous. So is too much oxygen. Until we know exactly how our tiny bowl of an atmosphere is reacting and recovering, then it is best if our reserves of carbon dioxide remain locked up in trees."

A brief discussion followed in which it was decided that four more supervised public barbecue areas should be established and that a leaflet explaining how to convert central-heating radiators to solar-powered water-heating panels should be published, and that a contract be awarded to Selby Engineering to produce a batch of solar cookers using Harding's four-metre parabolic satellite TV dish to make the mould.

"Made from what?" someone wanted to know.

"Papier mâché reinforced with net curtaining," Harding replied. "We've got the waste material to make the pulp, and enough net curtaining to last us until we can crop flax to make linen. The finished dishes are sealed with varnish to make them weatherproof, and the dish surface painted with aluminium wood primer. Supports and framework are made from hazel and chestnut. They are not efficient, but their size makes them effective."

The scientist looked at his notes. "We've forgotten what a marvellous material papier mâché is. Just about anything that's made out of plastic can be made out of papier mâché. It's light, immensely strong, and can be sealed with a varnish made from pine resin – shellac. Best of all, the sun can used for drying mouldings. Your Formica worktops are made from layers of paper bonded together by pressure-cooking, and Bakelite is really a sophisticated form of linen and papier mâché."

Gerald Young reported that there were now over twenty drinking-water standpipes installed in and around Pentworth, and four more public toilets would be completed the following week.

"Next report to consider is from Councillor Gavin Hobson's Agricultural Task Force," said Prescott. "Sorry you have to share minutes but we're economising on paper until production is increased. The report clashes with Emergency Council policy regarding the purpose of this meeting which is to get us through the coming month. But as the task force rightly say, we must act now to pool all vegetable seed and seed potatoes. Shops and garden centres have already handed over all their stocks. Now we need growers, nurserymen and the public to do the same."

"And supposing people refuse?" Ellen enquired.

Prescott regarded her frostily. "The co-operation with my appeals has been remarkable so far, Councillor Duncan. I'm sure most people will be pleased to hand over their seed in the common interest. I'm also sure that if problems arise, we'll be able to rely on Inspector Evans and his police force to exercise a degree of assertiveness."

Harvey Evans looked as though he were about to say something but remained silent.

"Anyway," Prescott continued, "let's see what happens first before we start needless worrying."

Ellen had a point before the report was voted on. "It includes a provision to purchase the Jet filling station's entire stock of petrol and diesel. How will it be paid for? Surely we're not using work vouchers for capital expenditure?"

"The same way that we've been paying our way for the past week," Prescott replied. "With IOUs."

"Promissory notes, Mr Chairman," Diana corrected.

"We've used them to buy up Pentworth Plant Hire's mobile generators and other equipment, and everything else we've needed," Prescott continued, eyeing Ellen with ill-concealed dislike. "All paid for at the going rate in euros. When the crisis is over, West Sussex Council or central government will have to bail us out by footing the bill. Let's worry about that when we have to."

Ellen had no further objections but by speaking out she had encouraged others to find their voices. Some farmers were unhappy with the idea of the crop-rotation practices outlined in the report because they had never used them.

"You'll have to get used to the idea," said Gavin Hobson bluntly. "We've plenty of grain in stock so we have to concentrate on vegetables. Plan your arable land this year – a quarter for brassicas; quarter for pulses – peas and so on; quarter for root crops; and a quarter lying fallow – good for running pigs and chickens on. Switch around the next year and so on until you've run through a four-year cycle. That way bugs and pests that depend on one crop don't have a chance to get established. I expect most of you have forgotten that peas and beans provide free fertiliser for follow-on crops by fixing nitrogen in the soil. OK – so you don't get the vast, unnatural yields that you've got used to but you will get healthy crops without having to buy pesticides and insecticides – which we won't have anyway." He glanced around the chamber. "And a lot of you know the difference between my eggs and the watery crap balls you mass-producers palm off on the supermarket buyers."

There were nods of agreement.

Dan Baldock's contribution, "A load of bollocks," produced some smiles.

"You have something to say, Councillor?"

"You're talking about a four-year plan," Baldock retorted. "As I keep pointing out, for all we know the bloody Wall might be gone next week."

"And it might not," said David Weir. "If we do something and it goes, we haven't lost anything. But if it stays and we do nothing, we starve – even with the four thousand tonnes of EU grain we're sitting on. It might go mouldy in this humidity. There might even be a scarcity of carbohydrates this coming winter, because what seed we have we'll have to let go to seed this year for next year's crop."

"The shortages will start to be noticed in the early summer before main crops are ready," Hobson remarked. "Be plenty of salad crops, though. People will have to change their eating habits."

"For the better," Millicent Vaughan added.

There was a silence in the room.

"Councillor Weir is right," said Prescott. "We have to assume the worst and plan our spring ploughing and harrowing now with a clear idea as to how we're going to make the best use of our land – the warm days and nightly rain means that the soil's incredibly friable so we're lucky in that respect, but there's no point in unnecessary ploughing. It's not so much sulphur pollution from diesel that's the problem – we've only just got enough fuel for this year and next year if we're careful. The fact is that we're going to rely on heavy horses in year three so we've got to start breeding them now. Councillor Weir has a pair of Suffolk Punch stallions and I've got a mare, and I know of two other mares."

"Horse-drawn ploughing," Baldock muttered in contempt when it was agreed that a heavy horse breeding programme should be implemented.

"We've done it for several hundred years," David countered. "The skills aren't dead." He grinned. "I came second in the ploughing contest last year. Five years ago the only ploughs I'd ever seen were on pub signs."

"It's going to be hard," said Prescott, "but we have to rethink our farming policy from scratch. We're back to the old system whereby the farms around the town fed the town. I've got around ten thousand chickens in my deep litter sheds; the Longs have around another forty thousand in their batteries. Pentworth doesn't need fifty thousand layers and we won't be getting feed for them anyway."

"An initial glut of boiled chicken," a councillor commented.

"We can use a lot of them to clear land for cultivation," said Gavin Hobson. "Fence a couple of hectares, dump a couple of hundred chickens on it, and they'll turn it into hard, bare earth for brassicas for free in no time without using weedkiller. They'll fertilise it for free at the same time, too, and you'll get top-quality eggs while they're doing it. Turn your weeds into eggs, I say." He glowered around the assembly, ready for an argument but it wasn't forthcoming.

"An excellent point," said Prescott expansively. "There you have it, ladies and gentlemen. Our market is no longer the size of a continent. We have to start relearning old techniques for raising and storing crops that most of us have forgotten. Growing sugar beet, storing potatoes in earth clamps, carrots in sand beds, and so on."

Health was the next item on the agenda. Millicent outlined her concerns. She pointed out that Pentworth did not have large reserves of drugs, vaccines and antibiotics. In that respect the community had been pitchforked back into the nineteenth century. But it did have one distinct advantage: the possession of the certain knowledge that pure drinking water, clean air, good diet, sanitation and housing were the most powerful weapons of all against epidemics. Clean air, sanitation and the water supply were being taken care of, therefore she proposed that a team of inspectors be trained to oversee the communal cooking facilities and visit private houses where they were cooking for several families.

"We'd best call them advisers – not inspectors," said Prescott. "At the moment everything is being done on a voluntary basis. It would be better to call them advisers until our plans have legislative teeth."

How long before that happens? Malone wondered.

The meeting lasted through into the warm afternoon and looked like it might outlast the daylight but at no time did it drag – there was an enthusiastic flow of ideas that were acted on swiftly. Millicent Vaughan and her colleagues were tasked with setting up a hospital and rounding up drugs. A working party was to be established to produce a whole shoal of guidelines ranging from refuse separation by householders for recycling, to the registration of ponies and all horse-drawn vehicles.

Ellen agreed to expand her herbal remedy production and was voted the necessary funding in the form of an allocation of work vouchers that would enable her to 'buy' labour to bring more of her land under cultivation.

The Freezer Fare supermarket had already been set up as a food-distribution centre; now there was to be a supplies depot, and there would be an appeal for the voluntary donation of books and journals, particularly reference and technical works, for the expansion of Pentworth Library into a learning centre with an increased permanent staff.

"That may well turn out to be the most important measure we've agreed on," was Harding's comment when the vote was passed. "We need a repository for all our learning. I've got about ten years' back numbers of the *New Scientist* that my wife's keen for me to find a home for."

"Next item," said Prescott briskly. "Radio Pentworth is our vital link with the people. Councillor Harding has proposed setting up a depot where people can swap their radio batteries for recharged batteries. Councillor Harding."

"It's one of the simplest things we have to do," said Harding. "All that's needed is about ten car batteries, a well-ventilated room, and use of a one-kilowatt generator for about four hours per week. We've several competent electricians who can trickle charge banks of ni-cad batteries and ordinary batteries. In fact the care of our stock of ni-cads and dry cells is vital. It would be better if the task was in good hands."

The proposal went through without dissent. Exhaustion was creeping in. The lengthening list of responsibilities falling on Diana's shoulders appeared to worry her. Malone noticed that she had shuffled her notes. Although he couldn't read them from where he was sitting, he caught a brief glimpse of the top document which appeared to consist of a single typewritten paragraph.

"Mr Chairman," said Diana hesitantly. "I've only done a rough calculation, but it looks like I'm going to need an admin staff of at least two hundred, and much bigger offices."

"Seems reasonable," said Prescott, looking around the table. "We're having to shoulder the responsibilities of central government and county council. Suggestions anyone? Town Clerk?"

Diana looked down at her notes and Malone's suspicions hardened. This was a set up.

"How about the old Court House in Market Square?" she suggested. "Four floors. It's been empty for the last two years. It's big enough to put everything in there: all the government offices and the library. The old courtroom could be used as a magistrates' court and council chamber. Mothercare next door aren't using their upper floors so we could take those over as well if necessary. And without telephones, it would be a good idea if all government departments were centralised." It was longest statement that the Town Clerk had ever delivered. Malone estimated that its length matched the length of her typed paragraph.

"Suggestions?" Prescott glanced around the table. "OK. We requisition the old Court House. I suggest we temporarily rename it Government House." He moved on to the next item without inviting discussion.

Set up – definite, Malone decided, and wondered what else would be sprung on the meeting when everyone was tired.

"Policing. Inspector Evans."

Harvey Evans preferred formality; he didn't have to stand yet he rose to deliver a carefully worded three-page report that had taken him half the night to write and had cost two candles. "That looks ominous, Inspector," said Prescott before the police officer had a chance to speak. "Could we have a summary, please. It's been a long day."

Evans was thrown. "I wanted the council to be informed of all the—"

"The Town Clerk will incorporate your report as an appendix in the minutes. We know that you're desperately under-manned. That's the first page taken care of. Yes?"

Evans managed a nod but Prescott jumped in before the police officer could continue. "And that there's been a spate of petty crime and a serious crime with that raid on Radlett's tobacconists. Town Clerk – minute a unanimous vote of thanks to Inspector Harvey Evans and his force for their tremendous efforts during this crisis. He deserves our full support therefore I propose that we hold urgent discussions with him to determine ways and means of expanding the police force. You've all had a lot dumped on your plates today so, if everyone is in agreement, I'll be happy to look into the problem with him."

Ellen was incensed. It looked like it was going to go through on another of Prescott's on-the-nod votes. She was on her feet, eyes blazing. "Mr Chairman! This is unconstitutional! Such an important matter *must* be discussed in open council!"

Prescott looked genuinely taken back. Either that or he was a better actor than Ellen realised. "Unconstitutional, Councillor? All

Inspector Evans and I are going to do is discuss ways and means of recruiting additional special constables. There is already a procedure in place whereby the Sector Inspector or Division Commander can submit the names of candidates to the Chief Constable for approval. Is that not correct, Inspector Evans?"

"That's correct, Mr Chairman." Even before he had finished speaking, Evans realised that his confirmation of the special constable selection procedure sounded like his approval of Prescott's overall plan. "But I would like to add—"

"Unfortunately, Councillor Duncan," Prescott continued, ignoring Evans, "Sussex Police's HQ is in Lewes so it might as well be on the moon. There can be nothing constitutionally amiss with Inspector Evans and myself coming up with a plan to strengthen the police force and putting it to the next full meeting." The motion was proposed, seconded, and passed with only Ellen's vote against. David's blood would've curdled in his veins had he the courage to look at her.

"Last point," said Prescott, his new-found astuteness ensuring that there wasn't a hint of a gloat in his smile when he looked at Ellen. "We need someone on hand to help deal with the thousand and one day-to-day problems that have been cropping up. I propose being in Government House every day during working hours to help with the smooth running of things. I'm more fortunate than most in having an excellent manager to run my farms."

Ellen snorted.

"Oh, please don't worry, Councillor Duncan – I shall be providing my services free of charge."

"Paying you what you're worth would be a very small burden on our resources, Mr Chairman."

Baldock had a sudden nasal problem. What little that could be seen of his face, hidden behind the handkerchief he had snatched from his pocket, was turning an alarming shade of pink.

Wonderful, thought Malone. *Oh hell – this woman is really getting to me.*

Prescott continued smiling blandly at Ellen but this time his eyes told her that he had filed that one away for future reference. "Let's take a vote on it," he said affably.

As before, one vote against.

Prescott beamed. "Thank you, ladies and gentlemen. We've got through everything in seven hours. A most gruelling day. You're all entitled to forty euros each for today's work."

While Prescott wound up the meeting and thanked everyone, David suffered another venomous curse whispered in his ear that, had Ellen had the powers to make it work, would have resulted in two important bits of him putrefying and dropping off.

Fifty-Five

Outside the Town Hall Ellen went for David like an unleashed Rottweiler that had endured a month of insults from a loathed postman. "You stupid, stupid idiot!" she railed. "Do you have any idea what you've done? Do you? You and all the other sheep have given that shit unlimited powers! He can reorganise the police force how he sees fit. You've even given him a presidential office, and as for his dealing with day-to-day problems, who decides what are day-to-day problems? He does! Like this Mickey Mouse luncheon voucher money we're stuck with. Was that decided democratically by the council? Was it hell!"

"It was something the banks—"

"Miss Duncan."

Ellen spun around. Malone was looking down at her. He smiled at David, and said quietly in Ellen's ear, "Well done, Miss Duncan. If I had voting rights in there, they would've been for you."

Ellen's answer took even the phlegmatic Malone by surprise. She threw her arms around his neck and kissed him passionately, pressing her breasts against his chest and grinding her pelvis against him in a response-provoking and decidedly unladylike manner. Malone judged that Ellen wasn't given to such overt displays in public. Having missed nothing of the tension between her and David Weir in the council chamber, he decided that its purpose was to shock the farmer into an appreciation of her anger. Much as he disliked being used, he found this sort of abuse tolerable. Some nearby youths tending horses whistled and announced their availability for similar ill-treatment.

"Thank you, Mr Malone," said Ellen stepping back and deriving satisfaction from David's surprised expression. "It's good to feel that there are some real men about."

"I'd be pleased to be of service to you at any time, Miss Duncan," was Malone's bland reply.

Ellen met his wide-set eyes and realised that he was in earnest. "Good," she said lightly to cover her momentary confusion. "Then

232

you'll join us for a beer in the Crown? David's paying. *Mr Baldock!*"
Escape was useless; Ellen had grabbed the passing pig farmer by the
arm. "Why, Mr Baldock?" she demanded.

Her victim was expecting this and had his excuses ready. "Because
it's been a long day. Because I was tired. Because the pain in the
arse from my chair was bigger than the pain in the arse in the
other chair."

"Your comfort and convenience comes before the interests of
those who elected you?" Ellen's tone was scathing.

"Prescott has given himself a shitty job," Baldock replied. "Who
better than a shit to do it? He's too stupid to do it properly. There'll
be a vote of confidence at the next meeting or the one after and he'll
be out."

"And you'll be in. You're Deputy Chairman."

"Like hell I will," Baldock growled.

There was a sudden commotion behind. Prescott had emerged into
the late-afternoon sunlight to be greeted by his coterie of admirers.
The reins of his horse were thrust into hands. He swung his heavy
frame easily into the saddle and waved to his fans.

"Lots of important matters thrashed out," he boomed in answer
to a barrage of questions. "I'll be talking to you all at nine o'clock
tonight." He rode off down the street, still fielding questions.

"Dear God – what the hell's got into everyone?" Ellen asked of
no one in particular.

"If you'll excuse me," said Baldock, "I've got a lot to do before
dark." He made his escape.

"So you'll have a jar with us, Mr Malone?" David offered.

"I'd be delighted to, Mr Weir. Although the Crown has probably
sold out of beer by now."

As it happened the low-ceilinged former post house had not sold
out of draught.

"The voucher scheme seems to be working," was David's comment as he set down the tankards on the table. "It's certainly stopped
a run on everything. One of the better ideas the banks have come up
with. Amazing that they should've been thought up, designed, and
printed in a day."

"The British flair for government and organisation," Malone
observed. He smiled at Ellen's and David's surprised expressions.
"Your incredulous looks underpin my theory. The British are good
at organisation and don't realise it, even though it's a rare talent. In
a major emergency, such as the Second World War, they organise
for simplicity of social structure. A coalition government, a single

233

supply ministry; a single fuel and power ministry – that sort of thing. In prosperity and peace, they organise for complexity, as we saw back in the 1990s when thousands of messy little organisations with overlapping responsibilities – quangoes – were spawned.

"The British like to reinvent and restructure everything to create a social order so complex that only they can operate it. Which is why the police have to complete about twenty forms to bring a shoplifter to book. Or rather, we did."

It was warm in the panelled saloon bar. Someone pushed a side door open and allowed in the smell of horse sweat and hay. After nearly a century as a car park, the Crown's yard was returning to its former function of stabling.

"And now the pendulum is swinging the other way in Pentworth, Mr Malone?" David enquired. "That we're heading for simplicity?"

"Perhaps it's too early to comment on Pentworth, but all dictators, even elective dictators, like simplicity. It makes for easier understanding and therefore control. The regulations such governments issue may be complex, but administrative lines are short and simple so that the sound of a cracking whip in the form of decrees reaches all ears quickly and effectively."

Ellen sipped her drink while regarding Malone. "Decrees about rationing, compulsory direction of labour – that sort of thing?"

"Yes. But they're usually called guidelines to start with," said Malone.

"What's the difference between government decrees and government guidelines?"

Malone gave a faint smile. "None."

"They make for bad law," said David, feeling that he was out of his depth in this conversation.

"They're no law at all," Malone replied. "But that doesn't stop them coming."

"You share my opinion that Prescott is likely to become an elective dictator unless he's stopped?" Ellen enquired.

This time Ellen found the strange compulsion about Malone's inscrutable, wide-set eyes even more disturbing. She realised that she was attracted to this enigmatic man and wondered why. Her ego was such that she liked to be in control, which was why she was content with her relationship with David. He had just the right degree of malleability to allow her to have her own way most of the time without him being a wimp. But Malone, she sensed, could undermine her ego with little effort and manipulate her into agreeable submission. He frightened her.

"I was talking in general terms, Miss Duncan," he replied. "But Pentworth is being well run, largely due to Diana Sheldon. She makes an effective head of the civil service provided she isn't overloaded. I don't think she's good at delegating. As Town Clerk of a small community, she didn't have to be."

"And Prescott's got her eating out of his hand," Ellen snorted.

"Until the novelty of having an attentive male hand to eat out of wears off," Malone replied. "Which it will when her pride reasserts itself."

"Ah! There you all are."

The company looked up at Bob Harding. The scientist was clutching a litre glass of cider. They made room for him at the table, which he paid for with several packets of peanuts. "Compliments of the landlord – he thinks we're doing an excellent job and that Prescott is the right man in the right place at the right time. Just like Churchill."

Ellen groaned. "I was enjoying this drink."

Harding chuckled. "That was funny what you said about his worth, Ellen. I won't forget that in a hurry, and I'm damn sure Prescott won't." He became serious. "David – I've heard that you've acquired some sort of steam-powered generator recently?"

"That's right. A Charles Burrell showman's engine."

"What exactly is a showman's engine?"

"What most people insist on calling a steamroller, but with a huge belt-driven generator mounted on the boiler. They provided electricity for travelling fairs in the days before the National Grid."

"Sounds interesting. Is it in working order?"

"In about two to three weeks. Charlie Crittenden and his family have been working on her, but a whole load of other priorities have cropped up. Her name's 'Brenda'. The road gear, boiler and steam mechanics seem sound. But we're not sure about the dynamo. We can't test it until the engine's running. It may be that the armature will need rewinding. That will involve stripping out the enamelled copper wire, reshellacing it, and rewinding. A big job."

"How much does 'Brenda' weigh?"

The question surprised David. "Well . . . I'm not sure. About fifteen to twenty-five tonnes, at a guess."

"Would it be OK if I came up and took a look at her tomorrow morning? About ten?"

"That'll be fine."

Harding stood and picked up his drink. "Thanks, David. See you then. Good day all. Suzi's with me. Better not keep her waiting."

"Most odd," Malone commented when the scientist had gone.

"Why?" queried Ellen. "It's his job to round up gen on all electricity generators. The only reason David hasn't mentioned it so far is that we don't know for certain that the mechanics are OK."

"My point exactly," said Malone. "It's his job to know about generators. But he wasn't interested in the engine's generating capacity – only in its weight."

Fifty-Six

M illicent Vaughan's views on home visits were such that her patients required considerable courage to summon her if their condition wasn't terminal or if they hadn't made an appointment at least a week in advance to be an emergency.

Normally icy silence on her part during a home visit was sufficient to convey her disapproval and ensure that the errant patient's condition got worse, but on this occasion, two weeks of unremitting frustration and exhaustion led to her expressing herself to Cathy Price in more direct terms.

"We've been working twenty hours a day since the crisis began – helping set up a hospital, training auxiliary staff, bullying retired staff back to work, rounding up drugs, dealing with a spate of injuries caused by people falling off or getting kicked by horses, or trying to burn themselves to death with candles, worrying ourselves sick about an epidemic. I'm having to cope with a trap pulled by the most bloody-minded pony on God's earth, and I've had hardly any sleep for two weeks. Your message said it was urgent and yet I find you looking fit, and you yourself said that you were OK. If it's another termination you want, you're out of luck – we don't have the facilities set up yet, and even if we had, I'm damned if I'd sanction their use for your—"

"If you would just listen—" Cathy began, having tried to interrupt several times.

"Listen?" Millicent snapped. "I don't have to listen! My eyes tell me that there's nothing wrong—"

"For Chrissake, will you please listen!" Cathy shouted.

The doctor jumped to her feet and seized her bag. She yanked the living room door open. "I have work to do. If you want to change your doctor, that's fine by me."

"If you won't listen, *look*!"

Millicent was about to slam the door behind her. She glanced back at Cathy with the intention of treating her to one last paint-stripper glare but her patient had done two things to make the older woman stand transfixed in astonishment, the colour draining from her face.

Cathy had stood and taken a few steps across the room towards her. For timeless seconds the two women stared at each other. Cathy was the first to speak. "It was two weeks ago," she said quietly. "When the electricity went off. My wheelchair battery was flat. I tried to reach it and found I could walk." She met Millicent's shocked gaze. "Well . . . sort of walk . . . It's getting a bit better each day. I can now manage ten or so turns around the room without having to grab something."

Millicent returned to the high-backed chair she had been sitting before she had torn into Cathy. She sat perfectly still, not taking her eyes off her patient for an instant. It was some seconds before she could bring herself to speak. "Do that again. Let me see you walk."

Cathy did a circuit of the room. There was a slight unsteadiness in her pace but she didn't need to touch any furniture or the gym equipment to maintain her balance. Her face was creased with pain or concentration when she finished – Millicent wasn't sure which.

"Can you stand on one leg?"

"Just about, now." Cathy wobbled a little but the demonstration showed that her balance was reasonable although not perfect.

She shouldn't be able to balance at all!

"I can even touch my toes. See?"

Several seconds passed before Millicent could marshal a coherent sentence. "Please sit down, Miss Price."

Cathy returned to the settee and sat. Millicent's mind refocused and she saw something that she hadn't noticed before, such was her preoccupation with her own problems. She had never particularly liked Cathy Price and her overt displays of flamboyance and sexuality – driving around the town in that ridiculous Jaguar, hood always down, even in the winter, and wearing next to nothing. It had all started, if the rumours were true, when she had taken up with some Londoner. But the doctor accepted that the young woman had worked hard, learned to live life to the full and make light of her disability. But now that vivaciousness and bravura were gone. Her face was drawn, almost haggard, and there were dark shadows under her now lustreless eyes.

Millicent reached across and covered Cathy's wrist. The response was startling; the young woman grasped the doctor's hands as though she were drowning. "When was that scan I sent you for, Miss Price?"

"Five years ago."

"As long as that? How time flies. I can't recall the details, but didn't the Atkinson Morley finally identify the damaged area of your brain that controlled balance?"

"There was some technical jargon in the report which meant 'beyond repair'," said Cathy dully. "I remember one of the consultants explaining something about undamaged parts of the brain being able to take over the functions of damaged parts. But not in my case."

"So they were wrong." Millicent paused and studied her patient. "Isn't that cause for rejoicing?"

"Rejoicing! Not knowing if it's going to last? Not knowing if a fall, or a sneeze, cough, or getting drunk, or even having sex, is going to throw me right back? Not knowing when I go to bed if I'll still be able to walk when I wake up?" Cathy stopped, choking back tears and a mind-swamping terror. "I can cope with not being able to walk – I've managed for years. It's the uncertainty . . . Not knowing . . . Not being able to pick up a phone and talk to someone . . ."

"How have you been coping since the crisis started?"

It was a deliberately prosaic question intended to shift Cathy's concentration. "The neighbours have been marvellous. They got permission for me to have my own chemical toilet, they installed it and look after it. Horrible thing but better than the public toilets, I suppose."

"They're quite civilised now. So you haven't told anyone about this?"

Cathy shook her head. And then she was close to tears again. "How could I? Not knowing if it's permanent? It's not as if I can walk properly. It hurts, Doctor. It hurts like hell, even after two weeks. I keep feeling that it's going to go away at any time – that it'll go just as easily as it went before."

"How long is it since your accident? Twenty years?"

"Twenty-two. When I was ten."

"Well, there you are. You've spent two-thirds of your life unable to walk. You're like a baby having to learn to walk without the advantages of being a baby. You're over ten times heavier than a baby; three or four times the height. Your brain is having to learn . . ." Millicent nearly lost her thread in mid-sentence, suddenly remembering using virtually the same reassuring words to a terrified Vikki Taylor two weeks previously – "is having to learn all over again, and all the dozens of tiny complex muscles involved in walking are bound to have wasted over twenty-two years, despite your exercising." She gently lifted Cathy's chin and looked into her eyes. "It won't go away. In two weeks you'll be doing somersaults – I guarantee it."

Cathy smiled. "Thank you, Doctor. You've been very kind. I'm sorry to have dragged you here."

Millicent patted Cathy's hand. "I owe you an apology, Miss Price. My wretched mouth tends to fire from the hip. I shouldn't have gone off at you like that. I really am very sorry."

An apology from the ever-frosty Millicent Vaughan! Cathy's look of surprise gave way to an embarrassed, dismissive wave. "Will you do me a favour, Doctor?"

"If I can."

"Please call me Cathy."

It was as good an opening as any for Millicent. She smiled. "Very well, but in exchange for a small favour from you. Tell me about the time you saw this spyder thing, as you called it."

"I had to give a proper statement to Sergeant Malone. There's really nothing much to say. I saw it at night through my telescope. It seemed to be following him."

"And it never got very close to you?"

"Good Lord, no. The nearest it came was about a quarter of a mile. Why do you look so disappointed?"

"Do I? Oh, nothing. Just curious."

"But I did dream that it got close."

Millicent looked sharply at Cathy. "How do you mean?"

"Please don't laugh, but I actually dreamed that it was in my bedroom."

Millicent didn't laugh but her pulse quickened. "What happened in this dream, Cathy?"

"It was only a dream. Well . . . I was in my bedroom and suddenly I felt a draught as if I'd left a window open – which I never do. And there it was at the end of my bed. A giant metal spider. Well – more like a crab really. It had manipulator things."

"And then?"

"And then I woke up feeling awful. A nice, bright morning and all the windows and doors were shut as they always are."

"Did you tell Sergeant Malone this?"

"Good Lord, no. He was only after facts."

"Can I mention it to him?"

"Well . . ." Cathy gave an unexpected smile. "He already thinks I'm a bit mad, so I don't suppose it'll hurt."

Millicent stood. "I'd better be going. You've no idea how much I've got on my plate."

"I'll see you out . . . Oh."

"What's the matter?"

This time Cathy laughed and the light returned to her eyes. "You don't know how wonderful it is to be able to say that."

"I think I can guess. So will you let the world know about your ability?"

"It's not much of a world now, is it? What will I say to people?"

"What's wrong with the truth? Doctors can be wrong, you know. Neurologists particularly so."

At the front door Cathy decided that there was no time like now and accompanied Dr Vaughan to her trap. The pony had made short work of the grass verge and was about to demolish the hedge. Cathy took his snaffle and rubbed him behind the ears. The animal nickered in pleasure.

"He seems to like you, Cathy. Cussed brute hates me."

"He likes being scratched. Just like all ponies. Do this now and then and he'll be your slave."

Doctor Vaughan boarded the trap and took up the reins. She looked speculatively at Cathy. "Do you think you could ride again?"

The bright sunlight sparkled in the younger woman's eyes. "I'm going to try as soon as I can. Looks like it's going to be the only way of getting around for a while." She hesitated. "You don't think my dream is important, do you?"

"No – of course not." Millicent flicked the reins. To her astonishment, the pony moved sedately off without need of further prompting or abuse.

Before returning to the house, Cathy sat in her E-type. She grasped the wheel, eyes closed, while imagining the throaty roar of the engine and the road disappearing under its absurdly long bonnet.

On her return to the surgery, Millicent brushed aside several matters clamouring for attention and shut herself in her consulting room with Cathy Price's file – a bulkier folder than most. Copies of the reports from two of the country's leading neurologists at the Atkinson Morley Hospital were among the more recent documents. Their findings were independent and unequivocal: Catherine Price would never be able to recover her sense of balance.

241

Fifty-Seven

As always when she was sitting in her cave, Ellen lost all sense of time. There was an indefinable therapeutic quality about staring at those wonderful hunting scenes of 40,000 years ago even though she now knew every brushstroke of those gifted, long-dead artists who could, with a few skilfully applied sweeping lines of red ochre, bring a bison to snorting, stamping life or a bloody, spear-riddled death.

But her attention was never long from the mighty life-size, woolly mammoth; the old bull's head lowered, its chipped, ancient tusks seeming to leap straight at her from the rockface as the great beast charged. The white glare from David's halogen lantern imbued the spectacular scene with the harsh reality of a bright sunlight that these artists did not have to aid their work, and yet it was as if the paintings were meant to be viewed under these conditions; the merciless light diminished nothing. It breathed a strange, surreal life into the creatures, particularly a herd of stampeding antelope, giving them weight, power, movement, sending a rippling tension surging through their graceful forms.

The lantern flicked and dimmed slightly. David put his arm around Ellen's waist and tried not to think about the tantalising pressure of the underside of her breast through her thin T-shirt. "We need the light to close up. Have you decided, m'dear?"

Ellen nodded, not taking her gaze off the mammoth. "As long as the Wall remains in place, we must say nothing to anyone about this place. I can't afford to keep an indefinite twenty-four-hour guard, and nor can you."

"I don't think the community as a whole could afford to," said David.

"So many people hate me," Ellen continued in a low voice. "To destroy this would be an easy way of getting at me."

"You exaggerate, Ellen."

"Do I? They vandalised my shopfront. And little bastards like Brad Jackson and his mob don't need the excuse of hate to vandalise anything. No . . . These wonderful paintings aren't mine, David – they belong to the world. Oh shit, I'm sounding like a pretentious little fart, but you know what I mean."

David gave her a hug and helped her to her feet. "You could never sound pretentious, m'dear, and I agree with you. They've waited four hundred centuries – they'll have to wait a little longer."

They crawled out of the cave. Working by the light of a three-quarter moon that blazed a trail of glittering silver across Pentworth Lake, they repositioned the hurdle in the tunnel opening that led to the cave and filled it in with soil. David stamped the turf home and filled the gaps. There was little to show the casual eye that the bank had been disturbed but, as a finishing touch, David whistled up his sheep and scattered handfuls of winter feed pellets so that their hooves would obliterate any signs of human activity.

"Just as well the public won't be seeing this cave," said David, sniffing. "I swear that the stink from that Chinese tree of yours is getting worse."

"It's no match for your sweat, David."

"My sweat is natural. The stink from that tree is anything but."

They trudged uphill, arm in arm, not speaking as they skirted the tumbling stream, sparking like a torrent of molten silver in the humid moonlight. Bats wheeled and swooped silently about them, feeding on the bonanza of midges that the warm nights produced. Above them the great scarp of the Temple of the Winds loomed dark and forbidding, the knotted scowl of its weathered sandstone face in full moonlight seeming to hurl a challenge at the distant and unattainable folds and humps of the South Downs as they were before Man gave them a name.

"Let's climb up to the temple," Ellen suggested on an impulse, and steered David along the path that led east. Ten minutes later they arrived at the foot of the steep, zigzag track that led to the summit.

David looked up at the sombre tor. "Not sure my legs are up to it, m'dear."

"You're turning into a young fogey, David Weir. Come on."

They emerged on to the plateau a few minutes later and stood in silence by the marker obelisk, taking in the scene: the lake, the stream below, the hills, all bathed in the moon's pallid, ethereal light, the faint glow of oil lamps from far-off farmhouse windows. Ellen stood in front of David and leaned against him, his arms around her waist while, with the lightest of touches, she traced her fingertips along the fine hairs and bold, knotted veins on his forearms. She took both his work-hardened hands and steered them under her T-shirt so that his palms gently cradled the weight of her breasts.

"Have you ever climbed up here before, David?"

"No, never. At least it's above the pong."

"It was Tennyson's favourite spot."

She idly guided David's hands so that each nipple was gripped lightly between a thumb and forefinger. As usual, this little encouragement he always seemed to need caused a little stab of irritation but she didn't want anything to spoil this moment.

"My mother used to bring me up here when I was a little girl and tell me hoary old legends about this place."

"Such as?"

"That the Beaker people used to make human sacrifices to their gods here. It was said that they used to throw virgins off the edge on to sharpened stakes below."

David nuzzled his way through her hair and kissed the back of her neck, moving the tip of his tongue along her jaw and gripping her earlobe between his teeth while his fingers started rolling her nipples in and out, with increasing difficulty as they hardened. He had discovered that this was something she liked, not as a result of any diligent research on his part, but because she had once told him – in some desperation.

"When I got interested in pre-history, I did some checking," Ellen continued, her voice catching in her throat. "There's not a shred of evidence that they did . . . Oh God, that's nice." She reached behind her and idly stroked David's hips. "But a witch was once scourged here."

"You're joking?"

"1646. An agent of Matthew Hopkins, the Witchfinder General, ordered the arrest of an Eleanor of Fittleworth. She was about my age. They brought her up here where she was stripped, beaten and raped. Then she was taken back to Pentworth and burned at the stake in Market Square." Ellen chuckled. "The buildings around the square were thatched in those days. Half the town burned down. Several local dignitaries had to pay fines because they used an illegal method of execution. In England witches were supposed to be hanged. After that the good people of Pentworth told Matthew Hopkins' rep to piss off."

"All a long time ago," David remarked. "Three centuries plus."

"You have to get time into perspective, David. There are certain to be some people alive today who were born in 1899."

"It's possible. So?"

"Their lives span three centuries."

David considered. "Yes. I suppose you're right."

"As a hundred-year-old dies, so a baby is born that will also live a hundred years or more. Four people link us with the scourging of Eleanor of Fittleworth right where we're standing. Just four people."

"I've never looked it like that," said David. "It makes it seem like it was only yesterday."

"It *was* only yesterday. Disease was rampant; children dying young; ergot-infected crops that caused healthy people to keel over and die. Cholera, smallpox. A thousand and one diseases whose causes we understand today so we no longer blame them on witches. Unless something surfaces again that causes misery and deprivation – something that people don't understand."

"Like the Wall?"

"Yes. You've been brought up in a city and probably find this hard to believe, but in the Weald towns across southern England people still believe in the supernatural. You produce a Ouija board at a party in London and your sophisticated friends will think it great fun. Produce one in Pentworth, Midhurst, and people will be too frightened to use it. And there were all those who came up here dressed in sheets to witness the 1999 total eclipse. They weren't the Bodian Brethren. The old superstitions and beliefs are still with us. Still an underlying but potent force."

"You don't have to tell me," said David with feeling. "The Crittendens are riddled with superstitions. Grandma Crittenden went berserk when a visitor took a photograph of her. She really does believe in the evil eye and possession of souls."

"A few people think I'm a witch."

"What?"

"Herbalism is often thought of as an offshoot of witchcraft. And I dare say Harvey Evans thinks I'm one."

"Why should he think that?"

They were silent for a few moments, enjoying the eroticism and closeness of each other.

"I used to love coming up here to sunbathe," said Ellen. "I never have the time now." She paused and chuckled. "The last time I did a little dance out of sheer exuberance. I'd been reading a book about a namesake of mine who liked dancing in the outdoors. I had my Walkman with me so I decided to try it. Naked. Harvey Evans saw me – he came zooming over in his microlight before I had a chance to grab a towel. Can you imagine a stuffy old biddy like me doing an Isadora Duncan stunt?"

"So it was you? We all heard about it from him in the Crown."

"Looks like it's common knowledge," Ellen grumbled.

"We couldn't prise a name out of him. Not for want of trying. All he said was that a voluptuous female with magnificent breasts was disporting herself naked on the Temple of the Winds, and that had he been flying a helicopter, he would've landed and arrested her."

Ellen laughed and brought her hands together, gently kneading him through the thick denim of his jeans.

"Anyway – it would hard to imagine anyone less like a stuffy old biddy than you, Ellen. Specially one doing what you're doing."

She suddenly turned around, pulled him close, and kissed him. "David – I want you to promise me something. This Wall thing could outlast us."

"How do you mean?"

"It could be here for hundreds of years—"

"Oh, really, Ell—"

"It could, and you know it could. I want you to promise me that you'll never reveal the whereabouts of the cave to anyone while the Wall is still there. Do you promise me?" Her fingernails were digging with unconscious intensity into the back of his neck.

David was at a loss. "I don't understand, Ellen. You sound so . . . so . . ." He groped for the right word. "Well – fatalistic."

"Realistic. You could outlive me."

"Statistically unlikely."

"But you *do* promise."

"Yes, of course – I promise."

David's word was enough. Ellen knew him well enough to have absolute faith in his integrity. She relaxed and kissed him again. When he returned her kiss, she wondered why an image of Mike Malone's brown, wide-set eyes intruded on her thoughts.

Fifty-Eight

"Fernbridge House used to be a Victorian mission hall, Mr Harding. It's been the Pentworth Museum since the Boer War," said Henry Foxley, leading the scientist down the central aisle of rosewood glass cases. Harding hadn't been able to get much of a word in since his arrival. The museum curator was a gifted talker.

"We were on the point of closure when Ellen Duncan discovered her Palaeolithic flint mine." The curator paused and pointed to a wall display of flint tools. "Suddenly we had publicity and a flood of visitors willing to pay for admission, so we were reprieved."

"If I could see your store room, please," said Harding patiently.

"Yes – of course. Bound to have some useful stuff. This way, Mr Harding."

The scientist followed the gnome-like curator and his endless chatter through a fire escape door and down a flight of stone stairs into a gloomy basement crammed with junk, or what had been considered junk before the crisis. Harding produced a pocket memo recorder and began dictating a catalogue of finds that included typewriters, sewing machines, bicycles, and even old printing machines.

"So much stuff that people have donated over the years," said Foxley. "We've never been able to exhibit a tenth of it. We give the dolls to the Doll House Museum, of course. My predecessor refused to throw anything away."

"Mangles," said Harding. "You mentioned mangles, old boiling coppers, and cast-iron Victorian irons."

"I thought you were joking."

"The council is considering setting up a couple of public laundries."

"What a sensible idea. Over here, I think."

They had to climb over bales of old magazines and newspapers to reach the far corner of the storeroom that was lit by a row of high windows. Foxley pointed apologetically to some tall display cases in need of repair, and stacks of bulging tea chests. "They're behind that lot."

Harding was impatient to get back to the installation of an intercom system in Government House. Not because of any great enthusiasm for the job on his part but because the building was well stocked with young girl clerks who were trying to come to terms with the warmth and humidity by wearing next to nothing. He started dragging the chests and cases aside. It needed both of them to haul the last and largest unit clear of the wall.

They stood staring at the mahogany cabinet for some moments. It was about the size of an upright piano.

"Well, I'm damned," Harding muttered, the girls in Government House forgotten.

"I'm so sorry, Mr Harding. I'd forgotten that the old switchboard was here. The mangles must be over—"

"It doesn't matter. This is much more important." Harding peered at an oval nameplate and read out: "*Western Electric Company. London. 1908. 100 subscriber exchange. Patents Pending.*" He pulled up one of the many jack leads from the desk panel and plugged it into one of the rows of labelled sockets on the jack field panel.

"So far as I know, it's never been exhibited," said Foxley. "That's its original position. It's screwed to the wall. Up until the beginning of the Great War, this corner was Pentworth's telephone exchange. That side door was for the ladies that manned it. The rest of the room was the mail sorting office."

Harding shook his head disbelievingly. His fingertip made a trail of gleaming, polished mahogany through the switchboard's dust. "Looks like this one's in better condition than the one in the Science Museum." He pressed his fingernail into one of the jack cables. "Insulation hasn't perished too badly, either. Could be because it's been kept in the dark. It's been here for a century?"

"So it would seem."

"Remarkable."

"I doubt if it would work now."

"Mr Foxley – these things are so simple that there's no way that they can't work." The scientist pointed to the rows of jack sockets. "Each one of those was connected to a subscriber's line. When the subscriber wished to make a call, they picked up their telephone and cranked a handle that sent fifty volts down the line to flash a light against their number here." He pointed to the jack field. "The operator plugged into the caller and asked them who they wanted to speak to. She then connected to the required number and cranked her handle – this thing. That rang the bell on the receiving subscriber's phone. If it was answered, she merely patched the two lines together on this jack field and she had two happy subscribers who found it good to talk."

"Sounds simple."

"It *was* simple." Harding studied faded labels on the jack field. "So simple that they hardly bothered with numbers. Look: the Rectory, Fishmonger, Undertakers, Greengrocer, Squire Prescott." He turned his attention to the markings on the nearby tea chests. He opened one and lifted out a small polished mahogany box that was fitted with a crank handle, a small, horn-type microphone, and an ivory-handled headphone dangling on a length of cable. "Voila! Telephones."

"No dial?" Foxley enquired.

Harding chuckled. "These were made about twenty years before Almon Strowger's automatic exchanges became commonplace. He was an undertaker, you know. He only invented the automatic exchange because he was convinced that a telephone operator in his town weren't sending business his way. The manual telephone operators in a small town had a lot of power in the old days – upset them at your peril."

"But how were these manual exchanges actually powered, Mr Harding? 1908 was long before Pentworth had mains electricity."

"Ah . . . Lead acid batteries. Big buggers in coffin-size wooden cases with rope handles."

"Ah! So *that*'s what those things are," Foxley exclaimed. "Follow me, Mr Harding."

Fifty-Nine

"**R**emarkable," said Malone when Cathy Price did a pirouette for him.

"Remarkable?" Cathy exclaimed. "It's a wonderful miracle!" She bounced on to the settee beside Malone, her breasts nearly falling out of her catsuit. "Bloody neurologists. Would you believe that they could be so wrong?"

"You certainly caused a stir in the town centre last week."

"I know," said Cathy happily. "Aren't people wonderful? All the problems and misery that everyone has and they wanted to celebrate like that."

"It was quite an impromptu party."

"Looks like it's going to be a big one in the square next Saturday." She clasped her hands together in anticipation. "A street carnival and barbecue! I'll be dancing till I drop."

"The council decided that the people deserved a special party after a month so they brought the May Day Carnival forward by two weeks," Malone commented. "Also there'll be a full moon so that people will be able to find their way home. Social events and special parties always used to be held on moonlit nights."

Cathy's eyes twinkled mischievously. "Do you reckon that you and me deserve a little special party, Mike?" She cursed herself before she had hardly finished the sentence. Such a crass, juvenile remark.

Malone regarded her levelly. "You have a short memory, Miss Price. My visit is in connection with your statement about the spyder. You gave Dr Vaughan permission to mention to me about your dream."

"You're cross with me for not saying anything about it when you first took a statement from me?"

"No. You stuck to the facts. I can understand your thinking that I might not be interested in a dream. But I am now. So perhaps you'd tell me about it, please."

Cathy recounted the events of the night of the Wall when

she had imagined or dreamed that she saw the spyder in her bedroom.

"Would you show me your bedroom please, Miss Price."

Cathy met Malone's hard gaze and decided that a suggestive response would not be well received. She stood and led the detective up the spiral staircase to her studio-bedroom. Malone took in the bed, the workstation and the remarkable views from the windows at a glance. He peered through the Vixen telescope. Cathy Price's bedroom would be an ideal stakeout.

"These octagonal rooms are fun but awkward," said Cathy. "It was easier to combine my sleeping quarters and workstation in this one room because of the wonderful views and good natural light."

"You were in bed when you dreamed that you saw the spyder?"

"Yes."

"And the spyder was where?"

"At the end of the bed."

Malone stood where she indicated. "Here?"

"Yes."

The police officer measured distances with his eye, and moved around the perimeter of the room, examining each window in turn, drawing aside the vertical blind louvres. "These are excellent windows, Miss Price."

"Top-quality glass. Optically flat. They cost a fortune."

Malone squatted and examined one pane closely where it abutted a mullion. "You should've asked for your money back with this pane."

"What?"

"Take a look."

Cathy looked closely at the window that Malone indicated. "What's wrong?"

"Look down at your Jaguar."

"Yes."

"Now move your head from side to side."

Cathy did so and was astonished at the rippling effect she saw. "Good God – that's quite serious distortion. I've never noticed it before."

"And some slight discoloration, too, if you look very closely," Malone added. His forefinger traced the outline of a large area of faint discoloration in the glass that could be seen only at a certain angle. He rapped the centre of the flawed area and an adjoining pane. They sounded different.

"Extraordinary," said Cathy. "I suppose I never noticed it before because the louvres are always in the way."

Malone straightened. "When was it you discovered you could walk?"

"It must've been a day or so after the start of the crisis. Yes – when my wheelchair had a flat battery." Cathy's eyes widened. "You don't think—?"

"Right now I don't know what to think, Miss Price," Malone cut in, regarding her steadily, "but I don't think your spyder close encounter was a dream. Somehow, it made and repaired a hole in the window pane, and it was right here in the room with you."

Sixty

Prescott was sitting in Harding's workshop, listening to the scientist's report in some astonishment. Even Harding's assistants, trying to breathe life into long defunct radio receivers, had stopped work to listen. "You mean the batteries actually took a charge? After the best part of a century?"

"After I'd topped them up – yes. Luckily they'd been well sealed and hadn't lost any acid."

"Amazing."

"Not really," said Harding. "You remember the Holland submarine that was on show at Pompey? Well, she'd lain underwater in mud for a nearly a century, yet her batteries turned out to be in good working order when she was raised."

"Wasn't there a flashlight from the *Titanic* that started working again when it was fitted with a new bulb and its battery cleaned out?"

"There was indeed."

"The Victorians built them well."

"Edwardians," Harding corrected.

"Will modern telephones work with this exchange?"

Harding looked doubtful. "Up to a point. They'd be able to receive calls but not make them. They can't send out fifty volts to signal the operator – the juice was generated by a crank handle on old phones. But there's at least thirty of them in the tea chests I looked in – possibly more."

"How about using existing lines?"

"No problem. We'd have to rig up some trunking from the main box in the High Street to the museum. About a fifty-metre run. At least a hundred man hours and that's without checking all the handsets. Some are certain to need attention. But it wouldn't be too difficult to make some. Selby Engineering can knock out anything."

"Manning the switchboard sounds like excellent work for the disabled," said Prescott thoughtfully.

"That's a very good idea, Mr Chairman."

Prescott grinned and stood. "Well done, Bob. Drop everything and get stuck in. Get Government House, the fire station, the hospital, the police station, and doctors' surgeries and vets hooked up first."

"What? Put all my team on it?"

"All of them. I'll sign the funding authorisations. Amazing. We're actually going to have a working telephone system."

Sixty-One

M alone decided that Anne Taylor was the second most beautiful woman in Pentworth. The extraordinary length of her golden-tanned legs just had to be an optical illusion due to her position.

"Good morning, Mrs Taylor."

Anne gave a start and nearly fell off the stepladder that gave access to her new cooker: a four-metre-diameter papier mâché parabolic dish mounted on a stout framework of cross-braced chestnut saplings. The huge, lightweight contraption was sitting in the middle of her lawn, aimed at the southern sky. She stopped stirring the contents of a large saucepan on the dish's cooking shelf and jumped down from the ladder. "Good morning, Mr Malone. Still jogging, I see."

"It's a good way of getting around. My apologies. I didn't mean to make you jump. I thought you would've heard my whistling."

Anne smiled at the police officer and gestured to the silver-painted dish. "It's amazing how that thing collects sound as well as the sun's energy. There's a skylark up there somewhere – I couldn't even see it, yet it was deafening me."

"How are you coping with it?"

"I'm getting the hang of it now. The first time I used it, it melted the knobs on my saucepan lids."

Malone chuckled.

"These dishes seem to be mushrooming all over the place," Anne continued. "Hideous things, but they certainly work well at this time of day."

Malone looked at the old central-heating radiator, still in the same position on the lawn, but now painted black and tilted at a more efficient angle to the sun. "And your hot-water system?"

"Absolutely brilliant. You were right about painting it black. And it said the same thing in a leaflet from the council. What a difference! Luckily we've got a big, well-insulated hot water tank so we have hot water round the clock now."

"I'm delighted to hear it."

255

Anne pulled a face. "You have to remember to turn it off at night. Otherwise it works in reverse and radiates all the heat back into space. And no proper tea or coffee. Probably a good thing – I'm sleeping better. And I've had to give up smoking – not that I smoked that much."

"I think we're all in better health now," said Malone.

"Well – I certainly feel on top of the world. And everything's growing like mad. Look at the apple and pear blossom. We're in for huge crops if we don't get any frosts."

Malone said that frosts seemed unlikely and added that the sudden explosion of blossom added to his enjoyment of jogging.

Anne breathed deeply. "It is wonderful, isn't it? The air seems so clean. I can hang washing out now without having it end up smelling of paraffin from jets going in and out of Gatwick. I started my seedbed two weeks ago and it's romping away. My tomatoes have reached the top of the greenhouse already and some are ready for picking." Anne's cheerful expression faded. "Only one thing missing . . . But – Oh well . . ." She pushed the sad thoughts aside. "I can offer you some of Ellen Duncan's nettle tea, Mr Malone. It actually tastes very good if it hasn't been brewed for two hours."

"How long has yours been brewed for?"

"Three hours."

They both smiled. Malone said that he would take a chance.

"I suppose you've come to see Vikki again about her clockwork crab?" said Anne a few minutes later when they were sitting at the picnic bench. "I'm sorry, but she and Sarah are in town helping get the May Day carnival ready. As they're both in their sixteenth year, they're allowed to take part in the main dance. Vikki's volunteered to be this year's witch."

"Good luck to her. I hope she's a good runner," Malone replied, smiling. "No. It's nothing to do with that. I expect you've heard on the radio about the increase in break-ins?"

"It's awful. Everyone's trying to pull together, and we have this to put up with. Mr Prescott said how over-stretched the police were."

Malone grimaced. "An understatement if ever there was. But prevention is better than cure, so I'm going around to outlying houses to check and advise on security." He finished his mug of tea. "Would you have any objection to my checking your house, Mrs Taylor? It'll only take a couple of minutes."

"Of course not, Mr Malone. Please help yourself. I apologise in advance for the state of Vikki's room. With Sarah staying with us, there's now two girls to keep it in the manner to which it's accustomed. You'll know what I mean when you see it."

Under the watchful gaze of a life-size poster of a Zulu warrior that dominated Vikki's bedroom, Malone found the same faint discoloration in a window pane that he had seen in Cathy Price's bedroom. The affected area was about the same size and was big enough to admit the spyder that he had nearly caught. So . . . Two definite visits by the device and two remarkable cures. There was no doubt in his mind now that Vikki Taylor's left hand was genuine and that the spyder, or rather its controllers, were responsible.

The police officer returned to the garden after a few minutes. "No problems with your windows, Mrs Taylor. All good catches. And your doors are fine. As you haven't got a door on your garage, I suggest you reverse your car in there hard against the wall. That'll make it difficult for thieves to get at the battery."

"I'll do that," said Anne, adding: "Sorry about Vikki's room. I never go in there unless I have to. Was it bad?"

"It's hell in there, Captain," said Malone, his face contorted in mock anguish. "It's taken a direct hit from a salvo of Klingon photon torpedoes." He was quite captivated by the way Anne Taylor's eyes sparkled like emeralds when she laughed. He added: "The poster's interesting. A pen friend?"

"That's Dario. Vikki's name for him. Most girls go for pop stars – my daughter likes Zulus."

"Actually, I've got two girls who refuse to accept that the dirty laundry basket has been invented. Not as old as Vikki and her friend, but trouble enough."

"Outside the Wall?"

Malone nodded, his face suddenly impassive. His daughters were always in his thoughts.

"I understand," said Anne sympathetically. "It's the same with my husband. Jack's in Saudi Arabia. Or was. I don't where he is now . . . I don't suppose I'll . . ." She made a small, dismissive gesture to minimise the pain. "Well – he used to spend a lot of time overseas, and when he was here, he was a fanatical do-it-yourselfer." She smiled wanly. "So I never really saw much of him anyway."

"Are you going to the May Day carnival, Mrs Taylor?" Malone asked abruptly.

"I don't think so. I'll listen on the radio. It sounds like it's going to be a youngsters' do."

"It's not," said Malone seriously. "It's for everyone – of all ages. I've made sure of that."

"Oh? How?"

"Other people's hobby horses can be boring."

"Well, I'd like to hear it. Look, Mr Malone – it's lunchtime. I've got some chicken stew in that pot. There's plenty for both of us. Surely there's nothing in regulations to say that you can't eat chicken stew on duty?"

Malone would've politely refused but for Anne Taylor's captivating green eyes. A few moments later he was sitting opposite her at the picnic bench and complimenting her on her cooking. The stew was superb.

Anne nodded with pleasure and glanced at the huge papier mâché solar dish. "You wouldn't have said that last week when I was getting used to it. Several disasters. You were going to tell me about your hobby horse."

Malone dipped a piece of home-made bread in his bowl. "Most people tend to look on the English pub as a cornerstone of English culture. It is in a way, and yet it has created the terrible alienation between age groups that has become a feature of English society. Pub bars are always self-service. The bartenders have no idea who is drinking what because they never venture out from behind their bars unless they're running out of glasses. The Rogers and Darrens of this world can ply their underage girlfriends with endless Bacardi and Cokes without the publicans having the slightest idea of who is drinking what on their premises."

"In France and Spain most bars take your order at the table and you're served at the table," said Anne.

Malone nodded emphatically. "Exactly. They retain control by having a waiter service, therefore it isn't necessary to exclude children. But in this country, as kids get older, they're excluded from just about everything their parents enjoy. Nightclubs, for example – not because it's illegal for them to dance, but because they have to be protected from the total lack of control of the English bar self-service system. So English kids don't go out with their parents and we imported the babysitter habit from America. They grow up accepting the alienation of age as normal and we've ended up with a stratified society that doesn't mix. Youth have their youth clubs; young adults have their pubs; the middle aged, their clubs. Young adults are the most vulnerable. They're allowed to drink and do so – heavily because that's what their fellow drinkers expect and encourage. They don't have the moderating influence of the young or old around them."

"You make ageism sound worse than racism," said Anne.

"In a way it's far worse," said Malone seriously. "It divides society at the family level. We've forgotten how to enjoy ourselves unless we're with people in our own age group and other age groups are excluded."

"A sad indictment."

Malone wiped his bowl clean. "I told the same thing to the council and the carnival committee. Both agreed with my point of view that in Pentworth we have a clean slate and that it would be a pity not to use it. So no bars tonight. Waiter and waitress service at the tables. Well – Elizabethan serving wenches."

Anne laughed. "You should've heard Vikki complaining about the blouse she's got to wear."

"She'll be waitressing as well?"

"Oh, yes. She and Sarah are hoping for good tips. She'll be interested to discover that it was all your idea."

"She copes remarkably well with her left hand," Malone remarked casually. He expected a sudden chilling but it never came.

"She's had over ten years' practice," Anne answered lightly and changed the subject by adding that Malone's banning of bars sounded like an interesting experiment.

Malone accepted the warning off and smiled. "I'd consider it an honour if you'd accompany me to see it how it works at first hand."

Sixty-Two

Prescott sat at his desk in Government House, contentedly admiring his impressive new office which had been the judges' chambers, now knocked into one room. It still wasn't quite right; the large, south-facing windows meant that the room tended to get uncomfortably hot. Underarm sweat would eventually rot the immaculate white safari suits that he now favoured as his working dress. Diana said they gave him an air of relaxed distinction. Blinds or air-conditioning were the answer. Preferably both. He made a mental note to find out if the uninterruptible power supply that consisted of banks of car batteries in the basement would be capable of running an air-conditioning unit.

He swivelled his chair and watched the bustle of activity four floors below in the Market Square. He was sure that this was going to be an excellent May Day carnival and congratulated himself on his foresight in bringing it forward. His intercom buzzed.

"Father Adrian Roscoe wishes to speak to you, Mr Chairman," said Diana.

"Splendid – put him through." Prescott pulled the antique telephone carefully across the French-polished expanse of that symbol of a vain man – an unnecessarily large and over-ornate desk, which had belonged to his father. He picked up the headphone. "Good morning, Adrian. What can I do for you?"

"You sound horribly crackly," said Adrian Roscoe curtly, his voice losing little of its richness over the antiquated system.

"Try shaking the headphone. It always works for a few minutes and then you have to do it again. Something to so with shaking up carbon granules, according to my engineers who did the installation."

Roscoe grunted. "That's better. Well – congratulations, Asquith. A working telephone system."

"You're my third call," said Prescott smugly. "It's going to make our work of effective administration so much easier. Official opening is on Tuesday. You've received your invitation, I trust?"

"I need to see you before then."

"Like when?"

"Like now."

"The carnival will be getting under way soon," said Prescott. "I'll put you back to my secretary who will be pleased to make an appoint—"

"It's an urgent matter which is in both our interests to discuss, yours particularly. I'll be around in five minutes." Roscoe hung up before Prescott had a chance to reply.

He replaced the headphone on the unfamiliar hook and turned to the window. He had a good idea of what was on the cult leader's mind and took a pair of binoculars from his desk drawer. It didn't take long to pick out Vikki Taylor's long, ash-blonde hair. She was wearing rubber gloves, helping soak chicken quarters in marinade. He focused on her left hand and noticed that the fingers were half-clenched, and when she needed to hold something using her left hand, she did so by holding it in an awkward manner against her body with her wrist. There had been a mistake, of course; the girl with two normal hands in the camcorder tape that Roscoe had him shown just *had* to be a different girl.

Ellen Duncan joined the girl and they chatted animatedly. Prescott wondered if Roscoe's justified hatred of the woman could be turned to his advantage. He had a rough plan worked out by the time Diana was showing the leader of the Bodian Brethren into his office.

"Adrian!" said Prescott expansively, slipping the binoculars into the drawer. "A rare pleasure. Please take a seat. What do you think of my new office? Impressive, eh?"

Roscoe was wearing his customary white monklike habit. He sat and trained the full power of his cobalt-blue eyes on Prescott without showing a flicker of interest in the office. "I've heard a most disturbing rumour that you're planning some sort of assault on the Wall, Asquith. Is this true?"

"Not true," Prescott replied, pleased that he no longer experienced discomfort when Roscoe fixed those hypnotic eyes on him. "But Bob Harding is hatching something."

"On your authority."

"On his own authority. We're a free society, Adrian. If a man wants to use his initiative—"

"Raising a hand against the Wall would be a blasphemy! It was placed there by God as a punishment for our sins, and will be removed by Him only when we have cleansed ourselves of the evil within."

261

Prescott had heard this before. Roscoe had taken to touring the town to preach his message from a phaeton, using his gift of oratory and those extraordinary unblinking eyes to gather surprisingly large and attentive crowds.

"He's good," Diana had reported to Prescott. "He held forth at the public loo near the fire station and I got the impression that a number of people believed him."

"So you're saying," said Prescott to Roscoe, choosing his words carefully, "that God will smite down anyone who raises their hand against the Wall?"

"I'm not saying anything of the sort, Asquith. What I'm saying is that such actions will add to the sum total of the stinking cesspool of sin in this community and make His removal of the Wall that much more unlikely."

Prescott nodded. "I understand your point of view on the matter, Adrian. Perhaps you'd listen to mine. The people want the Wall destroyed—"

"God's will is all-important!" Roscoe snapped. "What the people want is of no consequence!"

Prescott held up his hand. "They have suffered a great deal as a result of the Wall, Adrian. They do not see it in the same light as you do."

"We are winning converts every day," Roscoe interrupted.

"I'm delighted to hear it. But forgive me, Adrian, not everyone thinks as you do. I have to take all views into consideration. Bob Harding believes that the Wall has been put in place by extra-terrestrials that may be dead now for all we know. He is convinced that the Wall's physical properties must conform to engineering principles that we may be able to overcome even if we don't understand them."

"And you approve of this blasphemy?"

"I want to see that Wall destroyed as much as anyone," Prescott replied. It was a monumental lie – the destruction of the Wall would mean the end of his power and he planned to veto Harding's plan when it was put forward, but there was no harm in letting Roscoe think otherwise.

The cult leader gestured to the intercom. "Is that thing live?"

"We can talk," said Prescott.

"You remember the last time you dined at Pentworth House?"

"Indeed I do. An excellent meal."

"You got a little drunk."

"I did?" Prescott looked suitably shocked.

"Perhaps you were too drunk to recall that one of my sentinels, a rather lovely girl called Theta, took you back to her room for some massage treatment . . . I'm sorry to have to admit to this, Asquith, but a member of my staff is keen on candid photography. He's been a nuisance at times with his camera. Digital – just the thing for taking pictures in low light without flash. When I discovered that he'd taken pictures of you and Theta, I was naturally extremely angry. Imagine the fuss if such pictures got into circulation . . ."

The two men regarded each other. Prescott thought fast – his political cunning at its sharpest when his hide was on the line. He chuckled. "Please don't worry, Roscoe. They must be very boring pictures because nothing happened between Theta and myself."

"You are hardly likely to recollect what happened," said Roscoe pointedly. "You were drunk."

"Drunk in a friend's house? Dear me. I would never allow such a thing to happen. I rather pride myself on being able to hold my drink. Yes – we went back to the lovely Theta's room, and, yes – she did give me a massage." Prescott met Roscoe's eye and chuckled again. "An excellent massage, too – just as you promised. You see? I can recall your words. Naturally, seeing the excited state the girl was in, and not wishing to abuse your splendid hospitality, I deemed it best to pretend to fall asleep. On my stomach, of course. A little sex siren, that young lady, Roscoe. Why – she even tried to turn me over. But I'm a big man. So please don't worry. As I say, they must be extremely boring pictures." He paused and added, "As I'm sure you must be aware."

Roscoe had been a professional actor, therefore there was nothing about his demeanour to suggested anything other than an icy calm.

Prescott sat back and smiled blandly. His political antenna told him that Roscoe was shaken; he was pleased with himself for having turned everything to his advantage. The truth was that he had been drunk, but Roscoe had overdone the brandy – he would've gone along with the girl had he not fallen asleep. Like most seasoned drinkers, he could recall his activities when drunk. He knew he had fallen asleep on his stomach, woken in the same position, and correctly guessed that nothing had happened that he didn't know about other than his snoring.

"Next time you want my co-operation, Adrian, it might be best if you came right out with it instead of resorting to silly games."

Roscoe remained silent, temporarily wrong-footed by this unexpected political sleight from a man he had considered stupid.

"Let me guess what's on your mind, Adrian," said Prescott softly. "The Duncan woman? Correct?"

"God wants that daughter of Satan destroyed!" Roscoe snapped, recovering his spirit. "What I want is of no consequence. I am merely His servant."

"Yes – well, it may be that what God wants, what you want, and what I want, are one and the same thing," said Prescott smoothly. "For example, I could find a use for those security men you're stuck with."

"They've been useful on the farm," said Roscoe guardedly.

"That's not what I've heard, Adrian. I need a security team to guard this building, so it could be that you and I could do a little deal."

Roscoe left ten minutes later leaving Prescott feeling very pleased with himself. It was now only a matter of time before he was rid of Ellen Duncan, and possibly her lover. With those two off the council, persuading two more to stand down so that he could co-opt a couple of compliant friends would give him absolute control.

Of course, to do that would mean ruling out an election on the grounds of cost even if ten electors demanded it under the Representation of the People Act, but that shouldn't prove too difficult. Much depended on getting around Diana Sheldon.

That was the easy bit.

Sixty-Three

From the numbers arriving early to be sure of a good position, it seemed that the entire population of Pentworth was going to be crowded into the Market Square for the spring carnival.

"Looks like we needn't have bothered setting up the radio link," one of Bob Harding's assistants observed as he and a colleague tested the microphones that they had installed on the stage. "Radio Pentworth's first outside broadcast and there won't be anyone at home to hear it."

Helpers were carrying plastic garden tables and chairs from the Crown and stacking them around the square. Several consignments of folding trestle tables and folding benches had arrived on horse-drawn carts, the beasts less nervous and skittish these days having got used to the unfamiliar harnesses. Electricians were stringing coloured lights from the buildings overlooking the square and routing the supply cable to the big mobile generator parked in an adjoining street. The speakers, sound amplifiers and light show equipment that had been rented for the party at Pentworth House were also being pressed into service.

Aluminium kegs filled with raw but drinkable cider, and crates of plastic bottles of apple and pear juice were stacked around the town stocks. By tradition, the worm-eaten timbers of the ancient punishment device were still pressed into service for a few minutes every January 1st, amid much hilarity and lewd behaviour, as a ritual punishment for the first drunk of the new year. A large sign proclaimed similar treatment for tonight. The maypole had already been erected in its traditional position near the Crown. A custard pie vendor was setting up a stall. His wares had become the traditional ammunition to be used against the spring witch.

Vikki and Sarah, both dressed in denim shorts and halter-neck blouses at Sarah's insistence, had been among the helpers who had started work early that morning. Because they were under sixteen they had to do only six hours of community service at weekends before they could receive fully charged batteries from the power

265

depot for their tape players. Life without pop music was unbearable and helping with the carnival seemed an agreeable way as any of meeting their commitments. The long barbecue occupied one side of the square. Charlie Crittenden and his sons were unloading sacks of charcoal from a hay wain drawn by Titan, and a team of butchers were busy with cleavers and saws, preparing the sides of beef on makeshift shambles. Twenty beasts donated by Prescott Estates had been slaughtered for the event. Tony Warren, a master butcher who ran a family butcher's shop on the outskirts of the town, was in charge of the cooking. A big, powerful man – plagued with worries about there not being enough meat to feed a possible 6,000 revellers but delighted to have the chance to do some real butchering and cooking of prime beef. But the amateurs he had working for him . . . If the crisis continued there would have to be a training scheme.

"You're cutting those steaks too thick!" he bellowed at Sarah.

"Knife's got blunt again!"

Warren sighed and seized his steel. They didn't even know how to put an edge on knives without the aid of electric sharpeners.

"Vikki! Where the hell is that girl?"

"Right here, Mr Warren."

The butcher wheeled around. He found it impossible to be angry with such impossibly green eyes. "Go and find out what's happened to that wagon load of spuds."

"Right away, Mr Warren."

Vikki darted through the crowd to Government House. She was the messenger between the carnival organisers and Pentworth's centre of government. She no longer worried about people seeing her left hand simply because she had learned not to use it in a dextrous manner in public and always wore gloves now. There were the inevitable rumours about her having a special bionic hand that had cost her father thousands, but the few overt starers were thwarted by the gloves. Even her return to school hadn't been the ordeal she had expected, largely because her fellow pupils had been drilled by teachers over the terms into not taking much notice of her hand.

"And you think this is one of Prescott's better ideas," Ellen commented sourly to David, who was helping her on the tea stall to prepare bags of her herbal tea. Pentworth's stock of conventional was virtually exhausted.

David grinned. "Council meeting held in public? Followed by a barbie, and music and dancing? I thought you were in favour of open government, m'dear?"

It wasn't the first time that Ellen realised that she was beginning to find David's mode of address irritating. "I am. But we weren't given the chance to decide, were we? All we get now are faits accomplis. Like that requisition you received for the community to have the use of your wagons and horses for so many hours a week."

It was David's turn to be annoyed. "The rural museum isn't important now, Ellen, but the implements are." He stopped work and watched Charlie Crittenden piling empty sacks on to the hay wain. "In fact I get a real kick out of seeing my wagons being put to good use."

Ellen spotted Bob Harding's tall figure in the crowd and dived after him, telling David that she would be gone only a few minutes. She was back twenty minutes later. "Five councillors agree that we should have the chance to vote on the matter," she declared. "With your vote and mine, that ought to be enough to swing it."

David chuckled. "You mean we vote on whether or not to vote?"

"We vote to keep power with the council where it belongs!" Ellen snapped.

"Your lobbying had an audience," David commented. "Prescott is watching you from his office window."

Ellen looked up at the fourth floor of Government House just as Asquith Prescott was closing his sash window. "Bugger," she said succinctly. "I'd forgotten about his new lair. Do you think he's guessed?"

David shook his head uncertainly. "I don't know, m'dear. A month ago I would have said that he was too stupid to put two and two together and make anything other than three or five. Now I'm not so sure."

Sixty-Four

The bustle of preparations in the square below was muted when Prescott slammed the sash shut. The window tended to jam. It annoyed him that an important detail had been overlooked when the room had been prepared for him. Looking resplendent and relaxed in a fresh white safari suit, he stood gazing across the square at Ellen Duncan and David Weir for a few moments before turning to regard his visitor.

"Well, Harvey?"

The senior police officer shifted uncomfortably in his chair. Prescott's huge desk was intended to be intimidating but Harvey Evans was not easily intimidated. "I can't accept the idea, Asquith," he said bluntly.

Prescott perched his large frame on a corner of the desk and idly swung a leg. "Why not?"

"The dissolution of the police force—"

"That's not the word I used," said Prescott mildly. "I said, reconstitution."

"God dammit, man! It amounts to the same thing! I can't accept it."

"Unfortunately we're not in the position of being able to enjoy the luxury of personal choice, Harvey." Prescott pointed to a stack of papers on his desk. "Those are a whole host of council orders that need to be implemented quickly. They cover the ten per cent transaction tax that the bank working party has come up with, the requisitioning of food stocks held by growers, forfeiture of hoarded stocks, spot fines for unlicensed fires or illegal use of motor vehicles, and the handing over of all shotguns, cartridges, and CB radios. All unpopular measures and yet they must be enforced in the wider interests of the whole community. We've tried coping with the existing police force and we've failed. We don't want a repeat of the Howland's Farm debacle, do we?"

Evans did not have an immediate answer ready. The previous week two police officers had accompanied a government bailiff

268

with a search warrant to an outlying farm. The bailiff had found a tonne of seed potatoes which he decided to impound. The farmer had refused to recognise the legality of the search warrant or the authority of the bailiff. He used a CB radio to summons help and the whole thing would have turned into a major incident with serious injuries all round had Evans not ordered his men to withdraw. One of the officers was still off sick which meant that he had one WPC and two PCs on daytime response. All his other officers were committed on escort and enforcement duties.

The silence in the office was broken by the sound of the public address system in the square being tested. Evans stood and looked down at the activity below. Tables and chairs for councillors were being positioned on the stage, and more kegs of cider were being unloaded around the stocks.

"With respect, Asquith. These fun and games you're organising only add to the pressure on my officers."

"Bringing the May Day carnival forward is a big morale-booster, Harvey. And Sergeant Malone's novel ideas on the control of excessive drinking should ensure that it doesn't get too out of hand. Anyway, dealing with drunkenness is hardly a problem – nothing like the trouble we're getting with people refusing to accept the transaction tax or hand over their CBs and shotguns. You can't cope, Harvey. And you know you can't."

"There's my list of five specials to be recruited," Evans began.

"Five! What damned use are five? You said yourself that the ideal number to provide proper twenty-four-hour response cover would be at least fifty." Prescott picked up a list and gave them to the police officer. "Names and addresses of twenty volunteers that my staff have collected. Full-time. That starts to give us a sensible force with your five."

Evans ran his eye down the list. "Some of these are in my morris men side."

"Easier for training. Men you know."

"We haven't got uniforms for an additional twenty-five officers, Asquith. And before you lead off about trivialities and how great is the need for action, uniforms *are* more than merely important, they're vital. A uniform commands the sort of respect that you could never get with armbands or whatever it is you have in mind. A uniform in itself provides a large measure of assertiveness and gives its wearer a massive psychological advantage in any confrontation."

Prescott smiled. "I agree with you absolutely, Harvey. A distinctive uniform is vital." Evans gave the landowner a suspicious look.

"But providing twenty-five traditional caps, helmets, and tunics would be impossible for us," Prescott continued. "And they have to be a good fit, particularly peaked caps, otherwise they look ridiculous. You agree with that, Harvey?"

"Yes," said Evans uncertainly, sensing a trap.

Prescott sorted through some papers in a filing tray and pulled out a drawing which he held up. "How about this?"

Evans stared and would have laughed had he not been so surprised. The sketch showed a grim-faced figure wearing a broad-brimmed straw hat, a loose, long-sleeved white blouse, black breeches, white socks and black buckle shoes. He was holding a long ash staff. A shorter baton was hanging from the figure's leather baldric.

"Morris men kit!" Evans spluttered. "You can't be serious!"

Prescott looked from the sketch to his visitor. "I'm deadly serious, Harvey. Let's look at the advantages, shall we? Firstly, your morris men wear a very simple get up – very distinctive in black and white and very easy to make. The blouses can cover body armour or weapons most effectively when they're needed. The breeches can be made from ordinary trousers and dyed. The buckle shoes are ordinary shoes fitted with brass buckles. I understand that all your morris men have their own kit, and that your dance master holds about five kits in reserve . . ."

"Eight," said Evans woodenly, not taking his eyes off the drawing. "And my bagman has a spare kit."

"Even better," said Prescott. "And thanks to your scrapping of the handkerchiefs, and bringing in those brilliant sword and staff dances, everyone takes your morris men side seriously. They have a reputation for toughness and they're well disciplined. Exactly the qualities we need in our police force. I suggest that the straw hats are worn for ordinary duties and that white-sprayed crash helmets are worn when there's likely to be trouble."

Although Evan's initial instincts were to rebel at the suggestion, he was proud of the Pentworth Morris Men and knew that they were held in high esteem in the community. On reflection it seemed that Prescott's seemingly outlandish scheme had much to commend it, but he had grave reservations. "They would not have the powers of police officers," he ventured.

"Perhaps they shouldn't even be called police officers?" said Prescott expansively, sensing victory. "How about public safety officers? As for their powers, they should be no more than those of ordinary citizens in the maintenance of law and order. They could operate in teams with a police officer as their . . . What's the correct term?"

"Foreman," said Evans.

"Foreman," Prescott agreed, watching Evans closely. "So what do you think?"

"I take it that the matter will put to the full council for approval?"

Prescott looked at his watch. "Your side is opening the carnival in a couple of hours."

"The May Day fertility dance," said Evans. "They're getting ready in the Crown."

"Excellent, Harvey. Excellent," beamed Prescott. He stood and shook hands with the police officer, draping his arm across his shoulder and leading him to the door. "You've no idea what a relief it is having us in total agreement on this one, Harvey. A tremendous weight off my mind. Now, if I were you, I'd nip across to the Crown and acquaint your side with their new responsibilities."

Diana entered Prescott's office when he was alone. She closed the door behind her and looked at her boss, her expression a mixture of hope and adoration. She was dressing well now. The light summer dress she wearing suited her better than her usual somewhat old-fashioned business skirts and over-fussy blouses.

"Did you get all that?"

"Yes, Mr Chairman—"

"I've told you to forget that Mr Chairman nonsense when we're alone, Diana. Well?"

"He could've been a little closer to the intercom but it's clear enough on the tape, and Vanessa Grossman took a shorthand transcript." She smiled self-effacingly. "She makes an invaluable assistant. She's unbelievably efficient."

Prescott crossed the office and sat on the davenport. He patted the seat beside him. "Lock the door, Diana."

She did so and sat beside him, sitting upright and looking tense.

"A telephone system, a proper police force, and a special security team to guard this building, courtesy of Father Adrian Roscoe," said Prescott softly, resting a hand on her knee. Her legs were bare, which pleased him. She had good legs. "It's all coming together, Diana. You look lovely in this dress. I told you blue would suit you."

"Thank you . . . Asquith."

Prescott moved his hand along her thigh. She gave a little sigh and closed her eyes, relaxing against him, allowing her knees to part slightly. He was in no hurry; he liked to tease her.

"Where would we be without you, mmm, my little Diana?" Prescott's voice was soft and wheedling. Her answer was to grasp his hand and pull it higher, pressing herself against him with all the clumsy urgency of someone who feels that they have wasted a lifetime. Prescott kissed her. She responded – a desperate, yielding passion that had so surprised him when he had visited her home to apologise. Moments later she was moaning softly and biting his earlobe as her pelvis ground against his hand.

Prescott was a happy man; he had the world in the palm of his hand, and his chief executive officer around his finger.

Sixty-Five

The wail of anguish from the salad bar was that of a Mothers' Union commando unit who had used 200 eggs to brew a cauldron of mayonnaise that had gone wrong.

Sarah was about to commiserate when she caught a glimpse of Anne Taylor in the crowded square. She scrambled on to the barbecue for a better view. "Oh, bugger!" Her dismay equalled that of the grieving Mothers' Union.

"Oy – Miss Rhubarb Legs!" Tony Warren bellowed. "Down!"

Sarah poked her tongue out and jumped down. "That's dropped a spanner among the pigeons, Viks. Your mum's beaten me to it. She's sunk a million hooks into Mike Malone. Bang go my chances."

Vikki was alarmed on two counts. The presence of her mother at the festivities was bad enough – decidedly style-cramping, but the thought of her being with a man other than Daddy was doubly unsettling.

"But she said she wasn't coming."

"Well, she's here. Near the maypole."

A boy on a mountain bike pushed through the crowd. He was wearing the green sash of a government messenger – eminently suitable work for youths whose only skill was staying upright on a bike. He handed a slip of paper to Tony Warren.

"Right, everyone!" the butcher bellowed when he read the message. "We're lighting up!"

"Bit early, Tony?" Vikki queried.

"Order from the Chairman's office. The Health Officer wants the barbecue really hot for the chicken breasts." The butcher added moodily, "Bloody busybodies think I can't cook chicken." He thrust lumps of paraffin wax into the huge charcoal bed while bawling out some boys who were supposed to be scrubbing a mountain of potatoes.

The Mothers' Union ended their period of mourning and started making more mayonnaise.

There was a stir and some ragged cheering around the entrance to

Government House when the white-safari-suited figure of Asquith Prescott appeared. With much head patting, he chatted briefly to the school children who were being shepherded into position around the maypole by parents and teachers. Preceded by the red-coated Town Crier, he mounted the steps to the stage.

The crier rang his bell for silence and called upon the people of Pentworth to draw near and give heed to the Chairman of Pentworth Emergency Council.

Prescott stood at the microphone, beaming around, acknowledging cheers and waves of the crowd, radiating bonhomie and capped teeth. There were a few catcalls, even boos from the edges of the square, but he took them in his stride as he welcomed everyone to the May Day carnival.

"My fellow citizens of Pentworth . . ."

"Oh, Christ – a presidential address," Ellen muttered.

". . . we are all facing the most terrible problems. But you have risen to the challenge of those problems and confronted them in a spirit of fortitude, sacrifice, comradeship and co-operation that will be remembered in Pentworth long after this crisis is over. In the years to come our children, and our children's children, will look back with pride on these dark times and see them as your finest hours."

"Oh, God," Ellen complained. "Now he's going all Churchillian on us."

Some scattered jeering suggested that the anti-Prescott faction thought the same. Ellen scanned the crowd in the hope of spotting the malcontents, wishing that there were more. But at least there were some . . .

Anne Taylor turned to Malone. "Delusions of grandeur would you say, Mr Malone?" she asked her escort.

"I'd rather not say anything, Mrs Taylor," Malone replied solemnly.

Anne caught the flicker of amusement in his usually inscrutable eyes and decided that she liked Mike Malone's company. The detective returned his attention to the stage – not to the speaker, but to the people surrounding the stage. Prescott's vociferous coterie of about thirty admirers intrigued him.

"But today," Prescott continued, ignoring the ignorant fringe element – there were always some, "we are here to forget our troubles and the undoubted hardships that lie ahead. Today we are here to enjoy ourselves. Once the open council meeting is over – and I promise we'll keep it brief! – there will be food and drink and music, laughter and love, and dancing the night away! I declare the Pentworth May Day Carnival open!"

A pipe band that had assembled near the maypole struck up and the children started dancing around the maypole, under-rehearsed as always and bumping into each other. Two boys and a girl started brawling. Laughter echoed around the square.

Woman laden with baskets of spring flowers created a floral dance area near the maypole which was the signal for the thirteen spring virgins – one for each full moon of the coming year – to get ready.

Vikki and Sarah joined eleven other teenage girls crowding into Pentworth Antiques where they changed into flowing white chiffon dresses amid much ribald chatter and laughter. Mrs Williams, the antique shop's owner, clapped her hands for attention. She rebuked her charges because so few of them had attended the final rehearsal, and told them to watch the chief virgin for their cues.

"And I don't want a repeat of last year when a girl turned out to be inadequately attired. Those photographs in the papers were quite shocking."

Foxing Mrs Williams was becoming an annual tradition. Sarah was among three of the girls who had decided to forsake all underwear. Nothing could persuade Vikki to join them, particularly with her mother in the crowd. The thirteen virgins, an honorary title in Sarah's case, gathered near the door. With much moving about and swapping places they managed to pass Mrs Williams' inspection as being reasonably respectably dressed.

"Vikki!" she called. "Where's our witch?"

"Right here, Mrs Williams."

Mrs Williams smiled. "You're much too pretty to make a convincing witch, Vikki. Do you have to wear both those gloves?"

"I prefer to, Mrs Williams."

"Very well. Now for goodness' sake start your run the instant the Fool gives you the cue. Which is . . . ?

"He'll say, 'Run . . . Run . . . Run . . .' in a loud whisper," Vikki recited.

"Good. You'd better wear shoes. They've nearly sold out of custard pies."

Vikki laughed. "I can run quite fast bare-footed, Mrs Williams." Her laugh died when she remembered the night when she had fled bare-footed from Nelson Faraday. Mrs Williams clapped her hands again. "Quiet please, girls, otherwise I can't hear!"

The young children finished their dance and were hustled away.

The applause was Mrs Williams' cue. She threw the shop door open and her thirteen virgins raced bare-footed into the bright sunlight, skipping and whooping, and kicking up flowers as they ran to the maypole and gathered around it, each girl holding a ribbon. There was a stampede of youths to get into good positions. Some even climbed lamp standards; word had spread rapidly that half the girls were virtually naked.

The pipe band struck up again, this time a madrigal to which the girls moved with sinuous grace, entwining and untwining, circling each other to work a spiral pattern of coloured ribbon around the phallic symbol of the maypole. Some of them were out of step with the music but no one seemed to worry, least not the dancers, smiling self-consciously at the appreciative chorus of whistles and cheers from the boys.

"It gets worse every year," Ellen muttered disapprovingly. "Some of them aren't wearing bras, and look at the way Sarah Gale's flaunting herself."

"I am looking," David cheerfully assured her. "Actually, I think it gets better every year." It was an observation that earned him a playful dig in the ribs. He added, "God – what a lovely kid Vikki Taylor is."

On the other side of the square near the dancers, Anne Taylor informed Malone that she had once been a Pentworth May Day virgin.

Malone looked down at her. "I really can't think of an answer to that, Mrs Taylor."

The pipe band stopped playing and dispersed when their conductor heard the slow beat of a bass drum. The crowd fell silent and marshals cleared a bigger area around the Crown. Led by the chief virgin, twelve of the thirteen girls formed a wide circle around the maypole, facing outward, young breasts heaving, looking demurely down as they were showered with more flowers. For Sarah to look the most demure maiden of all was a notable achievement. Vikki remained at the maypole, dancing with an unconscious, sensual grace by herself, without music, taking hold of each ribbon in turn in her right hand to gradually unwind the work of the troupe. The double doors to the Crown's coaching yard swung open and the Fool appeared. He pranced into the sunlight, his bell pad and garters jingling, each silver bell in the form of a skull. In one hand he held an inflated pig's bladder on a stick, in the other an ancient, stick-like object that was removed from the museum once a year for this occasion. It was a pizzle whip – a bull's penis, a vicious object

276

capable of inflicting severe injuries that had been used in medieval times to drive demons from the possessed.

In all the other dances in the Pentworth Morris Men's Sussex tradition repertoire, the Fool was the collector – laughing and joking as he and his assistants rattled charity tins under the noses of onlookers, playfully beating with the pig's bladder those whom he considered less than generous with their donations. But for this pagan dance he wore a frowning mask to scare off witches and demons; this was the ancient fertility dance that had its origins in the Moorish (hence 'Morris') rituals of North Africa that predated Islam and even Christianity. It was a direct appeal to the old gods for fruitfulness during the coming year. Fruitfulness in the crops, in cattle and womenfolk – a ritual too important to be sullied with demands for money.

The crowd remained unusually silent, sensing that this time the ancient ceremony held a special significance. The people of Pentworth were alone, there was no one to help them. They had been trapped for a month behind an impenetrable wall created by forces or beings beyond their understanding. A wall whose very permanence told them that it could last many years. If the crops failed, they would surely starve. Under circumstances of such fragility of existence, it was all too easy to slip into a primitive belief in demons and witches, and vengeful gods that demanded constant appeasement and sacrifice if they were to heed the pleas of inconsequential mortals and accord them the insignificant gift of survival.

Behind the Fool came the drummer, virtually hidden behind his huge bass drum as he beat a slow but purposeful step. Following him was the hobby-horse: a towering, hellish creature with staring eyes, flaring nostrils, lips curled back in a permanent savage snarl to expose snapping teeth – its operator hidden under an enveloping black cloak. It lurched to the left and right, its fearsome wooden teeth gnashing and clacking above the heads of onlookers. Children who had been lifted on to shoulders for a better view screamed as the sinister apparition threatened to devour them.

Vikki felt sorry for them. She had a vivid memory of a time on her father's shoulders when she had shrieked in terror at the hobby-horse. She caught sight of her mother with Malone and exchanged waves while wondering if she would ever see her beloved daddy again.

There was a sudden tension in the air. The crowd pressed forward when they heard the measured beat of heavy, iron-tipped ash staffs on cobbles – a beat that kept time with the drum. Crying children were quickly hushed, and two columns of black and white-clad morris men appeared.

There were twelve of them – a full 'side'. They were all big, powerful men, four of them police officers. Their faces were grim, staring straight ahead, straw hats on straight, baldric buckles gleaming, the little silver skulls on their leather bell pads glinting and jingling in the sun as they stamped in unison into the square, sparks flashing from the impact of their iron heel caps and staffs on the granite cobbles.

The Fool danced ahead, half-crouching, leaping from side to side, sometimes confronting spectators, pushing up his mask and sniffing them up and down with much exaggerated, theatrical twitching of his nostrils. Children hid behind parents' legs when the scowling mask seemed to be looking at them.

Ellen had seen the witch-sniffing part of the dance at many May Day carnivals but this time she felt a cold, unexplainable and unreasoning fear welling up inside her.

EX2218!

The dread message flashed before her.

"Was your Eleanor of Fittleworth sniffed out, do you suppose?" David asked.

It was an innocent enough comment but its effect on Ellen was profound. In that instant the sun went out and the silent crowd became a yelling mob in rough homespun, brandishing blazing torches, and screaming abuse at a hysterical, naked young woman being driven around the square in a dogcart. The woman's raw and bleeding wrists were lashed to a crossbar that forced her to stand, her mane of once-lovely dark tresses now wild and unkempt; her thighs caked with blood, mucus and semen from the animal savagery of the mass rape she had been subjected to at the Temple of the Winds because it was believed that the semen of the righteous was poison to demons. But that treatment was nothing compared with the torture that awaited her at the stout oaken stake driven into ground in the centre of Market Square. The dogcart turned towards Ellen and for the first time she saw the face of the young woman, highlighted by the torches, and saw the abject terror in her eyes. It was a face she knew well.

Her own face.

"Ellen?"

EX2218!

The terrible scene faded as quickly as it had come, leaving the message of hate that had been sprayed on her shopfront flashing before her like a demented, subliminal neon sign.

EX2218 . . . EX2218 . . . EX2218 . . .

David sensed her distress. "Ellen! What's the matter, m'dear?"

"Nothing. Nothing. I'm fine. Just a giddy spell."

Questioning faces in the crowd were turned towards her. They were wearing gaudy T-shirts, bright tops, their eyes sympathetic. But they were the same faces as the faces of the mob in homespun.

"Ellen?"

She found herself resenting the security of David's arm around her. "It's OK, David."

He was looking at her in concern. "Can I get you a drink?"

"No – really. It was just a momentary dizzy spell. Nothing."

"You've been overdoing it."

"Maybe. But I'm all right now. Please don't make a fuss." She made a manful pretence at concentrating on the morris men who had now encircled the twelve virgins.

Still striking sparks from their slow stamping and pounding staffs, they stood facing the girls whose gazes remained demure and cast down, but they were surreptitiously watching the chief virgin because she knew the steps that followed.

The rhythm of the beating drum changed. The morris men enlarged their circle and slammed down their staffs in a spoke pattern so that each one was pointing at a girl. The chief virgin smiled coyly at her morris man and skipped disdainfully over his offered staff. The rest followed suit and became a dancing circle of fluttering white butterflies as they weaved in and out and around the morris men, their skirts flying high as they pirouetted, affording tantalising glimpses of clad and unclad pudenda. They kept this up until the prancing Fool had sniffed each girl in turn and pronounced them pure by touching their breasts and pelvis with the pizzle whip as a gesture of acceptance.

The tempo quickened. Each morris man seized a virgin to him so that the couples stood facing outwards, a pair of muscular arms around each girl while holding the staff upright which the girls also grasped to help maintain the steady, insidious pounding.

Smoke from the barbecue rolled across the square, causing a curious surreal effect as though the circle of dancers were enveloped in a primeval mist.

Ellen frowned and glanced across at Tony Warren and his helpers who were using bellows to breathe life into reluctant patches of glowing red in the barbecue's charcoal bed. She looked at her watch.

"They've started the barbecue early," she commented to David.

At that moment the Fool, who had been leaping around the dancers, 'noticed' Vikki by the maypole which she had now completely unravelled. He looked up at the freely fluttering ribbons and uttered a shrill scream.

The dancers froze, their staffs stopped pounding. The bass drum fell silent, and a shocked hush fell on the square. The Fool went through the circle of dancers and advanced on Vikki, brandishing his pig's bladder and pizzle whip like a village shaman confronting an evil spirit. He pushed up his mask and came so close to Vikki that she could smell the sweat streaming down his face, for he had hardly stopped his crazed gyrating since emerging from the Crown. He sniffed her from head to toe like a suspicious bloodhound and suddenly leapt backwards as though he had been stung. Vikki was both puzzled and surprised for the terror in the Fool's staring eyes seemed so real. No one had warned her that his acting would be this good.

"Mekhashshepheh!" he spat. It was the ancient May Day shout – used when a witch had been detected.

A solitary beat on the drum. "Mekhashshepheh!"

Another beat, louder.

"Mekhashshepheh!"

The staffs resumed their pounding on the Fool's third scream of the terrible accusation that dated back to rule of the pharaohs. And then a few in the crowd nearest the sweating morris men took up the chant in time with the drum's insidious beat.

"Mekhashshepheh! Mekhashshepheh! Mekhashshepheh!"

"Something's wrong," Anne whispered to Malone. "It's not usually like this."

The Fool backed a few paces away from Vikki, smoke swirling around him, his mask pushed up so that she could see the hatred in his wide, staring eyes. Her muscles tensed, waiting for his cue that would send her racing off on a circuit of the square.

"Mekhashshepheh! Mekhashshepheh! Mekhashshepheh!"

Suddenly the Fool uttered a wild scream and rushed at Vikki. He never gave the cue. She brought up her arm to ward off the blow but the pizzle whip struck her on the forearm. The stinging pain was all the cue she needed. The Fool's second blow struck at empty air for Vikki had become a blur of white as she plunged through the circle and down the roped lane in the crowd.

"Vikki!" Anne cried out and raced after her daughter. Malone overtook her easily.

Vikki's speed took those armed with custard pies by surprise; most of their ammunition splattered on to the cobbles in her wake but some quick-thinking youths ahead hurled their pies on the ground in her path. She skidded on the mixture of flour and water, lost her balance, and went sprawling, putting out both gloved hands to break her fall.

"*ENOUGH!*" Malone bellowed.

Youths about to hurl their pies thought better of it and looked sheepishly embarrassed when confronted by the police officer's commanding presence. Sarah and several of the morris men went to Anne's aid as she helped her daughter to her feet. Blood was streaming from a long but shallow gash on Vikki's left arm but otherwise she seemed more shaken than hurt.

"OK," snapped Malone, staring at the revellers. "You've had your fun. The dance is over."

Sarah spotted a boy who was less awed than most by Malone's hard stare. "You chuck that, Joe Collins," she warned, "and I'll kick you so fucking hard you'll be using your bollocks as eyeballs."

The boy was quickly disarmed by his neighbours and Vikki was led away. Satisfied that the situation had been defused, Malone signalled to the Town Crier on the stage. The crier announced into the microphone for the benefit of the majority who hadn't seen what had happened that the spring witch had been caught and suitably punished. There was cheering and applause.

Malone waited a few moments before pushing through the crowd and entering Pentworth Antiques where Vikki was being cleaned up by her fellow virgins and having her cut dressed. She was embarrassed at being the centre of attention and kept assuring everyone that she was fine.

"But you might've warned me, Mum," she said reproachfully to Anne. "It was just a little bit scary."

"Well it shouldn't have been," said Anne angrily. "It's meant to be fun. What went wrong? Why did that cretin attack my Vikki like that?"

The Fool entered the shop without his mask, bladder and pizzle whip. Mrs Williams pounced.

"Vikki said that you didn't give her the cue to run! What on earth got into you? Look what you did to her!"

"Vikki," said the Fool contritely, "I really am terribly sorry. I tried to give you the word but I got a sudden lungful of barbecue smoke at the crucial moment just before I charged at you, and nothing came out. I'm dreadfully sorry."

The girl readily forgave him and, in answer to his expressions of concern, assured him that she was fine. "But I don't think I want to be next year's witch," she added, smiling ruefully.

"It's never happened before," said the Fool unhappily. "Why the hell have they started the barbecue so early? Do you know, Mr Malone?"

At that moment the Town Crier's voice from the public address speakers was heard in the shop:

"And now, ladies and gentlemen, boys and girls. We start on the serious business of today. The open council meeting. You've heard the Chairman's promise that it won't last long. But first a slight change to the programme. Can we have all the tables and chairs out now, please. Yes – all of them. And will Councillor Robert Harding please come on to the stage. Councillor Bob Harding to the stage."

"No," said Malone in answer to the Fool's question. "I don't know. But I think we're about to find out."

Sixty-Six

P rescott waited at the microphone while the tables and chairs were distributed and nearly everyone in the crowded square was seated. The barbecue was well established, giving off little smoke but plenty of mouth-watering smells. Beside him Bob Harding was reading through his notes and making pencilled last-minute changes.

"I expect many of you know Councillor Bob Harding," said Prescott expansively. "It's thanks to him that we have Radio Pentworth. Also, as a scientist, he has made a close study of the Wall. He has a number of important things to say in his report to the council. Many of you have said that you'd like to ask him questions therefore I've asked him to give his report before the meeting so that you can fire questions at him when he's finished. Councillor Robert Harding."

There was applause for Bob Harding when he stepped up to the microphone. The stooping scientist was well liked. He was accustomed to addressing meetings, although none as large as this, and he spoke with authority.

"In September 1991," he began, "eight men and women said goodbye to Mother Earth and locked themselves into an artificial three-point-one-acre ecosystem in the Arizona desert for two years. Their giant greenhouse-like building was called Biosphere 2 – the Earth being Biosphere 1. It was, in many respects, similar to the situation confronting us in Pentworth. Biosphere 2 was airtight and contained everything needed to sustain life. Plants would make food and oxygen, insects would pollinate the plants, and algae and bacteria would break down waste and purify the water. The purpose of the NASA-sponsored research project (financed by a Mr Edward Bass) was to investigate ecosystems that would be needed to support crews on long space voyages, or in colonies on planets such as Mars.

"Biosphere 2 was complete with a miniature rain forest, some swamp, a four-million-litre 'ocean' with a wave-making machine, desert, savannah and marshland. There was a farm with goats, pigs, and chickens. Additionally, there were fish in the ocean, and about four thousand species of reptiles and insects in the swamp and forest. There were even birds. Everything was put in place to create a supposedly ideal environment for the eight 'biospherians' in which they would grow their own food, recycle water, while completely cut off from a sustaining outside world from which they would receive only sunlight."

Harding paused and looked up from his notes. He had the square's complete attention.

"It didn't work," he continued. "All the pollinating insects became extinct, which meant that many of the plants were unable to reproduce, causing food shortages. Soil microbes consumed more oxygen than predicted. As a result the occupants suffered from oxygen deprivation, which in turn led to violent mood swings and irrational behaviour. Trees became diseased, their roots rotted and they fell over. Water became polluted. Of the three thousand species of insects originally brought into Biosphere 2 only ants and cockroaches survived.

"The seven of the original eight biospherians who stayed in their huge ark for the two-year period of the experiment paid a price. They lost up to forty per cent of their body weight because they ended up competing for food with their livestock. For example, egg production went down but the hens ate just as much. The goats and pigs didn't breed nearly so prolifically. This meant that animals slaughtered for food were not replaced. As crops approached maturity, so the increased food supply triggered explosive growths of parasite populations that ate the crops. The biospherians could not use pesticides because that would have contaminated their water supply. They lost five staple crops and were always hungry.

"On the other hand weeds flourished, taking valuable nitrogen and nutrients from the soil resulting in the biospherians expending more energy in weeding than they were able to replace by eating their crops.

"In the post-mortem that followed, the general view of many researchers involved in the fascinating Biosphere 2 project was that the experiment was a failure because so many mistakes were made. I don't agree. Mistakes are an important element in any learning process. The all-important lesson learned in the case of Biosphere 2 was that we don't know, as yet, how to engineer a system that provides humans with the life-supporting services that natural ecosystems produce for free. *Our Earth remains the only known home that can sustain life.*

"The big problem with Biosphere 2 was its size. Or, rather, lack of it. It wasn't big enough to permit the drumbeat of nature to resonate. For example, their species of frog relied on the splatter of heavy rain to announce mating time. There was no rain, the frogs didn't breed, therefore there were no tadpoles to feed on water weeds to provide food for the carp that would be eaten by the crew. The food chain wasn't so much broken – it was never even started."

A child started crying and was immediately hushed. Harding glanced up from his notes at the sea of silent faces before him and was surprised at the close attention he was receiving.

"Walter Adey, one of the scientists involved in the Biosphere 2 project, observed that the biospherians were forced to provide a huge input of work to do the job that nature does for free. Populations of plants or animals that outran their niches were kept in reasonable range by human 'arbitration'. If the lavender shrub began to take over, the biospherians hacked it back. When the savannah grass shouldered out cactus, they weeded fiercely. In fact the biospherians spent several hours per day weeding in the wilderness areas, not counting the weeding they did on their crop plots. Adey said, 'You can build synthetic ecosystems as small as you want. But the smaller you make it, the greater role human operators have to play because they must act out the larger forces of nature. The subsidy we get from nature is incredible.'"

Harding paused. "I want you all to remember those words, 'The subsidy we get from nature is incredible.'

"Again and again, this was the message from the naturalists who worked on Biosphere 2: the subsidy we get from nature is incredible. The ecological subsidy most missing from Biosphere 2 was turbulence. Sudden, unseasonable rainfall. Flash floods. Wind. Lightning. A big tree falling over. Unexpected events that nature demands. Turbulence is crucial to recycle nutrients. The explosive imbalance of fire feeds a prairie or starts a forest. Peter Warshall, another Biosphere 2 scientist, said that everything was controlled in Biosphere 2, but nature needs wildness, a bit of chaos. Turbulence is an expensive resource to generate artificially. But turbulence is also a mode of communication, how different species and niches inform each other. Turbulence, such as wave action, is needed to maximise the productivity of a niche.

"Turbulence is an essential catalyst in ecology, but it was not cheap to replicate in a man-made environment like Biosphere 2. The wave machine that sloshed the lagoon water was complicated, noisy, expensive, and forever breaking down. Huge fans in the basement of Biosphere 2 pushed the air around for some semblance of wind, but it hardly moved pollen."

Those nearest the barbecue were becoming increasingly distracted by the smells of cooking. Tony Warren and his helpers were turning rows of chicken breasts, steaks, ribs, and potatoes on the grills. The marinade ladles were busy, sending up more smoke in the process. Ellen left David's side for a brief word with the master butcher.

Harding pointed to the smoke billowing from the barbecue. It rose above the rooftops and then drifted eastward towards Pentworth Lake.

"That breeze is doing a job that we could not replicate without a million horsepower of electric fans, and perhaps not even then, if Biosphere 2 has taught us anything. Not only is the breeze carrying the carbon from the barbecue's charcoal across the fields to feed plant life, but it's also taking moisture, such as our sweat, with it at the same time. It then rises over Pentworth Lake, and gives up its harvest of moisture to the colder air so that it falls as rain . . . Perhaps as much as a tonne of our body waste has been purified, transported, and redistributed since I started talking . . . All without any effort on our part. The subsidy we get from nature is indeed truly incredible.

"We should be thankful that Pentworth is just large enough to permit these natural turbulences and uncertainties of nature to operate – at least we have the natural water purification process of evaporation and condensation at work, we have rainfall and sometimes heavy dews.

"The three point one acres of Biosphere 2, roughly twelve and a half thousand square metres for eight men and women, sounds like a lot of room, but it wasn't. It was only one and a half thousand square metres each. By contrast, we are six thousand souls locked into a dome ten kilometres in diameter. That's over thirty square miles, giving us approximately thirteen thousand square metres each. Biosphere 2 was about seventy metres high; our dome is *nearly four miles* high at the centre, therefore the volume available to us is nearly a million-fold the volume the biospherians had. Also, as a conservative estimate, we have approximately five thousand cubic metres of water per person locked within our dome. It sounds a lot but let me sound a cautionary note – it's an infinitesimal percentage of the average amount of water per person on a global scale. Like the Earth's water, it is our only water. Like the Earth's water, we won't lose it, but we won't get any more therefore we have to take great care of it.

"And that applies to not only water, but all our raw materials. We do not know if the Wall will remain in place for a year, or ten years, or ten centuries. Therefore we must conserve and, above all, recycle. We have about a tonne of metals per person, which ought to be more than enough. But anything we make from those metals must be built to last. Obsolescence cannot become a component part of our economy. The regulations on separation of household waste before collection, on the avoidance of pollution, the strict controls on fires, may seem irksome, but by following them we are ensuring, not only our health, but the health and well-being of future generations. That we are entrusted with the present does not give us the right to raid the future."

Ellen returned to David, grim-faced. "Prescott's up to something. He told Tony Warren to start the barbecue early to ensure that the chicken breasts are well cooked."

"Sounds like a sensible precaution. You know, m'dear, your conviction that Prescott is turning into some sort of dictator is beginning to get a tad boring."

Harding finished his report. One of his assistants with a boom microphone moved into the crowd to take questions.

"Mr Harding. Will we starve if our population increases?"

"A population cannot outgrow its food supply," the scientist replied. "The ghost of Malthus was laid to rest on that point many years ago. Where there is famine, it is usually due to failures in government or in management. We've calculated that Pentworth can, with the help of heavy horses for ploughing and harvesting, double its population, and possibly triple it. Horses are vital. Mankind would not have flourished without the co-operation, and the power and stamina, of these good-natured beasts. But I must warn you that there will be shortages this year because what little seed we have must used to raise crops to provide the seed stock for next year."

"What about this hot weather we're having?"

Harding smiled. "Yes – we seem to moving towards a Mediterranean climate but with a higher humidity. Who's complaining? Seriously though, we've been watching the climate closely and it seems to be stable. Some traditional crops will flourish, others may not do so well. Crops that had to be grown under glass such as peppers, melons and aubergines are racing away in the open. Early indications are that we can expect bumper yields. The lettuces and tomatoes et cetera in the salad that you'll be enjoying soon are all two to three weeks early.

"If this weather pattern becomes the norm, it means that our heating problems next winter will be virtually non-existent and therefore our need for fires, which might lead to high levels of carbon in our precious dome of an atmosphere, will be greatly diminished. The magnificent weather is a bonus – especially with so many pretty girls around. God knows, we need something."

"Sexist old fool," Ellen muttered.

"Spoilsport," David countered.

The opening questioners encouraged spate of queries that Harding dealt with in detail and at length. The smell of cooking now pervaded the entire square and the crowd appeared to be getting restless with many frequent glances at the barbecue. The thirteen spring virgins emerged from Pentworth Antiques dressed as Elizabethan serving wenches.

Prescott mounted the stage. It was the cue for Bob Harding to wind up the question and answer session, thank everyone for their attention, and hand the microphone to the Chairman. The scientist seemed overwhelmed by the enthusiasm of the thunderous ovation he received.

"And now, ladies and gentlemen, boys and girls," said Prescott, blasting his capped-tooth smile around Market Square when the applause had died away. "I have some good news, some very good news, and some *extraordinarily* good news! First the good news." He held up a polythene bag containing a pinkish-white substance. "Salt, ladies and gentlemen. As some of you know, Ted Brewer's spring over on Macao Farm has always been slightly salty. Two weeks ago a small experimental salt pan to evaporate his spring water was set up and this residue is the result. Half a kilo of salt!"

Many faces in the crowd looked blank, particularly the younger ones. The only salt they were interested in was what they would soon be sprinkling on those delicious-smelling steaks just as soon as all this boring talk-talk was over.

"Salt is vital," Prescott declared. "Therefore we're going to build a much larger salt pan. The Romans used to pay their soldiers in the stuff – their *salarium*. That's where the word salary comes from – a man being worth his salt. Oh well – suit yourselves. The very good news is that we'll have the official opening of the telephone system on Tuesday. We have a small number of the very old-fashioned dial-less phones that work with the system, therefore we'll be giving priority to essential services although there will be a number of telephone kiosks working. Calls will be free . . ."

Cheers.

"But only because we haven't worked out a payment system."

Catcalls.

"Local calls only. You won't be able to make long-distance calls."

Laughter.

"You have to admit that the man knows how to handle an audience," said David.

"So did Hitler," was Ellen's sour rejoinder.

"And now for the extraordinarily good news," said Prescott. "We've come through a month of this curse. Thanks to all your efforts Pentworth is surviving and will go on to flourish." He pulled a typewritten sheet of paper from his pocket and held it up. "This is the agenda for the council meeting we're about to hold on this stage."

Groans.

Prescott beamed. "You've come here to enjoy yourselves. The last thing you want to endure is a council meeting, and that meat smells absolutely gorgeous." He suddenly tore up the agenda and tossed the pieces into the air. "The council meeting is adjourned! We can hold it some other time. Let's start the feast! Let's start living, everyone!"

A storm of applause, wild cheering and whistles greeted the announcement. The Bee Gees' 'Stayin' Alive!' burst from the speakers and there was a determined surge towards the barbecue.

"That," said David slowly, "was an extremely well-planned spontaneous decision." Ellen stood transfixed for some moments, unable to speak.

"Bastard?" David offered.

"*BASTARD!*" Ellen spat.

"How about 'unprincipled scumbag'?"

"Unprin— I can think up my own insults, you stupid nerd-brained streak of rancid toad smegma! How's that?"

"Not bad," said David admiringly. "But just because he's screwed you and your schemes—"

"Screwed me!" Ellen echoed in fury. "*Screwed me!* Don't you realise what that snivelling little bucket of curdled camel vomit has done?" She waved her hand at the eager queues forming at the barbecue and salad stand. "He's not just screwed me! He's screwed all of us!"

Sixty-Seven

A nne fanned herself and looked up at the few coloured lights that remained on, shining brightly against the humid night sky. The majority had been turned off at midnight to conserve fuel. Most of the light now was from flickering candles in glass goblets on each table, and a full moon edging above the rooftops.

"I'd forgotten what electric lights look like," she remarked to Malone, and closed her eyes, enjoying the music. "It was about a fortnight ago that I realised that my hand was no longer going automatically to the light switch whenever I went into the kitchen."

It was nearly one o'clock. Parents with young children, and most of the elderly, had left but the square was still fairly busy, most of the tables occupied by young adults determined to see the night out. Cathy Price was on the dance floor, seriously entwined with an admirer as they groin-wrestled to a slow waltz.

The general consensus was that the Radio Pentworth disc jockey was doing a good job, trying to please as many as possible some of the time. His evening's repertoire had been divided into thirty-minute segments of nostalgia, heavy metal, hard rock, house and garage, with volume levels ranging from loud to deafening. St Mary's striking twelve had been the signal to wind back the sound, turn off the light show apart from some coloured strobes over the dance floor, and play slower dance music to tempt exhausted couples back to the dance area.

A party of noisy late arrivals trooped into the square and picked over the remains of the barbecue. Tony Warren's worries had been unfounded; the food had lasted. Anne watched a horse-drawn bus – a converted hay wain – enter the square and pick up a few waiting passengers. She told herself that she ought to round up Vikki and Sarah and leave but she was in no hurry for the evening to end.

"You're a good dancer, Mr Malone," she said. "It must be all that jogging."

Malone smiled lazily. "I'm a lousy dancer, Mrs Taylor. I think it must be all that cider that's warped your judgement." He regarded his partner appreciatively. After they'd eaten, Anne had taken herself off to the ladies' toilets with the inevitable support group of other women and returned wearing a white slip dress that she had secreted in her handbag. It suited her golden suntan and long, straight-brushed hair.

"I hate the stuff," said Anne, opening her eyes. "But it didn't taste so bad after the first two glasses." She glanced across at Vikki, who was still taking orders for drinks. "My daughter must be dead on her feet but look at her. You must be pleased with yourself. Your theory worked. No one drunk. Kids mixing happily with parents. All age groups having a good time together."

Malone nodded to the Crown. "It's nothing new. There used to be assemblies in the Crown in the eighteenth century. Balls two or three nights a week. No age restrictions because babysitters and licensing laws hadn't been invented."

Anne yawned and apologised. "I've got used to going to bed when it gets dark, and getting up at first light. Funny thing is that I still spend as much time up and about and I'm as busy as I always was. Busier, really. I've trebled the size of my vegetable patch and I'm having to hoe weeds for about an hour a day."

"Our tempo of life is changing," said Malone. "We've been pitch-forked back into eighteenth-century England, without the impractical costumes, but with solar cookers."

Anne laughed. "And decent weather. And a wonderful radio service. Real local radio churning out news and information and swap shops, no ads, and just enough raunchy rock to keep me happy."

"Not forgetting telephones."

"Telephones." Anne pulled a face.

"Don't worry," said Malone, smiling easily. "Lines are being assigned to emergency and public services only."

"Don't get me wrong," said Anne. "The telephone is a marvellous tool. It's just that it's been prostituted into a device for blatant commercial exploitation and downloading mucky pictures. We'll have Pentworth Television next."

"Very unlikely," said Malone. "I asked Bob Harding the same question. He said that radio receivers need milliwatts of power. Even the transmitter uses only a few watts. But Pentworth would need a power station before it could have a television service."

The music changed to a ballad. Cathy Price and her partner carried on dancing.

"Well, that's something, Mr Malone. Television is one thing I don't miss. Would you think me silly if I said that there are some things about this mess we're in that I'm actually enjoying?"

"I'd say that you're being pragmatic and practical." He added, "But separation from loved ones is hard . . . So damned hard."

"No motor traffic – and clean air as a result," said Anne. "I used to have the most God-awful migraines. I've tried all sorts of diet fixes but none of them worked. But I haven't had an attack since the crisis started. Dr Vaughan said that I wasn't the only one. We're lucky that Mr Prescott took such quick action. And look at the way he got the radio station working so quickly. Did you listen to the radio play the Drama Society did yesterday evening?"

"I was on duty," said Malone. He enjoyed listening to Anne's small talk and guessed that she was alone a good deal.

"An R. D. Wingfield 'Inspector Frost' whodunit. It was very good. Wonder how they'll pay his royalty?" She broke off. "I'm sorry, Mr Malone. I must be boring you senseless."

"I promise you that you're not."

Vikki approached their table, her order pad resting on the side of her left hand. "Anything to drink, madam? Sir?"

Anne smiled. "Not for me. I apologise for my cheeky daughter, Mr Malone."

"I think she's just treating her customers even-handedly," Malone observed. "No thanks, Vikki – I'm fine."

"Bad luck, mother dear. Doesn't look like you're going to get him drunk."

"Vikki!"

Vikki fled.

"I'm sorry, Mr Malone. We shall have words later."

Malone grinned as he watched Vikki returning to the serving table. "Nothing to apologise for. I admire her spirit. And, if you don't mind my saying, I also admire her ability with her left hand."

Malone's plan to lead the conversation along lines of his making was thwarted by the DJ mixing back to a waltz. Anne kicked off her shoes and jumped up. "I haven't danced a barefoot waltz since I was a kid. If you would do me the honour, Mr Malone."

"I'd be delighted to, Mrs Taylor," said Malone, matching her solemnity. "But I fear that our recent gyrations have left me somewhat sweaty and smelly – a most objectionable partner."

"I will tolerate it as best I can with my customary fortitude, Mr Malone."

Vikki and Sarah took advantage of a lull in the demand for drinks to flop out in plastic chairs. They watched Malone and Anne dancing. Very respectably, very conventionally.

Sarah observed, "I worry about what the older generation's coming to these days. Last time I served them it was all 'Mr Malone' this, and 'Mrs Taylor' that."

"It still is," said Vikki, pumping her blouse. "I think their parents have got a lot to answer for. And it's long past my mother's bedtime. She'll be difficult and fretful in the morning. And so will I if I discover she's taken him home for breakfast. Hell – am I bushed."

"You've only been taking orders," Sarah protested. "We've been doing all the humping. Fetching and carrying humping, that is. We're going to have to 'out' that hand of yours soon, Viks."

"Don't, please, Sarah."

"You can't go on putting it off and putting it off."

The group of recent arrivals, now at a table on the far side of the dance floor, started yelling for service. Vikki groaned.

"I'll see to them," said Sarah, jumping up. "You rest and relax, your ladyship."

"Bitch," said Vikki, laughing.

Sarah took a short cut across the dance floor, dodging the couples, and approached the table. "Well," she said. "What have we here? Father Roscoe decided to let you bleeders out of your cage tonight?"

"Sarah!" said Nelson Faraday warmly. "How lovely to see you. This is Sarah, everyone. She was at the party on the night of the divine curse."

The girl exchanged brief nods with the others, but she had eyes only for Faraday, devouring him hungrily with her eyes. He was dressed in his customary black cloak, Cavalier boots, and broad-brimmed black leather hat.

"You've been hiding from me, Nelson."

"We've been busy, my precious – helping keep Pentworth supplied with milk, bread and butter."

"We have some unfinished business from that party," said Sarah reproachfully, making no attempt to disguise the fact that Faraday appeared to be bending the needle against the stop on her F scale. The women in the party were aware of Faraday's weakness for very young girls, and assailed the skinny, besotted interloper with stiletto-dagger looks that encountered an armour of youthful indifference.

"We have indeed," said Faraday, grinning broadly.

Sarah's answer was to throw her arms around his neck, push

293

herself on to his lap and kiss him with uncontrolled passion, thrusting her tongue into his mouth, only coming up for air to chew on his earlobe and whisper gross indecencies into his ear while power-wriggling her buttocks into his groin with knowledgeable provocation. Faraday laughed and stood with Sarah still entwined around him like clinging ivy.

"Mustn't let this little one down," he said, grinning broadly at his friends. "This won't take long."

He hardly had a chance to finish the last sentence because Sarah was dragging him towards a side street. Two minutes later this demented little nympho had him pinioned in a doorway in Barton's Lane, her lips pressed against his, and her eager fingers tugging down the zip on his fly. Faraday liked to exercise control but he let this little bundle of sex-starved mischief have her way because his plan was to drive her crazy once she was dependent on his co-operation to achieve the fulfilment of her impassioned cravings. He even let her pull down his leather pants as best she could and roll down his underpants. He tried to guide her head for his own gratification but Sarah suddenly straightened up, her eyes large and luminous in the moonlight.

"Do you know what I'd like to do to you now, Nelson, darling?" she whispered dreamily, fondling him with both hands.

Faraday's eyes glinted, his expression now a sneer of buoyant anticipation at the grovelling humiliation he was going inflict on this stupid, randy little cock-teasing child-bitch.

"The same that I'd like you to do to me," he replied.

"Oh – that's good," said Sarah brightly. She tensed and drove her knee into Faraday's groin with all the power she could muster. Her knee glanced against his thigh and reduced its force, but it was enough.

The sudden glaze of shock in his eyes as Sarah felt his testicles absorb the crushing impact was most satisfying, but even better was his scream of agony as he doubled up and keeled over.

"That's from Vikki," she said dispassionately. She was tempted to spend a few moments savouring her victim's writhing agony but his howls were certain to attract the attention of his friends so she took off fast, weaving around side streets to return to the square from a different direction.

Sixty-Eight

It was the first time Malone had visited Harvey Evans' home. He looked around the comfortable, book-lined, low-beamed living room with interest as he and the senior police officer sipped nettle tea. Outside the cottage's latticed windows bees buzzed around a row of hives that extended down the side the paddock. At the far end of the close-mown field was Evans' Durand 'Aerocraft Ultralight'. The flimsy two-seater microlight biplane was parked under a sailcloth gazebo that served as a hangar. Two tethered goats did the job of a mower by keeping the grass short for his landings and takeoffs. He was provided with an allocation of fuel for fire-spotting flights and survey work.

"One of Ellen Duncan's concoctions," said Evans. "Quite good. I think I'll stay with it even if we manage to grow ordinary tea."

"Evasion," said Malone.

"What?"

"You haven't answered my question, sir."

Evans smiled. "I'm now out of the rat race and you decide to start calling me sir."

"That's because I've decided to appreciate you now that it seems you won't be around any more."

Evans laughed outright at that. "My only regret is that I'm retiring before I've a chance to fathom you out."

"Let's make a start now," said Malone. "Firstly – I know that taking early retirement is a euphemism for your being pushed into resigning. I also know that you're not the sort of person to give in to a bully like Prescott."

"He wasn't always like that," said Evans. "A bit pompous at times. Hopeless with women. But always prepared to laugh at his golf handicap . . . God – how that man has changed. I can't see him laughing at himself now."

"If it's any consolation, I misjudged him as well," said Malone.

Evans was surprised. "Now that I do find hard to believe."

"True," said Malone. "I thought I was manipulating him over the first Radio Pentworth broadcast, and he ended up manipulating me. So what happened?"

Evans drained his cup. "He called me into his office and told me that Adrian Roscoe's Southern Area Security mob were to become a separate force responsible for the security of Government House and the centre of Pentworth, under the command of Nelson Faraday, who would be answerable to him. It was totally unacceptable. I said that if he wanted to appoint them as a private security team inside Government House, then that was up to him, but I wasn't prepared to accept them as police officers outside Government House – especially with a thug like Faraday in charge of them. The only thing he agreed to was that they should have a different uniform. Black.

"I told him that for every inch of concession I'd agreed to, he'd grabbed a yard, and that enough was enough. So Prescott invited me to resign. He promised me a reasonable pension, which I accepted." He broke off and smiled ruefully. "I was thinking of early retirement long before the Wall. Don't worry about me. I shall become Pentworth's biggest honey producer. My wife started the hives when we first moved here. When she died . . . Well – I couldn't bring myself to give them up. And I'm keeping my flying hours up with aerial survey work for the council."

"So Prescott has appointed himself police commander?"

Evans nodded. "He said he'd run the force with morning briefings in his office. He wants you to run the CID. I'd like you to stay on, Malone. I'd be happier knowing that there was at least one sane officer left in the nick. It'll be that much easier picking up the pieces if and when the Wall goes."

"I'll stay," said Malone. "But I'm not going to find it easy taking orders from Prescott."

Evans threw back his head and laughed. "That's rich. You've never taken orders from me, Malone. You've always acted on suggestions."

Malone smiled wryly and stood. "I'd better be on my way. Thank you for confiding in me, sir."

Malone jogged back to Pentworth, turning the conversation over in his mind. As he had suspected, Prescott and Roscoe had done some sort of deal and that Roscoe's handing over of the security team to Prescott was only part of the deal. Whatever it was, Prescott would be unlikely to agree to anything unless it consolidated his grip on Pentworth. On the other hand Roscoe's ambitions were more concerned with the next world so in that respect the two men were not in competition. Strange really: when the crisis had started, Malone had seen Roscoe as the real threat. So what did these two very different men have in common?

The answer was so obvious that Malone lost his pace when it jumped out on him like a mugger: Prescott and Roscoe shared an implacable hatred of Ellen Duncan.

Sixty-Nine

N evil Cross lived up to his name. He glowered at the three morris police on his doorstep, told them to piss off, and slammed the door in their faces. He returned to his kitchen but the thunderous hammering on the front door made listening to the radio impossible. He stormed back to his front door, determined this time to really give these buggers a piece of his mind, but it was thrown open the instant he turned the latch. He was grabbed and dragged, protesting and yelling, to his front gate.

Apart from being outnumbered, it was an unequal match from the physical point of view; Nevil Cross was a little runt and the morris police weren't, particularly Russell Norris, their foreman. He was two metres of muscle and calm assertiveness. His two colleagues held Nevil Cross off the ground and Norris kicked the householder's wheelie bin over so that a cascade of household refuse spilled on to the pavement. Even tins, which were becoming rare in domestic rubbish these days. Net curtains on the neat housing estate twitched excitedly.

"Did you listen to Pentworth Drama Society's performance of Dylan Thomas's *Under Milk Wood* on the radio last night, sir?" Norris enquired with exaggerated politeness as he rescued some tatty paperbacks from the rubbish. The question had to be repeated before Nevil Cross stopped yelling and deigned to admit that he had heard the broadcast.

"It was excellent, wasn't it?" said Norris, beaming. "Well, sir, I'm not going to ask you to put your pyjamas in the drawer marked pyjamas as Mrs Ogmore-Pritchard required of her husbands, but I am asking you to put your organic waste in the big bin marked organic waste at the end of your road. I am also requesting that you sort your refuse into separate boxes or heaps for plastic waste, plastic bottles, tins, cardboard, paper, woody garden clippings, and miscellaneous junk. And throwing away books is a serious offence – they have to be handed in to the library."

Nevil Cross's protests that how could be expected to remember

298

all that were countered by Norris's observation that the details were on the instruction sheet circulated to all householders.

"The tins are being sprayed with hot shellac resin for re-use," said Norris affably. "And as for woody garden clippings, they're ideal for pulping to make paper and papier mâché mouldings." The three morris police closed around Nevil Cross, hands on staffs, and stared dispassionately down at him. "I'm sure we can look forward to your eager co-operation in this little matter, sir. Like right now."

Five minutes later Norris's hopes were fulfilled, not only in respect of Nevil Cross's dwelling but several other houses on the estate – news of the morris men's presence had spread resulting in a sudden flurry of rubbish-sorting activity.

"Excellent," said Norris when the work was finished to his satisfaction. "Unfortunately we have to make a thirty-euro supervision charge for our time, and there's a further ten euros to cover our counselling fees as a result of the shock we've suffered at our having to deal so assertively with you."

Cross swore roundly and told Norris that he did not have forty euros.

"Not to worry, sir," was the cheery reply. "In that case we'll seize goods to the value of forty euros. We'll give you a receipt so that you can recover your goods within ten days from the government supplies depot at a most favourable rate of interest. We'll start with your radio."

Nevil Cross suddenly remembered that he had the required sum.

The morris police toured the rest of the housing estate in their pony-drawn gig and found all refuse awaiting collection to be graded in accordance with regulations. Their next call was nearby Burntwood Farm where Norris inspected a recently walled mountain of cow dung, steaming nicely in the sun.

The morris man pointed to several rivulets of brown liquid that were escaping from the base of dung heap's retaining wall and merging into one before streaming down the farmyard approach road and pouring into a drainage ditch. The pollution had first shown up on photographs taken on the recent aerial survey that Harvey Evans had undertaken for the government in his microlight biplane.

"That has to stop, Mr Allen," Norris told the farmer. "You've already had two warnings."

"But dammit, man, we had heavy rain last night," Allen protested. "I've lined it as best I can, but there's no way I can stop it."

"It *has* to be stopped from getting into rivers and streams,

Mr Allen," said Norris seriously. "And that's exactly where that ditch is taking it. You'll have to break this heap and top dress with it."

"What with? My spreader's been collectivised and I've no diesel allowance left, and no fields that can take any more top-dressing anyway, and I've been told that it'll be another two weeks before the direct labour force can build me a methane digester. Meanwhile my cattle go on producing crap."

Norris considered. He was a farming man and understood the problem Allen was facing; Burntwood Farm was a major supplier of Pentworth's dairy produce needs. His instructions were to go easy on farmers such as Jeff Allen, but to make it clear that pollution would not be tolerated.

"I'll see if I can move your digester up the list, Mr Allen. Meanwhile you'll have to spread it around the yard – give the sun a chance to dry it."

"My wife will kill me! There's about a hundred tonnes of the stuff!"

Norris signalled to one of his men who rummaged in the gig's boot and produced an envelope which he handed to Norris.

"In that case, start a new heap ASAP," said Norris. "Make sure it's properly lined and transfer about a quarter of this heap. Cover what's left with a layer of top soil and sow these."

Allen opened the envelope that Norris gave him and shook some of the contents into the palm of his hand. He picked up one of the seeds and examined it suspiciously. "Melons?"

"Marrows," Norris corrected, making notes in a book. Allen was a dairy farmer who knew nothing about raising crops. "They'll go berserk, growing on a manure heap, specially in this weather. They'll suck out all the contaminated water from that lot, purify it, and pump it into the marrows which you'll be able to sell, and you can store the surplus. They keep well if you hang them from ribbons made from video-recorder tape. Actually, melons aren't a bad idea either if this weather holds. I'll see you get some seeds." The morris man turned to leave and pointed to the oxtail-soup-coloured stream of nitrate-enriched water. "Divert that crap into a soakaway please, Mr Allen. We'll return this time tomorrow. If it's still discharging into the ditch, there'll be an on-the-spot thousand-euro fine."

The morris police drove off, leaving Allen thinking nostalgically of the days of Ministry of Agriculture, Fisheries and Food guidelines: toothless documents – the equivalent of verbal reprimands

– which allowed farmers to do more or less exactly as they pleased.

Those days were gone.

Perhaps for ever.

Seventy

Victoria . . .

V Vikki stirred in her sleep. The voice was faint, a far away murmur on the very edge of her consciousness.

Victoria . . .

"No one calls me Victoria."

A pause, then: *What are you called?*

"I can't hear you."

What are you called?

"Vikki, of course."

Vikki Of Course?

"Just Vikki."

Will you come to us, Just Vikki?

Vikki opened her eyes. Moonlight filled the bedroom. A slight breeze stirred the curtains at the wide open windows but otherwise all was still in the hot little room. Sarah was asleep in the spare divan, pushed hard against her bed in the cramped bedroom. She was breathing shallowly, lying on her back with the duvet thrown off. As always when waking, Vikki automatically flexed the fingers of her left hand although the fear that she would wake up one day and find it gone had largely faded with the passing months.

"Are you happy with your hand?"

A nudge of alarm at the realisation that this wasn't a dream. She knew she was wide awake. She sat up and stared around at the familiar surroundings. Soft moonlight illuminated the poster of Dario. The Zulu warrior stared back at her. Sarah gave a snort and rolled on to her side.

"Sarah!" Vikki hissed. "There's someone in the room!"

Sarah slumbered on. Vikki was about to shake her friend but the distant voice stilled her hand.

Come to us, please, Just Vikki.

The mistake over her name and the friendliness of the voice did much to allay Vikki's fear.

Voice? What voice? It was neither male or female. It seemed to be nowhere and yet everywhere. She drew the duvet fearfully to her chin and stared around the room.

"Where are you?"

Water. A picture of a lake formed in Vikki's mind. It was if as the image was being shaped with difficulty for it came and went. Fading into noise and reappearing. And then, for a few seconds, it was startlingly clear: moonlight making a river of molten silver on a familiar stretch of water.

Pentworth Lake!

Almost immediately the image wobbled, as though the sustaining of such a sharp picture in her mind was absorbing a considerable effort, and then it faded away.

"Come to us."

It was then that Vikki realised that there was no voice, no one in the bedroom, hiding in the shadows. What she was hearing was a coaxing, reassuring voice-picture shaping persuasively in her mind in such a manner that it banished the last vestiges of her fear. For some moments she was undecided, still thinking that perhaps it had been a dream.

Come to us.

Why? she asked. For some unaccountable reason she sensed that it was not necessary to speak out loud. Her mind trapped a faint *too far* in response.

It wasn't a dream; the voice that had no body was real and yet she was not frightened. A strange compulsion held her in a gentle grip and urged her to move. She slipped from her bed and changed into a T-shirt, jeans, and trainers, moving carefully to avoid waking Sarah. There was little she could do to prevent the creak of the narrow stairs but night visits to the outside toilet were normal. Once clear of the house, she set off at a fast pace down the lane and, keeping the moon to her left, struck out across Prescott's fields. Following the lane would have been easier but she was anxious to travel in as straight a line as possible on her three-kilometre trek to Pentworth Lake.

Moving in a straight line across country was easier now. The countryside was undergoing a profound change. Patches of long-neglected, ivy-choked woodland were being cleared to provide biomass for alcohol production, and trees thinned out to give deciduous saplings a chance to flourish as a source of hardwood in years to come. A few surviving elms from the ravages of Dutch elm disease were receiving particular care because wheelwrights needed elm to make wheel hubs on their lathes. Broad verges once abandoned to weeds were now close-cropped by tethered goats and sheep, and she had to make several detours around hurdled enclosures that penned chickens, guinea fowl and geese. Not since the Second World War had the land been so productive.

Her determination to maintain a straight line faltered when she crossed cropped fields and came to a stand of maize. This was not the usual shoulder-high sweetcorn that grew in England, but an alien, towering forest. Warmth, high humidity, pure rainfall had enabled Pentworth's precious supply of maize seed to achieve its full potential. Midges arose around her as she pushed her way through the tall fronds. Tasselled ears of corn, nearly the size of rugby footballs, brushed against her hips.

Rather wishing she hadn't become such an avid reader of horror novels now that there was no television, Vikki thrust steadfastly through the dense forest, telling herself that the scurrying noises at her approach were caused by creatures more scared of her than she was of them. Nevertheless Stephen King's bloodlust *Children of the Corn* tormented her imagination and she was immensely relieved when the stand of maize ended abruptly, giving way to clumps of sunflowers separated by wide fire breaks. Like the maize, the crop was valuable; its progeny would provide the seed stock for the basis of large-scale vegetable-oil production if the Wall persisted. All the crops were early; there had even been talk on the radio of the possibility of a second crop between autumn and Christmas.

Fifteen minutes later, her hair slicked with perspiration, her ankles weary from the cross-country trudge, and her arms aching from futile flailing at mosquitoes, she emerged on to the road that passed David Weir's Temple Farm.

She was about to cross when she saw the flare of approaching headlamps. For a second she was blinded by the lights before she threw herself flat into a newly cut drainage ditch. The two-man morris police patrol swept past in their commandeered Range Rover. There was a trial period curfew on children being out after dark. As Sarah had discovered the week before after returning in the small hours from seeing her latest boyfriend, it was no use lying about one's age because every police patrol, even those that used ponies and traps, had a CB radio link with the police station which maintained a card index on everyone in Pentworth. Vikki waited a few minutes before resuming her journey. She knew that David Weir's employees, the Crittendens, had dogs so she took a wide arc around Temple Farm, crossed several pastures close-cropped by David's sheep, and found herself in the more familiar territory of Ellen Duncan's land. She breasted a rise and climbed a stile. To her right rose the brooding scarp of the Temple of the Winds. Straight ahead was her objective: Pentworth Lake spread below her, silver filigreed in the moonlight. It had shrunk to its normal size from the huge expanse of flood plain of March. The margins were still soft underfoot but no longer dangerous. Ellen and the council had given up persuading people to stay away. Instead the council had recognised that people needed a bathing and picnic spot, therefore a roped-off sandy lido and beach had been created.

The coolness of the water was a pleasant shock. Vikki stopped when it covered her ankles and stood still, staring across the water. "I'm here," she said in loud whisper.

The response took Vikki by surprise. She was engulfed by a sudden sensation of warmth – welcoming, yet overpowering in its wordless intensity. Her instinct was to turn and run but the warmth smothered her reactions. A thousand questions swam crazily in her mind. She plucked one at random.

"Who are you?"

The answering kaleidoscope of images and concepts of free will and endless searching for the truths of the universe were meaningless to the girl. They seemed to realise this and condensed their answer to a single concept that shaped in her mind as a single word: *Seekers.*

"Where are you from?"

The myriads of star patterns and constellations that Vikki saw confused her. But she knew what a star map was and made a desperate attempt to understand. As before, this must have been sensed because the star maps disappeared and she felt a compunction to turn her head to the south-east.

Sirius, the Dog Star, had just risen above the line of distant hills that were now paling with the first light of dawn. It was the brightest star, the only one visible during the close, humid nights and consequently one that Vikki could recognise. But with the coming of the dog days of summer, when it rose and set with the sun, early morning and late evening were the only times of day when it could be seen.

"Is that where you've come from?"

A picture of a brilliant sun shining on a landscape of forests and mountains came and went leaving a lingering image that said: *Home.*

"Is it far?"

The distance that was expressed caused Vikki to cry out at what her mind automatically rejected in self-defence. The image was fleeting, snatched away as if those who had projected it understood the distress it could cause.

"Why have you come?"

It was more than merely a sensation of loneliness that over-whelmed Vikki; it was utter desolation of the spirit, terrible in its intensity, frightening in its consequence. Like the concept of the awesome distance to Sirius, the emotion was banished the instant it was expressed before she had a chance to fully understand. She crossed herself, more out of fear than any religious belief.

Why did you do that?

She concentrated on the meaning of the gesture and felt her immature thinking suddenly shaped into a deeper meaning that was quickly sucked from her. She sensed that her gesture was appreciated. And then she was spoken to clearly with perfectly formed words: *We will be sending a man to you who will explain but he is not yet ready.*

"I don't understand."

We will call you when he is ready. You will understand then.

The clarity of the reply emboldened Vikki to venture the question that was now uppermost in her mind. "Did you make my new hand?"

"Just what the hell do you think you're playing at?"

The images withdrew with a suddenness that left Vikki clutching frantically at an implosion of nothingness. She whirled around to be blinded and transfixed by a powerful flashlight.

"I said, what the hell are you playing at?" The voice was harsh, demanding. Nevertheless she decided to brazen it out. "Nothing."

"Name?"

"Boadicea."

"It's Vikki Taylor," said another voice. She couldn't place it at first and then realised that it belonged to the Fool. The flashlight snapped out and two morris police confronted her. Their white blouses shone like ghostly shrouds in the moonlight. The skull-shaped silver bells on their bell pads and shoes had been muted so that they could move unheard. Vikki was scared, but at least they weren't the feared Government blackshirts.

"What are you doing out at this time, Vikki?" The Fool's voice was not unfriendly.

"It's such a hot night – I thought I'd go for a swim."

"Fully clothed?" demanded the first morris man.

Feeling somewhat foolish, Vikki squelched on to dry land. The morris police Range Rover was parked about a hundred metres away. She agreed with the first morris man that she shouldn't be out at night and invited them to sue her.

"We saw you when you tried to hide outside Temple Farm," said the Fool.

"What's going to happen to me?"

"For starters, you're under arrest."

"No," said the Fool. "We'll run her home. I owe her a favour."

"We have to account for every bloody eggcup of diesel!" the Fool's colleague protested.

"She doesn't live far," said the Fool. "Come with us, Vikki."

"Thanks, but I can walk."

"You will come with us!" snapped the Fool.

Ten minutes later the Range Rover dropped Vikki at the end of her lane. During the short drive, she had persuaded the morris police not to tell her mother. They watched her to be sure that she kept her promise to go straight home.

The dawn chorus was in its stride when she reached her bedroom. Sarah was still sound asleep, sprawled on her back. Vikki edged around the beds to the window and leaned out. Sirius was much dimmer now that dawn was commandeering the eastern sky.

She stared at the fading star in wonder. They had come all that way just to end up submerged deep in the silt at the bottom of a lake. Why? And yet she felt that she knew the reason; the clarity had slipped away; now it was a shadowy, ill-defined concept, flitting furtively just beyond her grasp around the margins of her understanding. Who was the man they would be sending? Would she recognise him? Did they want her to be the messenger? To announce his coming? She looked down at her left hand. And why had they singled her out to make her whole? So many unanswered questions.

She tried to clear her mind and concentrated hard on Pentworth Lake, begging for answers.

None came.

She marshalled her powers of concentration and forced herself to think of one question:

"Did you make my hand? Please give me an answer."

None came.

An owl hooted.

"Please! I must know! Did you make my new hand? Is it permanent? Will you take it away from me?"

Silence.

Perhaps she had imagined the episode at the lake?

But her recollection of the startling clarity of their voice to tell her that a man was coming, the state of her mud-caked, sodden trainers, and a thousand itchy mosquito bites told a different story. She changed into her nightdress and returned to bed – the sheets and pillow now blissfully cool. She stared up at the ceiling, fingered her crucifix with her wonderful left hand and prayed for an answer to the questions that were now a torment.

None came.

But there was always tomorrow.